Gripping her hair ti[...]
knife deep into he[...]
blade back across h[...]
continued, but now [...]
She slumped agai[...] [...]here,
suspended by the ropes binding her to the frame. The
blood from her torn throat gushed onto the glass,
warm and salty, steaming slightly, hissing, bubbling.

The mirror exploded into a maelstrom of light.
Jagged streaks of colour ran from one edge of the glass
to the other. The image reached out to match the
position of the young woman tied to the glass. Only
now when it pressed itself against the glass did Frazer
clearly see the glass bow outwards. He saw its fingers
stretch the surface of the glass like jelly, and then break
through one by one, and wrap themselves around the
girl's face, pulling her close to the glass to where its
lips pressed against the glass around the gaping
wound in the woman's throat. Its tongue – long and
dark and moist – lapped at the spurting blood.

MICHAEL SCOTT

SPHERE BOOKS LIMITED

A *Sphere* Book

First published in Great Britain in 1991 by Sphere Books Ltd
a Division of Macdonald & Co (Publishers) Ltd
London & Sydney

ISBN 0 7474 0884 X

Photoset in North Wales by
Derek Doyle & Associates, Mold, Clwyd.
Printed and bound in Great Britain by
BPCC Hazell Books
Aylesbury, Bucks, England
Member of BPCC Ltd.

Sphere Books Ltd
A Division of
Macdonald & Co (Publishers) Ltd
165 Great Dover Street
London SE1 4YA
A member of Maxwell Macmillan Publishing Corporation

To the SKUA crew – Remember Patrick's Island?

To the SHA crew – Remember Babe's Island

PROLOGUE

THE glass was cold against her naked flesh.

She turned her face slightly, pressing her cheeks against its coolness, feeling its sensuous touch against her breasts, belly and thighs. She shuddered, spreading her arms to clutch the edge of the plain wooden frame, opening her legs to the touch of the mirror's moist surface.

She felt her nipples hardening, her breathing quickening.

'Forever and ever?' she whispered.

The shadowy figure behind her – barely glimpsed in the mirror's dull surface – moved closer. 'Forever and ever, unchanging, unchanged. I swear it.'

'Yessss,' she hissed. She closed her eyes, visualizing herself spreadeagled up against the mirror, face to face, breast to breast, belly to belly with her own image. Her heart began pounding with ever-increasing force, throbbing against the glass, and the heat moved down into her groin, rippling through her muscles . . .

At the precise moment her orgasm took her, arching her body, the thin sliver of sharpened stone ripped through her throat.

Ultimate pleasure became absolute pain.

Blood hissed and steamed on the glass. Her mouth opened in a soundless scream as the shadowy figure moved closer, bending his head to her face. Her lips moved, words forming, bloody froth bubbling on them. 'Thank you.'

Chapter
ONE

IT stood seven foot tall, four foot wide, an enormous mirror, dirty, speckled, the glass warped, the images it showed slightly distorted and blurred. It was quite grotesque.

And Jonathan Frazer had to have it!

He stood at the very back of the small crowd in the foul-smelling auction room and waited impatiently while the bored auctioneer made his way down through the catalogue of 'the property of a gentleman'.

'Lot 66, a French gendarme's side arm saw sword, with a double-edged steel blade, bronze handle and cross guards, complete with leather scabbard . . .'

Jonathan Frazer had strayed into the auction rooms almost by accident. He had decided to take the later flight and spend the last day of his holidays in Dublin, exploring some of the side streets. He usually passed through Dublin briefly on his way to the west of Ireland for his regular twice yearly fishing holiday. He had spent a pleasant morning walking around the surprisingly small city, and had eventually found himself standing outside the imposing Four Courts on the River Liffey. He glanced at his watch: it was a little after one. He turned around and began the long stroll

3

down the quays towards O'Connell Bridge, where he would be able to orientate himself and find his hotel. His bags were packed and it was simply a matter of picking them up and heading out to the airport. His flight was at five and he'd be in London by six.

There were numerous small antique and second-hand shops along this side of the quays and he stopped at all of them; now that his holiday was over a sense of professional duty was beginning to take over. He wasn't expecting to find anything: the really good stuff was usually traded amongst the dealers and collectors and rarely reached the shops, especially shops like these. As expected, a lot of what he saw was rubbish, or its condition was so poor as to render it worthless.

He had been tired by the time he reached O'Connell Bridge and he almost walked past the auctioneer's. Furniture, none of it interesting, was strewn about on the street outside the premises and through the large windows he could see a motley assortment of people facing a young man at the far end of the room. The auctioneer's sing-song chant drifted out through the open doors.

Jonathan Frazer stepped into the shadowy interior of the auction rooms, blinking until his eyes adjusted to the dimness, and then began to wander around amongst the larger objects which were piled up at the back of the room.

'Lot 68, a gentleman's half-hunter pocket watch . . . in need of repair . . .'

The mirror was at the very back, behind a woodwormed wardrobe and an early Edwardian dresser. He squeezed between the wardrobe and the dresser, initially attracted to the sheer size of the glass. He was six foot tall and it was least a foot taller than he was. He spread his arms, judging the width from experience: it was at least four foot wide. There was a

4

surprisingly plain wooden frame surrounding it, complete with brass clips for securing it to a wall, although it was now mounted on a stand which enabled it to be swivelled. The stand was a later addition, he decided.

Jonathan Frazer ran his hand down the mirror, drawing long streaks on the glass; it was filthy, the glass itself covered with a greasy layer of grime. He ran his handkerchief around in a circle at about head height and peered into it, but, what with the dimness of the auction room and the dirt on the glass, he could barely make out his own reflection. He licked his finger and rubbed it against the mirror, his breath catching when he felt its chill, but even that had made no impression against the grime.

Without examining the back of the mirror he had no way of accurately dating it, but, considering the slightly bluish tinge to the glass, the perceptible distortion around the perimeter and the curious bevelling in towards the centre, it was certainly old. Seventeenth century, possibly earlier.

'Lot 69, a large antique wooden-framed mirror, approximately seven feet tall by four feet wide. An imposing piece.'

Frazer took a deep breath, suddenly glad he was wearing his rather ordinary holiday clothes. He cast an experienced eye over the small crowd: he knew no one, and he couldn't spot any obvious dealer types. He hoped anyone looking at him would assume he was just another guy in off the street looking for a bargain.

'Now who will open the bidding at one hundred pounds?'

Frazer could hardly believe his ears. The mirror was worth at least twenty times that. But he kept his head down, not looking at the auctioneer, showing no interest.

'Seventy-five pounds then. Come along, ladies and

gentlemen; it's here to be cleared. Seventy-five for a fine piece of glass like that. A handsome piece in any house.'

'You'd need an awfully big house,' someone quipped in a flat Dublin accent.

The auctioneer smiled. 'Fifty pounds, ladies and gentlemen. Fifty pounds, or I'll have to pass it.'

Frazer looked up and caught the auctioneer's eye. He nodded slowly.

'Fifty pounds is bid. Any advance on fifty pounds. Come along ladies and gentlemen, this is a real bargain. Any advance on fifty pounds?'

No one moved.

'Fifty pounds I'm bid. Going once, going twice . . . sold!' He looked in Frazer's direction and nodded. 'Now Lot 70 . . .'

A young man, wearing blue overalls, made his way through the crowd and handed Frazer a slip to fill in.

'Can you ship it?'

'We can of course, sir. Shipping is extra.'

'Of course.' Frazer handed across his business card. 'To this address.'

The young man turned it over. 'Frazer Antiques . . . we haven't seen you here before, sir.'

'Just passing through.' He glanced back at the mirror. 'My lucky day.'

The young man smiled. 'You got a real bargain. The right man in the right place at the right time.'

Chapter
TWO

'**IT'S** quite something.' Tony Farren ran his hand appreciatively down the length of the glass. 'The frame's horrific, but we'll see if we can do something about that.'

Jonathan Frazer crouched down in front of the enormous mirror, pointing to the black speckling that ran around its edges. 'Let's see what we can do about these too, eh?'

'No problem.'

Jonathan stood up and brushed off his hands. 'What do you think?'

Tony Farren tucked his hands into the pockets of his faded shopcoat. He had been with Frazer Antiques since James Frazer, Jonathan's father, had started the business just after the war. Small, stout, and completely bald, his knowledge of most aspects of the antiques business was phenomenal. When Jonathan had been a boy, he had spent most of his summers in these crowded, musty converted stables at the back of the house in Kensington, which was almost in sight of the Victoria & Albert Museum. The long low building contained the overflow from the shop as well as serving as workshop for Tony Farren and Diane

Williams, his longest serving assistant to date.

'It's a fine piece,' he said eventually. 'Very fine.'

'Can you put a value on it for me?' Jonathan smiled. This was high praise.

Farren ran his hands over the glass, and then used a small pocket torch to throw a light onto the mirror. He repeated the procedure with the wooden frame, and then moved across behind the tall mirror to examine the back. He ducked out from behind it. 'It's an interesting piece, no mistake about that. The glass is Venetian possibly, late fourteenth, early fifteenth century, although it's very difficult to say. Could be even earlier for all I know. The frame looks early sixteenth century, it's in the style certainly, although the wood looks older . . . and it's a peculiar wood too, birch or alder.' He stepped back, sinking his hands into his pockets, his head tilted to one side. 'On reflection it would seem a shame to remove it from the frame, unless we could put together a more ornate one – but finding a frame of this size would be virtually impossible.'

'The price, Tony,' Jonathan gently reminded him.

'Twenty thousand . . . give or take a few bob.'

'What!'

Farren grinned at the younger man's surprise. 'Why, what were you going to charge for it?'

'A couple of grand, three, three and a half maybe . . .'

'For twenty-eight square feet of what is possibly Venetian glass with what looks like an Elizabethan frame on it! Come on lad, that'd be like giving it away.'

'Could be a fake,' he murmured.

Tony Farren snorted rudely.

Jonathan Frazer moved away from the huge mirror, looking at it in a new light. He sank down onto a badly made copy of a Chippendale and began to laugh gently. 'I paid fifty Irish pounds for it, and then

8

another fifty for carriage.'

Tony shook his head. 'It's a once in a lifetime bargain.'

'Piece of good fortune, eh?'

Farren smiled. 'Every dealer – whether he's dealing in books, stamps, coins, furniture, pictures or silver – turns up one special item in his lifetime.' He rested his hand against the glass, a damp palm print forming on the glass only to disappear almost immediately. 'This is your special item.'

Frazer fished in his waistcoat for his pocket watch. He looked at the mirror for a final time. 'Isn't it just, though – you take special care of that for me, Tony.'

'I'll start refurbishing it immediately. I'm quite looking forward to it,' he added.

Tony Farren had left the army after the war with no skills other than how to handle and fire – with extraordinary accuracy – a Vickers Mk 1 medium machine gun. But war-torn London had little use for machine gunners; instead they needed carpenters, builders, plumbers, glaziers, painters and decorators. Farren drifted from trade to trade, learning enough to be competent in each, but eventually finding each task remarkably boring. He was on the point of emigrating in 1948 when he chanced to meet his old Captain, James Frazer of the Queen's Own. He was in the process of opening an antiques shop, antiques of various types – both legitimate and otherwise – being plentiful in post-war Britain. And James Frazer needed a handyman, someone who could fix the leg of a chair, polish a table top, touch up a painting.

Tony Farren lied; he told him he could do all these things and more. And there was no one more surprised than he was, when he actually discovered that he could. He improved his basic skills by studying, and his solutions to the problems presented to him on a daily basis, while unorthodox, usually worked.

James Frazer claimed he was a genius; Tony put it down to the fact that he was finally doing something he enjoyed. Every day was different: one day he might be working on chairs or tables, the next refurbishing a crusader's sword or a suit of armour, the next day touching up a fine book binding.

Tony Farren had spent over fifty years in the business, and had become one of its master craftsmen as well as a recognized authority on the history and development of bladed weaponry. He had seen just about every type of antique and artefact liable to come up for auction sale ... but he had never seen anything like the mirror.

He walked slowly around the mirror, certainly the largest he had ever seen. It was a solid sheet of glass set into a plain wooden frame, with a solid wooden back fixed to the frame. Obviously the back would have to be removed before he started work. He fished into his pockets and removed a magnifying glass, and then bent to examine one of the clips which secured the back to the frame. He hissed in annoyance: the heads of two of the screws had been entirely destroyed, the groove completely worn smooth. He moved onto the next screw, and frowned; this too had been destroyed. Moving slowly from clip to clip – and there were twelve in all, two screws to a clip – he discovered that the heads of all twenty-four screws had been worn completely smooth, the grooves hacked and torn away.

He rubbed a callused palm against the wooden backing. 'Whoever put you on, didn't want you coming off.'

However, the problem wasn't insurmountable.

The trick was to cut new heads in the screws, make a groove deep enough to give him purchase for a screwdriver. There was always the danger that the screw would snap – and that would be a bitch, but he'd cross that bridge when he came to it.

Tony Farren moved over to the long work-bench that ran the entire length of the stables. It was littered with tools and half completed projects and had been the despair of numerous assistants down through the years. While they searched frantically for tools, he had always been able to go exactly to the place he had last left it.

He chose a small Black & Decker and fitted a circular abrading stone to it. He slipped a pair of tinted protective goggles over his head and pulled on a pair of gloves. And then, with infinite patience, he carefully cleaned the ragged metal off the heads of the crude screws. It took him the best part of an hour, starting with those he could easily reach and then climbing up onto a step-ladder to complete the job. When he was finished, the heads gleamed silver and sparkling in the light. Returning to the bench, he replaced the Black & Decker with a diamond-tipped drill. He took a few moments to review what he was about to do and then, satisfied, knelt on the floor beside the mirror. This was the tricky bit.

'Don't try this at home, children,' he murmured, as he manoeuvred the drill in a reasonable straight line down the centre of the first screw. Sparks flew and the soft, musty air was tainted with the sharp tang of scorched metal. It took him about three tense minutes to cut the groove, but when he fitted the screwdriver head into the groove, it slotted neatly into place. He hissed in quiet satisfaction. No problem.

Tony Farren had actually cut twenty-two of the twenty-four screws when the accident happened.

He was tired; he'd been working for over an hour just cutting the grooves and his neck and shoulder muscles bunched and his eyes felt gritty, nerves

11

twitching in the eyelids. He should have stopped for lunch over an hour ago, but far better to get this bit finished, grab a bite to eat and then proceed.

He moved the ladder along to the last clip and climbed up it, with the drill clutched in his right hand. He had just about reached the top when the ladder shifted. Farren yelped with fright and dropped the drill, scrabbling to catch the expensive piece of equipment, missing it, hearing it crack onto the concrete floor. He toppled forward, instinctively clutching at the top of the mirror for support. He immediately realized what he was doing and attempted to push himself back, terrified that he was going to push the mirror to the ground. The step-ladder swayed with the violence of his movements, metal legs screeching on the floor.

Tony Farren crashed to the ground, feeling his hip pop with the sickening force, shards of metal from the shattered drill digging into his flesh. Luckily the heavy metal step-ladder had been pushed away from him as he fell and went clattering across the floor.

Tony lay on the floor for a full twenty minutes, defiantly resisting the urge to vomit. Every movement was agony, and from his stomach down was a solid mass of anguish. Paradoxically – in spite of the pain, because of the pain? – he was losing feeling in his legs ... but he guessed that was just the shock, or maybe there was internal bleeding.

'*Stupidstupidstupid.*' His voice was a strangled hiss of pain. Finally, when he had decided he had come to terms with the hurt, he began the painful process of crawling across to the telephone on the wall above the bench. How he was going to get it down was another matter, but one thing at a time. He hoped Jonathan was still at the house; he knew Cecilia – Mrs Frazer – was still skiing in Switzerland and wouldn't be back for another few days, but Emmanuelle was home from college; she might be there. And he could always phone the shop. Bugger the shop! He was going to phone an ambulance.

Digging his fingernails into the scarred concrete floor, Farren pulled himself forward, moving awkwardly around the mirror which was in the centre of the floor directly in front of him.

Blood was pounding in his head, roaring in his skull. His breathing was a loud rasp. Concentrate . . . one thing at a time . . . he was going to have that engraved on his tomb: *One Thing at a Time*. Right now he was concentrating on the edge of the floor, where the strip of tattered carpet ran beneath the work-bench. When he reached it he would rest.

Pressing his palms to the floor he pushed – and nothing happened. He couldn't feel his legs now. His shoulder muscles were aflame, his arched spine ached as he dug into his reserves, attempting to pull himself along the floor.

With an almost superhuman effort he reached the edge of the faded, dirty carpeting and clutched at the leg of the work-bench. With something to hold onto how, he made one final effort to drag himself across the floor.

Something shifted.

Tony Farren turned.

His left foot had become caught up in the ornate base of the mirror. He had been pulling the mirror with his every movement, and the flesh of his ankle was rubbed raw. He hadn't heard it because of the noise in his head, hadn't felt it because of the numbness in his legs. He sat up and attempted to extricate his leg using both hands, jerking it towards him.

The seven foot tall mirror shifted on the stand, the top swivelling, dipping downwards.

Tony Farren opened his mouth to scream, but no sound came. He knew what was going to happen.

Trapped, unable to move, he could only watch in horror as the mirror shifted, turning on its stand.

With a slow, almost ponderous movement, the entire thirty stone – four hundred and twenty pounds – weight toppled forward.

Farren managed to scream once before it crashed into him, snapping through his outstretched hands, impacting the bones deep into his body, cracking and then flattening the skull, crushing the ribs deep into the lungs and internal organs.

Blood and gore spurted once – briefly – before the weight of the mirror pressed the corpse onto the ground.

It took four policemen to lift the mirror off the crushed remains of the man. There were two surprises in store for them: the mirror was intact despite the fall, and there was a complete lack of blood.

Chapter
THREE

FOREVER and ever. Unchanged and unchanging.

And so it was.

Limbo, soundless, soulless, grey agony. A shadowland, grey and sere, black and white . . .

Forever and ever. Unchanged and unchanging.

Until now.

The colour ran through the Otherworld, bringing memories, awakening desires.

It experienced a quickening . . .

Chapter
FOUR

HE was, Dermot Craig thought, one of the biggest and certainly the ugliest mothers he had ever seen. He'd been watching the man for the past few moments peering in through the auction rooms' large windows, shading his eyes with his hands to see into the darkened interior. Finally, he moved in off the quayside and stood in the doorway effectively blocking it. He was not the sort of guy you'd want to meet in a lighted alleyway, Craig decided, never mind the other kind.

Dermot Craig moved through the bewildering assortment of furniture he was presently listing in preparation for the usual weekly auction, stopping a few feet away from the large shadowed figure. 'Hello, can I help you? Action's not till Wednesday, and there's no viewing until Tuesday morning.'

The big man moved into the large circular room, ducking his head slightly as he came into the room. He was dressed entirely in black, the outfit vaguely clerical, except that he wore a black polo neck jumper instead of a roman collar.

Craig, who himself stood six foot, and weighed fourteen stone, found himself looking up at a man who topped him by at least four inches, and who had the body of a professional wrestler. He stopped in the centre of the room, his head swivelling on his thick neck. He had a shock of snow-white hair, though his eyebrows were coal black, and much of his face was lined with a tracery of scars which were especially evident along his cheekbones and forehead. His nose had once been broken and badly set and his chin was deeply cleft. When he finally turned to look at Craig, coal-black, stone-hard eyes stared unblinkingly at him.

'Can I help you?' Craig demanded more forcefully. As casually as possibly he began to move over to a collection of umbrellas and walking sticks in an elephant's foot stand. There was a sword cane in one of them, though God alone knew which one. The auction rooms had been raided once, and on two previous occasions they had been approached and asked – no, *told* – to pay protection money. Despite threats of burning they had refused to pay, and they had heard nothing further.

But the big ugly mother was an enforcer if ever there was one.

'You're auctioning a mirror,' the big man said finally, his voice surprisingly mild and cultured. Craig detected a trace of a Cork or Kerry accent in it.

'No . . . no . . . sir, we're not. Not this week anyway.'

The big man frowned. 'I was told there was a large mirror coming up for auction in these rooms. I have travelled a long way to purchase this mirror. Now, is there a mirror for auction?' His voice was a rasping whisper as if his throat had once been damaged.

'Well no, sir,' Craig said nervously, completely disconcerted by the man's sheer presence. 'We had a large mirror for sale in last week's auction . . . perhaps you have been misled about the dates.'

'Have you the catalogue for last week's auction?'

'Yes sir, but I can describe the mirror to you. I

actually catalogued it myself.'

'Describe it.'

Craig glanced nervously around the room: where were the assistants? Surely they should have been back from lunch by now?

'It was a large mirror, measuring approximately seven feet by four feet, set into a plain wooden frame, the whole lot mounted on a hinged base which allowed the mirror to be tilted back and forth. It weighed a ton,' he added with a grin, which faded at the expression on the other man's face.

'That is the mirror I was looking for.' He took a step forward. 'I take it it was sold.'

'Yes sir.'

'To whom?' he demanded.

'I . . . I'm afraid we're not at liberty to disclose that sort of information.'

'Disclose it!'

'Now hang on a minute, mister . . .!'

'Who bought that mirror?' Although his voice was still little more than a whisper, there was a definite menacing tone in it now.

'Sir, we guarantee client confidentiality. I'm afraid I cannot disclose the purchaser of the mirror.' Craig felt beads of sweat pop out on his forehead as the man stepped nearer. The scars on his face stood out palely against the darker tan of his flesh. He looked as if he'd gone straight through a windscreen. Craig glanced longingly at one of the nearby walking sticks; he wasn't sure he'd be able to get to one before the stranger was on top of him.

'Why make trouble for yourself?' the man asked pleasantly. 'I can make it worth your while.' He pulled out a roll of Irish currency and began peeling off the larger blue notes, the twenties.

Dermot Craig stared at him until the man had counted out five twenties.

18

'Frazer Antiques,' he said suddenly. 'London address, purchased by Jonathan Frazer for fifty pounds and shipped by Europe Air Freight which cost him another fifty.'

The stranger smiled thinly, and the wad of money disappeared back into his coat. 'Thank you.'

'Hey,' Craig said, affronted, seeing his hundred disappearing along with the rest. 'What about my money?'

'I never said I'd give you money,' the man said turning away.

'We had a deal; you said you'd make it worth my while.' Forgetting his earlier fears, he reached out and grabbed the bigger man by the arm.

The large man turned and looked into Craig's face and stared for at least a minute and then he smiled. Craig dropped his hand and stepped away: that smile had been the most frightening thing he had ever seen. He backed into the elephant's foot, scattering umbrellas, walking sticks and canes all over the floor. He looked down involuntarily, and when he looked back, the big man had vanished.

Dermot Craig wiped his face on the sleeve of his shop coat. He felt chilled although he was bathed in sweat: for the first time in his life he realized he had experienced real fear.

The place wouldn't be the same without him. When people in the know talked about Frazer Antiques, they were generally talking about Tony Farren. Jonathan's knowledge was limited, and he was still learning; Tony's knowledge had been encyclopedic.

Jonathan Frazer wandered down the silent work-room, still wearing the black suit he had worn to the funeral. This was the first time in the past week that he'd come into the stables, and the long room – even though it was crowded with antiques – still felt empty.

He sat down in Tony's much battered chair and looked around the room, dust motes spiralling upwards in the afternoon stillness. He had lost a friend. He hadn't looked on Tony Farren as a father, but rather as an uncle. Oh, he'd had his faults: he could be petty and spiteful, quarrelsome, and he hated to be proved wrong, and in recent years he had become far too fond of old wine and young men, but he had been a friend.

His eyes were drawn to the tall, imposing mirror and the dark stain on the floor in front of it. Christ, but what a freakish accident! There had been an autopsy of course and a coroner's court: Accidental Death had been the predictable verdict.

The sequence of events was easy enough to reconstruct. Jonathan found his eyes going up the mirror, visualizing Tony working on the screws, cleaning them all off, and then laboriously cutting new grooves in them. He'd overstretched and fallen, breaking his hip, damaging his spine. The mirror had tilted, shifted, and then fallen forward on top of him. The police had estimated its weight at about thirty stone, four hundred and twenty pounds, but he thought it might be heavier. It was small consolation that Tony had died instantly.

Jonathan smiled bitterly. Tony always said he thought he would like to die in this room. Well, he'd had his wish.

May God have mercy on his soul.

The door cracked open, the hinge screeching, startling him.

'Sorry Mister Frazer, I didn't expect to find you here.' Diane Williams, Tony Farren's assistant, stepped into the long room, allowing the door to swing closed behind her.

'It's not the same without him,' she said quietly, traces of her Cockney accent coming through, even though she always tried to speak 'proper' around him.

She wanted to work in the shop some day. She was dressed in a black suede skirt and white blouse today – the first time Frazer could ever remember her wearing a skirt – and her shaggy blonde hair was hidden beneath a rather large black hat. She was wearing dark glasses to hide her red and swollen eyes. Although she had fought long and bitterly with Tony, they had both been very fond of one another.

'There was a good turn-out,' she said numbly, the silence of the long room oppressive.

'He would have been proud.' Frazer nodded. Just about every major antiques shop in London had sent along a representative, along with the numerous friends, colleagues and contacts Tony had built up over the years. Frazer's only regret was that his wife had categorically refused to cut short her skiing holiday to attend the funeral. Manny, his daughter, had taken her place, but it wasn't the same of course.

'Mister Frazer . . .' Diane began tentatively. She pulled off the hat and ran her fingers through her short, shaggy hair. 'I know this isn't the time, and this probably isn't the place . . .'

'What is it, Diane?' Frazer asked gently.

'It's that mirror, Mister Frazer, that fuck . . . that bloody mirror! I'm not working on it. I couldn't!' She began crying then, the tears which flowed so freely at Tony's graveside until she thought she had cried herself out, returning again. She pulled off her glasses and pressed a tiny lace handkerchief to her eyes.

Jonathan went and took her in his arms, pressing her head to his chest, brushing her hair, crooning slightly to her. She would be about the same age as Emmanuelle – Manny – he guessed, around eighteen, and he had soothed and salved enough tears in his twenty-year marriage to be counted an expert on the subject. He pressed his handkerchief into Diane's hands. 'I wasn't even going to ask you,' he lied. He

21

hadn't even thought about the subject. 'Now, listen to me. I want you to take a couple of days' holiday – we'll call it compassionate leave. Come back to me Monday, and we'll work out something. I need you now, Diane, and I need you on top of your form. Only you know all of Tony's tricks. Don't even think about the mirror. I'll probably dispose of it.'

'I'm not superstitious, Mister Frazer, you know that. But that mirror is bad luck . . .'

'Diane . . .' he began.

'Look . . .' Taking his hand, she manoeuvred him around in front of the mirror. 'What do you see?'

'Beneath a layer of dirt, I see two unhappy people,' he said gently.

'I polished that mirror four times since it arrived here. The first day I spent nearly two hours removing every speck of dirt from it. Tony insisted.'

'It probably got dirty when it . . . when it fell,' he said reasonably.

Diane took Jonathan's arm and turned him so that he was facing her. 'Please Mister Frazer, dispose of the mirror, break it up, throw it away, burn it, but please, don't keep it here.'

Frazer took hold of both her arms, squeezing tightly. 'You're overwrought, Diane. Now, go home, get some rest. We'll sort everything out on Monday.'

'Yes sir,' she said meekly.

'Off you go now.'

When she had gone Jonathan Frazer walked up to the mirror and ran his fingertip down the length of the glass. It came away black with grime.

He presumed it had got dirty when it had fallen, but wasn't it amazing that it hadn't shattered when it had fallen on poor Tony. It had emerged from the accident completely unscratched . . . even the frame . . .

A sudden thought struck him and he knelt on the floor, unconsciously standing in exactly the same spot where Tony had been killed. He examined the edges of the wooden frame. They had been splashed with blood, they should be stained, the wood scarred where they had struck the concrete floor . . . but there was nothing.

And then he noticed something else: the black speckling around the edges of the bottom of the glass had disappeared!

Chapter
FIVE

JONATHAN Frazer turned his Volvo Estate into the driveway and was surprised to find his wife's new BMW 5-Series parked carelessly across the double garage doors, effectively blocking both. Hissing in annoyance, he pulled the Volvo into the verge and then trampled up the gravelled driveway, lifting the duplicate key for the BMW off his own keyring.

It would have taken her two minutes to park the car.

Jonathan sat into the BMW, smelling its newness and the richness of the leather upholstery, now overlain with his wife's latest perfume, Opium. She changed her perfumes with extraordinary regularity. Before starting the car he took a deep breath to calm himself. She could have parked the car, or at least not blocked the doors . . . it was just thoughtlessness. Or maybe it was something more than that.

He suddenly grinned into the mirror. He hadn't had an argument, hadn't felt like this in a month . . . which was exactly how long Cecilia had been away.

The last time he had had an argument with Cecilia – which was just before she left for Switzerland, or wherever the hell she'd been this time – he had slammed out of the house, climbed into the Volvo and proceeded to back it into one of the ornamental fauns on the lawn. The faun had toppled off its pedestal and shattered the back indicator lights. In some obscure way he felt that just about summed up their relationship.

But the bitch could have parked the car properly!

When his breathing had returned to normal and his heart had slowed its angry pounding, he started up the BMW, carefully reversed it down the drive and then tripped the garage doors with the remote control. With a series of wheezing and hissing gasps the left-hand garage door rose smoothly upwards. When it had settled into its cradle, he drove the car slowly forwards. Cecilia had had a trick with the previous car – one of the older BMWs – of tripping the garage door when she was driving in through the double gates at the end of the drive and shooting straight into the garage without waiting for the roof to settle. Jonathan had been waiting for the day when either she would drive straight into the garage door which had refused to open or the door would stick half-way up and take her head off.

With her car safely parked, he strolled down the drive to his own car, breathing in the cool evening air. He had had a particularly frustrating day, having lost two items at an auction to one of his rivals because he hadn't been paying attention. Indeed, at one point, he had found himself bidding for the wrong lot; luckily he hadn't bought it. He should have taken the day off, he realized now. Tony's tragic death and the funeral yesterday had completely unsettled him and, of course, he hadn't really had a chance to settle back into a work routine since his holiday.

Unfortunately, tomorrow was Saturday, one of the busiest days in the shop, and he couldn't afford to take it off. Next week maybe.

He parked his own car carefully – the garage was

just a little on the small size to accommodate the Volvo Estate, but the car was eminently practical for carrying purchases away from auction or bringing them to or from the shop.

He locked down the garages and strolled around to the hall door, and there his anger flared again when he put his key in the door and it immediately opened silently inwards. It hadn't been locked. Standing on the step, he pushed the door all the way open.

The marbled hallway was littered with Cecilia's luggage and numerous bags. A pair of skis were leaning against the highly polished oak banister of the curving staircase.

Moving through the mess, Jonathan gently lifted the skis away from the wood, licking his finger, rubbing it on the spot where they had scored the varnish.

Aware that an argument was almost inevitable now – recognizing the signs, feeling his shoulder and stomach muscles beginning to knot – he slowly climbed the stairs.

The master bedroom was littered with clothes, and through the closed door of the adjoining bathroom he could hear the shower drumming steadily. Frazer cracked open the door and peered into the *en suite*, wincing as steam billowed out around him. He could just about make out his wife's form through the frosted glass.

'Hello . . .' he called. The hissing of the water lessened. 'Hello, it's me . . .'

'Oh, you're home. I'll be out in a minute.' The shower resumed with full force.

By the time Cecilia Frazer emerged from the shower and strolled, naked and dripping, into the bedroom, Jonathan had tidied up most of the scattered clothes, bundling the majority of them into the laundry basket, and hung the rest up on their hangers in Cecilia's wardrobe. She kissed him perfunctorily on the cheek, even though she hadn't seen him in a month, as she passed him, while reaching into the open wardrobe to pull out an ivory silk nightdress. When she pulled it on it immediately stuck to her wet body.

Jonathan Frazer found he could look at his wife without feeling anything. Even though they hadn't slept together in a month and hadn't made love in twice that time, he wasn't in the least aroused by the sight of her naked body. An ever-present diet had stolen much of the flesh off her, and constant exercise had replaced it with muscle, which gave her flesh a slightly lumpy appearance. Her breasts, which had always been small, had almost vanished as she had developed her chest and shoulder muscles, and although she only stood five six – and even he didn't know what she weighed – he guessed that she was stronger than he was.

'Are you not going to ask me how my holiday went?' she said eventually, not looking at him as she unpacked her clothes, dropping them in a pile on the floor beside the laundry basket.

'You left the hall door open,' he said shortly.

'Oh. I thought I locked it.'

'There's little point in having a fifty thousand pound security system installed, if you're going to leave the door open.'

'It wasn't fifty thousand pounds dear . . .'

'That's not the point,' he snapped. 'You left the bloody door open.'

'I forgot.'

'Why didn't you just hang a notice on the door, "Please come in and steal." '

'I'll do that next time.'

'Jesus, Cee!'

Cecilia dropped a bag onto the bed and snapped the catches. 'I forgot. All right, I had a lot to carry in. I was in a hurry. I've been on a plane for two hours, and then I sat on the motorway for another hour. I was tired. I felt grubby. I wanted a shower. Right?' They glared at one another across the expanse of the king-sized bed.

Finally, Jonathan shrugged. 'Right,' he said tiredly. 'You could have come home for the funeral,' he said softly, realizing that this was at the heart of his anger.

'It would have been awkward.'

'He was an employee . . . a friend.'

'He wasn't my friend!' Cecilia snapped. Tony Farren had had little time for Cecilia and her fashions and moods, and hadn't bothered to hide his distaste. Their aversion was mutual. She disliked him; she detested the very thought of him working – *working* – at the bottom of the garden in the converted stables. 'He was an employee, in fact he was nothing more than a glorified handyman!'

Frazer allowed the rage to engulf him, paradoxically enjoying his anger. 'Let me tell you something,' he said icily. 'Tony Farren is the reason Frazer Antiques is as successful as it is today. When antique shops were springing up all over the country, bigger shops offering a better choice, a more exotic range, cheaper prices, the only reason we kept our edge in the market was because we had Tony Farren. The shit I bought for half nothing he turned into antiques of value. He is the only reason we survived!'

He hurried from the room before she could see the tears in his eyes. All the things he should have said to Tony; all the things they should have talked about.

Everything he had said had been true.

Maybe he had over-emphasized the case for Cecilia's benefit, but it was still true. Frazer Antiques had survived because of Tony Farren's skill and knowledge; it wasn't going to close up tomorrow because he was gone, but there would be a difference. He had had the gift of taking rubbishy bits of junk and turning them into antiques – and an antique is in the eye of the beholder.

And now he was dead.

Killed by a fifty quid mirror.

With the rage still bubbling inside him, leaving him cold and empty, he stormed out into the stables. The mirror stood in the centre of the floor, outlined in the late afternoon light, the glass a milky-pale, non-reflective sheet.

Frazer grabbed a hammer from the bench and stood before the mirror, chest heaving.

Killed by a fifty quid mirror. Fifty fucking quid!

He raised the hammer and approached the glass.

It was worth twenty thousand pounds. At least.

The thought stopped him cold.

Breaking it would give him a great deal of satisfaction, help work off some of the anger he felt at Tony's needless death. But the need was there to strike out, to hit something, hurt something. OK. So perhaps he had a just reason for arguing with Cecilia; she'd been in the wrong. She should have come home for the funeral, two lousy days wouldn't have made much difference to her holiday. She should have parked the car properly, she should have closed the front door behind her.

But that didn't make him any more in the right.

They had been married for twenty years now; he should have become used to her ways by now.

He raised the hammer again; surprised to find that he could barely see himself in the glass. He reached out and rubbed his finger down the length of the mirror: it came away encrusted with a thick sooty grime.

He looked at the hammer in his hand. And then allowed it to fall to the floor.

Break the mirror and what would he achieve? It would give him a momentary satisfaction . . . and he would lose twenty thousand pounds. And the first person who would call him seven sorts of a fool would be Tony Farren.

He turned away and stopped at the door, glancing back at the mirror. He'd clean it up and sell it – cheaply too, just to get rid of it.

As he closed the door, colours, like oil on water, ran down the surface of the glass.

Chapter
SIX

THE insistent buzzing woke him close to three in the morning.

Jonathan Frazer rolled over, arm flailing blindly, assuming it was the alarm clock . . . and then suddenly snapped awake.

The alarm!

He sat up quickly, rubbing sleep from his eyes, blinking sleepily at the lighted square panels on the small white plastic box, wanting to turn on a light to read the handwritten labels, but afraid to do so. The monitoring device kept track of the sophisticated alarm system that girded the house, garages, outhouses, even the exterior gates and portions of the walls. It looked as if the outhouses – the converted stables – had been burgled . . . or, more likely, were in the process of being burgled now. The alarm was a silent one, there were no strident, jangling bells – Cecilia didn't want that – but it buzzed in the bedroom, alerted the local police station, and the security monitoring station simultaneously.

Jonathan Frazer slid from the bed, shivering in the early morning chill. He usually slept naked, regretting it now as he wasted precious moments slipping on a pair of dark trousers and a black jumper, sliding his feet into house slippers. Ignoring the advice of the security company and police – *'if the alarm goes off, do not, under any circumstances, investigate yourself'* – he raced down the stairs, heart pounding. He stepped into the kitchen and stopped. Ducking down below the level of the windows, he moving cautiously to the glass panelled back door and peered out across the tiled patio to where the converted stables were barely visible through the trees.

Light flashed, flickered, died.

There was someone there!

At the back of his mind he had half-thought – hoped! – that it might have been a false alarm, although the alarm company had guaranteed that the system it had installed was self-regulating, incapable of going off for no reason. Now, he stood in the kitchen, beginning to shiver with nerves as well as the night chill. The police would be – should be – here at any moment, the alarm company's patrolling car as well . . . but whoever was in the stables could be long gone by then, taking goodness knows what with them. And there were some very valuable pieces in there that were easily portable: the four Russian icons Tony had been repairing for the Soviet Attaché, the collection of gold coins he'd been making a display box for . . .

There was a set of kitchen knives on a magnetic rack to the left of the sink, each naked blade gleaming dully in the grey light. He pulled off the longest knife, a heavy eight-inch butcher's knife, and hefted it in his hand, wondering if he would have the nerve to use it.

Wondering if he would have the nerve to even open the kitchen door and step out into the night!

Realizing with a wry smile that he was merely making excuses for not going down to the stables to investigate, hoping the police would arrive, Frazer stooped down and undid the bolt at the bottom of the door. He pulled back the top bolt and quietly turned the key, and then cracked open the door . . . and immediately swore. He had forgotten to turn off the alarm. Now two alarms would have gone off in the security company and the police station . . . well, no matter, perhaps it would bring them all the sooner.

Clutching the knife like a talisman, he stepped out onto the patio, the leather soles of his slippers clicking on the path. He moved quickly onto the grass. The garden was bitterly cold, the grass sodden with an icy dew which quickly soaked through his soft suede slippers. The chill air bit through his jumper, and by the time he reached the stand of trees and bushes that partially hid the stables from the house, he was shivering almost uncontrollably.

He stood in the bushes for what seemed like a long moment, berating himself for his cowardice: James Frazer might have been a war hero, but his son certainly hadn't inherited any of his father's characteristics. For him, something heroic was outbidding a rival at an auction.

Something fell inside the stables with a dull clanking, the sound abruptly spurring him into action. Switching the knife from his right hand, he wiped his sweating palm on the leg of his trousers and then gripped the knife tightly again.

Keeping on the grass, avoiding the gravelled path, he darted from bush to bush, moving up to the stables, checking the windows on this side of the building. They were all discreetly barred, a decorative latticework taking the place of ugly bars, and none of them had been broken. The skylights possibly . . . but as he rounded the corner – and he was now out of sight of the house, he realized – he discovered that the stable door was open.

The door was secured by three heavy mortice locks, one at top and bottom, one in the middle. The hasps were sunk into concrete and not the frame of the door and the door itself was two and a half inches thick, and was itself a relic from a crofter's cottage.

The only way in was with a key.

But the only people with keys were Tony and himself . . . and he abruptly realized he hadn't got Tony's keys back yet. OK. So maybe a friend of Tony's? Maybe friend wasn't the right word. He knew Tony preferred the company of younger men . . . possibly one of his men friends who knew what he was doing and where he worked had found the keys amongst his possessions and had just taken advantage.

Jonathan Frazer stood beside the door, listening intently, but he could only hear his own thundering heartbeat. Finally, he pushed it open with enough force for it to slam back against the wall and simultaneously slapped at the light switch.

The stables snapped into light, fluorescents buzzing into life in three long banks that ran the entire length of the long building.

'Who's there?' He was surprised at how calm his voice sounded.

Something fell to the floor at the far end of the stables.

'I know you're there. Now come out.'

The lights overhead began buzzing, flickering annoyingly.

Something moved at the corner of his vision and Jonathan whirled, knife upraised . . . and the lights overhead exploded with a bang!

Frazer screamed with fright and then pain as tiny slivers of glass rained down on top of him. And then, one by one, in a long series of rattling detonations, the banks of fluorescents exploded down the length of the room. The air was suddenly rank with acrid fumes and the brittle stench of electricity. One light remained at the far end of the stables, and it was buzzing furously, flickering on and off, strobe-like.

Frazer staggered to his feet, turned – and screamed aloud!

There was a figure facing him, tall, pale, gaunt, hollows where the eyes should have been, a disembodied face. Frazer brought up his arm, thrusting the knife forward . . . and the figure copied him, producing a knife of his own. He waved the knife left to right, and the figure moved with him.

The wave of relief that washed over Frazer almost made him lightheaded. He was facing the mirror. He was looking at himself in the fucking mirror!

He'd hardly recognized himself in the dirty glass: his face looked positively skull-like, and he looked as as if he hadn't slept for a week! With the light at the far end of the room now flickering madly, he put his back to the glass, and looked out across the clutter. It had been a mistake to come in here, he knew that now. He should have waited outside, trapped the person inside.

There!

A shape. Tall, dark, ahead and to his right, alongside a collection of medieval militaria he had bought months before. The thought made him suddenly nervous: there were knives, swords, axes, maces, spears and morningstars down there.

The shape moved, the light-dark light-dark in the room reducing his movement to slow motion.

At the moment the final light at the end of the room exploded, the hand dropped onto his left shoulder, long hard fingers biting deeply into his flesh. With a scream of absolute terror, Frazer leapt forward . . . and in a blinding flash of light found himself facing a slavering nightmare: long yellow pointed teeth, huge golden eyes, the entire face covered with long coarse hair. The creature howled at him, fetid breath washing over him, making him gag.

'Sir . . . sir . . . it's all right now . . . sir?'

The cool, neutral voice cut through his terror.

'Sir. Mister Frazer, sir. Mister Frazer,' the voice said more forcefully.

Jonathan Frazer opened his eyes, and attempted to straighten up. Strong hands gripped his arms, hauling him to his feet. He found himself looked at two impassive faces, both men wearing the uniform of TSE, The Security Experts, the company who had installed the alarm. They were both carrying long black torches, the type that doubled as truncheons, which shed a stark white light over Frazer and his surroundings. On a short leash, now sitting quietly, head cocked to one side, regarding him quizzically, was an enormous Alsatian. One of the men bent to lift the kitchen knife, and handed it, handle first, to Frazer.

'We had a report that your alarm had gone off,' the smaller, seemingly older of the two men, said.

'Yes . . . yes, that's right. And there was – there is – someone here, I saw him. Down there.' He pointed towards the back of the room.

'Yes, sir. Now, if you'll just step outside, we'll have a look around for you.'

Frazer allowed himself to be led outside by the younger man. His older colleague, holding the dog, remained inside.

'Will they be all right?'

'They'll be fine,' the man said softly, the trace of a Scottish accent in his voice. 'You should have been told not to investigate any disturbance of this nature yourself,' he added quietly.

'I was, but . . .'

'I know,' the man said understandingly. 'But you have to understand, when we go into a place like this where we know a silent alarm has gone off, we're likely to be just as nervous as you. When we went in there for example, we were confronted by – if you'll pardon the expression, sir – a wild man wielding a knife. If Max hadn't been holding Betty, she'd have taken your arm off.'

'I know, I just . . .'

The scream was high-pitched, chilling; the cry of a creature in mortal agony. It lasted a couple of seconds and the silence that followed was, if anything, even more frightening.

The security guard pushed Frazer back. 'Stay here,' he hissed. He reached down to his belt and pulled up a small circular transmitter. 'Mobile One needs assistance.' He turned back to Frazer. 'Now, don't move!'

There was a second scream, and this time the sound descended into a recognizable whine.

'That's Betty. Where's Max?' Pulling a long baton from his belt, holding the torch away from his body, the security guard pushed open the door with the baton, moving the light from left to right in a sweeping pattern. Light sparkled off metal, slid off polished wood, briefly winked on the mirror.

The guard moved into the shadows, although Fraser could follow his progress down the length of the building as the windows briefly lit up.

Where were the police?

He had half turned his head back towards the house, when he saw the flicker from the corner of his eye and turned back . . . just as the shape appeared from the doorway. Black against black, it was almost completely invisible. There was a vague oval of a face, the startling white of eye and teeth. And then the shape lunged towards him.

His cry caught in his throat, and he struggled to bring the knife up. There was a suggestion of movement before his face before the night exploded into light. He sailed backwards into the bushes curiously aware of the wetness on his face, running down his nose, tasting the copper in his mouth.

Chapter SEVEN

DEATH.

Violent bloody death.

Colour in the Otherworld, the soul of a creature ripped from the life. It experienced the creature's confusion, pain, anguish . . . and then the immediate fading of consciousness, of awareness.

An animal then.

The little soul of an animal.

The memories were returning . . .

Chapter EIGHT

IT was dawn by the time the police, the security people and doctor had left, all of them promising to return.

Frazer sat in the kitchen, his head cradled in his hands, an enormous bandage around his head, a thick pad, already faintly stained, in the centre of his forehead. He stared blankly at the two painkillers the doctor had left, moving them to and fro with his forefinger. He disliked taking pills, but he knew if he didn't take something for this headache soon he would go mad.

Cecilia moved quietly around the kitchen, wan and shaken after the night's events. She had woken to hear screaming coming from the stables, and she'd been horrified when she'd rolled over and discovered that Jonathan was missing. She was actually phoning for the police when the sirens had woken up the whole neighbourhood and blue flashing lights began to pulse in the darkness beyond the window. However, by the time Jonathan had been carried in, stunned and bleeding from a gashed forehead, her initial fear had turned to anger. Why hadn't he let the security company handle it? That's what they were paid for. Of course this was typical of him: hire someone to do a job and then do it himself anyway. Stupid bastard could have been killed! Anyway, maybe now he'd think about moving the contents of the stables into some sort of secure storage, and she could do something about the eyesore than ran the entire width of the garden at the rear wall. She sat down across the table from Jonathan and pushed a cup of coffee over in front of him.

'How do you feel?'

Jonathan attempted a smile. 'How do I look?'

'You look like shit.'

'That's how I feel.'

'Do the police know what happened?'

He shrugged, and then winced as his shoulder and neck muscles protested. 'It was an attempted robbery . . . or maybe they actually stole something, I don't know, I haven't been back to the stables yet. The police want to go over it for fingerprints first. The alarm went off . . .'

'You should have waited for the alarm company to come,' she said coolly.

He started to nod.

'Or phoned the police.'

'The alarm is hooked into the station. Anyway . . . and this is the scary part – when I went into the stable, there was someone in there, watching me, waiting.' He shivered, and then wrapped both hands around the cup to steady them. 'The security people arrived first; their mobile patrol was in the area, so they were here within minutes. They went in, and took me outside. Then, one of the men went back in with the dog. There's some confusion about what happened next. The security man, Max, either slipped or was pushed to one side. He loosed the dog.' Frazer drank some of the coffee quickly to take the sour taste from his mouth. 'Whoever was in the stable killed the dog.'

'That was the scream I heard.'

Frazer nodded.

'But there were two screams.'

'Do you want to hear this?'

'Tell me.'

Staring into the cup, he continued, his voice devoid of emotion. 'From what I can gather, the dog was first pinned to the side of the captain's oak sea-chest with an ancient long-tined pitchfork. And then one of the fake medieval broadswords I bought a couple of years ago was used to hack the dog's head off.'

'Oh, Jesus!'

'The first scream was when the dog was pinned to the wooden chest with a single blow. So whoever did it was obviously immensely powerful. The second scream was when he attempted to cut off the head; the sword was blunt. It took him two tries.'

Cecilia pushed her cup away.

'The second security man then went into the stable. But the intruder slipped past him, and met me outside! He struck me once just here.' He touched his forehead tentatively. 'The police say it was probably with the heel of his hand or some sort of martial art punch. I don't remember anything else.'

'You could have been killed,' Cecilia whispered.

'I could,' Jonathan said quietly, the realization only beginning to sink it. He barely made it to the bathroom before he began to throw up.

'Jesus Christ Almighty, place looks like a fuc . . . an abattoir.' Diane Williams ran her fingers through her shaggy blonde hair, pushing it back off her face.

Frazer glanced sidelong at her. 'It's a bit of a mess,' he agreed. There were glass fragments from the shattered lights everywhere, covering everything in a fine glittering white sand, crunching underfoot as they moved.

Diane smiled. She was wearing purple-black lipstick

41

to match her eyeshadow, and he found the whole effect rather startling. 'That's a bit of an understatement.'

One end of the stable was blood spattered. Long tendrils of thick crusted brown gore were spattered high on the walls, speckling the ceiling, spattered on every single object within a six foot radius of where the dog had been butchered. The sides of the sea-chest where the dog had been killed were torn and gouged, the tines of the pitchfork having bitten deeply into the wood, and the dog's own pathetic attempts to extricate itself clearly visible in the long scraped furrows in the wood. Dark hair matted the deep cut in the side of the chest.

Jonathan and Diane stood looking at the chest for a few moments and then they both turned away without a word, each absorbed in their own thoughts, Frazer realizing that it could just as easily have been him, pinned to the box, like some bug on a needle and then butchered, Diane beginning to have second thoughts about working here in the first place. She turned suddenly: she had seen something moving out of the corner of her eye. But when she turned there was nothing.

Christ but she was edgy!

Hardly surprising was it? Some madman wandering around butchering animals. Could just as easily have been one of the security guards . . . could just as easily have been Mister Frazer.

Diane Williams turned slowly, eyes drawn to stare at the mirror, hands on her hips. She was wearing all black today, partially in mourning for Tony, whom she genuinely liked, though he could be a crotchety old bastard, but principally because she usually wore black, and she could just about make out her reflection in the warped glass.

She turned her head to one side, staring hard at the glass. There was something . . .

'What's wrong?' Jonathan asked quietly, startling her.

'No . . . nothing. Have you made any decision about the mirror, Mister Frazer?'

'Ahem, no, Diane. I really haven't had a chance to think about it . . .'

'I'd like to work on it.'

Frazer blinked at her in astonishment. 'But I thought you said . . .'

'That was then and this is now. I was upset, I wasn't thinking clearly. I'd like to work on it as a sort of a tribute to Tony. Putting everything he taught me into practice, completing the last piece he worked upon. Do you think he'd like that?'

'I think he'd like that very much.'

Diane walked forward and rubbed her hand down the length of the mirror; it came away covered in a thick grimy soot. 'Hey, I cleaned this mirror before I left the other day.'

'I've noticed that about it too. It seems to attract every particle of dirt and dust.'

'I'll see what I can do about it,' she murmured. 'I think I had better go and clean up some of the mess around here though. I'll have to draw some petty cash for washing-up stuff,' she added, glancing at Jonathan.

'Take whatever you need; just leave the receipts in the box.' He returned again to the sea-chest where the dog had been killed and bent down, taking a pencil from an inside pocket, attempting to measure how deeply the tines had been driven into the wood. Deep enough. Whoever had done this had possessed tremendous strength. But what had they been looking for? Granted there were a lot of valuable antiques around, but disposing of them would have been particularly difficult and, as far as he could see on a cursory examination, nothing had been taken. The police had dusted for fingerprints and had found nothing out of the ordinary. There were plenty of weapons around: he had briefly considered that it might have been some local kids breaking in for the knives or swords or crossbows, but the police had said that that was unlikely; most of this stuff was too big for them, they liked something small and concealable, and hiding a six foot tall Gallowglass broadsword was going to be difficult in a pair of Levis.

He stood up and dusted off his hands. He could understand killing the dog; if he'd had a weapon to hand when he'd first seen the creature, he'd have taken a swing at it himself. But chopping off its head was . . . what? Unnecessary?

And that reminded him . . .

He returned to the mirror and looked deeply into its grimy surface. When he'd been standing with his back to it he could have sworn he'd felt a hand on his shoulder . . . ridiculous, of course, but it had been so real. Real enough to make him jump with fright. He touched his left shoulder, wincing as his fingers touched bruising.

Maybe it had been a real hand. Maybe the intruder had crept up behind him and had been preparing to grab him or attack him when the security people had walked in and ruined his plan.

'It's only since that mirror arrived,' Diane Williams said quietly, coming up to stand beside Frazer. 'It could be cursed,' she said dramatically.

'Probably . . .' he agreed. He was glad he was disposing of it. It made him, in some vague way, uncomfortable.

'Yes, can I help you?'

He turned at the sound of Diane's voice, the strident quality in it bringing him back to the present. There was a man standing in the doorway, one of the biggest men Frazer had ever seen, though with the sun behind him, it was almost impossible to make out his features.

'I'm looking for Mister Jonathan Frazer.' There was a curious accent, a lilt to his voice, Irish, Scots or Welsh.

'I am Jonathan Frazer.' He stepped forward, his sense of unease growing. No one was allowed down to the stables. 'Can I help you? Can I ask how you managed to make your way down here?'

'I was given your name,' the man said, not answering the question. 'I understand you have a mirror here for sale, Mister Frazer,' he said directly, stepping into the room and looking around. Jonathan suddenly – immediately – knew that this was the same man who'd been in the stables the previous night. He looked at his size and obvious strength, and his unease turned to fear.

'I'm afraid you've been misled, sir: nothing in this building is for sale, it is all under repair. However if you would care to visit our retail establishment, I'm sure we . . .'

'I was told you had a mirror here for sale,' the man repeated doggedly. He took another step into the room, looming larger over Frazer. Now that he no longer had the sun at his back, not only his size but also his physical appearance were intimidating. His cheeks were deeply scarred, his nose had been broken and badly set, long lines cut into his forehead. His eyes were coal-black and penetrating, and his shock of pure white hair seemed to make the disfigurement all the more shocking.

'May I . . . may I ask who told you?' Jonathan asked, turning the tremor in his voice into a cough.

'Anthony Farren.'

And Jonathan immediately knew he was lying. Tony had never been known as anything other than 'Tony'.

'It is a family heirloom,' the man continued inexorably, and Frazer was beginning to wonder what was going to happen when he refused him. 'It should never have gone up to the auction in Dublin.'

'I'm afraid the mirror is not for sale.'

45

The big man leaned forward. 'Make it for sale, Mister Frazer.'

'I must ask you to leave now,' he said, as quietly as possible, attempting to keep his voice from shaking.

Diane Williams appeared by his side, a cocked and loaded eighteenth-century French hunting crossbow cradled in her arms.

'If you don't go now sir, I shall be forced to call the police,' he said more forcefully, encouraged by her presence. 'You are trespassing.'

The big man glared at Frazer and then stared long and hard at Diane, his dark eyes moving slowly over her face as if committing it to memory. He turned and left, moving surprisingly quickly for such a big man. Jonathan and Diane turned to look at one another: without a doubt, it was the intruder from the previous night . . . and they both knew he would be back.

Chapter
NINE

MAYBE she'd ask Mister Frazer for a few days' holiday. She could go away, she had a few bob put by. She'd been saving it for a new motor-bike, but she thought that a little holiday right now might be a very good idea.

The way that guy had just looked at her!

That big guy had scared the shit out of her, and no mistake. The size of his hands, and he hadn't got those scars on his face playing chess. Give him the fucking mirror if that's what he wanted. Gift wrap it too.

But it looked like Mister Frazer was going to try and play cute with him; the only problem was, people like the big guy didn't know how to play cute.

No, she'd take a couple of weeks off and maybe by the time she got back, this mess would have sorted itself out.

Diane walked the length of the stables, glass fragments crunching beneath her boots – she thought she'd cleaned them all up! – checking all the windows. The cumbersome crossbow was awkward in her arms, and there was a First World War bayonet strapped to her waist. So what if she looked ridiculous, she felt a lot safer. Frazer had gone back to the house, scampering along the gravelled path like a frightened rabbit, to phone the police, the phone in the stables no longer working for some reason. She'd locked the heavy door behind him, the windows were locked and barred, and the skylights were all sealed but she was still hanging onto the weapons. She was taking no chances. He'd got in the previous night, hadn't he? Well, what was to stop him doing it again?

The weapons were stored at the back of the room, close to where the dog had been killed. A lot of them were in poor state of repair – which is why they had been here in the first place – but she was wondering if there was anything more useful than the crossbow – like a .44 magnum for example.

There was a brace of ornate duelling pistols on a shelf, beside a long-barrelled western Colt. But she'd no ammunition for either gun, and even if she had there was no guarantee that they wouldn't explode when she pulled the trigger. Tony had once demonstrated that for her with a fake Purdy shot-gun, wiring up the triggers and standing well back. She smiled, remembering the man's delight at being proven correct, and Frazer's horrified expression when he saw the guns he'd just purchased for a couple of hundred pounds disintegrate into scrap metal.

'Cheap Indian fakes for decorative purposes, never intended to be used,' Tony had grinned.

He had known so much. What a waste. What a way to die.

Diane turned and walked back down the room to stand before the mirror, staring at its grubby surface. She pulled a cloth from the work table and worked it in a circle, grimacing at the amount of muck that came off the glass: she thought she must have cleaned this mirror every day since it had arrived: where had all this shit come from?

Carefully placing the crossbow on the ground within

48

easy reach, she lifted a bottle of cleaning fluid from the top shelf. Starting at eye level, she rubbed furiously at the grime.

Ten minutes later, with a fine sheen of sweat on her forehead, and an aching arm, she stepped back to examine her handiwork. There seemed precious little result for so much effort. Bringing her face close to the glass, she rubbed at a patch she'd just cleaned with her fingertip. The glass was slightly greasy, clammy to her touch.

The movement caught her completely unawares, sending her stumbling backwards with a scream. She whirled around, clutching at the knife on her waist, dragging the long blade free, holding it before her in both hands. The room was empty. The door was still closed, bolted. Dust motes spiralled in the air.

Maybe that's what she had seen moving. The glass was slightly distorting. Feeling slightly foolish, she lowered the long blade and turned back to the mirror, grinning at the unexpected picture that presented itself: black dress, white hair, white face, the purple-black lipstick and eye shadow lending her a skull-like appearance. She laughed shakily; Tony's crazy death, the funeral – she hadn't been to a funeral in years – and now this strange business had her all on edge.

There *was* movement. Definite movement, a twisting shifting flicker.

Heart pounding she spun around, bringing the bayonet up again. She had glimpsed the movement behind her right shoulder, which would have put it – there! A hideous Victorian easy chair lay on its side, most of the underside removed, horsehair carefully laid out on sheets of newspaper. Behind it were three straight-backed kitchen chairs. There was no place for anyone to hide. And yet she wasn't alone in here, she knew that.

Maybe if she turned away, they would appear. Still clutching the long knife, she turned back to the mirror.

There!

The temptation to turn was almost irresistible, but she continued staring at the mirror. She frowned, attempting to make sense out of what she was seeing, but the mirror was distorting the image ... Transferring the knife to her left hand, she rubbed at the glass with the palm of her hand – and yelped!

Something like a spark had leapt from her flesh to the glass. She rubbed her hand furiously against her thigh: static. She sometimes sparked when she touched metal, door handles, some cutlery, especially motorbikes, but never glass.

She tentatively touched the glass again, but this time there was nothing. The surface of the glass felt unpleasant, slightly greasy, vaguely damp.

The flickering was still perceptible over her left shoulder. A twisting, shimmering movement, like a heat haze on a summer's day, with some darker, deeper thread inside it, like coiling smoke.

Diane glanced back over her shoulder, but there was nothing moving except the coiling dust motes. She turned back to the glass, frowning. The disturbance was within the glass!

She drew back in shock, heart thumping. She leaned forward, forefinger touching the slick glass. With her finger still pressed to the glass she turned her head again: there was still movement within the glass, but nothing behind her.

OK, so it was an imperfection in the glass, after all it was five hundred and more years old, some trick of the light, refraction or reflection or whatever it was called.

She was about to turn away when the flickering seemed to intensify, becoming even more agitated, the twisting, coiling smoke seeming to speed up. Diane watched it, mesmerized by its movement, fascinated by the way the colours ran along its length, like oil on water.

It was . . . it was the mirror, she thought, magnifying the whirling dust motes behind her . . . that's . . . that's . . . that's what it was.

She blinked, and then blinked again, realizing that she'd been day-dreaming, watching the spiral dance. The shimmering was hypnotic.

She straightened, attempting to pull her hand away . . . and couldn't. Cold fire ran up the length of her arm, tingling into her shoulders, down into her breasts, deep into her stomach. Black spots danced before her eyes and her breath came in great laboured gasps.

She was asleep and she was dreaming and there were pins and needles in her arm and she was going to wake up.

But she was awake.

She dropped the bayonet and gripped her right wrist with her left hand and pulled. But it was firmly stuck, fingers splayed . . . and yet she could only remember touching the glass with her forefinger.

There was a rational explanation for this . . . there was . . . there was . . .

Her hand was becoming warm, pleasantly so. The warmth rushed up through her arm – she could actually feel the movement – across her shoulders, down into her chest, tingling in her breasts, into her belly, down into her groin, along her thighs to her feet. She shuddered, abruptly conscious of the weight of her breasts, her nipples hard against the rough fabric of her dress, the tingling in her groin. Another shudder rippled through her, and she felt her legs grow tremulous. She dropped to her knees, her hand still stuck to the glass as another spasm rippled through her body, more intense than any orgasm.

And then ice-cool flesh touched her hand.

The scream caught in her throat as she attempted to stagger to her feet, hauling herself upright, using her trapped hand as leverage.

There was flesh beneath that hand. Soft, rounded flesh, like . . . like a woman's breast.

She could barely catch her breath now, and her heart was pounding so hard it was actually painful.

The shimmering in the glass had become almost frantic in its intensity . . . and then Diane realized it was throbbing in time to the beating of her heart. As she watched, the coiling, throbbing threads coalesced into a face, smoky, intangible, the planes of jaw and forehead and cheeks moving, sliding. Mouth opening, smoke coiling from the maw, matching the wreathing steam that took the place of hair.

The mouth opened wider and wider . . . and then a second face appeared within the gaping maw, smaller, the features sharper, clearer because of its tiny size.

And it was Tony Farren!

Diane found her voice then. The scream that tore from her throat was audible even up at the house.

Desperately jerking her hand away from the glass, feeling tendons and muscles pulling, she screamed and screamed until the sound was raw, and she tasted blood in her mouth.

Release came suddenly. So suddenly that she was almost flung backwards – straight down onto the point of the crossbow quarrel. The broad pyramid-shaped point pierced her skin, entangling in her dress, bringing her shockingly to her senses. She twisted, turned, and the trigger mechanism snapped.

The broad bolt ripped through flesh and bone, erupting just below her left breast, continuing on up into the ceiling.

From the gory mess embedded in the ceiling blood dripped down into the surface of the glass.

Chapter
TEN

POWER.

Raw coursing strength.

Confusion, pain, anguish . . . it had felt these before, but these were stronger, much stronger now.

Human. A human soul in mortal agony.

The colours in the Otherworld now were bright . . . bright. Sharp, clear, clean colours slicing through the greyness.

The quickening was upon it. Memories were returning. Promises made, oaths sworn.

For ever and ever.

A petty life, a female life, not a virgin, but responsive. It savoured the life, a foretaste of the feast to come.

Blood dripping.

The tang of it in the dust of the Otherworld. The colour. The life.

Blood dripping.

Life quickening.

Chapter
ELEVEN

ONE death was messy, but two – obviously connected – meant piles of paperwork.

Inspector Margaret Haaren leaned forward, peering between the seats, looking at the impressive façade of the Frazer house. In real estate terms she wondered what she was looking at: a million, a million and a half? Without knowing a thing about them, she guessed there'd be two cars, one child, probably with an exotic name, and a dog. She knew the type.

'Just like my gaff,' Bill Russell murmured, changing down as they drove up the long gravelled driveway.

'I thought you lived in a one-room squat in Hackney, Bill,' Margaret Haaren murmured. The sergeant laughed, but the inspector caught the startled look from the WPC in the passenger seat. She was young, just out of Hendon, new to the Met; this was her first murder investigation, and she was obviously in awe of Inspector Margaret Haaren, whose reputation was fearsome.

'What do we have, Bill?' Margaret asked, sitting back into the seat, picking up the report again.

Sergeant Bill Russell was a second-generation London bobby. He'd spent twenty-five years on the force and while much had changed in that time – the types of crime, the frequency, the violence, the types of people committing them – there were still some things, like motive, which remained satisfyingly the same.

'I think we've got a case of money problems, ma'am.'

Margaret Haaren sat forward, listening intently. She had known Bill Russell since she had joined the force a lifetime ago, and when she made inspector, eight years ago, she had requested him as her sergeant. She respected his advice and intuitions.

'First we have the accidental death of one of the workmen, then a break-in, and the savage killing of a guard dog. Next, we have the appearance of the big guy with the scars, followed, almost immediately by the death of another of the employees.' He smiled ruefully, looking into the mirror, catching the eyes of the woman in the back seat. 'Someone is leaning on our man.'

'The same thought had crossed my mind.'

Bill Russell caught the look of puzzlement on the young woman police constable's face, and explained patiently. 'This Mister Frazer is obviously very wealthy. Now let's say someone wanted to make him pay a little insurance, a little protection, and he refused, then what better way of gaining his attention than by knocking off two of his employees, terrorizing him in this way.'

'But two people are dead,' Carole Morrow said, horrified. In her disgust, she forgot her fear of the inspector and half-turned in the seat to look at her, 'No one would kill for that reason – just to threaten someone, would they?' she asked plaintively.

'You're assuming that other people place the same value on life that you do, that most normal people do,' Margaret Haaren said gently, 'I think you'll find that that's not always the case.'

'Yes . . . yes, ma'am. Thank you, ma'am.' Carole Morrow turned around, realizing that she'd spoken to the inspector like an ordinary person.

There were two police cars neatly parked in the gravelled driveway, and a BMW rather more sloppily parked closer to the door. As they pulled up, the hall door opened and a short, stout man, who would have looked like a doctor even if he hadn't been carrying his bag, walked out onto the step. He was talking to a slender blonde-haired woman sporting a marvellous tan that looked too good to have come from a sun-bed. The doctor walked down the steps and climbed into the BMW.

Haaren leaned forward and tapped the WPC on the shoulder. 'Stop him. Find out what's wrong. He's probably sedated someone, if so find out how long it'll be before I can ask questions.'

'Yes, ma'am!'

Bill Russell stood on the brakes, scattering stones, but effectively blocking in the BMW, allowing the WPC time to hop out of the car and hurry across to the doctor. Margaret Haaren popped the back door and strode up the steps to where the woman remained standing in the open doorway. Their mutual dislike was instinctive and almost immediate.

Margaret Haaren produced her ID. 'Inspector Margaret Haaren, London Metropolitan Police.' She heard gravel crunching behind her and, without turning around, she said, 'My sergeant, William Russell. And WPC Morrow.' She looked at the younger woman, waiting for her to introduce herself.

'Cecilia Frazer,' she said eventually. 'We have some police here already.'

'And I am here to take charge.' She walked past Cecilia Frazer into the high, wide hallway. 'May I come in?'

Margaret Haaren had been forty last birthday and looked older. A tall broad woman, with a square mannish face, emphasized by hair cut straight across over her eyes, curling around by her cheeks. There

56

were strands of grey in her brown hair which she didn't bother disguising, but her strength and determination showed most clearly in her startlingly bright green eyes. She was dressed in a two-piece suit that was almost, but not quite, the same colour as the police uniform. A frilled French blouse softened the suit's rather severe line. Her nickname in the force was Mata Hari, for no real reason that anyone could remember. The last constable who had used it in her hearing had ended up walking a beat for the best part of a year. Her reputation was formidable.

'You will not be able to speak to my husband for some time I'm afraid,' the woman said curtly, obviously resenting the intrusion. 'He was quite distressed by the death of the young woman and the doctor had to be called to sedate him.'

'When can we speak to him?' the inspector asked, glancing up the broad curved stairway.

'Tomorrow.'

'Tomorrow,' Haaren repeated slowly. 'Tomorrow might be too late. He might have seen something which might be of immediate use.'

'He saw nothing,' Cecilia Frazer said quickly.

'You were with him when he discovered the body?'

'Well no, but . . .'

'We will take your statement shortly, Mrs Frazer.' Haaren turned to the WPC who had stepped into the hallway, and raised her eyebrows in a silent question.

'A mild sedative, valium in liquid form to relax him, the doctor said. You should be able to talk to him.'

'Thank you. Is your husband up here, Mrs Frazer?' Margaret Haaren started up the stairs.

'Yes, but I don't think he'd want to be disturbed.'

Margaret Haaren smiled sweetly. 'Best to get it over with, don't you think?'

She found Jonathan Frazer lying on an enormous bed in a room that her entire apartment could have been squeezed into. He was fully dressed, and appeared to be dozing.

She tapped on the open door. 'Mister Frazer, Jonathan Frazer?'

He opened his eyes, blinking sleepily at her. 'Hello . . .?' he murmured.

'Inspector Margaret Haaren, London Metropolitan Police.' She stepped into the room and crossed quickly to the bed. 'I know you're tired, and you've had a terrible shock, but I want to speak to you now while the memories are still fresh.'

'Of course . . . of course . . .' He started to sit up and swing his legs out of bed.

'No, no, please stay where you are.' She wanted Frazer in the bed; it gave her a certain psychological advantage, and the fact that he'd been sedated meant that his defences would be down. She pulled over a high-backed, plain wooden chair and sat down on it. 'Now sir, in your own words, try and remember everything that happened, no matter how trivial . . .'

'Either he's not telling us everything or he knows nothing,' Margaret Haaren said to Bill Russell thirty minutes later as they approached the converted stables.

The sergeant nodded. 'From what I can gather from the gardener, the maid and the cook, the wife's a cool enough bitch. They all like him, he's a gentle sort apparently, but she's one of these rich bitches, likes to lord it over the servants.'

The inspector stopped at a bend in the path and turned to look back at the house. She could make out the kitchen window and part of the bedroom, so that part of Frazer's story was borne out. 'Anything else?'

'There's a daughter, Emmanuelle, Manny for short. She's home on holidays from some fashionable school in Paris, last year it was Rome and undoubtedly next year it'll be New York.'

'Little jealousy, Bill?'

He grimaced. 'Nah, not really. At least me and my missus get on together.'

Two uniformed police officers were standing outside the door to the stables chatting to WPC Morrow. They came to attention and saluted as Haaren and Russell approached.

'Anything to report?' the sergeant asked.

'Nothing sir. No one been around since the technical people finished and the coroner's people took away the body.'

'Anything else?'

The second constable, younger, round-faced, red-cheeked, looked from Haaren to Russell. 'We did hear noises at one point sir . . .' He continued despite his companion's disgusted face. 'But when we investigated we found nothing.'

'What sort of noises,' Haaren asked.

'Sort of moaning, groaning sounds.' He looked desperately at his companion.

'Can you be more specific?'

The colour in the young man's cheeks intensified.

'Cries of pain, of agony, panting . . .? Be more specific.'

'Sort of . . . of pleasure, ma'am.'

'Pleasure?'

His eyes flickered from the WPC to the inspector. 'We thought . . . we thought there was someone inside . . . doing . . . *it*.'

'But there wasn't?' Margaret asked seriously.

'No, ma'am.'

'Stay alert then.' She stepped into the relative darkness of the stables, blinking to allow her eyes to adjust to the dimness, desperately resisting the urge to burst out laughing. She could tell by Bill Russell's expression that he was controlling the same emotion.

'Where do we get them from Bill?'

'Don't know, ma'am, and that's no mistake. This is supposed to be the liberated nineties, people able to talk about sex and drugs and rock and roll.'

'*Doing it*,' she repeated wonderingly. 'How long has it been since I last heard that expression?'

'You're getting old, ma'am, if I may say so.'

'You may. But I'm not alone there.'

Their noses led them to the spot where the young girl had died, the peculiar – once smelt, never forgotten – odour of blood and excrement pervading the dry atmosphere.

'Talk me through it, Bill,' Margaret said quietly. She stood back and folded her arms across her broad chest, her left arm raised, chin cupped in the palm of her hand.

'The big guy with the scars appears and frightens the shit out of both of Frazer and the girl, Diane Williams. He was talking about a mirror – this mirror, which he said he wanted to buy. When he was told that it wasn't for sale, he became obstreperous, and vaguely threatening. The girl picks up a loaded crossbow – some antique thing apparently – and he leaves, and they think they've frightened him off.'

'Something like that wouldn't frighten someone like that,' she murmured, and he nodded in agreement.

'Anyway, Frazer goes up to the house to phone our lads, because he's convinced that it was the intruder from last night.'

'Why did he have to go up to the house? Was there no phone here?'

'It seems that the phone on the wall behind you wasn't working, for some reason. I checked it out myself: the wire's been cut. Anyway, he waits until she's locked in before he leaves her. Frazer phones us, and is walking back to this storeroom – they call it the stables – when he hears the deceased, Diane Williams, scream.'

'How far away was he at this time?'

'On the patio.'

'So he was almost in sight of the stables.'

'Just so. The cook heard the screams and she described it as blood-curdling, raw and terrified. Frazer races down the path – and he would certainly have seen someone lurking about – and attempts to gain entry to the building. But it's locked from the inside. When he looks in through that window there, he sees the girl lying on the floor, blood everywhere. He had no doubt from the quantity that she was dead.'

'How did she die?'

'Shot at point-blank range by the same crossbow she was holding. The bolt passed right through her body and lodged in the ceiling.'

'The implication is that the big man who threatened them, returned, gained entry and killed the girl.'

'Yes, ma'am. But from the angle of the crossbow in the ceiling, there is evidence to suggest that the crossbow was on the floor when it was fired.'

Margaret Haaren nodded. 'Accident? Carelessness?'

He shrugged. 'The door was locked on the inside. When our lads arrived, they had to break their way in with a sledgehammer.'

'No other way in I suppose.'

'None that I know of. The windows are barred as are the skylights. There might be another door hidden amongst all this mess, but that presupposes two things: that there is another door and that someone knows about it. And both deaths look like accidents.'

'Let's not get too complicated,' Margaret warned. 'Let's keep it simple. One accident I could believe, but two . . .? What have we got: two dead people, one employer. Motive?' she asked.

'Putting pressure on Frazer for money.'

Margaret Haaren nodded. She looked around the cluttered room, finally stopping before the tall, ugly mirror.

'And this is the mirror the scarred man talked about?'

'Said he wanted to buy it. Frazer bought it very recently at auction in Dublin. The big guy said it should never have been sold.'

'Ugly looking thing,' she murmured, staring at its grimy surface.

'That's the sort of thing they put on the ceilings of those love motels in America,' Bill Russell remarked, 'for when the couples are doing *it*.'

'Well you certainly wouldn't get it on the ceiling of my apartment ... doubt if you'd even get it in the door.'

'What do you want to do now, ma'am?'

'Let's take a closer look at Mister Frazer and his antiques business.' She strode towards the door. 'And God help him if anyone else turns up dead around him!'

Chapter
TWELVE

TRACING the mirror had been easy enough. There was a stink to it that anyone with half a talent could sense. Recovering it would be a lot more difficult.

The mirror had been purchased by an antiques dealer named Jonathan Frazer. He didn't know the man, didn't know the name, but he obviously needed to be looked at, and he would have to do some research into his background.

There might be no connection, it might simply have been a coincidence, but Edmund Talbott didn't believe in coincidence. Frazer had been lured to the mirror, drawn to it, like a bee to pollen. And he was prepared to gamble that somewhere in the man's past – in previous generations even, for the mirror knew no time – the mirror's path had crossed that of one of the Frazers.

The big scarred man moved restlessly around the tiny flat which had been loaned to him by a London contact. It was situated on the edge of Soho, above a Chinese take-away restaurant, next door to a dilapidated adult movie house. It was shabby and anonymous, and it suited him perfectly. Before settling in, he had taken some basic precautions and removed the spotted mirror from the bathroom, blackened or covered all reflective surfaces, and finally covered the windows with newspapers. He was doomed never to look upon his own reflection, never to allow himself to be aware of his own image in a mirror.

He had been in danger from the mirror before, mortal danger. It had come close to claiming him, but he had always managed to defeat it . . . but now? This was the first time in generations that the mirror had been uncovered for any length of time, and already it was gathering its strength.

It had taken one life, a man, almost immediately.

He had been asleep when he had felt the cry of the soul in torment. He had been drawn to it, pulled from sleep into that shadowy astral Otherworld in pursuit of the cry of the lost soul. But it had vanished, leaving behind no echo, no resonance, as if it had never existed. Although he had searched through the Otherworld until he had endangered his own body's massive reserves, he had found nothing. And he knew then that the mirror had swallowed it, trapped it within its ancient core.

It had fed off animal next, but that had been his doing.

He had traced the mirror to Frazer's house by fixing on the last location of the death cry. Once he was close to it, he could feel the insidious chill of the glass, though now he noticed that the residual trickle of power he always associated with the mirror had grown sharper, slightly stronger.

He hadn't thought the building would be alarmed, and that had been his first mistake. And he rarely made mistakes; he was usually the most meticulous and careful of men. His predecessor's mistakes had cost him his life and his soul. Edmund Talbott hadn't made a mistake of this nature for . . . for a long, long time. Unless of course, his reason had been clouded, his judgement awry. And if so, then he had every reason to be afraid, to be terribly afraid.

He had been close to the mirror when he had become aware of Frazer's approach. Instinct had driven him away from the glass, deep into the furthest corner of the stable. When Frazer had thrown the light switch the bulbs had overloaded, sputtering and exploding with sharp pops down along the length of the stable.

And that had been none of his doing either.

He should have known then that the power was gathering in the stable, that the mirror was drawing in its defences.

Then the security people had arrived.

The dog had been alarmed, frightened, aware with that residual sixth sense that was once part of the human kind too, that something was wrong here. It sensed a presence, and it had been torn between orientating on the mirror or on him. Eventually, it had latched onto him as being a tangible, human target.

Talbott knew that the animals were not trained to kill, but as the beast had loomed up out of the darkness, teeth bared, saliva running in ropes down its jowls, he knew that if it hit him, it would tear his throat out.

There were weapons and implements to hand, knives, swords, flails, spears. His questing fingers wrapped around the haft of a tall pitchfork just as the crazed animal leapt. He pirouetted, extraordinarily deftly, surprisingly swiftly, for such a large man, holding the pitchfork close to his head, pointing downward. As the dog blundered past, he had plunged it into the creature, pinning it to a large wooden chest.

It was a mortal wound, it should have killed the animal. It didn't.

The beast screamed once, a terrifying sound,

human-like in its intensity. Even then it had turned on Talbott, snapping furiously, bloody saliva spraying everywhere. What was even more frightening now was that it was snapping at him in silence, its front paws scrabbling at the wooden chest, tearing into it. The big man picked up a sword, hefting it in both hands. As if sensing what he was going to do, the dog's frenzied silent snapping intensified, actually turning itself around on the pitchfork's tines to come closer to him.

Talbott swung at it, the sword biting deep into its neck. The creature screamed again, and Talbott's next cut sent its head bouncing across the floor, spurting blood that was black in the vague light. The stench of blood – tart and metallic – suffused the air.

He hated having to kill so close to the mirror but he had no choice . . . or had he? Was this further evidence that his judgement was clouded?

He had made another mistake when he had gone back and asked about purchasing the mirror. Neither Frazer nor the girl Williams – especially the girl – had been intimidated by his presence. Indeed, that little ruse had gone badly wrong. The girl was killed shortly afterwards, and naturally, suspicion had fallen on him.

He was unsure what his next move was. He couldn't go back near the Frazer house, not with the police presence. And he didn't think Frazer would be offering the mirror for sale in the immediate future. The man's interest in the mirror had been aroused. He was frightened – but intrigued.

And what if he tried to break it?

The thought was terrifying, but Edmund Talbott immediately dismissed it. The mirror itself had its own battery of protections and defences, he would be very surprised if it allowed someone like Frazer to come even close to it with *evil* intent.

His only choice now was to wait. Wait for the next

move. But that time would only allow the mirror's strength to increase and grow. It would have time to feed. But all he could do was wait.

And he was very good at waiting.

He stripped naked and then washed himself as thoroughly as was possible with the small cold-water sink. His mind was elsewhere, and he didn't feel the chill water that raised goose-bumps on his arms and shoulders, the cold flesh tightening around the extraordinary network of scars that began on his face, patterned his shoulders and ran down onto his chest and back. Many of the nerves beneath the skin had been damaged during the accident and both heat and pain were dull, vaguely perceptible feelings on his flesh.

Edmund Talbott would be fifty next birthday, but looked – and sometimes felt – older. He was too old now to go hunting this object; this should be the time of life when he should begin to instruct his own son in the legend of the mirror. If he had a son. But Edward had been dead ten years now, destroyed in the same accident that had shredded his own body. He'd been strong, he'd survived, but the child hadn't . . . nor had his wife, dearest Elizabeth, five months pregnant at the time. No man's fault, an accident, terrible, tragic, front page headlines for exactly one day, a brief mention on the television news headlines. A court case that ran for three years and a record amount of compensation that warranted five lines on the back pages of some of the newspapers.

It had taken him the best part of a year and a half to recover from his terrible wounds, and when he had finally been released from the hospital he had returned to Ireland, his first stop the tiny graveyard close to the house where the bodies had been buried. He had squatted on the damp ground and wept then, the first tears since the accident, laying to rest his memories of them, putting aside all thoughts of vengeance.

It hadn't been an accident. He knew that, but he could prove nothing. And he was powerless to do anything about it.

Talbott rubbed his face vigorously, squeezing his eyes shut as the cold facecloth rubbed across them. If he wanted to, he could convince himself that the moisture on his face came from the cloth.

Ten years ago, and about three miles away.

It had been a glorious day, the details of it were etched on his memory, warm and sunny in the first week of June. They had spent a marvellous weekend in London; he had renewed some old acquaintances, they had seen some shows, Elizabeth had shopped.

And at some time over the weekend his defences had dropped.

The lift was bullet shaped, a tube that crawled up the exterior of the building, the view over the city centre absolutely breathtaking. Little Edward had watched it move up and down the building with all the concentration that a ten-year-old can muster, and had then begun to pester his parents with that same concentration and determination. He wanted to ride in the lift. Eventually they had agreed.

The journey up was uneventful. He had been sure Edward was going to be terrified, but the boy had been fascinated with the view through the heavy perspex walls, ceiling and floor. Elizabeth had felt slightly nauseous and Edmund had had to admit that he felt slightly off balance himself.

They were alone in the lift as it began its descent. The sensation of falling was more pronounced now, even the boy falling quiet.

'Look straight ahead, don't look down,' Edmund had advised, and, of course, everyone had looked down, seeing their reflections in the floor.

Beware the image, it will steal your soul away.

Edmund Talbott opened his mouth to scream a warning, his hand scrabbling for the emergency stop, his eyes locked onto the reflected images.

The lift immediately ground to a halt, lurched and settled. As he watched, he saw the reflections in the perspex change, alter, become something else, something hideous, flesh slewing off muscle, muscle liquefying off the bone, hair lengthening, falling out, their features twisting, turning, changing.

Skeletons.

One reached out and touched the wall, mimicking his movement, mouth opening in a parody of a cry. Another, the female – Elizabeth – pressed both hands to her stomach, the bony fingers disappearing into the cavity, dress folding in around them.

And the lift fell.

It plummeted twenty-seven of the thirty floors, pulling free of its moorings almost immediately, smashing the frail cocoon off the heavy glass windows of the office block. Glass – supposedly unbreakable – shattered, showering the occupants with slivers of razor sharp glass. Hands locked rigidly around the handrail – later the rail would have to be cut off because of his unopenable grip – Edmund Talbott could only watch as his wife and son were smashed repeatedly against the perspex walls of the lift, rolling in the slivers of glass that had burst in through the rent in the perspex close to the roof and along one wall. Their skin was flayed from the muscle, their flesh torn open to the bone. At some point, close to the ground, the metal hawsers, which had been hissing upwards as the lift fell, became entangled around the falling tube. They sliced through the perspex with ease, snapping the tube in half, catching Edward's tiny body, mangling it before his father's eyes. He squeezed his eyes shut and when he opened them again, both bodies – Elizabeth's and Edward's – were gone, tossed out like refuse. Before the lift finally exploded across the London pavement he still had the presence of mind to commend their souls to God and was strangely glad that at least they would all die together.

But he hadn't died, though in the eighteen months that followed, he wished many a time that he had.

It took London's fire brigade nearly four hours with cutting equipment to free his body from the wreckage. Men who had worked on some of the most horrific accidents for much of their adult lives turned away as the mangled mess that had hours before been a human being was finally recovered from the wreckage. He should have been dead. The fact that he still lived was a miracle ... or an evil joke. Both legs were broken, multiple breaks which practically guaranteed that he would never walk again. Only two ribs remained intact, most of them having impacted inwards, puncturing or tearing most of the internal organs, collapsing both lungs. Arms, wrists, shoulders and collarbones were shattered. Jaw, nose, cheekbones and skull were fractured.

And his flesh, especially around his face, had been flayed by the countless thousands of pieces of glass and perspex in the lift.

Months later, one of the plastic surgeons had handed him a jar filled with glittering specks. There was a scrawled note on the side of the jar, which said simply, '2234'. 'That's how many pieces of glass we took from your flesh,' he said simply. He had tilted Edmund's face slightly, looking at the ruin, and then smiled ruefully. 'Well, you'll certainly never look in a mirror again.'

But Edmund Talbott had made the same promise to himself a long time ago. One moment of weakness had destroyed everything he loved. Then, ten years ago, he had thought revenge impossible. He had been weak and ignorant, but ten years' research had given him certain knowledge.

And he would have his revenge.

He swore it.

Chapter
THIRTEEN

HE blinked, rising up from a dream in which he saw himself reflected a dozen times in every direction.

'Hi Dad, how're you feeling?'

Jonathan Frazer opened his eyes and looked at his daughter sitting beside his bed. He wondered how long she'd been sitting there, wondered how long he'd been asleep. The room was dark, hazy, as if it was late afternoon.

He reached out and took her hand, turning it slightly, looking at her long and slender fingers lying against his soft palm. Her fingers tightened over his, squeezing gently. There was sympathy and under-standing too in her coal-black eyes, but without the pity he had seen in his wife's face.

Emmanuelle Frazer was eighteen. She was a stunning classical beauty, large eyed, fine-boned, whose resemblance to her mother was slight, although she was the very image of her grandmother – Jonathan's mother – who had been a great beauty in her youth. One of her features had been her mane of thick black hair, and her father had been horrified when she had returned from Paris and he had discovered that she had had her head shaved in what he called a skin-head, but which she insisted was a Number Two haircut, which left a slight fuzz of hair across her skull. It was, she had assured him, quite the latest fashion, and he had to agree that, while he didn't particularly like it, it did emphasize her high cheekbones and her huge black eyes.

'How are you?' she asked again.

'OK. I've felt better. You heard . . .?'

'I heard,' she said shortly.

'What did your mother tell you?'

Manny shrugged. 'She said there's been an accident; Diane had been playing with a loaded crossbow and she must have dropped it and it had gone off.' Her fingers tightened on her father's hand. 'It's scary Dad, two people dead within days of one another.'

'Its something to do with that scarred man,' he muttered.

'What scarred man?' she asked, frowning, her forehead and the skin on her almost bald head crinkling comically.

'Before . . . before Diane's accident, this big ugly guy had come around asking about that mirror I bought in Dublin . . .'

'Hang on, hang on a sec, Dad. What mirror? The mirror you bought at auction? Remember, I've been away for the past few days. I don't know what's been going on around here.'

'You remember I told you about the mirror I bought in Dublin at some quayside auction house. Tony was working on that mirror when it fell on him.'

She nodded slowly, unsure where this was leading.

'There was a break-in last night . . .'

'Mother told me about that.'

He nodded slowly. 'I'm convinced it was the same guy who was here today – he gave me this little present last night.' He touched the ugly purple swelling in the centre of his forehead.

'How did he get in?'

'The police think he might have had a set of keys – possibly Tony's. You know he'd had a long-term relationship with a man about ten years younger than himself ... well, the young man didn't attend the funeral, nor has he been seen for the past few days. The police are now interested in his whereabouts.'

'You think something might have happened to him?' she asked, almost breathlessly.

'I don't know. All we know is that he's not around, and that possibly Tony's keys were used to open the door, because the lock wasn't forced.'

'And then the dog was killed?'

'That's right. The same person who belted me, killed the dog. The police speculated that it must have been someone of immense strength, because he had managed to pin the dog to the wooden box with a single blow, before decapitating it. So today, when this big ugly guy – must be the ugliest man I've ever seen, terrifically scarred – turns up at the stables wanting to buy the mirror, you don't need to be a genius to work out that they're one and the same man.'

'Did he look powerful?'

'He was tall – six three or four – with huge shoulders, broad chest, massive arms. He could have taken care of the dog without even breaking into a sweat.'

'And he wanted the mirror?'

'He said it was a family heirloom, and it had been sold by mistake.'

'Had he an Irish accent?'

Jonathan frowned. 'No, not exactly Irish, but there was a ... a sort of Celtic tinge to it. I'd more properly describe it as a country accent. He was frightening, everything about him was intimidating. I was beginning to wonder what was going to happen when Diane appeared beside me with a loaded crossbow.

74

The man left then, but we both knew he'd be back. I tried the phone in the stable, but it wasn't working. So, Diane locked herself in while I went to phone the police.' He stopped and swallowed hard. 'I was on my way back down to the stables when I heard her scream. When I got to it, the door was still locked and all I could do was look inside. She was lying on the floor before the mirror . . .'

Manny's fingers tightened on her father's damp hand.

'She . . . she'd been shot in the back with the crossbow. The bolt had gone right through her.'

Manny took a deep breath. 'How did it happen?' she whispered.

'I don't know. The police weren't prepared to even guess. Your mother thinks that she may have put the crossbow on the ground and, because it's such an old weapon, the cocking or firing mechanism may have slipped, and she just happened to be standing in the line of the bolt . . . I don't know.'

'But you think the big guy's involved?'

'I'm sure of it. I know the police are certainly interested in him also. And the mirror's involved somewhere,' he added, almost as an afterthought.

'How? In what way?'

'I don't know.' He leaned back on the pillows, and closed his eyes. 'The scarred man said that the mirror had been sold by accident, that it was a family heirloom and that it should never have gone up for sale. He seems to be making a lot of effort to recover his heirloom.'

'Is it especially valuable?' Manny asked.

'Tony estimated twenty thousand plus. But I've got more valuable pieces in the shop.' He smiled crookedly. 'Diane never liked the mirror, she said it was bad luck.' He laughed shakily. 'I'm beginning to believe her.'

*

The door had been replaced by a temporary rough-hewn construction made up by a local handyman. The remains of the old door, which had been sledgehammered by the police, lay propped up against the side of the stable, the shattered timbers bright against the dark stained wood.

Emmanuelle lifted the key she had taken off the ring behind the kitchen door and slid it into the gleaming new lock. It snapped smoothly open. She had already disabled the alarm from the panel in the kitchen, but when she stepped into the long dim building and pulled the door closed behind her, she discovered that the alarm hadn't been reconnected to the new door.

There was a peculiar smell in the room, not the usual sweetly pleasant smells of must and dust, mould and rot, but a different, sharper odour. There was blood too, the smell heavy and cloying on the dry atmosphere, and she could distinguish the sharper stench of urine and the heavier odour of excrement.

Wrinkling her nose, she made her way through the piled artefacts to where the mirror was a tall pale rectangle in the shadows. Having heard so much about it, she just had to see the mirror that had been responsible either directly or indirectly for the deaths of two people.

And she was disappointed.

She had expected something different, something more impressive, maybe with an ornate, heavy frame worked with evil symbols, but instead it looked just like an ordinary mirror – a little larger than most perhaps – in a plain wooden frame.

There was a rust brown stain across the bottom of the wood close to the base of the mirror, and it took her a few seconds to realize that she was looking at Diane Williams's blood. She was surprised that she could look at it quite so dispassionately.

Moving closer to stand directly in front of the mirror,

she stared at it impassively, hands on hips, head tilted slightly to one side. Her own reflection was barely visible behind a patina of dirt. There were clear streaks in the glass, bright speckles at the bottom as if the mirror had been washed with liquid, more of the liquid had run down from the top of the glass, to the foot, long clear streaks bright against the grime.

Manny stepped forward and peered into the glass and something – no, someone – looked back!

For a moment she thought her heart had stopped. The image had lasted a second – less than a second – a brief flickering that might have been a face or might have been her imagination. The face had been superimposed over her own, coal-black eyes matching hers exactly, the same high cheekbones, though she had the impression that the images were slightly rounder, fuller. Full, red lips, like her own. And hair. That was the chief difference: the image had had a full head of wavering, twisting, wreathing black hair.

A deep, convulsive shudder ran through her, breaking her concentration, losing the picture. She shivered, suddenly cold, goose flesh along her bare arms and legs. She stepped back from the glass, reluctant to turn her back on it.

Maybe it was some of that dope she'd been smoking throughout the school term. She had read somewhere that some of that stuff could linger in your system for years, and that something – light, a smell, a sound – could set it off again. Maybe that's what it was, some sort of residual after-effect of the drugs.

She was almost at the door when she sensed the presence standing behind her. She screamed, at the same time flailing backwards with the point of her left elbow as she'd been taught in self-defence classes. It caught the figure dead centre in the chest, dropping him to the ground. She spun, fists clenched, all her fear now transformed into anger, pumping adrenalin . . .

and found her father gasping on the floor.

'Dad, oh Dad. Jesus I'm sorry. I thought you were someone . . . I just felt someone standing behind me, and I thought . . .'

'It's OK,' he gasped, taking Manny's arm, allowing her to haul him to his feet. He was ashen, his breath rasping through tortured bruised muscles. 'I'm sorry, I just saw the door was unlocked and I thought . . .' He stopped. He hadn't been thinking. He had opened the door purely on impulse, just in time to see the faceless figure coming towards him, barely distinguishable in the gloom. And then he had felt the pain. 'At least it's nice to know that the martial arts classes you're taking worked.'

'Dad, I'm sorry . . .'

'Don't worry about it. But what were you doing here?'

Manny shrugged. 'I just came for a look.'

'Curiosity killed the cat,' he said and then immediately regretted it.

'It's a very ugly mirror.'

'It is,' he said, looking into the shadows where he knew the mirror was standing.

'What do you think of it?'

Manny shrugged again. 'Not much. It's ugly, it's . . . plain. I'd been expecting something else.' She didn't add that the mirror disturbed her. But the image of the face in the glass had already faded to a vague memory, in which she could barely remember the features on the face she'd seen, except that it had been female . . . yes, definitely female. 'And what are you doing down here anyway? I thought you were supposed to be in bed.'

'I was.'

Manny suddenly noticed the item he'd been casually holding away from her, partially shielding with his body. 'Dad, what are you doing with the shot-gun?'

of the room, around a chaise longue that had seen better days. With great difficulty he had manoeuvred the mirror into this clearing, with the entrance to the cleared area directly facing the door. Anyone entering through the doorway would be immediately visible, though he, hopefully, would be invisible in the shadows.

'And what happens if someone comes looking for the mirror?'

Her father glanced over his shoulder, his bruised face pale in the gloom. 'Then I'll hold him for the police, and maybe I'll ask him a few questions before they arrive.'

'And the shot-gun?'

'For personal protection only,' he muttered, turning away, not meeting her eyes.

'Dad . . .'

'Yes.'

'Be careful Dad . . . Don't do anything . . . anything heroic.'

Jonathan Frazer straightened, dusting off his hands. 'Don't worry. You know I'm a coward.'

'Yes, that's why you came charging in here the other night, and damn nearly got yourself killed. That's the sort of thing cowards do.'

'You sound like your mother,' he said gently.

'Dad!' she said in disgust, turning and walking away into the evening.

Jonathan Frazer spent the next two hours wandering around the stables, looking through the multitude of pieces Tony had been in the process of repairing. Some of them had been there for years; many, he knew, would probably never reach the shop. It was no way to run a business, but then the antiques business was no longer his primary source of income, although he wasn't completely independent yet. His father had made the money, and then secured it with shrewd investments; all he had had to do was to consolidate. He still needed the business for the cash flow though. He wondered what he would do now without Tony. Every firm that dealt in antiques – whether it be miscellaneous antiques, or books, prints, pictures, furniture, militaria – had someone like Tony Farren, someone whose knowledge was essential to the running of that establishment. Without Tony, things would be different; he could try to find someone else, but finding someone with knowledge and experience was going to prove extraordinarily difficult – and expensive. He would have to start taking a more direct hand in the day-to-day running of the business. And the first item on the agenda would be to sell off much of this stuff in storage: he had tens of thousands of pounds tied up here.

He pulled aside an ancient battered chesterfield, wincing as glass slivers from the shattered striplights stung his hands. Diane had done a good job of cleaning up most of them, but ... but she'd never completed the job. First thing in the morning he'd get someone in to replace the fluorescent lights, and to check the fuses – obviously something had overloaded them, some power surge from the house maybe, or the alarm ... yes, that was it, the alarm had overloaded them, though he was surprised they simply hadn't just died rather than exploding so spectacularly.

Then, maybe with Manny helping him, he could close the shop for a couple of days and bring Robert, his shop assistant, in to help him clean the place up, do a little re-organization. Maybe he'd sell off some of the junk – and without Tony's expertise to transform it much of it was junk – to one of the country dealers.

He only realized the light was almost gone when he found it impossible to read the title on the spine of an enormous atlas Tony had been rebinding. He reached for his pocket watch, but he was wearing a cardigan over faded cords, and had left his watch in his waistcoat back in the house. Well, it was late, and he was hungry, but reluctant to go back up to the house and possibly have another argument with Cecilia. And he didn't want to leave the stables.

He manoeuvred his way through the mess and lay down on the chaise longue, wincing as something prodded the small of his back. He folded his arms across his chest and stretched out, crossing his feet at the ankle. The shot-gun was on the floor beside him within easy reach.

Six feet away, the mirror was a pale rectangle against the shadows.

If you dealt with antiques for any length of time, you soon learned that there certainly were some pieces which were *unlucky* – cursed was probably too strong a word for them. He recalled a cavalry sabre a friend of his had bought at auction, a relic of the Light Brigade's charge. As he had slid it from its sheath he had sliced open the palm of his hand on the edge of the blade. An accident. Because the dealer had more than a passing interest in bladed weaponry, especially those with historical connotations, he had brought it home and added it to his personal collection. A few days later, his three-year-old son had somehow managed to lift the sword off its wall hangings, slide it from its sheath and stab himself in the foot. An accident. Deciding to sell the sword after all, he had put it on display in his Oxford Street shop. One of the sales assistants tore through the flesh between index finger and thumb while sliding the sword back into its sheath. An accident.

But three accidents with the same piece? Upon investigation it was discovered that the sword had belonged to an officer accused of cowardice during the Crimea campaign. Upon the eve of his court-martial – when the weight of evidence was against him – he had fallen upon his sword in his tent. Since then the weapon was deemed to be cursed.

But such stories weren't unusual in the antiques trade. There were many unlucky pieces, and the stories about cursed jewels were legion.

So was it impossible that the mirror could be cursed in the same way? Or was he simply allowing his imagination to run away with him?

Tony was dead. But Tony had had accidents before; Jonathan smiled, remembering the time he had become locked in the eighteenth-century sea-chest, and then again when he'd become trapped in a fourteenth-century suit of armour – God alone knew why he'd climbed into it in the first place. He took risks, he did stupid things . . . and he drank. What was to say that he hadn't been drinking that day, over-balanced and pulled the mirror down on top of him? Accidental death, the coroner had said.

And Diane?

Well, she knew the rules about playing with the weapons. He'd once found two young apprentices duelling with sabres, both weapons razor sharp. He'd dismissed them both on the spot, and made the rule that the militaria were not toys. What did she know about crossbows, especially one as delicate and as difficult to manoeuvre as an antique hunting crossbow? It could have been an accident, nothing more.

And the scarred man? Why had he broken into the stables? – for the mirror certainly – and yet it wasn't exactly hidden the night he had broken in. And even if he had found it, what was he going to do with it? It had taken four policemen to lift it off Tony Farren's body; how was one man going to haul it away? But hold on, hadn't he mentioned Tony's name? Maybe he'd been involved with Tony, maybe there'd been an argument and the mirror had been pushed down onto him. The same scarred man had shot Diane in the back . . .

Jonathan Frazer sat bolt upright, pressing both hands to the sides of his head. This was craziness. He could feel his head spinning, his thoughts chasing one another. He was thinking like a madman, curses and plots and murders. He must still be feeling the effects of the sedatives the doctor had given him, that was it, that's why he was confused, sleepy.

But what would happen if he fell into a drugged sleep now? What would happen if someone broke into the stables tonight? His heart began to pound in a panic attack. All the windows were barred, so the only way in was through the door and the door was bolted on the inside. He climbed up out of the chaise longue and lifted a bucket of nails from the work-bench and scattered them over the floor. He tied a length of fishing wire across the entrance to the little clearing where he had positioned the mirror so that anyone approaching him wouldn't be able to do it without making enough noise to waken the dead . . .

Frazer began to laugh, a dry hissing sound, the thought of waking the dead – suddenly seeing Tony Farren's and Diane Williams's faces – highly amusing. The laughter went on for two minutes and then became gentle snoring.

The full moon was high in the heavens, the sky clear and cloudless, its light cold and sharp across the dirty streets. Edmund Talbott stood at the window of the flat and looked down over the almost deserted Soho streets through a tiny rent in the newspaper he had pasted over the glass. The young woman in the blonde wig and the too-tight, too-short dress with the too-high heels had finally left her post across the road, obviously hoping to pick up a late customer coming out of the Chinese restaurant.

The big man looked up into the heavens, gauging the time. He folded his arms and leaned back against the wall, watching the way the moonlight moved across the bare floorboards, the light still distinct even through the newspapers.

Talbott closed his eyes, concentrating, trying to remember the layout of Frazer's stables, orientating on it, and then fixing the mirror in relation to the windows, then determining the fall of the moonlight. Finally, he relaxed, shoulders slumping; providing everything had remained untouched, the mirror was out of the direct moonlight – and anyway there'd be no one in the storehouse to see anything.

The moonlight moved down the length of the long room, gradually illuminating each of the small barred windows in turn before moving on. It was close to three in the morning before the luminescence finally reached the mirror. Liquid silver ran down the length of the glass, bringing it to startling, brilliant life. A trembling shadow drifted down the length of the tall glass.

Jonathan Frazer opened his eyes and looked into a wall of silver light.

Shapes moved within the light, ghostly, flickering images . . .

Chapter
FIFTEEN

SMOKE coiled and twisted around the enormous pillars, thick and grey, almost glutinous. Lower down, closer to the floor, tendrils of dank mist rose up through the cracked and shattered slabstones. Water dripped in the distance, the sound echoing hollowly through the high-ceilinged chamber. There was water on the floor, large shallow pools washed silver in the vague light, and the pillars were streaked green with fetid moisture. The air felt damp, heavy, cloying, tainted with excrement, seaweed and fish.

The cloaked and hooded figure moved through the swirling mist, seemingly unconcerned with the chill or the odours, moving confidently across the maze of broken stones and the other, less easily definable debris that littered the ground. There were natural pot-holes strewn around the huge echoing chamber, as well as other, man-made traps. Even if someone managed to breach the outer security defences without raising an alarm, they would have to be very lucky indeed to make it past this sanctum without succumbing to one or other of its defences.

Moving deeper into the huge chamber there were sounds, distant and indistinct, occasionally broken by a rasping shriek that might have been metal on metal. There was light too, an archway illuminated by warm, golden light, incongruous in this dark and drear place. There were newer, though possibly even less pleasant odours, overlaying the stench of the place.

Two men suddenly appeared out of the shadows, the wan light running off their leather jerkins, the swords and knives in their hands. Their faces were flat, impassive, their eyes wide and unblinking, their pupils tiny.

The hooded figure stopped and straightened, throwing back the hood, shaking out a mane of thick black hair, coal-black eyes regarding the two men impassively.

The two men stared at the woman, their mouths slack, saliva running onto their chins, into their beards. She stared them down, knowing that even though they had been trained to accept her, they could still tear her apart if she showed the slightest fear or hesitation.

Without a word they both saluted with their swords and stepped back into the shadows. They were effectively the last line of defence and even if one were lucky – or unlucky – enough to breach the multiple defences, it would be impossible to pass these. They were brothers, taken from their mother since birth and trained in the same way the hunting dogs and pit bulls were trained, beaten, starved and tortured, until they were completely loyal to their master. Narcotics kept them docile and obedient, especially the weed that had originally been brought back by the Knights returning from the Crusades.

The woman moved into the arched doorway and stopped, unwilling to intrude now, knowing that the work was at a very delicate stage. When he was finished, he would notice her.

There had been some improvements in the place

since she had last been here. Equipment had been brought in, a table and chairs, a brazier.

And the mirror.

She caught herself looking at it, staring deep into its grimy depths before she realized what she was doing and tore her gaze away, forcing herself to concentrate on the room. The chamber was actually below the level of the Thames in a rotting wharfside warehouse, surrounded by filthy slums. And even in this overcrowded disease-ridden part of the city, the building remained unoccupied. People who entered its dank interior – tramps, vagabonds, some of the women who plied their trade on the wharf – had been found dead in the street the following morning.

The building was cursed. As simple as that.

The woman smiled. How primitive these peasants were; how easily controlled. A few dead bodies and they spoke of curses. Aye, the building was cursed, but the only curse on it was the two half-human creatures. This might be the age of discovery and invention, and men might talk of the Americas and the Indies as if they actually knew what they were talking about; they might admire the new weeds, the fruits, the vegetables coming back from the New World, but in all their quest for knowledge they were ignoring a greater, larger, far more mysterious world. A world of magic and power.

There was a man in the centre of the room, tall, thin, a shock of red hair and beard emphasizing his pale skin, highlighting his green eyes. His clothes had once been white and cream, but now his silk shirt and hose, and pale doeskin boots were soiled with the filth of the place. His hands were on his hips and he was looking at the floor.

Without turning around he raised his left hand, fingers crooked, calling her forward. She moved lithely through the debris littering the floor to stand beside him, her arm moving around his waist, her head resting on his shoulder. 'Kelley,' she murmured.

There was a pit at his feet, ten feet deep by ten feet wide. Thick iron bars, already speckled by rust even though they were barely weeks old, had been set into a stout wooden frame, which in turn was bolted to the floor.

And within the pit was a man.

The woman stooped, taking care to lift the hem of her dresses and long cloak off the floor.

'He is young?' she said. It was difficult to make out his features or age in the dim lighting.

The tall red-haired man brought the lantern from the table and held it high, shedding warm yellow light into the pit. There was a quick scrabbling movement as the rats scurried for cover and then the young man came to his feet. He was naked, his pale body patterned with bruises and scrapes, covered in filth and matted straw. His hair was thick – filthy now with grease and straw – but there was a distinctive bald patch in the centre of his head.

'A cleric!' she said, delighted.

'A cleric,' the big man nodded. 'He believes I am the devil.'

She smiled, showing long yellow teeth. 'He is almost right.'

The big man smiled humourlessly. 'I wonder what he will make of you.' His accent was flat, dull, almost crude.

'And he is a virgin?'

The red-haired man shrugged. 'Who can tell these days? But he is young, fanatical, not the type to give himself to the sins of the flesh.'

'Wash him,' she said, turning away.

Kelley shouted aloud in a guttural language not unlike Gallic and one of the guards appeared. He pointed to the terrified man in the pit and spoke again in the same harsh tongue. The brute looked into the pit for a moment and then moved away, returning moments later with an enormous bucket of water which it dumped unceremoniously over the man. He screamed with shock and and surprise: the water had been pulled from the Thames and was freezing.

'*Aris*,' Kelley grunted. Again.

More water was emptied down onto the terrified young man. He was now shivering so badly he could barely stand, and the water had turned the floor of the pit into a quagmire. The pit was then unbarred and the dead-eyed guard dropped the ten feet into the sodden mire of straw and filth and hauled the young man to his feet. Although he was barely conscious, he attempted to beat at the guard with his fists. The guard slapped him once, a single blow that rocked his head from side to side.

Kelley lowered a makeshift ladder – a length of wood with pegs set on either side – and the guard climbed up, the young cleric tossed over one shoulder. '*Anseo!*' Here. He pointed to the long wooden table that had been set up before the mirror. The guard dumped the young man onto the table, allowing his head to bounce off the wood.

Kelley and the woman approached the table and looked at him critically. He was perhaps seventeen years old, physically perfect, all his limbs, fingers and toes intact. His back teeth had gone, but his eyes were unclouded by cataracts, the whites reasonably clear, tainted around the edges by yellow. His armpits and groin were free of growths or nodules and there were no cankers or pustules on his penis. Perhaps this one was a virgin. They had been unsuccessful on two previous occasions: both young men had been diseased.

Kelley looked at the woman. 'Well?'

'Well enough.' She looked around as she unhitched her cloak. 'Fetch me some more water – and not that swill you were drowning him in,' she snapped. 'Proper water, hot too if you have it.'

Kelley stared at her for a few moments longer, his long, delicate face impassive. She was just beginning to wonder if she'd gone too far when he suddenly nodded and walked away.

She busied herself preparing the narcotic, a mixture of henbane, wormwood, hashish from the East and brandy. Crouching beside the young man, she allowed the mixture to trickle between his lips and down his throat. He coughed once and she saw his throat working as he swallowed the liquid.

Kelley meanwhile had returned and stood behind the woman, remaining half in shadow, a wooden bucket of tepid water and a half dozen rags in his hand. 'Well,' he said eventually, when she had managed to feed the youth the entire mixture.

The woman raised her hand for silence, and then she laid her head on his chest, listening intently for his heartbeat. It was slow, but strong and steady. They had killed two people experimenting with the strength of the narcotic. Finally, she looked up, eyes blazing and nodded.

Kelley handed her the bucket and cloths and stepped back. Not normally an excitable man – he had lived his entire life suppressing his emotions, using the controlled energy in his experiments and craft – he could feel the blood beginning to pound in his veins now. They were close, very close. He could feel it.

The young man opened his eyes.

There were memories of fear and pain, of hunger and thirst, of cold and wet and ... fear. The overwhelming memory had been one of fear.

He had been ...

He had been in the Church of St Mary, doing a novena to the Virgin, when there had been the cloying stench of something thrown over his head. Blows on his body, kicks . . .

And the pit! He remembered the pit! Adrenalin surged through his body and he sat up straight, only to fall back down again as bruised, stiffened muscles refused to obey him. His head pounded against wood.

The woman came to him then. A beauty, an angel. She had rescued him from the pit and taken him . . . taken him where?

Was he dead?

Had he died and gone to heaven? He was warm and dry and the filth was gone from his body. He felt rested and relaxed, at peace with his surroundings.

Now the woman was bending over him, raven tresses brushing his face, tickling along his chest. He felt their touch with a strange intensity, and then he realized he was naked.

A man should not show himself . . .

The woman's lips brushed his face, his forehead, his lips, her hair now moving across his skin like trailing fingers.

And then, to his horror, he felt his body begin to respond! No angel this, a demon then, a succubus. He attempted to lift his arm, but it barely responded. He opened his mouth to cry out, but the woman pressed her mouth to his, and he shuddered as he felt her tongue against his, licking at his lips. She straightened and allowed the cloak she'd been wearing to drop from her shoulders. She was naked.

The young cleric attempted to squeeze his eyes shut, but he could still feel, exquisitely, the woman climb onto the table beside him, could feel her breasts against his skin as she pressed herself to his body. He attempted to pray, but the demon was whispering words in his ear, foul, obscene words that managed to arouse him ever further. He shrieked aloud as he felt the woman's moist flesh envelope his, and he knew then that he was lost. He was dead and damned. He was in Hell. That is why he could not pray, that is why he could not concentrate on the holy images.

Opening his eyes, he saw the woman sitting astride him, her hands on his shoulders, moving rhythmically, her eyes closed, mouth open, tongue moving across her moist lips. He watched the movement of her breasts, fascinated, the sweat trickling down between them, across her flat stomach. She suddenly stopped moving and opened her eyes . . . and he found he had taken up the rhythm, moving inside her. She smiled triumphantly. Almost of their own accord, his hands moved up to her hips, across her stomach to cup her breasts. He felt . . . he didn't know what he felt. He had never experienced this before. He had never been with a woman before.

He was moving frantically now, and the woman had to clutch his shoulders to remain atop him. His heart was pounding, the veins in his forehead and neck visibly swelling, and his face and chest and thighs were bathed in sweat. He was dimly aware, as the tingle began deep in his groin, that the woman had looked past him, and nodded, but he was too far gone in his passion to stop even if he wanted to.

There was a shadow behind his head. A shape. The glitter of metal. And pain.

The knife was curved like a sickle. It tore through his throat seconds before his orgasm took him. Blood arched from his torn throat splashing down the body of the woman, more of it spouting into the plain wooden goblet Kelley held to his throat. The young man's last conscious sight was of the woman rubbing his blood into her body, licking the drops from her fingertips.

Blood-spattered and sated, the woman climbed off the body of the young man and picked up the cloak, draping it casually around her shoulders. Timing was essential: virgins had to be slain when their blood was hottest, but before orgasm. Once their passion had taken them they were useless. She watched as Kelley approached the mirror, holding the cup in both hands like an offering. With careful, deliberate movements, he spilt some of the liquid onto the dirty surface, allowing it to run down, scouring through the dirt.

For an instant the mirror cleared, and images flickered within the glass.

The red-haired, red-bearded man spattered more of the blood onto the glass, not touching the mirror himself, allowing the liquid to find its own way down the glass.

The images were clearer now; there were faces, dimly glimpsed buildings, shadows.

Standing back, he threw the remainder of the contents of the goblet at the glass, splashing it at about head height. The steaming gore dripped in long sticky strands down the glass, wiping away the encrusted slime.

The images were clearer now; sharper, brighter. There was a face, a woman's face . . . eyes wide, mouth open . . . and then it faded.

Edward Kelley swore and then he turned back to the woman. 'Again; we will have to do it again!'

Jonathan Frazer came awake as the moonlight slid off the glass. He was freezing and his heart was pounding painfully in his breast. The dream had been so vivid, so real.

He sat forward, head throbbing . . . and then realized that his trousers were wet. He was horrified to discover that he'd ejaculated in his sleep.

Chapter
SIXTEEN

THE memories were returning, and with the memories came strength and knowledge. It knew now that it was not without power.

To lure, with images and shadow shapes.

To court, with desires and promises.

These were its memories. This was its power. This was its strength.

This was its skill.

And now the trap had been baited, the prey sighted.

Now there was the time of waiting . . . but it had waited for so long – forever and ever, unchanged and unchanging – it could wait a little longer.

Chapter
SEVENTEEN

MARGARET Haaren sat across from Jonathan Frazer in the plush office above his shop. To the inspector's mind, the room was exactly what an antique shop should look like – cluttered, jumbled, chaotic – in stark contrast to the shop itself, which was brightly lit, cool and pristine, resembling a modern art gallery, with each piece individually displayed on glass shelves.

When she had walked in out of the bright morning sunshine, the chill of the air conditioning had rather taken her breath away, and she had had to squint against the glare from the stark white walls, and the cold, impersonal lighting and fittings. There was also a white carpet on the floor, and she reckoned the cleaning bills for that alone must be enormous. There was no cash register in sight and nothing was priced. The shop was actually a series of small rooms, the clever use of mirrors lending the shop a size and giving it a breadth which it didn't possess. Each room was laid out with different objects: there was glassware in one, ceramics in another, a third room held militaria, another contained books, prints and a small selection of pictures. Two interconnected rooms were filled with miscellaneous objets d'art. There was no obvious security system that she could see, which meant that the system was discreet and expensive.

The assistant had materialized out of one of the rooms, a slim, raven-haired, dark-skinned young man who looked vaguely Latin, but whose English put hers to shame.

'May I be of some assistance, madam?'

'I am looking for Mister Frazer.'

Margaret Haaren was wearing her usual two-piece suit over a silk blouse, but she still felt shabby standing before the assistant's three-piece white Italian silk suit with a red silk tie. She tried her usual trick of estimating the value of his clothing, jewellery, tie and shoes, and then began to wonder how a shop assistant – albeit one in a place like this – could afford to wear upwards of five hundred pounds to work.

'Mister Frazer is engaged at the moment. I'm not sure if . . .'

She smiled coldly. 'Tell him it is Margaret Haaren. He will see me.'

The assistant's smile faded to a bare curve of his lips, and he nodded once before disappearing back into the room marked Books & Prints. He reappeared almost immediately. 'Mister Frazer will see you now.' He stepped aside and allowed the inspector to precede him into the brightly lit room. Here the books were displayed on dark oak shelves, with concealed strip lighting bringing out the gleaming polished leather, the gilded buckrams and decorated cloth bindings. Framed prints hung on the walls between the shelves and there was one wall devoted to miniature watercolours.

The assistant touched a concealed switch on the side of one of the shelves and an entire section of shelving swung out to reveal a staircase. Footsteps clattered on the stairs and Jonathan Frazer appeared, hand outstretched. 'Inspector Haaren . . .'

98

prefer something gentler, something I don't have to work at enjoying.'

'I know the feeling,' she smiled.

'I had a couple of hours to kill in Dublin. I wandered around just seeing the sights and on my way back to the hotel I spotted this auction house on the quays. I went in out of professional curiosity. There was an auction in progress, rubbish mostly, but the mirror was there. And no one bid on it, I think because it was so big. But I recognized its age and I bought it for fifty pounds.'

'And it's worth a lot more?' she asked.

'I would have thought it was worth a couple of thousand, but Tony Farren – who knew a lot more about these things than I do – estimated it around twenty thousand.'

Margaret Haaren looked up in surprise. 'Twenty thousand pounds! So it was quite a find then?'

'It certainly was. A sort of once in a lifetime find.'

'Then what happened?' She lifted a discreet black leather notebook from her bag and began to make notes.

He shrugged. 'The mirror was shipped back here . . . and that's when the trouble started.' He looked up suddenly. 'Was Tony's death an accident?'

'There is no evidence to suggest otherwise, but we shall be re-investigating the circumstances in the light of Miss Williams's tragic death.' She rubbed her slender black pen against her cheekbones. 'Mister Frazer – and I must ask you now to be honest with me – do you owe anyone any money, do you have any gambling debts, or have you done anything which might leave you open to blackmail?'

The shock in his face was genuine enough, and she knew the answer even before he said, outraged, 'No! Absolutely not. I don't gamble and I don't . . . leave myself open to blackmail. This is a reputable business.'

'I'm sure it is, Mister Frazer, but you will appreciate that we have to look at every angle.'

Frazer drank his tea in angry silence. He was insulted that they should even think . . .

'Tell me about your assistant, Mister Frazer,' Inspector Haaren continued, as if nothing had happened.

'Who . . . Robert?' he asked, surprised.

'The young man I met downstairs.'

'He is Robert Beaumont; he's French and a friend of my daughter's. His references are excellent and while he doesn't know a lot about antiques, he's a superb salesman.'

'Is he wealthy?'

Frazer shook his head. 'No. He came to London to study design, but unfortunately found the city a little too expensive for him. His savings ran out and he was forced to find himself a job. He asked Manny – that's my daughter, Emmanuelle – and she knew I was looking for someone . . . someone presentable for the shop. I interviewed him and found him perfect.'

'Do you pay your shop assistants especially well, Mister Frazer?'

'Inspector Haaren . . . I really don't see what this has to do with . . .!'

'Just answer the question, sir.'

'He is paid a salary of eight hundred a month, plus two and a half per cent commission of any sales he makes or initiates during the month.'

'That's not a particularly enormous salary.'

'I think it is very fair,' he said coolly.

'I notice he dresses very well.'

'Very well.'

'Would he wear the same suit to work every day?'

'No, quite the contrary. It's something of a running joke that he has a larger wardrobe than I have.'

'And is he living in a flat?'

'I have his address here . . .' Jonathan pulled open the file and pulled out a single sheet of paper, and then added photocopies of letters to it. 'These are his references,' he said. 'May I ask why you're interested in Robert? Surely you don't think he has anything to do . . .?'

'Is he honest, this Robert Beaumont?' Inspector Haaren pressed on. 'Have you ever had any suspicions about him?'

Jonathan Frazer stared at her for a few moments and then he smiled. 'I underestimated you, Inspector.'

She smiled innocently, but said nothing.

'Well, yes . . . yes, I have suspected him of . . . of irregularities. We had an occasion recently where there was a shortfall in the cash, but he explained it away by saying he had sold certain items at a discount but had then inadvertently entered the full amount into the ledger.'

'Has he the authority to discount items?'

'There would be leeway on just about everything, yes. In order to make the sale, he would have the authority to reduce it slightly, but to do it in such a way that the customer thinks it is being done as a personal favour to him or her. I would rather sell the item at a reduced price than lose the sale altogether.'

'Any other times you suspected him?'

'On occasion small items have gone missing . . . coins, small items of militaria, especially daggers, medals, decorations, buttons.' He shrugged. 'Well, there are only the two of us in the shop.' He waved at the small television screens, which flickered from picture to picture at ten second intervals. 'Anyone coming into the shop shows up on the monitors.'

'But you're not always here.'

'No.'

'So we have a young man who, by his own admission, has no money, earning two hundred a

103

week, plus commission, living in a flat, with a very fine, very expensive wardrobe. It probably has no bearing on the present case, but I'll look into it just the same.'

'What should I do, Inspector?'

'Find another assistant, Mister Frazer.'

Robert Beaumont scuttled away from the door as soon as he heard the conversation come to a close. His heart was pounding and his fine silk shirt was stuck to his skin. He had heard most of the conversation . . . the important parts anyway. He had heard that bitch do the number on him with Frazer. How could she have caught onto him so quickly?

Because he'd been stupid. It had happened before for exactly the same reasons.

Robert Beaumont was a small-time thief with big ideas of his own worth. He had made a career out of working the better class shops first in Paris, and then later in Deauville, Marseille and Lyon, before moving onto the Riviera, where his good looks and charm found him employment in some of the best establishments. He preferred boutiques, either men's or women's, where the pickings were easy, light, portable and re-saleable. Antiques shops were his second choice: again the goods were portable and pocketable, and it wasn't difficult to find someone to take them off your hands.

Now this job had proved a real dream. Frazer was rarely in the shop; he was a simple trusting sort, good-natured, good-humoured, and a fool. Beaumont almost felt guilty taking the few bits and pieces from him, but some people deserved it, some people almost asked for it. And Frazer was one of them.

Most of what he stole went to support his great passion – clothes. He had grown up on the backstreets of Paris, wearing rags and hand-me-downs, cast-offs from his brothers and sisters. He had stolen his first item of clothing – a shirt – off a washing line when he was seven years old. With the realization that these things were out there for the taking, he had embarked on a life of petty crime, hampered only by his greed and his stupidity. He stole from his employers too often, and he couldn't resist wearing his fine clothes. He had been caught that way too often before.

But he had never been lucky enough to have any warning before. Maybe he was getting smarter in his old age.

He folded his arms across his thin chest and then immediately allowed them to drop to his sides, unwilling to crease his suit. He looked around the shop, wondering what little 'going away' present he might give himself. The problem was everything here on display was marked, listed, catalogued and photographed.

There were voices on the stairs behind him and he moved quickly through the shop, hurrying from room to room, away from the stairs, so that when Frazer and the inspector came into the shop, he was in the militaria room, busily buffing an embossed shield.

He glared at Margaret Haaren. Bitch!

And all because that Farren bastard and his stuck-up assistant had had a stupid accident at the stables they used as a storehouse.

It took long moments for the idea to trickle through to his subconscious mind, and he stopped, frowning, looking at his reflection in the shield. He had never been in the stables, but from what he had heard, it was crammed with antiques and artefacts: unmarked, unlisted, uncatalogued and unphotographed antiques. There for the taking and no record of them ever existing in the first place. Why, Frazer wouldn't even know they were gone.

Keys. He'd need keys. He glanced at the Rolex on

his wrist: close to twelve-thirty. Frazer would be on his way to lunch soon; the weak fool would probably need to fortify himself before he came back to sack him.

He checked his pocket: he still had the key to Frazer's office he'd stolen weeks before. There was sure to be a key to the stables in there.

Chapter
EIGHTEEN

EDMUND Talbott spent the remainder of the day in the British Library reading rooms. He felt it was reasonably safe there, and very probably the last place the police would think of looking for him.

Now that the mirror had become active again, he needed to renew his knowledge of its history and, outside of the Vatican, the British Library possessed one of the finest collections of books on occult and related subjects.

In the past the Talbott family had been the keepers of the mirror, although how it had come into their hands in the first place had been lost in the mists of antiquity. But now the time for simply guarding the mirror had passed; it was time for it to be destroyed. Fear – fear of the unknown, of the devil, of evil – had nearly always prevented even the most foolhardy from prying too closely into the mysteries of the glass. But now, in this secular age, when these fears had been dulled and almost forgotten, the danger had assumed terrifying proportions. He was hoping that here, amongst the British Library's occult collection, he would find some answers.

Talbott had attempted to disguise himself, stooping

to shield his height, while wearing a loose fitting, voluminous coat that concealed his size. There was nothing he could do about his scarred face. The doctors had given him the option of plastic surgery, but he had rejected it, wearing his scars proudly, and as a constant reminder that his wife and child had been taken from him. It was a reminder too that he must never look in a mirror again.

He sat down at the long table and pulled the slip of paper from his pocket. Jonathan Frazer. Anthony Farren. Diane Williams. Was there some connection between the three, something in their past? And yet they were from widely differing social classes, age groups and backgrounds. What could they possibly have in common? There was nothing that immediately came to mind, but possibly there was some connection in previous generations perhaps? The mirror seemed linked to certain families, certain lines, and when it became active it always worked through a male and female. But what sparked it from its quiescent state? His father had told him that it was nothing more than moonlight on the surface of the glass, but was there something more?

Was the key to its ultimate destruction somewhere in these meagre clues? He would find it: he had to before it killed and killed and killed again!

And every death fed it, making it stronger. Deadlier.

Margaret Haaren was convinced that the police should police and secretaries should secretary, and while a secretary wouldn't do police work, neither should police officers do a secretary's job. She had once attempted to work out how many hours she spent filling in forms, making reports and generally doing secretary things, and had eventually given it up in disgust and despair. Then the ratio was running at two to one: twice the amount of secretarial work to police work. Outside her office, she knew, there were at least three able-bodied police officers sitting at their desks when they could have been gainfully employed elsewhere. There was a tap on the door and Bill Russell entered, scores of computer printer paper bundled loosely in his big hands. 'I thought you'd want this immediately,' he said, by way of an apology.

Margaret Haaren gladly shoved the monthly report forms to one side, making space in the centre of the desk for the reams of paper.

'It's the report from the Garda Siochana in Dublin about the auctioneers who sold Frazer the mirror.'

'And?' Margaret asked impatiently, aware that Bill was leading up to something. 'Are you going to tell me that they don't exist?'

'Oh, they exist all right; that's not the problem. They hold an auction every week, sometimes twice a week if they have a lot to clear. Apparently everything they have for sale is catalogued on computer, which explains this mess of paper.' He rested his hand flat on the accordioned pile. 'They have checked their records for the past eight weeks . . . and they have sold no mirror, such as we described to them.' Margaret Haaren sat up straight. 'Furthermore, they checked their records and they have no record of ever having dealt with Frazer Antiques.' He glanced up and smiled. 'It gets better.'

'I'm sure it does.'

'I then checked with their usual freight company – just in case there was an oversight, you understand. Again; they checked their computer records and they have never made a delivery from Ireland to Jonathan Frazer of Frazer Antiques.'

'Why did he lie?' Margaret Haaren wondered.

'And such a stupid lie.'

'Surely he knew we'd check with Dublin; why did he give me names and addresses?'

'Maybe he didn't think we'd check.' Bill Russell grinned. 'He's smart this Frazer, you know that, far smarter than us mere bobbies,' he added sarcastically.

'I didn't think he was that type,' she admitted. She had thought that Frazer had some respect for the police; far too often people of his class thought that their money and connections made them some sort of superior being. Maybe she'd been wrong.

'Did he ever show you any documentation from the auctioneers or the freight people?' the sergeant asked.

'No.' She smiled, showing her teeth in a fixed grin. 'Let's go and visit Mister Frazer again, Bill.'

Fuck him! That was his considered opinion. Fuck him. He wasn't going to hang around until after lunch so that Frazer could build up a head of steam. He was going to be long gone by the time he got back.

With a slender Gold Cross fountain pen he scribbled a quick note on the firm's ivory parchment note paper.

> *Monsieur,*
> *My mother is close to death in Paris. She has hours to live. My brother has arrived with a ticket for the next flight home. Please allow me four days leave.*
> *Respectfully,*
> *Robert Beaumont.*

Frazer was such an idiot that he'd believe him too. He was tempted to take what cash there was, but that would give the lie to his story. What he needed to do was to give himself a couple of days' grace before Frazer decided to contact the police. It wasn't something he could do with someone brighter, but Frazer was such an idiot. Well, fuck him!

Carefully locking the shop door so that he couldn't be disturbed, Beaumont made his way up to the office. He could still smell the woman's perfume on the heavy dry air, something cheap, whorish too he had no doubt. There was nothing feminine in her, everything about her was cheap, from her mannish suit to her common haircut. He knew the type; he had met them before, worked for them. Women pretending to be men. She thought she was so clever, discovering him. Well, he'd show her.

Sitting in Frazer's chair, he opened the drawers on the right-hand side of the desk. There was a set of keys lying on top of a pile of mail. Beaumont looked at them in dull surprise: he couldn't be so lucky, could he? Well, perhaps he deserved a little luck. Pocketing the keys, he picked up the mail and looked through it. Most of it was circulars, subscriptions for magazines, but the last envelope was from an auction house in Dublin, a computerized invoice for 'Lot 69: A large antique wooden-framed mirror, approximately seven feet tall by four feet wide'. Pinned to the back of it was another computerized receipt from a freight company for transporting the mirror from Dublin to the house in Kensington.

There was something about a mirror ... Wait a second! That woman and Frazer had been talking about a mirror he had bought at auction. Added to what he had been able to pick up over the past few days, Beaumont realized that this must be the same mirror that the mysterious scarred man had offered to buy before Diane Williams's death. Frazer had warned him that if a large, particularly ugly man with a mop of white hair entered the shop, then he was to phone the police immediately. And Frazer had told the police woman that the mirror was valued at twenty thousand pounds. And this letter contained the provenance, which proved the title to the piece. When the mirror came to be sold, this piece of paper would be invaluable for conferring the title to the piece. And suppose *he* wanted to sell the mirror – maybe to the scarred man if he could make the connection – then this piece of paper would prove the legitimacy of the sale. Sliding the envelope into his inside pocket, he returned the letters to the drawer and closed it, carefully locking it behind him. He glanced at his watch. Just one-thirty. Frazer would be back soon, and he had no intention of being here when he arrived. His thin lips twisted in a smile as he surveyed the office for the last time. Once he had left, Frazer would be forced to stay in the shop for the rest of the afternoon, or close early, and he didn't think he'd do that. Maybe now would be the perfect time to visit this Aladdin's cave of a stables. If everything went according to plan he'd be well away before Frazer arrived home for tea.

Jonathan Frazer strolled down the street arguing with himself. He was a soft-hearted, blind fool. He knew that. He'd always been soft and, curiously, he didn't consider it a character fault. The alternative was to be someone like Cecilia – hard, unyielding, caring only for oneself – and he was definitely sure he didn't want to end up like that.

So Robert Beaumont had taken him in; well, it wouldn't be the first time he'd made a fool of himself, nor would it be the last. He'd paid the young man well, and in return, his Latin charm had wooed some customers, especially the female ones. And if he'd stolen from him, well . . . what was done was done and could not be undone. He would dismiss him now – immediately, even though that was going to mess up the shop for the next few days. Maybe Manny would stand in until he found a replacement: she should, seeing he had been her recommendation. And he wasn't going to give him a reference either. He'd probably stolen some headed paper in any case and would write his own!

The shop was locked.

He stood, pushing stupidly at the door, while the fact sunk in. The shop was locked. He looked at his watch: it was just gone a quarter to two. Where was Robert? His heart began to pound. Was something wrong? Had there been a robbery; was he tied up in the back of the shop someplace . . . or . . . or maybe he had just popped out for something – he'd done it before, even though he'd been warned never to leave the premises unattended during working hours.

Shading his eyes he peered inside.

'Is there a problem, Mister Frazer?'

Jonathan whirled, startled. 'Inspector Haaren!'

'Is there a problem?' she repeated, her face hard and expressionless. She hated to be treated for a fool and so far as she could see, this man had done nothing but.

'I don't know, Inspector . . .' He turned to look back into the shop, hoping to see Beaumont appear. 'I've just come back from lunch and I've discovered that the shop is locked.' He rattled the handle for emphasis.

She continued to stare at him, saying nothing.

'Well, Beaumont should be there.' He lowered his voice. 'I was wondering if there's been a robbery, or something.'

Margaret Haaren looked back over his shoulder, and Bill Russell immediately stepped out of the unmarked car.

'Yes, ma'am.'

'Mister Frazer's shop is locked, and he fears there may have been a robbery. Anything on the radio?'

'Nothing.'

'Do you have a key, Mister Frazer?'

He handed it over without a word.

Bill Russell turned the key in the lock and stepped inside, followed by Haaren and Frazer. The sergeant walked swiftly from room to room, moving surprisingly quietly for so large a man. He returned moments later, shaking his head. 'There's no one on this floor.

But I did find this on the desk over there.' He handed Frazer the single sheet of folded paper with his name scrawled across it.

Jonathan read it aloud, and then glanced at Haaren. 'This young man takes me for a fool,' he said angrily.

'It's not a nice feeling is it, Mister Frazer?'

The tone of her voice caught his attention. 'Is there something the matter, Inspector Haaren?' he demanded, transferring his anger onto her.

'I think it's you who has been taking me for a fool, Mister Frazer. You told me you purchased the mirror – the cause of all your recent problems – at auction in Dublin. That does not appear to be the case. Neither the auction house nor the carrier have any record of ever having dealt with you.'

'That's nonsense!' he snapped.

'You will of course have receipts and invoices from both sources then?' she demanded.

'Of course! And I must say I find your attitude and your suggestions offensive.'

'Just show me the proof, Mister Frazer, and I will apologize,' Margaret Haaren said, suddenly turning away. 'Sergeant Russell and I will wait down here for you.'

'Is there another way out up there?' Bill Russell asked softly as Frazer disappeared behind the swinging bookshelves.

'Not that I could see. Anyway, where's he going to go, eh?'

They wandered around the main showroom, not talking. The inspector had warned Bill about the security monitors and they were both aware that Frazer could see them in his security monitors, although they weren't sure if he had an audio pick-up. Five minutes later, Margaret Haaren looked at her small-faced wrist watch and glanced at Bill Russell. 'How long does it take to look out an invoice?'

They had both started towards the stairs, when the section of shelving swung back and Jonathan Frazer, wide-eyed and white-faced stepped out.

'Let me guess, Mister Frazer,' Inspector Haaren smiled. 'You can't find them at the moment. They've been misfiled.'

'No, no,' he shook his head violently, 'they were in the top drawer of my desk. But they're gone,' he said wonderingly, 'and the drawer was locked. They must have been stolen!'

'How very convenient,' Bill Russell said. He glanced at the inspector. 'We often have people stealing invoices from locked drawers; there's a big market in stolen invoices.' He took Frazer by the elbow and steered him towards the door. 'Let's go down to the station and have a little chat, eh?'

Chapter
NINETEEN

IT had been easy, pathetically easy.

He had walked past the house twice just to make sure that neither Jonathan nor Cecilia Frazer's cars were there and, on the third occasion, boldly walked right up to the front door and rang the bell long and insistently. Then, with his hands folded together in front of him, he turned his back on the door and looked out over the expanse of neat lawn and carefully trimmed garden. Like everything else about Jonathan Frazer, it was unspectacular, conservative.

Robert Beaumont had no appreciation of gardens, but he appreciated land and property prices and Frazer's property was certainly in the big league.

And here he was earning a lousy two hundred a week. If he needed an excuse for extracting a few things – which he didn't – he had it now. Frazer wouldn't even miss them.

The door clicked open behind him and he turned, smiling automatically, until he discovered that it was Emmanuelle, and the smile turned genuine.

'Bonjour, Mademoiselle,' he murmured, bowing elegantly. When they had first met in Paris, she had mocked his too-elegant old world manners.

'Robert,' Manny said, blinking sleepily. She had been out until the early hours of the morning – home with the milkman, her father would have said – and she had drunk far too much, smoked a little too much and had been dead to the world until the persistent jangling of the bell had awoken her. Idly wondering where the cook was, she had pulled on a long candy-striped tee-shirt that came down past her knees and which did duty as a nightdress when she needed one and padded down the stairs. She had peered out through the fish-eye spy hole, but the caller had his back to her. She glanced at the clock – two in the afternoon – and debated ignoring the caller. Of course . . . it might be the police. She looked out through the spy hole again and noted the caller's short haircut and neat suit. Probably a Jehovah's Witness she decided, as she turned the lock and swung back the door. She discovered then that the suit was far too bright and far too expensive for a Witness. It took her a second to recognize the smiling young man. 'Robert,' she said, digging the heel of her hand into her eyes, and smothering a yawn. 'What are you doing here?'

He smiled ruefully and ran his fingers back through his slick coal-black hair. 'Business I'm afraid.' He showed Manny the keyring he had taken from the desk drawer. 'Your father asked me to come out and collect a few things from the stables.'

She stood back and allowed him to walk past her into the hallway. He caught a hint of her perfume – now heavy and musky with sleep – and the sourer, sharper odour of alcohol.

'You were partying I take it,' he murmured, glancing surreptitiously around the hall.

'I did have a late night – or an early morning,' she admitted, and then added philosophically. 'And now I'm paying for it, I'm afraid. And I'll pay for it tonight when Dad gets home.'

'He doesn't know what you got up to in Paris then, eh?' His dark eyes caught and held hers.

A touch of colour appeared on her cheeks and then she threw back her head and laughed aloud. 'No,' thank God, and don't you even think of telling him.'

'Mademoiselle!' he said in mock outrage, 'it is – as the saying goes – more than my job is worth.'

'Have you got time for a coffee?' she asked, moving past him.

'Not really, but I'll have one in any case.' He watched her move down the hall, the realization that she was completely naked beneath the tee-shirt exciting him. He had seen her naked many times when they had been lovers, but that had been a long time ago, and he wondered . . .

Shaking his head from side to side, grinning at the very idea, he followed her down the hallway into the kitchen.

'How are you enjoying working for Father?' she asked as she pulled open cupboard doors looking for coffee and a percolator. *Where was the cook?* 'I can't find a thing in this place,' she admitted. 'I'm sure the cook hides everything to make herself indispensable.'

Robert went to stand by the back door looking out over the back garden, across the paved patio and down through the trees to where the edge of the stable was just visible. 'Your father is . . . well, he's fine really. I don't see him often enough to form any opinion. The shop isn't really his main business you know, most of it is done through catalogue and mail order, and his invaluable list of special customers.'

'You always had the trick of not answering my question,' Manny glanced over her shoulder and grinned. 'Come on, be honest: what's he like to work for?' She suddenly pulled out the coffee. 'Success!'

'He'd a bit of a – what is that charming English phrase . . .?'

118

'Robert, your English is better than mine, so don't give me any of that Gallic nonsense, "how do you say".'

Beaumont laughed. 'It was your sense of humour that first attracted me to you, you know that don't you? Anyway, your father is a fuddy-duddy. He is old-fashioned, slow, unimaginative and uninventive. How he has survived in business so long eludes me.' He was watching Manny's reflection in the window and saw the smile fade from her lips, and realized that he had gone too far. 'And yet,' he added brightly, 'just remember, I am working for him, so if there is a last laugh going around, he has it.' He suddenly changed the conversation. 'That building down there, is that the stables?'

Manny glanced over at him and nodded. 'That's it. They were actually used as stables apparently once upon a time but my grandfather had them converted into one long building. Mother hates it,' she added. 'She hates the very idea of having a storehouse and a workroom in sight of the house. She had a landscape-gardening firm come in and gave them instructions to hide it. They put down the trees and bushes. Eventually they'll screen even the small corner of the building you can see.'

Robert glanced at his watch. 'I tell you what. While you're preparing the coffee, I'll go on down and see if I can find the few things your father asked me to get for him.'

'Sure. I'll give you a call when its ready.'

Robert turned the key in the back door and stepped out onto the patio. There was a rich scent of flowers and herbs in the still air, and it was difficult to believe that this was still, figuratively speaking, the heart of London.

First the stables, and then a quick cup of coffee. The thought of it appealed to his sense of irony. It was another way of thumbing his nose at Frazer. Then he'd have Manny call him a cab, go straight to the flat, pick up some clothes and his passport and then head directly to Dover and onto Calais. Simple. Neat and effective.

What a pity though he hadn't a little longer to hang around; he would have enjoyed taking Manny Frazer to bed again. Wouldn't that be the ultimate insult: take Frazer's goods and his daughter on the same day? However, discretion being the better part of stupidity, perhaps not now . . .

His first shock came when he realized that the stables were bigger than he'd first thought. There was no way he was going to be able to conduct anything like a proper search in the twenty or thirty minutes he'd allotted himself. He'd just have to count on striking it lucky.

He got his second shock when the key he'd taken wouldn't fit the lock fixed to the surprisingly crude looking door. He stood, looking stupidly at the heavy Chubb padlock, and then turned the keys in his hand to read the names on their sides. None of them matched. Well, he hadn't come this far for nothing . . .

Manny was surprised to find Robert back so quickly. 'Get what you came for?'

He spread his hands in a typically French expression, his head tilted to one side. 'I can't get in.' He held up the keyring, 'none of the keys fits the lock.'

'Oh, he's given you the wrong keyring,' she laughed. 'The locks were changed after . . . after the accident,' she added, the smile fading from her lips. 'He's been so addled lately he's probably forgotten.' She plucked a keyring from its hook behind the door and handed it across. 'It's one of the new keys on that ring, but I'm not sure which.'

'You are an angel,' he smiled, clutching the keyring and heading out the door, moving quickly now, eager to make up for the time he'd lost.

It was the third key on the ring, and the heavy Chubb lock snapped open immediately. He stepped into the dim, musty interior of the stables and pulled the door closed behind him.

Afternoon sunlight shafted in through the barred windows and the dusty skylights, catching the silently whirling dust motes, glinting off the wood and metal, glass and leather piled high around the room. There was a long work-bench running along the length of one wall. Beaumont moved his way swiftly along it, figuring that Tony Farren would have been working on pieces destined to end up in the shop in the immediate future. Valuable pieces. He discovered two pocket watches, a hunter and a half-hunter sitting on the shelf above the bench. He wound them both and they began to tick, sounding surprisingly loud in the absolute silence. The young man slid them both into his pocket, and continued down the bench. There was an antique pearl necklace, the pearls of different sizes in small plastic bags, obviously waiting to be strung, and beside them a pearl choker with a broken clasp. They were just what he was looking for: they were light and portable and, more importantly, easily concealed. At the far end of the bench, close to the militaria, he discovered a fifteenth-century psalter in a jewel-encrusted leather binding. He didn't know enough to determine whether the jewels were genuine or not but, again, it was pocket sized.

Moving swiftly now, he made his way down through the centre aisle, but everything here was too big – chairs, tables, ugly ornaments, enormous clocks piled high on either side. There was obviously a fortune stored here. At one point the centre aisle was blocked and he had to retrace his steps back around by the walls back to the door. Standing with his back to the door he looked around the room for a last time, wishing he had more time.

He had missed it the first time round, because he had turned right at the door to follow the bench, but there, directly in front of him, was an opening into the centre aisle. He could see a couch . . . and the mirror.

Robert Beaumont wove his way through the piled up artefacts, realizing that this was what had blocked up the centre aisle. A clearing had been created in the centre of the room, with a battered couch placed facing the huge mirror. Beaumont walked right up to it and grinned, and his reflection, shabby, twisted and distorted by the dirty glass, leered back at him. He had actually come here to steal this thing! When Frazer and the police woman had been talking about it, he had formed the impression that it was a small object, probably jewelled or something like that, but he'd never imagined this monster. Craning his head, he looked up, trying to gauge its height: no wonder it had killed Tony Farren when it had fallen on him: it must weigh a ton.

When he looked down again, Emmanuelle Frazer was standing behind him.

He opened his mouth to speak, but she raised a finger to her lips, shaking her head. He was about to turn when she pointed her index finger at the dirty glass.

With a smug grin, he folded his hands across his chest, not thinking of his fine suit now, concentrating on the image in the mirror.

Without saying a word, Emmanuelle lifted the long tee-shirt over her head, holding it in front of her body, barely covering her breasts and groin for a few tantalizing moments, before allowing it to fall to the floor.

Beaumont felt his breath catch in his throat.

She was even more beautiful than he remembered, and he felt himself becoming immediately aroused. He reached out and brushed his hand across the mirror, attempting to wipe it clean at face level; although her body was clearly reflected in the glass, her face was smudged and in shadow. With the grime on the glass, it looked as if Manny had a thick head of hair.

His hand came away filthy, and he fumbled in his pocket for his handkerchief, his eyes still locked on the glass, roving over the woman's body. It had filled out a little since he had seen it last; her breasts were fuller, heavier, though her nipples seemed smaller then he remembered. Her stomach was slightly rounded too, and her groin was now covered in a thick mat of hair, whereas formally she completely depilated her body.

With his breath caught somewhere at the back of his throat he watched Manny run her hands down her body, slowly caressing herself, catching and cupping her breasts, thumbs flat against her nipples. She brought her right arm across her body, her hand pressing itself flat to her left breast, her forearm across the nipple of her right breast. Her left hand moved down across her rounded belly, fingers splayed, fingers probing deep into the thick hair.

With his right hand, he reached for his belt, fingers fumbling with the buckle. His left hand went to the mirror again, rubbing at the grimy, greasy surface with the handkerchief . . .

The shock that lanced through his system was like an intense orgasm. His heart was pounding, his breathing ragged as he rubbed at the glass, almost *feeling* the touch of her skin beneath his fingers, moving down to brush the silk handkerchief across her reflected breasts.

It was a game now. An intensely erotic game, voyeurism taken to another degree. She was behind him, he could almost feel the heat radiating off her body, could smell the heavy musk of sex in the dry air. And yet he wouldn't touch – not yet anyway. That was part of the game.

123

He was stroking himself now, a faintly ridiculous figure with his trousers down around his ankles, his eyes fixed on the mirror.

Manny's head was thrown back, the smooth column of her throat taut, nostrils flaring, lips wet and parted as her fingers worked deep inside her.

And still with no sound.

Beaumont was aware of his own harsh, ragged breathing, his rapid gasps as his own orgasm approached, but there was no other sound . . . no other sound.

His concentration faltered . . . and so did the image. For one brief moment the woman behind his back was not Manny Frazer, but another, older woman, long haired, full bodied, long haired . . . long haired . . . long hair . . .

His hand slowed its pumping as the realization struck home. It wasn't Manny Frazer standing behind him. He was almost afraid now to turn around while behind him the woman continued to arouse herself with complete abandon. He leaned forward, resting his forehead against the cool glass, supporting himself with his left hand . . . and screamed!

The agony tore through his body, enveloping his face and hand first. There was fire before his eyes . . . inches before his eyes.

Fire in the glass.

Fire *on* the glass.

His flesh blistered, scorched and then cracked, bubbling in the heat. It fell in blackened strips from his hand, flesh and fat bubbling in the intense heat. His hair crisped, then ignited, the styling gel in his hair running in boiling liquid strips down his back. The silk suit melted onto his body as the flesh burnt off his face and neck, his eyes sizzling, boiling in their sockets, tongue shrivelling in his mouth. He sucked in breath to scream – and swallowed flame – and his shout was accompanied by a vomited ball of flame.

And his last conscious thought before the agony totally consumed him was the sudden jerking throb of ecstasy as his orgasm took him.

Chapter TWENTY

THE howl of triumph ripped through the Otherworld.

Raw power, naked energy, bright corruscating colours rippled through the grey landscape, the vibrations taking a long time to die away.

Another soul, trembling, afraid, in agony had been dragged into its trap.

It savoured the pain. It fed off the agony. It drew strength from its terror.

It had taken the creature's death, accepted it as its due.

It was close now, so very close. It needed sustenance; it needed blood.

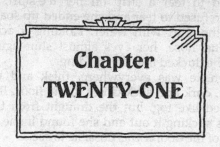

Chapter
TWENTY-ONE

THE smell brought Manny running. The sickening, cloying foul smell of burnt meat and leaves, of dried wood and leather. Oily black smoke was curling from the stables, twisting in the still afternoon air.

She couldn't imagine what Robert had done, probably dropped a cigarette onto a seat covering. But he hadn't smoked when she'd known him.

She slowed down when she reached the stables, the nauseating smell troubling her already delicate stomach. She felt her gorge rise. The smoke coiled around her, making her eyes water, clinging to her tee-shirt, adhering to her skin, coating her lips, her mouth.

'Robert? Robert? Are you there, Robert?'

Where the fuck was he?

'ROBERT!'

Ducking beneath the billowing smoke, she ran to the nearest window and, pressing her face close to the glass, cupping her hands over her eyes, peered inside. The thick white smoke blanketed everything, but there seemed to be no flames . . . nor was there any sign of Robert. Maybe he'd been overcome by the smoke . . .

She ran back to the outdoor cold water tap hidden in

amongst the bushes at the edge of the path. She attempted to tear a strip off her tee-shirt, but the material refused to tear and she ended up soaking the hem of the shirt with water. Holding it across her mouth and nose, her eyes almost shut against the smoke, she ducked into the building.

The smoke was everywhere, thick and white at eye-level, dark and slick closer to the floor. It twisted and curled like fog, but the draught from the open door was sucking it out and she found if she stood to one side of the door it was possible to see.

'ROBERT?' Her voice, muffled by the wet tee-shirt, was lost in the stables. Rubbing her streaming eyes, blinking away the tears that clung to her long eyelashes, outlining everything in glistening rainbows, she pressed forward, looking for the source of the fire. Where were the fire extinguishers? As far as she could recall, they were somewhere close to the work-bench which ran along the wall. Her father had refused to install a sprinkler system, saying that if there ever was a fire – which was extremely unlikely – the water would probably do more damage than the flames.

She barked her bare shins and hopped back, swearing, tears of pain springing to her eyes. Where the fuck was Beaumont?

She caught the movement out of the corner of her eye and turned quickly, moving forward. The smoke twisted up, thicker now. 'Robert?' she mumbled, moving closer.

The fire was around her somewhere. The smoke was thick and cloying, the stench appalling. She swallowed hard, bitterly regretting the amount she'd drunk and smoked the previous night.

Again the movement . . . a flicker . . . a face?

'Robert?'

The smoke cleared and Manny screamed! She staggered back, heart pounding, legs beginning to tremble with reaction. She attempted to laugh, but the sound caught at the back of her throat: she had been looking at herself in the mirror. She hadn't recognized herself in that sudden, brief glimpse of a pale-faced, wide-eyed, semi-naked woman.

The smoke seemed to be coming from directly in front of the mirror. She stepped forward, frowning. There was a pile of smouldering rags on the floor.

Manny stooped to look closer at them.

On some deep subconscious level, she had already recognized the incinerated man-like shape on the floor, but refused to accept what she was seeing. She poked at the seared cloth with her forefinger, cinders spiralling upwards to dance briefly in the air. Metal glinted, gold against the blackened mess and she touched it, hooking it out of the ash.

It was a watch, a gold Rolex watch. The face was cracked, the heavy gold casing melted to sludge in the intense heat, the enamelled face bubbled and warped. Engraved on the back, barely visible beneath the patina of soot was the line, 'Robert Maurice Beaumont.'

And she suddenly recognized, she suddenly *accepted* what she was seeing.

The watch dropped from her nerveless fingers, falling onto the burnt meat, sinking into the chest cavity, a tiny blue flame dancing about the hole.

She scrabbled away, wrapping her arms around her knees, hugging them close to her body, swallowing again and again, bile flooding her throat and mouth. She closed her eyes, squeezing them shut, but the images – vivid, bloody images, of whitened bone and blackened flesh, a charred skull, strips of flesh clinging to it, of an arm that ended in a knotted stump – all the images remained.

And the smoke.

The smoke coiling sinuously from the body, flowing

upwards, crawling across the surface of the mirror, clinging to it, wreathing across the surface, forming shapes, forming pictures, forming faces.

Tony Farren . . . Diane Williams . . . Robert Beaumont.

Face upon face, image upon image. Eyes wide, mouths open in soundless agony.

Calling to her . . . pleading with her . . . enticing her . . .

Emmanuelle Frazer opened her mouth and screamed until her throat bled.

'This is ridiculous, absolutely ridiculous. Your insinuations are absurd.'

'Perhaps you wish to wait until your solicitors arrive, Mister Frazer . . .' Margaret Haaren suggested quietly.

'I don't see why. Your allegations are unfounded. I am innocent of these ridiculous charges,' Frazer continued, almost trembling with rage.

'There have been no charges, Mister Frazer. You are merely helping us with our enquiries.' She looked up as Bill Russell came into the small office, his broad face completely impassive, a manila folder in his hand. Without a word he came around the desk and placed the folder before her, and then took up a position at the door, arms folded, eyes fixed on her face. Even before she opened the folder, she knew it was bad news.

'You must appreciate our position, Mister Frazer,' she continued, speaking to him while her eyes ran down the single typed sheet. 'You told us you bought a mirror in Dublin, the same mirror which inadvertently caused the death of one of your employees, the same mirror which a mysterious man offered to buy, the same mirror another employee died guarding. And yet the auction house in Dublin has never heard of you, they have no record of ever having dealt with you before, and there was no mirror of the size you describe sold at the auction that day. We contacted the

130

freight people whom you said delivered the mirror and, again, they have no record of ever having dealt with you. We are left with the conclusion,' she finished softly, having absorbed the impact of what she had just read, 'that you have lied to us, Mister Frazer.'

'But why,' he began, almost desperately, 'what possible reason would I have to lie to you . . ?'

Margaret Haaren stood up and reached for the coat draped across the back of the chair. 'I think you had better come with us, Mister Frazer.'

'Why, where are we going?' he demanded, not moving.

'We're taking you home. There has been . . . an accident.'

'An accident! What sort of accident?'

'We're not sure. A fire in your storeroom. Your daughter seems to have been injured.'

Frazer looked at her in horror.

'I've no further details, I'm afraid,' she lied, not telling him about the grisly carcass that had been discovered in the stables.

They drove without speaking through the crowded London streets with a motor-cycle escort and sirens blaring. Jonathan Frazer was wide-eyed, white-faced and trembling and both Haaren and Russell could smell his fear.

An ambulance screamed out of the cul-de-sac as they turned in, and they pulled up in front of the house just as a bagged corpse was being loaded into the back of a second ambulance. Frazer gave a scream of anguish and leapt from the moving car, screaming all the time as he ran across the drive towards the startled ambulance drivers. Still shouting, he managed to pull the zip of the body bag down and revealed a burnt and tattered eyeless face before Bill Russell grabbed his arms and physically hauled him away. 'She's alive, she's alive. That's not your daughter. She's alive.'

131

Frazer collapsed onto the steps, his head buried in his hands, sobs racking through him. Bill Russell sat down beside him and put his arm around his shoulder. 'It's OK guv', its not Manny. She's fine, she saw the body and fainted we think, but the ambulance boys say she wasn't injured.'

'I thought . . . I thought . . . I thought . . .' Frazer hiccupped.

'I know what you thought. I've a girl about Manny's age myself. I know what you were thinking.'

Frazer rubbed his hand across his eyes and attempted to stand, but his legs felt like water and the sergeant helped him to his feet. As the ambulance pulled away, he looked at the policeman. 'Well if that wasn't Manny, who was it?'

'We don't know sir. The body was found in your storehouse, burnt beyond recognition, all identity burnt with it. All we have left is some rags and a pair of shoes – men's shoes.'

'Then the stables . . .' Frazer gasped.

'Untouched.'

Frazer looked at him uncomprehendingly. 'How?'

'I've seen it once before sir, many years ago when I was a beat bobby. I was called in to investigate an old man who hadn't been seen for days. We found him in his flat sitting in his chair. But although he was burnt to a crisp, the chair he'd been sitting on had only been scorched. The pathologist told me it was called spontaneous combustion. Happens to maybe twenty people a year; they just burst into flames, from the inside out as it were.' He attempted to smile. 'No one knows why or how it happens; just one of life's little mysteries, I guess.'

'What was he doing in the stables?'

'We'll look into that, sir.'

'I'd like to see the stables.'

'I'm not sure . . .' Bill Russell caught Margaret

Haaren's nod, and then smiled. 'OK then. Let's go.'

The two men walked around the side of the house, with the inspector trailing along discreetly. As they neared the stables they could see police milling about, while from inside the stables light flashed at regular intervals as the scene of the death was recorded.

Frazer moved through the crowd, shouldering his way into the darkened interior, blinking quickly to adjust his sight. He walked right up to the mirror, looking closely at it before realizing he was standing on the scorched concrete floor.

Haaren looked at Russell. Neither of them had told Frazer where the body had been discovered. And they were very big stables, the body could have been anywhere.

Frazer abruptly turned away, his face set and expressionless. When he stepped out into the sunlight, he was breathing quickly, and his face had an unhealthy cast to it.

'Mister Frazer . . .' Margaret Haaren stepped up beside him, touching his arm.

'There!' he hissed. 'There. THERE!'

She followed the direction of his stiffly pointing arm. There was a tall, broad man standing at the corner of the house, his face in shadow, only his shock of white hair visible.

Frazer's fingers closed painfully on her arm, his eyes were wild with excitement. 'That's him! That's the scarred man.'

'I'll get him,' Bill Russell murmured, hurrying past them. The stranger turned away. 'Shit,' he murmured, putting on a spurt of speed. He was too old for this. 'STOP!' he shouted.

The inspector turned, pointing to the two constables who had come to investigate the shouting. 'Go with him. Quickly.'

Bill Russell pounded up the garden, wishing he'd a

weapon of some sort – even a police-issue truncheon would do. He raced around the corner and had time to register the shape before he was grabbed by the arms and hauled off his feet. He was slammed hard against the side of the house, the back of his head snapping off the wall, dazing him.

'What happened back there?' The voice was hard, the accent vaguely rural, Scots or Irish. The huge man began shaking him, holding him inches off the ground, rattling him from side to side. 'Answer me,' he grated.

'F-f-f-fuck you . . .'

'Hey you!' The two constables rounded the corner and were almost on top of Talbott before he – or they – realized it. The younger of the two men shouted aloud before Talbott, still holding Russell pinned to the wall, kicked him high in the chest with the flat of his foot. The force of the tremendous blow snapped ribs, driving them deep into the lungs and actually lifted the young man off his feet, punching him back into the second officer. Both men went down in a tangle of limbs.

Talbott returned his attention to Russell. 'Answer me.'

'Fuck you!'

Talbott kneed him efficiently in the groin. 'Tell me.'

Bill Russell attempted to double over, but he was still pressed to the side wall of the house. He could feel moisture on his head, running down into his neck, had seen – dimly – what the man had done to the constable, had felt the incredible fire in his groin. He was forty-seven years old . . . too old for this. He was going to throw up.

'Answer me.'

'There was a fire, a man, burnt to death.'

'Where?'

'In the stables,' he whispered.

'Where?' the big man demanded, raising a huge fist.

'Before the mirror.'

The fist descended, smashing his head against the wall.

Chapter
TWENTY-TWO

IN two separate hospital rooms, a floor apart, two families kept vigil.

Jonathan and Cecilia Frazer sat in the private room on the top floor, watching over the sleeping form of their daughter, Emmanuelle. Outwardly, she was unmarked and the only piece of hospital equipment in the room was the respirator to assist her breathing which was slightly laboured due to smoke inhalation.

Cecilia Frazer had fallen asleep, curled up in the large uncomfortable chair. Jonathan sat perched on the edge of a chair, watching his daughter intently, not thinking, not daring to think, only grateful that she was still alive.

On the floor below them, Bill Russell's wife and two teenage daughters sat, awake, alert, unable to sleep, watching over the form in the bed. In the stillness of the room, a heart monitor blipped softly, the respirator hummed and, although the drips were silent, the three women all imagined they could hear each drop thundering into the IV feed.

Bill Russell's principal injuries were a cracked skull and concussion. A portion of the skull had been depressed inwards and the doctors had initially feared that it was pressing on the brain, but a series of emergency ECGs and CAT scans had removed that worry. There was extensive bruising to his face, and the imprint of finger marks were clearly visible on his upper arms. There was a flat ugly weal on his forehead where the palm of a hand had struck him with tremendous force. The doctors had also found extensive bruising around his testicles.

In the room beside him, without family or friends – they were on their way down from Birmingham – was the more seriously injured of the two officers. He had received a tremendous crushing blow to his chest, which had impacted several ribs into his lungs, collapsing them both. He had actually stopped breathing before the ambulance had got to him and there was a grave possibility of brain damage.

Even though her manpower was stretched to the limit, Margaret Haaren had placed two officers outside each door with strict instructions that no one was to be allowed in unless they were family or medical staff, and provided that they could prove it. Frazer's description of the scarred man, now backed up and improved by the description furnished by the uninjured officer, had been circulated to police within the Greater London area. Margaret Haaren's orders had been precise: anyone even vaguely matching the description of the man in the vicinity of the hospital was to be held for questioning.

The situation had now changed dramatically: in the *them* and *us* attitude of both police and citizens in most modern cities, the police tended to look upon an attack on one of their own far more seriously than a similar attack on a citizen.

The attack, too, had been cold-blooded and brutal, possibly murderous in its intent, and the description of the scarred man had warned that he was 'violent and dangerous'.

Bill Russell had been a respected and well-liked

137

member of the force; the younger man had only recently come down from Hendon and was still something of an unknown quantity, but he was one of their own. The hunt was now on for their attacker.

Across the city in the quiet Kensington suburbs, the moonlight washed across the mirror, seeming to cling to the surface, swirling along its greasy face, creating patterns, images, shapes.

And faces.

Wide-eyed, open-mouthed, the face of Robert Beaumont peered from the mirror, soundlessly screaming. The image seemed to rush from the distance to explode against the glass. Within its open mouth, a smaller face appeared, distorted by fear and pain, barely distinguishable as the face of Diane Williams and within her open mouth a smaller face again, that of Tony Farren, eyes like stones, mouth agape threatening to split his face in two. Within his open mouth there was movement, coiling smoke-like figures.

Had there been anyone there to see, the faces appeared again and again as the moonlight flowed down the mirror. When the glass was completely bathed in light, the shadow faces vanished and were replaced by the Image. It was visible for a single moment, and then it vanished.

Jonathan Frazer came suddenly, startlingly awake, arms flailing, surfacing from a dream in which he had been drowning, unable to breath. In his semi-conscious state he realized that he still couldn't breath. There was pressure on his throat.

When he opened his eyes he looked into the implacable mask of a madman.

'I can kill you.' The eyes – black as coal, glittering

138

like polished stones, with only the barest thread of white visible – bored into him. 'Remember that,' the big man hissed, 'I can kill you.' Abruptly the pressure was gone from Frazer's throat and he slipped from the chair to the floor, gasping, hacking for breath.

'Silence!' the man snapped. He walked away from Frazer and went to stand by the bed, looking down at the sleeping Emmanuelle. A muscle twitched at the corner of his eye, and when he turned back to Frazer there was something approaching pity in his eyes. 'It is always the innocent who suffer,' he muttered.

'Who . . . who are you?' Frazer croaked, massaging his injured throat. The man was even bigger than he remembered, taller, broader, and the scars that criss-crossed the man's face were even more pronounced. 'What do you want?' he asked.

'The mirror,' the scarred man said shortly. He bent to look at Cecilia Frazer and nodded slightly. When he glanced up a smile had twisted the corners of his lips. 'If you'd given it to me when I'd first asked for it, your young woman would still be alive, another man would not have lost his life and this tragedy would not have happened.' He turned to look at Manny again.

'But she's going to be all right!' Frazer said quickly, briefly forgetting his fear of the big man as he came to his daughter's bedside.

'No.' He shook his head sadly. 'At first she will seem to be fine. She will act as she normally acted, but then, if you watch closely, you will notice changes.'

The two men faced one another across the hospital bed. 'What sort of changes?'

'I don't know. It affects different people differently. It brings out something in their characters.'

'What does?'

'The mirror,' the big man whispered and walked away from the bed. He stopped with his hand on the handle of the door. 'You should have given it to me when you had the chance, Jonathan Frazer. Now it's too late.'

'Who are you?' Frazer asked again, his words abruptly slurred, his tongue thick in his head.

'We'll talk next time,' the big man said, opening the door and walking out of the room.

'Wait . . .!' Frazer raced to the door and jerked it open.

The two police officers surged to their feet, one man's hand going under his coat in a way that suggested he was armed.

'Can we help you, sir?'

'That man. The one who just came out . . .' He glanced up and down the corridor, but it was deserted. 'Where did he go? Why didn't you stop him?'

The two men looked at one another. 'No one came out of the room, Mister Frazer.'

'No! He came out a moment ago. The man, the big man, with the scarred face, white hair . . .' He looked at them both, seeing the disbelief in their eyes replaced by anger.

'No one went into your room, no one came out Mister Frazer.'

He touched his throat. 'He grabbed me here, there must be some mark . . .' He tilted his head back for inspection.

One of the men dutifully looked at Jonathan Frazer's throat. 'There's no mark on your throat, sir.'

'Perhaps you were dreaming,' another suggested, not unkindly.

Frazer looked from man to man, suddenly feeling chilled. There *had* been someone in the room with him, he had felt the man's fingers around his throat, smelt the strange spicy muskiness that clung to him, seen his scarred and torn flesh. There had been someone there. 'No marks,' he muttered, touching his throat again.

'No sir.'

He turned away, aware of the police officers' eyes on his back. 'Maybe it was a dream,' he whispered.

Edmund Talbott lay naked on the thin mattress in his room, his hands by his side, breathing easily. To the casual observer he was sleeping peacefully, though if that same observer had looked closer, he would have seen that the man's broad chest was barely moving and that behind his slitted eyelids, his eyes were moving frantically. Although the room was hot, muggy with the stale smells from the restaurant below, his flesh was cold to the touch, chilled, bathed in an icy perspiration.

Edmund Talbott opened his eyes and began to breathe again, great gasping breaths, filling his lungs with the warm air. He began to shiver and when he swung his legs out of the bed he had to wait while the room stopped its crazy spinning. Reaching for the towel that was draped into the sink, he rubbed it briskly across his body, drying himself.

He had only mastered the skill of astral projection with the greatest of difficulty. Although the ability to shift the spirit out of one's physical body was inherent in most people, and occurred naturally while the body slept, controlling the spirit, directing it to a specific location, required great skill and concentration. Now Edmund Talbott used it to track those associated with the mirror, but never the mirror itself.

Perhaps the astral body was the soul – he didn't know, wasn't qualified to even think about it – but he wasn't going to risk it by going anywhere near the glass.

Visiting Jonathan Frazer had been a risk, making contact with him, actually impinging on the sleeping man's consciousness, had been an even greater risk. The man's association with the mirror, his prolonged exposure to it, and especially Emmanuelle's contact with it at a time of a violent death – when it had been feeding – meant that they had been tainted. He wasn't sure how far the mirror's influence extended, he used to think one had to be in sight of it for it to have any effect, but now . . . now he didn't know the extent of its power or influence. He was aware though that it was gathering its forces, flexing its muscles.

He had been shocked when he had first entered the grey, usually formless astral world. Now snaking lines of power, tainted with electric colours, principally reds and deep purples, were clearly visible flowing across the landscape. Fully conscious of the danger, he had followed the twisting, coiling lines across the astral equivalent of London, until he had seen the swirling grey whirlpool that marked the presence of the mirror in the physical world.

The customary silence of that desolate landscape had been breached too by a thin, high keening that was emanating from the midst of the whirlpool. In the gritty dusk, he had been able to make out figures trapped in the maelstrom, faces, shapes, the newest souls closest to the surface, the souls it had taken previously now lost deep in its twisting core.

The image-haunted mirror had awoken from its century-old slumber.

To survive, to remain sentient, it needed souls and blood. And he wondered how long it would take before it claimed both.

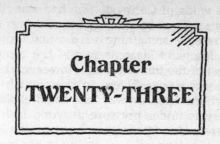

Chapter
TWENTY-THREE

IT was close to midnight before Margaret Haaren reached home. She was exhausted, the adrenalin rush of the afternoon having sapped her energy and then the resultant hassle, the emotionally draining process of informing wives and families, the mentally demanding procedure of gathering and preparing reports while the events were still fresh, had all conspired to completely drain her vitality.

And there was more of the same to look forward to tomorrow.

Her tiny apartment was stale and dry, close after the heat of the day. Without bothering to turn on the light, she draped her coat over the back of the chair and kicked off her shoes. She padded down the short corridor and into the kitchen. In the darkness, the answering machine light blinked red. She thumbed the play button as she filled the kettle.

Hi, Aunt Margaret, it's Helen. Just to let you know that the train gets in at twelve-thirty tomorrow. There's no need to meet me. I'll get some shopping and call round to the station for you about five. Love.

Margaret Haaren closed her eyes in dismay. She had completely forgotten that her niece was due in this

143

week for a few days' holiday in the Big Smoke, away from the wilds of Cornwall. She had started coming eight years ago, when she was ten, and over the years it had become something of a ritual. And, to be truthful, Margaret Haaren enjoyed the company . . . well, most of the time anyway. However, at least this year the girl was eighteen, so she shouldn't be too much of a burden. Anyway, she could explain to her that she was under pressure at work, Helen would understand. Her father was an inspector too. The tradition of policework was strong in her own family: her father and his brother, and her two older brothers had all entered the force. When she'd left school at eighteen, there really hadn't been anything else she'd even thought about doing.

There were days, like this one, when she wished she'd done something else.

She was forty years old, unmarried, unattached, unpursued by male companions, and likely to remain so at this stage. She had the disadvantage of being a successful professional woman and a police officer. A lethal combination in any man's eyes and, whereas many relationships within the force were made with other members of the force, with like-minded souls who understood the pressures and were aware of the difficulties of policework, the fact that she was a senior officer precluded that.

She wasn't particularly happy with her policeman's lot, but she was content.

She made herself some herbal tea to relax and then debated whether she'd have a bath or take a shower. The shower won out simply because it was easier to stand under the shower and let the water do all the work.

She walked back out of the kitchen into the hall and turned into the bedroom. She could have afforded better, but what was the point, she reasoned. If she bought herself a house, she'd never use it; and an empty house was simply an open invitation for burglars and once it became known that she was a police officer and out all day into the bargain, she could almost guarantee that it would be turned over with monotonous regularity. In this quiet block of residential apartments, she allowed people to think she was a simple filing clerk in the local nick and, because she was a woman, they believed it. It also meant that they didn't make a point of being nice to her, thinking that one day they might need her or that she might be able to do them a favour, like fixing a driving ticket or a minor summons.

Without turning the light on, Margaret Haaren stood before the half-closed blinds and stared down into the quiet street. There had been some reports of a prowler, possibly a peeping tom, in the area over the past few months and although this had become something of a nightly ritual, so far she had seen nothing.

Finally, closing the blinds and drawing the curtains, she undressed and padded naked into the bathroom. She climbed straight into the shower, turned the water on as hot as she could bear and then simply allowed it to flow across her shoulders and down her back. She consciously refused to even think about the day's events, they would still be there in the morning, the same questions looking for answers.

She stood there for about five minutes until the water abruptly turned icy cold, sending her leaping from the shower with a muted scream. That was always happening! If someone upstairs turned on their hot tap, it 'stole' the hot water from her! Dancing on the bathroom lino – why didn't she get carpet? – she towelled herself dry, standing before the square mirror above the sink. Maybe it was time to have something done about the hair, she decided, it was looking a little on the butch side, and a colour in it wouldn't go amiss,

there were far too many grey hairs there for comfort.
Tucking the towel in around her breasts she stepped
closer to the mirror and began to apply cold cream to
her face. She knew her nickname in the force was Mata
Hari: it came from the Margaret Haaren, and because
Haaren was Dutch. Her parents had met close to the
end of the Second World War, her father had been in the
Dutch resistance, her mother had been his London
contact; they had spoken together for three years before
they actually met. Margaret Haaren wasn't sure if she
approved of the nickname or not: Mata Hari, although
reputedly beautiful, had actually been quite plain.

She blinked: her image in the glass was becoming
fogged. She ran her hand down the moist glass . . .

The image appeared for a second: a woman's face,
pretty, with strong rounded cheekbones, full lips over
yellowish teeth, black, impenetrable eyes and thick
black hair.

And then the glass split right down the centre. Jagged
splinters of glass tore into the soft flesh of the palm of
her hand. The larger pieces shattered into the sink, tiny
flecks stinging the bare skin of her arms and legs.

The inspector staggered back, shaking with fright
and reaction, cradling her torn palm. The remaining
pieces of glass in the mirror were smeared in her blood,
and there were bright red droplets on the sink and floor.

Already her conscious mind was beginning to rationalize the event – she had pressed too hard on the glass
. . . the heat of her hand against the cold glass . . .

And the face, the woman's face? Imagination.

Just that. Nothing more.

In a hospital bed two miles away, Emmanuelle Frazer
twisted and turned in a nightmare in which she was
trapped in a block of ice. No matter how she hammered
or shouted or screamed, she couldn't get out, couldn't
attract attention.

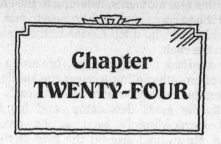

Chapter
TWENTY-FOUR

DAWN was breaking when Jonathan Frazer returned to the house in Kensington. The small cul-de-sac of exclusive, private houses was quiet and completely deserted; no milkman – indeed, no traders – drove into the tiny estate. A private landscape-gardening firm attended to the small green around which the houses were built and a discreet security firm ensured that there were no unwanted interlopers.

And of course that begged the question: how had the scarred man got in yesterday? Of course, with all the police activity and the ambulances coming and going, he supposed he had just slipped in amidst all the confusion.

Although the inspector had told him that she was assigning officers to keep an eye on the house, it was still a shock to find an unmarked police car sitting outside his house. The doors opened and two men moved out of the car when they saw the Volvo slowing to approach the gates to his house. One of them must have recognized him, or the registration of the car, and they returned to their car. From the corner of his eye, he saw one of the men writing on a clipboard, obviously noting the time of his arrival.

He parked the car neatly in front of the garage and then sat for a few moments, listening to the engine tick quietly. He had come back to the house to pick up a few things for Manny; he'd left Cecilia in the hospital, still dozing in the chair.

Frazer stepped out of the car, breathing in great lungfuls of air, attempting to clear the sterile hospital odour from his nostrils and mouth. The early morning was chill, the grass dew-damp, and his footsteps sounded extraordinarily loud as he crossed the driveway. He walked around the side of the house, pausing to look at the dark brownish smear high on the wall where the big man had pounded the sergeant's head against the stone.

It felt colder in the rear garden, and here tendrils of white mist coiled across the grass. The sprinkler system was on a timer and came on just after sunset and just before dawn, damping down the garden in anticipation of a fine day. It had obviously just switched off. The air smelt damp and earthy and water droplets glistened everywhere, dripping off the overhanging branches and dipping leaves. He walked down the pathway to the stables, his breath pluming before his face, digging his hands deeper into his pockets, suddenly conscious of the chill that clung to the garden, but unable to distinguish if it was simply a natural phenomenon of the pre-dawn chill or something else . . .

He stopped in the middle of the path, abruptly realizing that he had accepted – *had actually accepted* – that something very strange, that something very different, that something frightening was happening here.

And it was all somehow connected to the mirror.

People had died around that seven foot tall piece of glass. He was thirty-eight years old and he had never seen a dead body before. In the past week he had seen three.

The heavy padlock on the door was cold, slick with the morning's dew, the key stiff in the lock, his fingers numb, and it took him several moments before he finally got the door open.

When he stepped into the stables, he was immediately aware of the smell, a strange, almost sickly sweet odour that was tainted with burnt cloth and human flesh, and another stink, of something rotten. It was warm and close in the stables and he pulled off his coat and loosened the collar of his coat. He stood for a few moments, absorbing the atmosphere of the place, almost frightened by the change that had come over it.

This had always been his favourite place – indeed, his office was in some ways an attempt to recreate the atmosphere he felt in this place. Whenever he had wished to escape from Cecilia's nagging, or simply to be alone with his thoughts, he would retire to the stables and walk along its narrow aisles, looking, touching, handling the objects of the past, absorbing the peace and tranquillity of the room.

Now the warmth, the comfort he had taken from the antiques was gone: it had been replaced by an atmosphere of menace.

He breathed deeply, gagging slightly on the tainted air and walked directly towards the mirror. He could see his reflection in the glass, not distinctly or in detail, but far clearer than he had seen it before. The glass seemed brighter, some of the distortion and bubbling effects had vanished although as he approached, he could see that the layer of grime still clung to the glass.

He walked right up to the edge of the mirror, put his face close to the surface and attempted to stare *into* the glass. Only his own frightened, hollow-eyed face stared back at him, ghostly pale, deeply shadowed in the dirty glass.

'What are you?' he whispered.

The silence mocked him.

Jonathan Frazer backed away from the glass and sat down in the chaise longue he had set up before the mirror, wrapping his arms across his chest, holding himself.

High above him, still perfectly visible in the pale morning sky, the full moon shone down through the grimy skylights.

The woman stood naked in the small wooden tub while the other two women moved around her body, rubbing the soft flesh with pumice stones, massaging the scented oils and unguents into her skin. Her rich dark hair had been bathed in dew skimmed from the grass in the last moments before the dawn. She had been told it was of the purest quality and certainly her hair now glistened like burnished metal. The slightly abrasive touch of the pumice had brought the blood flushing to her skin, giving it a rich glow, and the oils had soothed the slight irritation caused by the volcanic stone.

There was a chill draught as the door opened and the tall, red-haired, red-bearded, green-eyed man stepped into the room. He shook snow from the shoulders of his cloak, brushed it from his beard and strode to the fire to kick off his boots. He looked at the woman dispassionately, 'Are you nearly ready?' he demanded.

She turned in the tub to face him, spreading her arms wide, a smile twisting her lips. 'Do I not look ready?'

'Clothes?' he grunted.

'I wasn't going to wear any,' she leered.

'Then you'll catch your death. It's freezing. There were folk walking on the Thames earlier today. The Queen complained that she was so cold that they actually began to burn some of the old wooden furniture, and that was fine until they began chopping up a fine chest that had once belonged to Henry, and you know how fond she was of her father.'

The woman laughed dutifully. This was as close as the dour Kelley ever came to humour. 'You have found someone else, someone suitable?' she continued, ignoring the two women servants, both of whom had been made deaf by having their ear-drums punctured.

Kelley suddenly looked evasive. 'Yes . . . no . . . possibly.'

She knew better than to mock him, but she found this sudden indecisiveness a little frightening.

'Get dressed,' he commanded. 'We can talk then.'

'We can talk now; my nakedness doesn't bother me.'

Kelley strode over to her and gripped her small face in his large hands, squeezing along the line of her jaw and cheekbone. 'You may think what you wish of me, but I am still a man, and I would be less than a man if I were not aroused by the sight of your nakedness, so cover yourself, wanton. We have much to discuss.' He turned away, returning to stand before the fire.

The woman swallowed hard and stepped out of the tub. The two women, who had retreated before Kelley's approach, returned with towels.

'How is your master?' she asked, exacting a little revenge for his treatment of her.

'The good doctor is well. He has prepared yet another horoscope for the Queen, which delights her no end, and he has promised her further delights when he has mastered the art of crystallomancy.'

'You told him!' she accused.

'I had to give him something,' he said defensively. 'It was a hint, nothing more. I spoke to him about scrying.'

'But it is a gamble,' she said, climbing onto the high-soled wooden shoes, while the two maids fixed the ornate ruff around her neck.

'He has some art, you know that, but no talent. He has some mathematical and alchemical knowledge and he has the contacts at Court, not only with the Queen, but also with Sir William Cecil and Sir Francis Walsingham. Now, we can never oust him from that position – he is too close to the Queen – but if we can control him, it places us in an extraordinarily powerful position. We will have power without the dangers.'

'What would you have me do?'

'Dismiss the women,' Kelley commanded.

'They are deaf.'

'But not fools. Dismiss the women.'

The woman turned, and waved her hand to attract the attention of the two servants who were busying themselves around the tub, mopping up the water that had been splashed out onto the wooden floor. When they looked up, she pointed to the door.

One – the older of the two – indicated the tub and raised her eyebrows in a question. The dark-haired woman shook her head and pointed to the door again, her face tightening into a frown. Both women scurried from the room.

When they were alone, Kelley turned to the woman and grabbed her forearms, pulling her close. 'How badly do you covet immortality?'

'To live forever?' she asked dreamily.

'For ever and ever,' he promised.

'I will do anything. You know that.'

'Even marriage?' he asked.

'In light of what I have already done, marriage would be the least of my crimes,' she smiled.

'And to conceive a child?'

She looked into his mad, bright green eyes and frowned.

'And to conceive a child?' he repeated.

'If it was necessary,' she said cautiously.

'And to give up that child, unbaptized, to me.'

'Why?' she whispered.

'To allow me to fulfil my promise to you: to grant you immortality, to enable you to live for ever and ever . . .'

'But surely we could buy a child on the street . . .?'

'It would not have those especial gifts from its parents. It would lack your own power, your consummate skill, your devotion to the carnal senses.'

'And the father? What of his skills?' She almost expected him to nominate himself as the child's father. Though they had never slept together, and at times she thought him a catamite or a eunuch, she knew he was prepared to do almost anything in the pursuance of his art.

'The father is a mathematician and an astronomer of some note. He possesses a little knowledge of natural magic and the arcane arts and much of alchemy.'

Realization flooded through her, and she suddenly laughed, almost with relief. She had thought he was going to suggest union with a demon.

'That's right,' Edward Kelley smiled. 'I want you to wed John Dee, our noble Queen Elizabeth's Astrologer Royal.'

Jonathan Frazer's eyes snapped open and he came to his feet with a shout. He stood swaying before the mirror, his heart tripping in his chest, while overhead rain pattered against the roof of the stables.

The dream had been so vivid, so clear . . . and he abruptly remembered his previous dream. That too had been clear, vivid, alive. And he had experienced that while sleeping before the mirror.

And the nameless woman and the man Edward Kelley had been in both.

With a growing sense of elation, he realized he was close to something. He had clues now, clues he could pursue. To solve the mystery of the mirror he would have to trace those references back to their source.

And soon.

Before the mirror exerted its baleful influence on anyone else.

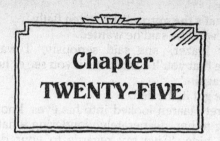

Chapter
TWENTY-FIVE

JONATHAN Frazer met Inspector Margaret Haaren at the hospital. He would have avoided her if he could; he knew she held him responsible – indeed, he held himself responsible – for the injuries to the two policemen, and he knew that she suspected his involvement with their attacker ran far deeper.

'How is your daughter, Mister Frazer?'

'She is very well, thank you, Inspector. Tired, distressed by what she witnessed, but she's young and strong.'

Margaret Haaren nodded.

'And your men, inspector?' he enquired.

She shrugged. She had just been into to see both men and while Bill Russell seemed to be improving, the younger constable, Martin Moore, was still in a coma.

'Bill Russell will pull through, but the other lad . . .' She let the sentence trail, and then stopped, her hand on Frazer's arm. 'Are you sure there is nothing you can tell us about the man who did this?'

'I've told you before. I don't know the man. I never met him before . . . and even if I did know him, don't you think I'd tell you? I've seen what he's done to your people, what'll he do to me if he doesn't get what he wants.'

'And that's the mirror,' she stated flatly.

'That's what he said he wanted.'

'Mister Frazer,' she said seriously, 'I want your assurance that you'll contact me if you see or hear from this man again.'

'You've got it,' he lied.

Margaret Haaren looked into his eyes, knowing he was lying to her, desperately wondering what he was trying to hide. 'Give my regards to your daughter, Mister Frazer.'

'I will. Thank you, Inspector . . . and . . . I'm truly sorry about what happened to your men.'

'It had nothing to do with you, had it? There was nothing you could do, was there?' she said, almost in an aside. In her experience people usually apologized when they had something to hide.

'I suppose I feel responsible because it happened on my property.'

'Well, you know I've placed a twenty-four hour guard on your house, Mister Frazer,' she said. 'That should give you some measure of security.' What she didn't tell him was that, as well as the highly visible car parked in front of the house, there was another very discreet watch being kept on the house from across the road, where the owner – a retired British Army colonel – was a personal friend of the Chief Inspector and had been only too delighted to do a favour for a friend and to assist the police in any way he could.

Jonathan Frazer watched the woman stride down the corridor, her gait long, quick and decisive, almost like a man's. But there was something else about it – and then he realized that she was moving in complete silence. She was wearing leather-soled shoes that made no sound on the tiled floor.

Footsteps made him turn and he saw Manny, linked

by Cecilia and a nurse, walking towards him. 'Dad, they think I'm a child. I can walk to the car by myself.'

'Hospital regulations, miss,' the nurse said primly, 'we have to see you off the premises.'

Jonathan stared into his daughter's large brown eyes. 'Are you sure you're fit enough to come home? I really would prefer if you would stay another day or so.'

'I'm fine, Dad, really I am. And I know if I stay here another hour, never mind another day, I'm going to go stark raving mad.'

'Home to bed then,' he said sternly.

'To bed,' she agreed. 'I'm looking forward to sleeping in a comfortable bed,' she added, glancing at the nurse, who ignored the jibe.

They drove home in virtual silence. Manny dozed in the back of the car and Cecilia, for some reason unknown to Jonathan, was treating him to the cold shoulder. He had more than enough on his mind at the moment to pander to her games and ignored her, and this only served to infuriate her even further. When they drove past the unmarked police car before the house, her reserve finally collapsed.

'This is intolerable!' she snapped. 'What do they think this is, a police state? I shall complain to the Chief Inspector or my local MP.'

'I'll bet you don't even know who your local MP is,' Jonathan teased her. 'And anyway, the police are there for our own protection. In case that maniac comes back.'

'But what must people be thinking . . .?' She glanced out at the houses, clearly visualizing the people in the airy drawing-rooms and stylized conservatories or over dinner in the formal dining-rooms discussing the Frazers and the sudden police activity up at the house.

'To be honest, I don't give a fuck what people are thinking!'

The obscenity stopped her cold. Jonathan rarely swore; he prided himself that he didn't need to resort to foul language. 'Three dead bodies have been taken from this house,' he said coldly, glancing in the mirror, checking that Manny was still asleep. 'Two men have been very seriously injured, a dog has been butchered, I've been attacked. Our daughter almost lost her life.' He had been speaking slowly and clearly, but his voice suddenly rose to a shout. 'So don't give me any fucking shit about the neighbours!'

'Jon ... Jon ... you're tired, you're overwrought ...'

'And don't fucking patronize me,' he snapped, standing hard on the brake, bringing the car to a stop in a shower of pebbles, gouging long straight lines in the gravel. He swivelled in the seat to face her, his face pale, sheened with sweat, eyes sunk into his head. 'I'm tired, very tired. Unlike you I didn't sleep very well last night, nor did I sleep the night before. I've got things on my mind. Like some fucking maniac who delights in kicking the shit out of people.' He took a deep breath and visibly controlled himself. 'Leaving aside everything else, let me put this in a context which you may be able to understand: with Tony Farren and Diane Williams gone, I'm going to have to close down the workshops, because I have no one to do the repairs. With Robert Beaumont gone, I have no one to run the shop. No shop means no money. It's as simple as that. And need I add that we've a lot of money tied up in stock in the shop, and even more tied up in the stock in the stables. And what you seem to have failed to realize is that I do not have bottomless pockets ...'

Cecilia turned to look out the window.

'So you see, dear, I do have one or two things on my mind at the moment.'

'Mum ... Dad ...' Manny Frazer came groggily awake. 'What's wrong?'

'Nothing's wrong dear, we're home. And . . .'
'I know that,' she smiled, 'straight to bed!'

It was great to be home. Jesus, but that hospital – even though she had been in a private room and all that – had been grim. And the bed; the bed had been unbelievable. And she couldn't get the idea out of her head that other people had slept in that bed, other people had died in that bed. That had been her one abiding thought in the hospital during her lucid hours. She'd been troubled by extraordinary nightmares in which she actually heard the voices of those who had passed away in that room, crying out to her, calling her name, begging her to help them, to ease their suffering, to help them for the love of Jesus to help them to *helptohelptohelptohelptohelphelphelphelp* . . .

She could rationalize it away; she was tired, distressed, she'd just seen her first dead body, it was only natural she'd think of death, especially now, in a hospital, but the dreams had been nonetheless frightening.

Manny walked around her room, simply enjoying the peaceful atmosphere of it, the aura of calm, the knowledge that this room was her place, and was such a reflection of her personality that she felt completely at ease here.

The room had been decorated quite simply in reds and pinks, with the darker colour starting at the floor level and rising until about waist height when it began to lighten, until it was a pink tinted white by the time it reached the ceiling. The carpet was a deep blood-red and there were fleecy pink clouds painted on the ceiling. Her mother claimed the room was childish and had attempted on a couple of occasions to have it redecorated, but Manny, with her father's help, had resisted.

Manny stepped into the small en suite bathroom

159

and undressed quickly, dumping her clothes into the tall wicker basket. They stank of the hospital, and she imagined she could smell the same sharp odour of chemicals and disinfectant from her own skin. Stepping into the shower, she turned it up as hot as she could bear and allowed the water to run off her shaven head and down onto her body, aware of the knotted muscles in the shoulders and at the back of her neck relaxing. She scrubbed at herself with a harsh sponge, bringing the blood flushing to her skin . . .

. . . *the rasp of pumice stone against her skin, across her sensitive breasts* . . .

. . . and then rubbed in odourless shower gel.

The small shower stall was suddenly flooded with the sickly sweet scent of a heavily perfumed unguent.

Manny stopped, head tilted back, smelling the moist air. What was that smell? Like dead flowers or bees wax.

A cold wind suddenly wafted across her moist body, as if a door had been opened, and she shivered. She peered through the frosted perspex door of the shower, trying to see if she'd left the bedroom door open, but she could see nothing. She blinked moisture from her eyes and rubbed at the glass door . . .

. . . *a tall, red-haired, red-bearded man, cruel faced, green eyed, in a heavy snow-capped cloak* . . .

The scream caught in her throat, and she floundered backwards against the icy tiles, hands automatically covering her breasts and groin. The figure seemed to be looking directly at her through the glass, his mouth opening and closing as if he spoke. Water splashed into her eyes and she blinked rapidly. When she could see clearly again, he had gone.

Manny flung open the door and stared wide-eyed out into the empty bathroom. The door leading into the bedroom was still locked, the bolt thrown across from the inside.

Hallucinations ... the residue of drugs in her system.

Shivering almost uncontrollably now, she staggered from the shower and wrapped herself in a thick dressing-gown, rubbing at her head with a towel, hearing the lengthening hair rasp against the cloth. She opened the door and stared out into the bedroom, feeling like a child checking for the bogeyman beneath the bed. And then a quick scramble beneath the covers, only tossing away the dressing-gown when she was safely tucked in. She snuggled down beneath the sheets, luxuriating in the feel of the fabric against her naked skin. She was tired ... overtired. That was all. A good night's sleep was what she ...

Manny awoke once during the night, and that was close to two in the morning. Moonlight streamed in through the window, the harsh light turning her soft pink room black and ominous. She turned over and closed her eyes against the glare.

This time he knew what he was doing. This time he was conducting an experiment. Twice before he had experienced something in front of this mirror, he had dreamed dreams, seen images, learned something – clues perhaps – to the mirror's past. This time he had come prepared.

He had positioned the video camera directly behind the chaise longue facing the mirror, and he had set it to shoot one frame every five minutes. A double-cassette player had been placed closer to the mirror, and there were two C120s loaded and ready. When one was finished the other would automatically take over, and it meant that he had effectively one hundred and twenty minutes of playing time, two hours. His Nikon lay on the chair beside him, loaded with a roll of 36 mm high-definition film.

With a deep breath, Jonathan Frazer settled back against the chaise longue and folded his arms across his chest.

Tonight he would have some answers.

Chapter
TWENTY-SIX

'**SHE** is magnificent,' the tall grey-haired, grey-eyed man agreed, turning to look at the woman.

'And she desires you, lord,' Edward Kelley said eagerly. Gone was his previous air of authority and learning; now he was nothing more than an Irish servant, fawning, ignorant and ill-educated.

They were sitting in a smoky tavern just off the bridge that was much frequented by alchemists and those dabbling in the occult. It was often used as a meeting place by those wishing to join a Circle or by a master looking for a servant with a knowledge of the occult. Dr John Dee had met Edward Kelley here, four years previously, in 1569. His previous assistant, Barnabus Saul, had turned out to be nothing more than a charlatan, foisted on Dee by his enemies, jealous of his privileged position with the Queen. Saul had promised much and delivered nothing.

Dee considered himself fortunate indeed in stumbling upon Kelley, an itinerant Irishman, fleeing the grinding poverty in his homeland, hoping to find his fortune in the big city, only to find a similar poverty in London, with nothing to his name except some skill as a medium. Kelley's talent as a medium and scryer was prodigious and the man soon became an integral part of Dee's life and work. The man's knowledge of the occult was extraordinary, far surpassing Dee's, although curiously this knowledge was only in evidence when Kelley was in a trance under the influence of his spirits.

'Tell me about her,' Dee said, glancing sidelong at the woman again. It was not unusual to find women in this tavern, though women of such beauty and presence were certainly rare indeed.

'She is a natural talent, neither witch nor sorceress, a practioner of some natural magic. Look at her, lord; tell me her age,' Kelley urged him.

Dee looked at the woman again, and then shook his head. 'Five-and-twenty, eight-and-twenty?'

'She was born in 1491, the same year Henry VIII, the Queen's father, was born.'

Dee looked at the woman in astonishment. Why, that would make her eighty-two! He turned to look at Kelley, his thin eyebrows raised in a silent question. The red-haired man nodded. 'Kept young by her magic.'

'And she wants to speak to me?' He sounded almost surprised.

Edward Kelley lowered his eyes. 'You have a reputation, master. That has drawn her.'

'I'll speak to her,' Dr John Dee said decisively.

'But not here, master. Too many eyes, too many ears.'

Dee nodded. He trod a particularly dangerous path; he was a known occultist close to the Queen, he had prepared the horoscope that had shown that the young princess Elizabeth would indeed be queen and had then prepared the horoscope which decided upon the most auspicious day for the Coronation. Although his travels in Europe had established much that had been of military or economic use to the Queen's

164

advisors, he had also made many enemies, and the church especially despised him, labelling him a practitioner of black magic and a heretic. He was in little danger while the Queen still lived, but should anything happen to her . . .

And there were always those eager to report his every movement to Elizabeth's enemies, looking for signs of weakness, trying to blacken his name with her.

John Dee made his way through the crowded room and stepped out into the street, pulling his cloak up around his shoulders. The night was bitterly cold and the frigid air was tainted with the stench of the streets and the pungent effluence from the river. He lived in Mortlake, a village on the edge of London, and so was particularly conscious of the difference in the air of the city and the country, but he knew that Londoners were rarely aware of the stench of their own city.

Kelley came out a few moments later, with the woman following close behind.

Sensitive to odours, Dee caught the scents of herbs and spices from her, expensive bath oils sweetening the foul night air. She had pulled up the hood of her heavy cloak and now the pale oval of her face stared at him from shadow, her eyes huge and dark against her face.

'I am Doctor John Dee,' he said formally.

The woman curtsied before him, but did not extend her hand and did not proffer her own name. Dee glanced at his assistant, but Kelley shook his head slightly, warning him to say nothing.

'You have an interest in Natural Magic,' she said suddenly. Surprisingly, her voice was uneducated, her accent placing her somewhere to the north of the Thames.

'I am used to dealing with people with names,' Dee said shortly.

'Names are symbols with which we chain others; the knowledge of names grants power.'

'That is a superstition and applies only to magical names. To know a person's magical name is to have power over that person.'

'Untrue. A name – any name – conjures the image of that person. Knowledge of the name – any name, be it true or false, so long as it is used consistently to represent that person – grants power.'

Dee bowed slightly, conceding the point. Her accent may be that of an uneducated woman, but her knowledge was evidence of learning and education, and that was a privilege of the wealthy.

'You have an interest in Natural Magic,' she repeated.

John Dee nodded. 'I have.' He nodded to Kelley. 'My assistant tells me you were born in 1491.'

'It is true.'

'And you have preserved your youth through this Natural Magic,' Dee asked, keeping his voice carefully neutral. As an alchemist, he had heard of the Elixir of Life, the magical formula which granted eternal life to the user.

The woman looked up suddenly. 'We should not talk here. Follow me.' She turned and walked away, her wooden heels clicking loudly on the few pieces of paving that still remained this close to the river. Dee looked at Kelley and shrugged. The doctor touched the knife on his belt and he was relieved to find that Kelley was wearing his sword. This was a particularly unsavoury part of London.

The woman led them down through the warren of side streets and alleys that ran parallel to the docks. Rats scurried across their path, huge creatures that could easily be confused with a cat or a dog. Dee was horrified to discover that even though it was after midnight on a bitterly cold winter's night, there were

166

still women and children on the streets, begging and selling themselves for the price of a meal. If he could truly discover the Elixir of Life then surely he should be able to put it to some use to ease man's suffering?

He was becoming nervous now. They were in the heart of the dockland, a vicious, dangerous no-man's land, where even the watch rarely ventured. He clutched at Kelley's arm. 'Where are we going?'

'She has some sort of base close by,' he said carefully. 'Her Natural Magic draws its power from the river.'

Dee nodded, not completely satisfied with the answer. His every instinct warned him of danger, but his desire for knowledge, his thirst for information, was greater.

They stopped outside a rotting wharfside store and the woman produced a brightly shining key from the depths of her cloak. The key turned easily in the lock and she stepped into the darkness. After a moment's hesitation, Dee and Kelley followed her.

Flesh touched his, and Dee stifled a scream as he recognized the woman's hand on his, her soft flesh wrapping itself around his fingers, pulling him forward. Kelley's heavy hand dropped onto his shoulder as they moved into the darkness. He wondered how she could see in the dark, and supposed that it might be a side effect of her Natural Magic; perhaps the senses grew more finely tuned as one aged, rather than degenerating as they did at present.

Or perhaps she was a demon leading him to Hell.

They moved down into the bowels of the rotten building. The smell of decay, of ordure, of corruption, was stronger now, and there was a ripe dampness in the air that caught at the back of his throat, eased its way into his lungs. Still in total darkness, the nameless woman led them across an echoing chamber, boots splashing through water that, by the smell it exuded, had been standing long stagnant.

And then there was light.

Dee didn't realize he was holding his breath until they reached the lighted chamber, and then he took a great sobbing breath that he turned into a cough.

The room was set up as an alchemical studio, a long table laden down with instruments occupying one wall, a broken chair beside a rough cot in the corner. There was a second, completely bare wooden table shoved up against another wall.

But the room was dominated by the mirror.

The woman walked into the centre of the chamber and threw off her cloak, while Kelley took up a position at the door, arms folded across his chest. Dee walked up to the mirror, mesmerized by its size: he had never seen a glass so big.

'Do not stare into its depths,' the woman advised.

Dee immediately whirled around. 'Why not?'

Her lips moved in a smile. 'It has certain . . . properties.'

'Properties?'

'Properly activated it can be used as a scrying glass, for example,' she said, repeating what Kelley had told her to say.

Dee turned to look at the glass again. Scrying – the ability to see the future in a glass – was becoming one of his especial interests. 'And how does one activate it?' he asked, running his long fingers along the smooth wooden frame. Yet again, he cursed his lack of any Talent or Ability. He glanced over at Kelley, wondering why he didn't approach the glass. Did he know something, did he see something with his second sight that disturbed him? 'How does one activate the glass?' he repeated when the woman didn't answer him. He glanced over his shoulder – and stopped.

The woman was naked.

She looked at him, lifting her arms, running both hands through her thick black hair, exposing herself to him. 'Blood will bring it to life,' she said, 'clean blood, with the proper incantation from the Key of Solomon. Semen, too, will bring it to life.'

Dee turned from the woman and stared at the mirror again, watching it from the corner of his eyes, his agile mind evaluating these snippets of knowledge. He had heard of such glasses – though never on such a scale before – and they too had to be fed with the body's sacred fluids, blood, semen or tears. But once fired they showed many, many wondrous things, the future, the past, Heaven, Hell.

'But we did not come here to discuss the glass,' she continued, 'we came her to discuss Natural Magic.'

Dee dragged his gaze away from the mirror and turned back to the woman. She was now wearing a blood-red cloak over her nakedness, though the cloak hung open down the middle, and he found the tantalizing glimpse of flesh even more arousing than the sight of her fully nude.

'Natural Magic,' the woman said walking past the man to stand with her back to the mirror, hands on her hips. 'We are all of us vessels of power, repositories of magical energy. But few realize that, few can tap the unlimited power of their own bodies.'

Dee nodded slowly. His own theories ran very much along these lines.

'I have developed a system of Natural Magic that can tap the power of the human body,' she continued, her large dark eyes now locked on Dee's face. As she spoke, her right hand had moved off her rounded hip bone and slid into the dark patch between her legs. 'This is the oldest magic in the world,' the woman continued, her fingers moving, probing, 'sacred in some parts of the world, shunned in others. The druids knew of its power, the witches, their

169

successors, knew a little also. The Egyptians knew the secret of this special magic, and we know the savages conduct their ceremonies naked.'

Dee said nothing, mesmerized by the sight of the woman arousing herself so brazenly. He was conscious of the odour of the woman's body in the room, aware of his own arousal.

'The power is only evident at moments of great emotion: pain, anger, desire, arousal, orgasm. These are the most potent of all the emotions . . .' Her fingers were moving swiftly now, delving deeply into her body, and her breath was beginning to come in great gasps.

And suddenly Dee was aware of the mirror behind her. Rainbow hues were flickering down the length of the glass, shimmering tints that hinted of pictures, half-seen images. He started forward, his gaze fixed on the glass.

Edward Kelley bent his head to hide his smile. They had Dee now. Much of what he had instructed the woman to tell Dee had been true, and the display on the glass was an almost natural phenomenon, triggered by the proximity of the woman and the intensity of her orgasm.

'At the moment . . . of orgasm for example . . . the natural magic of the human . . . human body is available. All one needs to do . . . is to . . . to capture that magic, utilize it. I have used . . . the magic of my own . . . body to remain young. Properly employed there is no limit to its . . . POWER!' The last word was a scream as the woman collapsed into a writhing heap on the ground, her entire body shuddering in the throes of orgasm. But Dee's eyes were not on the woman; he was watching the undulating display of rippling colours on the glass. There were pictures in the glass, images, half-seen, barely glimpsed. But they were there.

And what would he see if he were to properly apply the laws of Natural Magic to the glass, if he were to feed the glass . . . with blood and semen and tears.

Manny Frazer writhed on the bed, the sheets a tumbled ball on the floor. Her hands were busy at her groin, her breath coming in heaving gasps, her entire body covered in a sheen of sweat.

She dreamt she was standing before a huge glass mirror, masturbating before an old, grey-haired grey-eyed man . . .

Chapter
TWENTY-SEVEN

SHE was perfect.

Such power, such passion. It fed off her sensations, savouring their intensity. It was one of the mysteries of the human body. Such a frail delicate shell, and yet it was capable of such response. It was a mystery that had never failed to intrigue, a paradox.

There had been others, women always. The image of the naked woman was one of the most potent symbols of power it possessed in its armoury. It had experimented with the men, but men were tools, to be used, to bring the offerings and to perform the petty mundane tasks necessary for keeping the gateway open and safe.

Perhaps because it had once worn a female form, it felt happier in that guise and, in truth, it never trusted the male species since the Betrayal.

But woman-kind.

Since time immemorial they had kept the secrets, fed the fires, given freely of themselves and their great passions to honour the mysteries.

And yet it could not dismiss the male. There were always two, male and female, one was never enough: a male to feed the symbol, a female, made in its image.

172

Across the Otherworld, colours flickered and the seething column of power trembled with anticipation. In its core, the souls of those who had fed its hunger down through the countless centuries screamed their agony.

Chapter
TWENTY-EIGHT

Image.

The mirror, the topmost left-hand edge touched with moonlight.

Image.

The mirror, the moonlight now further advanced down its length.

Image.

The moonlight now completely bathing the tall length of glass.

Image.

A solid rectangle of white light, flat and featureless.

Image.

A twisting strand of reddish-purple colour about three quarters of the way down the length of the mirror.

Image.

Patches of oily colour on the glass now, irregular circles dotted around the mirror, clustered close to the top and middle, reds, purples, blues and greens predominating.

Image.

A face.

Image.

The moonlight sliding off the glass, the topmost corner washed in darkness.

Jonathan Frazer examined the photographs under an illuminated magnifying glass. The pictures had been taken every five minutes, and these eight frames represented the vital forty minutes when the activity had occurred on the glass. The audio-tapes had been useless; he had one hundred and twenty minutes of hissing static, and – despite his best intentions – he had fallen asleep, so the Nikon had been useless.

He had transferred the video cassette to the larger video format and run it through his video player, fast forwarding, watching the moonlight run down the glass and off it again. He missed it the first time, and it was only on the second run, when he slowed the machine to a frame-by-frame examination at the point when the moonlight began its inexorable slide down the glass, that he spotted the shifting swirls and circles of colour on the glass. And then the face.

Using the high-definition film, he had photographed the television screen, shooting four shots of each frame using different apertures and settings to attain the best results. A colleague who photographed the antiques for his regular catalogues developed the roll of film and, if he was curious about the subject matter, he said nothing.

Now, with the video frozen to the image of the face and the ten by eight blown-up print on the table before him, he pored over it with the glass. The face fascinated him. It was a fragment, nothing more, the shadowy outline of a nose, the twist of a mouth, indentations of eyes, a blur that might have been hair.

And it was familiar. But familiar in the way that any such photograph would have been, the features could have been almost anyone's. The video image, because of its fractionally better quality, was slightly sharper, but the image was no less distinct.

Finally, he sat back rubbing his throbbing eyes. There was a dull pounding at the back of his head and, when he looked at the clock, he was surprised to find that it was close to one-thirty. He wondered where Cecilia was; he hadn't seen her all morning. He supposed she was still annoyed with him because he'd spent the night in the stables.

He turned off the video and shuffled the photographs back into their brown envelope.

There was a jotter by his side, and he looked at the notes he'd made, drawn up from the clues he'd gathered from his *dreams*, if that's what they were, although he was inclined to think that they were much more.

Dee.

He recognized the name ... a magician or something in the court of Queen Elizabeth I. He'd been her spy in some of the continental courts.

Kelley.

He didn't know the name, though if he was associated with Dee he shouldn't be too hard to trace.

The woman.

Nameless, though he had a perfect image of her: long face, uptilted black eyes, rounded cheekbones, yellowish teeth, full lips. And then there was her hair, thick and black, that was her distinctive feature, and he was a little embarrassed when he realized that he also knew that she had full, heavy breasts with small dark nipples and thick dark pubic hair.

The mirror.

That was just as important a player in this game. The mirror was the key ... either the mirror or the woman. But in his own mind they were interchangeable.

The British Library was quiet, afternoon sun streaming in through the high windows, catching the tiny dust motes that whirled upwards. This portion of the library was virtually deserted, only two other people there beside Frazer and the attendant in the enormous circular room. The atmosphere was dry, the odour of leather and aged paper and the slightly sickly sweetness of leather preservative on the air. The attendant nodded to Frazer who was a regular visitor to the library where he researched into the history and background of some of his more expensive artefacts.

Ignoring the catalogue, which he still found totally bewildering, he began to work his way down through the shelves, not sure what he was looking for, picking titles at random, checking the indices for references to Dee, and finding several, but nothing of any real use. There were some listings for Dee's own works, which he noted, but wasn't sure if there was any point in looking for them yet.

He was considering going back to the catalogue when he rounded a bookcase and almost collided with an old man, white-haired and stooped with age. A heavy leather-bound book slid from his grip and clattered to the floor.

'I beg your pardon, excuse me.' Frazer stooped and lifted the book, brushing his hand down the length of the spine, surreptitiously checking it to see if the ancient looking binding was cracked.

Majister Johannes Dee.

The title stopped him cold. Ignoring the old man's outstretched hand, he opened the title page.

Majister Johannes Dee, Wim van den Berg, Antwerp, MDCX.

He quickly translated the Roman numerals into 1610. That meant it was written two years after Dee's death in 1608. There was a wood engraving of Dee facing the title page and Frazer felt his heart begin to pound. It was the man in his dream. The same long face, the same tall, thin man.

'Sir . . .' he began excitedly, and then he stopped, looking at the old man in horror. The bent back had straightened, the tired, slack and wrinkled face seemed to become animated and when he had straightened to his full height, which was fully four inches over his own six feet, Frazer found himself staring up at the scarred face of the nameless man.

'The book is full of lies and half truths,' he said easily, smiling at Frazer's surprise. 'In reality, Dee was a far more interesting man that many give him credit for. The occultist tag has somewhat tarnished his reputation.'

'Who are you?' Frazer whispered, anger beginning to replace his fear.

The big man grabbed him by the arm and pulled him to one of the small tables. 'Sit down, Mister Frazer. I did say we would meet again,' he said pleasantly.

'Who are you? How did you come to me that night? What do you want the mirror for, what did you mean about it affecting my daughter?'

'So many questions?' he smiled. 'I suppose you are entitled to answers.' His coal-black eyes stared into Frazer's face. 'I would ask you not to go to the police with the information I am about to give you, but once I tell you what you want to know, I don't think you'll be going to the police anyway.' He placed a broad hand in the centre of his chest. 'I am Edmund Talbott, which might not mean very much to you. However, you might be interested to know that an ancestor of mine, called Edward Talbott changed his named to Edward Kelley, spelt KELLEY, and was employed by Doctor John Dee.'

'What do you want?' Frazer asked quietly.

'The mirror. What I wanted from the beginning.'

'Why?' Frazer was gazing at Talbott with fixed intensity.

'Because it is mine by right of inheritance if nothing else, and because only I can control it.'

Frazer continued to stare at him, saying nothing,

realizing that Talbott would tell him more if he wasn't pressed.

'Let me tell you what you saw, Mister Frazer . . . was it last night, or the night before? You saw Doctor John Dee, and his assistant Kelley – though Kelley was more than just an assistant – and a woman, a mysterious dark-haired woman. Did you see Kelley and the woman feed the mirror with blood? If you didn't then you will, at the time of the next full moon. That is when the mirror is at its strongest. Its power waxes and wanes with the moon; when the moon is full the images are at their clearest, and that is when the mirror is at its strongest. Although I should add that once moonlight has touched the glass, it remains active even at the dark of the moon or when the moon is occluded.'

'How did you know what I saw in the mirror?' Frazer asked in a whisper, glancing around. There was a young man at the end of the aisle, but he was absorbed in a book.

'That is one of the most powerful images in the mirror; it is always the first to surface. When I first looked into the mirror, that was the image I saw. The more often you look, the more sights you will see. Paris during the Terror, Florence during the Medici reign, Rome during the days of the Roman Circus. There are said to be other, stranger sights to be glimpsed in its surface, but I have never seen them.'

'What is this mirror? Who is the woman?'

Talbott's smile was bleak. 'The woman appears in most of the images. She changes – although she is usually nameless and long black hair is another usual prerequisite. I think perhaps she is an ordinary woman, whom the mirror has taken over, absorbed, possessed if you prefer. I don't know what the mirror is: but it is powerful. Men have died to possess it, men have died to protect it.'

'And you, what is your interest in the mirror?'

'My family have – with some exceptions – protected the mirror down through the centuries. Edward Talbott-Kelley was one of those exceptions. He attempted to exploit the mirror's powers. And its powers are tremendous. Once it's fed – with human emotions, with blood, sweat, tears, semen – its powers are limitless. It can show wonders – or terrors – on its surface.'

Jonathan Frazer looked up suddenly, aware that the young man had moved closer and was staring openly at the two men, his head tucked unnaturally into his jacket. When he looked back there was a twisted smile on Talbott's lips.

'Company, I see.' The big man stood up, his chair scraping on the scarred wooden floor. 'We will speak again, Mister Frazer.' The young man was moving purposefully down the aisle, a walkie-talkie now clearly visible in his hand.

Edmund Talbott rested both his huge fists on the table and leaned across to stare into Frazer's wide eyes. 'Beware the image, Mister Frazer, it will steal your soul away!' He turned as the young policeman grabbed at his right arm with his left hand. Talbott pivoted, his left hand coming up, fingers straight, locked and rigid. They caught the young man a tremendous blow in the precise centre of his chest. He collapsed forward onto Frazer without a sound, driving them both backwards onto the floor.

By the time Jonathan Frazer climbed out from under the young man, Talbott was gone, and the young officer was dead.

'People die around you, Mister Frazer,' Margaret Haaren said tiredly. She glanced up at the clock on the wall of her office. It was twenty to ten. 'Let me tell you about the man who died today,' she continued when Frazer said nothing. 'He was twenty-eight years old, married with a two-year-old little girl.'

'He only hit him once,' Frazer said wonderingly.

'That's all that was needed. A massive blow to the solus plexus can kill. In this case, it ruptured both sets of ribs, driving them into the lungs . . .'

'I tried to give him artificial respiration . . .' Frazer whispered, tears starting to his eyes.

'I know that, Mister Frazer,' the inspector said, her voice softer. 'And the officer's last radioed report did say that you seemed to be held against your will,' she added. What she didn't add was if the dead constable hadn't said that, she would have held Frazer as an accessory. 'And you have nothing to add to your statement?'

Jonathan Frazer shook his head. He had told the police that the man had demanded money with menaces, threatening to burn down his house and his shop unless he received a hundred thousand pounds. He still wasn't sure why he'd told the lie . . . except perhaps that he didn't want the man Talbott captured just yet.

He wanted answers, and only Talbott could provide the answers.

Or the mirror.

Frazer abruptly realized he had stopped breathing.

The mirror could provide answers . . . if it was asked the correct question.

The idea was so obvious.

So simple.

He looked up at Margaret Haaren. 'If you're finished with me, Inspector, I'd like to go home. I'm very tired.'

'Go home, Mister Frazer. Get some rest; tomorrow is likely to be a long day.'

But Frazer was staring through the office window at the thin silver moon that was just visible behind rapidly moving clouds. But Talbott said that the mirror would remain active even if the sky was clouded over.

181

As he hurried down the police station steps, he found his desire to experience the mirror's images almost frightening in its intensity.

What was it Talbott had said? *Beware the image, it will steal your soul away!*

Chapter
TWENTY-NINE

JONATHAN Frazer stood before the mirror, fascinated and fearful. A couple of days ago he would have laughed at Talbott and then phoned for the men in white coats ... but that had been before he'd seen vivid images of sixteenth-century London, before he'd talked to a man who wasn't there, before he seen three people die before the mirror, one of them burnt to a crisp. Spontaneous combustion might be what they were calling it, but only a supernatural energy was capable of reducing a man to charred bone, and he didn't care what anyone else said.

He reached out tentatively, running a fingertip down the greasy glass, staring hard at his shadowy reflection in the mirror.

He was not an overly religious man – he attended church at Christmas and Easter – but that didn't mean that he didn't believe in a God or a Devil or Good and Evil. There were relics which performed miracles, and on the other hand there was evidence aplenty of evil in the world, and was it quite so difficult to imagine that an object should become associated with evil?

There was the famous Spear of Longinus, the spear that supposedly pierced Christ's side on the cross. It was notorious in the antiques trade, with 'genuine' spears being offered for sale with surprising regularity.

And yet hadn't Hitler made every effort to obtain the spear?

He recalled an ugly black-handled knife he had once bought amongst a job lot of Victorian cutlery. The handle had been crudely carved into the likeness of a man and woman copulating. The man was horned, tailed and cloven hooved. Within minutes of him displaying it in the shop it had been purchased by a collector, who subsequently informed him that the knife had belonged to a famous North of England black magic coven, and there were rumours that it had been used in sacrifices.

And Frazer had believed him.

One of the reasons he had put the object out for sale so cheaply and quickly was because he had found it difficult to touch the object without feeling cold, and almost physically ill.

So, yes – he could accept that the mirror was a focus for something, some power, some sort of negative energy . . . but that didn't necessarily make the mirror evil. Surely it was the intent with which the mirror was used? Could it not be used for good as well as evil?

Talbott had said that it was powerful – he hadn't said that it was evil.

Jonathan Frazer brushed at the glass with the palm of his hand, scraping off the black gummy coating on the glass. What exactly had Talbott said about the mirror? He said that it was powerful, but that it needed to be fed . . .

'Once it is fed – with human emotions, with blood, sweat, tears, semen – its powers are limitless. It can show wonders – or terrors – on its surface.'

It can show wonders . . .

Jonathan reached into his waistcoat pocket and took out a slender flat Hoffman pocket knife. The two-inch blade opened with a tiny click. He stared at the blade for a moment and then, gritting his teeth, he jabbed the point into his index finger, hissing with the sting. A tiny bead of blood appeared on the tip of his finger.

His hand was trembling as he reached for the glass . . .

She remembered the last time she had made love to Robert Beaumont.

Emmanuelle Frazer twisted on the bed, caught up in the erotic dream. She was semi-conscious, aware that she was dreaming, yet still conscious of the fact that she was lying in her bed, naked beneath the cool cotton sheets, her left hand resting flat against her breast, the fingers of her right hand moving across her belly, teasing herself.

She had met Beaumont shortly after she had first moved to Paris. She was not so naïve that she didn't recognize him for what he was – an opportunist possibly, a gigolo occasionally, a conman certainly. But he was also her entrée to a segment of Parisian society that she would never, in normal circumstances, have been able to experience. And if she had to pay for that privilege, then so be it.

That they should end up as lovers was almost inevitable. She was fascinated by him, the way he looked, the way he moved, the way he dressed. She had never known a man who paid so much attention to his clothing, and he was one of the very few men who delighted in going shopping with her. He took an especial delight in choosing underwear for her.

He had been the first to comment on her fine bone structure and to suggest that she should shave her head and, although she had initially resisted, they had got drunk one night and when they had woken, they had discovered that her head had been completely shaved – although neither of them could remember it happening.

She had never loved him and he had never loved her. That was an accepted part of their relationship. They got on well together, they eventually lived together, they slept together, and when she had left Paris she hadn't thought about him again until they had met by *accident* in London and he had asked her if she could do something about getting him a job.

But they had had good times together.

And he had been a good lover.

She wasn't a virgin when she met him, but she was still inexperienced. Her previous boyfriend had been unimaginative and the night she – and he as it had also transpired – had lost her virginity, it had been a painful, messy and altogether uninspiring event.

But Robert had taught her how her body could respond, he had shown her how to bring herself to orgasm. Often he would just sit across from her watching her arouse herself with her fingers, and then, when she was close to orgasm, he would come over to her, and press his lips to hers while his fingertips trailed down her body, until they finally closed over her hands.

And she felt him.

Had she fallen asleep; was she dreaming?

She felt his hands on hers.

She was still in her semi-conscious state, she was aware that she was dreaming.

She dreamed that she lay on her bed with her eyes closed while Robert Beaumont bent over her, pressing his lips to hers, squeezing her fingers with his free hand, urging her on. She was aware of his hairless chest against her breasts, his breath on her face, his lips and tongue, moist and damp against her lips. His hands spread her legs and he moved atop her body, mounting her smoothly. She lifted her legs, wrapping them around his buttocks, her long fingers digging into his shoulders . . .

*

His finger left a single dot of blood on the glass.

Even as he watched the crimson bead was absorbed into the mirror, leaving a brown flaking spot in its wake.

Frazer squeezed more blood onto his fingertip and smeared it down the glass, the thin liquid cutting a strip – like a window – through the grimy coating, revealing, for an instant . . .

. . . *Cecilia Frazer wrapped in the arms of a muscular blond giant* . . .

Dried flakes of blood see-sawed to the floor.

Jonathan Frazer stared in horror at the glass. What had he just seen?

Almost without thinking he drew the blade across the palm of his left hand. The flesh parted like a leaf unfolding, blood welling into the wound. With his fingers splayed, he pressed his hand to the glass, and rubbed it in a circle, smearing the surface of the mirror with his blood.

. . . *Cecilia Frazer wrapped in the arms of a muscular blond giant. They were both naked, and she had rolled atop him, moving herself to and fro with a frenzy which she had never demonstrated in their own marriage bed.*

Dragging his gaze away from the couple, he looked at the surroundings, noting the bedclothes, the room's furniture . . . the ski boots tossed carelessly on the thickly carpeted floor.

Frazer drew back from the mirror with a gasp.

He sat down on the chaise longue and stared at the length of glass, cradling his torn hand, his thoughts in turmoil. He had known – deep in his heart and soul – he had known that Cecilia was having an affair. He had just never admitted it before.

Becoming aware of the burning in the palm of his hand, he raised it up to look at it in the bad light. The flesh was filthy with the dirt from the mirror, the edges of the long cut encrusted with the slime that coated the glass. And then, as he watched, a scab formed along the edge of the wound, it thickened and hardened before his eyes, and then the edges began to peel and flake away. When he carefully picked away the crust, he found that the cut was completely healed, leaving only a thin black line in its wake.

His head was buzzing with questions and possibilities as he started for the mirror, and then something stopped him. If he wanted to see anything else, he would need to feed the mirror again. He looked at his hand again: it was possible to give of oneself without obvious cost, but were there dangers? What were the consequences?

Only Edmund Talbott could answer those questions.

In the Otherworld, the astral body of Talbott watched the silent whirlpool of power that circled above the mirror shudder, a crimson twitch rippling through it. It had tasted blood.

Deep in its core, he could see the white threads that ran its length, like thick worms, now pulsating with an ever-increasing rhythm. It was feeding off sexual excitement.

Someone was feeding the glass.

Deeply troubled, Talbott glided away from the area immediately surrounding the whirlpool. Even though he was separated from it by an enormous gulf, he was aware of its tremendous pull, and he knew that it was growing enormously powerful. It had shown that it was capable of influencing events in the real world, but what would happen if someone were to begin consciously feeding it?

Or unconsciously?

She could feel him deep inside her body, his stomach flat against hers as he strove to drive himself even deeper into her. Sweat trickled down her body and into the valley between her breasts. She was aware of him licking it off, his tongue rough against her skin. His fingers teased at her nipples, brushing, touching, squeezing, pinching – hurting – even as his pounding intensified, swamping the pleasure with the pain.

Manny Frazer opened her eyes – and looked into horror!

It was Robert Beaumont who had made love – who was still making love! – to her. The charred and incinerated corpse of Robert Beaumont, the flesh hanging in strips from his skull, his moist tongue a charred stump in his mouth. The fingers that had played with her sensitive nipples were burnt down to the bone, filthy, blackened stumps, some still leaking ichor. His smooth and hairless chest was a slab of raw meat, and his manhood which had been so deeply inside her – was nothing more than a charred and bloody stump.

And, even as she opened her mouth to scream, a part of her mind was attempting calmly to rationalize the fears away. But it was a very small voice, and her fears were very great.

And when she screamed herself back to wakefulness, she could still feel the burnt and blackened flesh against her skin, could still smell the stench of burnt meat in the air . . . and her breasts were red and bruised, and her groin was raw.

Chapter THIRTY

IN the Otherworld the whirlpool marking the occult presence of the mirror spun, drifting from side to side, shifting off its axis . . .

Bad Bill had been living on the streets for nearly ten years. He'd survived so long because he took care of himself, rarely mixed with the other down-and-outs, and didn't drink or smoke – except in huge binges. He was a quiet unassuming man, good-humoured, good-tempered – except when he drank, and then his personality underwent a complete change. And when he was bad he was very bad . . . and that's where he got his name. He was forty-two years old, looked twenty and more years older and didn't confidently expect to live to see forty-three. Nowadays he couldn't remember why he'd gone on the streets, and that bothered him, but shit, nowadays he sometimes couldn't even remember his own name.

Tonight wasn't so bad though. It was dry and there was no wind, and he found a discarded fridge box behind an electrical shop in Kensington High Street. It had taken him most of the day to flatten it down and drag it back to Kensington Gardens. Smuggling it into the park hadn't been too difficult, and he eventually got it into the centre of the stand of gorse bushes almost in sight of the Peter Pan statue, which was his equivalent of home. Then, with grass, leaves and mud, he had daubed the box in camouflage colours, rendering it virtually invisible. The effort had exhausted him, but it had been worth it. Fridge boxes were the tramps' equivalent of a limo: big and spacious yet thick and comfortable; a man could live in a box like that and not want for anything else, even in the coldest weather. Tomorrow he'd get some plastic to cover it and keep it dry, that would increase its life by a couple of months. He'd be able to leave it here, in the centre of the bushes, and know he'd have a safe place to come back to every evening.

Sometimes he thought the park keepers knew he was there and let him alone, although he had occasionally been moved on out of the park. He never argued, simply walked away . . . and walked right back in by another gate.

One of the advantages of living in the centre of the bushes was that it was reasonably secure at night. Far safer than sleeping on a bench, or under a bridge. If the police didn't move you on, then some kid's idea of fun was to beat you up or kick you around, and he'd heard stories of kids pouring petrol over tramps and setting them alight just to watch them dance.

He couldn't sleep tonight though, even though he was tired after the effort of hauling back the box. He rolled over in the box, tense and aching, listening, his senses buzzing. There was an ache in his stomach, a tightness in his chest and the pain went down into his left arm. Bad Bill staggered to his feet, clutching his arm, his right arm pressed across his chest. He made his way through the bushes, knowing from experience that a walk would ease the pressure.

He kept to the shadows, knowing that while it was

unlikely that the park keepers would be around, there were other less savoury characters that sometimes used the park for their business dealings – although you weren't going to get anyone to admit that. He followed the path that led along by the Long Water up towards the fountains. The water had been turned off so there was no misting spray to wet him, and he sat down on the low stone wall, forearms resting on his thighs, head drooping between his knees, attempting to catch his breath. He sat up, breathing deeply, and turned to look into the pool. The water was smooth, polished, a perfect mirror.

It took him a few moments to realize what he was seeing, and then his rheumy eyes opened wide with something approaching delight. His heart began to trip alarmingly, but he was barely aware of it. His lips curled back from his almost toothless gums as he bent his head to kiss the brackish water.

The image lured him down, the icy water enfolding him like a lover, sucking at his mouth, his tongue, lapping at his cheeks, his eyes.

Bad Bill grew aware of the sensation, the powerful eroticism of the water, the enfolding warmth, the pulse pounding rhythm. It reminded him of . . .

Abbey Meyers had been a widow for twenty years, since her husband, the colonel, had died suddenly and spectacularly at a regimental reunion. He had been toasting Queen and Country when he'd simply fallen down, a massive heart attack taking him in a manner and at a time and place which, she thought, he would have totally approved.

Twenty years was a long time, but she still thought of him, especially now, in the middle of summer. Summer had been their special time; they had met in that long hot summer just after the war, they had married the following summer, their first child had

192

been born the following summer, and finally the colonel had died in the summer. There were some nights – like now – when the air was warm and dry, when the sky never truly darkened, when she could almost feel his presence around the house in Kensington.

This had always been his favourite residence, and after his death she had sold off the country farm and that little apartment they had kept across the river. Nowadays, she regretted both decisions when she saw the fabulous sums that property was fetching, but there had been no way she could have looked after them, and their upkeep would have drained their resources. Maxwell, her son, had suggested that she put the house up for auction, and she knew herself that it would realize a huge amount of money, but she didn't really need money at the moment, whereas she knew that Max did. Anyway, it would all be his when she was gone.

She'd gone through a phase when the very idea of death terrified her. Now, she supposed she almost looked forward to it. She was seventy years old, she supposed she had achieved all that she was ever going to achieve . . . and if she were being perfectly truthful, she had really lost interest in most things since the colonel's death.

Abbey Meyers turned the key on the small book-lined study that had been the colonel's favourite room. Sometimes she imagined she could still smell the shag tobacco he favoured.

Here his presence was very strong. She hadn't deliberately kept it as a shrine to him; he was far too practical, and so was she, to do something like that. But she had kept it the way she thought he would have liked it. There was still the wall of leather-bound books, still the army trophies and citations, the medals, the awards, the framed photographs. There were the swords and knives in their decorative displays on the end wall above the fire. His desk was very much as he had left it, an old Royal typewriter – a collector's piece now she supposed – still taking pride of place. He had been working on the definitive story of the fall of Berlin when he'd died. It remained unfinished and, although she had often thought about completing it from his notes and references, she imagined that other, far more competent historians had already done that work.

In the top right-hand drawer of the desk were the photographs. They were mostly wartime snaps, but there was one which was her favourite. It showed Geoffrey as she liked to remember him, tall and proud, in his full colonel's uniform, wearing the Victoria Cross and George Cross, standing outside Buckingham Palace. He had always refused to have the photograph framed, saying it was too much like boasting and, when he had died, she had respected that wish.

Abbey stared at the image, concentrating on Geoffrey's face, remembering the young man, and later the hero, she had known. He never talked about his wartime exploits, and she never asked, but she had seen a boy go away to war and watched a man come home, and when he had started awake at night, shouting and crying, she had held him until the terrors had faded.

She looked at the image on the paper . . .

. . . *and the image looked back.*

She had never noticed how the eyes in the photograph seemed to follow her every move, how the lips twitched as if they were about to smile. Why, looking at it, she could almost imagine that she could see the chest rising and falling, the material stretching across his chest.

Twenty years a widow and she still missed him. She missed the touch of him, so strong, so gentle, the smell of him, leather and tweed and tobacco, the feel of his skin, so soft, surprisingly soft for such a big man. And the way his moustache would tickle her face, her throat, her breasts . . .

She missed him.

But it wouldn't be long now. She would join him soon. She wasn't a deeply religious person, but she believed in an Afterlife. She believed that they would be re-united one day . . . soon. She believed she'd feel his arms around her, feel his breath on her face, the tweed of his jacket, hear his gravelled voice.

Soon.

Abbey Meyers sat down at the desk in a creaking leather chair and propped up the photograph of her husband against the typewriter.

Abbey looked at the photograph and the image looked back.

The knife on the desk was a Fairbairn-Sykes Fighting Knife, made by the Wilkinson Sword Company for the British Commando Unit. Geoffrey Meyers had brought it back as a souvenir and had used it as a letter opener.

The long needle-pointed knife was cold and heavy in her hand as she pressed it in below and to the left of her jaw, her eyes still riveted on the image, a smile of complete satisfaction on her face . . .

Martin Stephens had really wanted the new Wang sixty megabyte 386 AT computer with a VGA colour graphics screen. His parents, who knew shit about computers, but who'd balked at the price, had opted instead for an IBM clone made by someone he'd never even heard of before, some Korean company, with only forty megabytes, and it was a 286 AT, with EGA colour graphics.

He'd been disappointed, and he'd let them know it. He'd been quite specific about his wants, and instead they'd bought him a totally inferior machine. He was sixteen years old and he deserved a little respect!

He'd sulked in his room for most of the day, and eventually, when his parents went out to some gallery opening, he had settled down to remove the computer from its various boxes and begin to set it up. He was still smarting over the fact that they hadn't got him what he'd wanted, when another grand or so, maybe fifteen hundred, would have been enough to buy it. For Christ's sake, some of the guys in college were already carrying portables and lap-top computers . . . but that was going to be his Christmas request.

He set up the screen on top of the processing unit and linked them up with their cables and then inserted the keyboard plug into the back of the processor. He plugged in the single plug – the good machines had a separate plug for the screen and the processor – and powered up the machine. It came to life with an ascending whine, and he spent the next hour setting up the various colours on the screen and creating numerous subdirectories on the machine to hold his files and programs which he'd copied off the old ten megabyte IBM he'd been using. It was a delight to see some of the programs running in colour. Most of what he put onto the machine were games, some of which he'd bought, others which he'd been given or swapped with his friends. He put them onto a directory buried a few levels down so they wouldn't be immediately obvious to his parents should they ever look at the machine – which was highly unlikely anyway, since they weren't really interested in him . . . as was immediately apparent by the cheap present they'd bought him.

However, at least now he'd be able to run some of the games that wouldn't run on the IBM which had a monochrome screen. Some of them, he knew, his parents wouldn't fully approve of.

His favourite was a game of strip poker, played

against the machine. There was a cartoon of an overendowed female on the screen whom he played against. When she lost a hand, she removed an item of clothing and, although he'd got her down to bra and panties on friends' machines, he'd never had the chance to take her any further, principally because to take her that far took about two hours, and time had always been against him. However, he had heard lurid stories about what happened when she removed all her clothing. There were a couple of other programs which he'd heard of, but not got yet, which showed couples actually doing it in different positions . . . and now he had colour graphics, they were a must. It was close to ten when he began to play the strip poker. He had changed into his pyjamas and dressing-gown and now lounged back on his bed with the keyboard on his knees, his total concentration on the screen.

By twelve-thirty he was beginning to pull ahead. She was again down to bra and panties and he was holding a winning hand. His eyes were also beginning to buzz and there was a throbbing headache at the back of his skull, but he couldn't give up now, not now, not when he was so close.

He played on, and won the hand.

Onscreen the cartoon woman removed her bra, revealing huge breasts.

Now this was more like it!

Although it was nothing more than a cartoon drawing, Martin felt himself becoming aroused, more with the tension and excitement at coming so close to winning the game than anything else.

At one-thirty he paused the game, freezing the images on the screen, while he pressed the heels of his palms into his eyes. He hadn't progressed anywhere in the past hour and he was down to his last twenty dollars. It would be absolutely frustrating to come so close and lose now.

He stared at the image on the screen. Big, blonde and busty – his type, he nodded smugly. He'd seen a few porno videos, and he decided he was definitely a breast man . . . not that he'd ever seen a breast in real life, or should that be a real life breast? But he'd a good idea what they were like.

Summertime now was his favourite time; lots of young woman in Kensington Gardens, which was close by, wearing no bras, breasts bouncing beneath their tee-shirts, and he'd recently taken up tennis, not for the exercise, which he needed, but because it allowed him to watch the young women playing in the courts on either side, with the short, short skirts, and their frilly knickers – and sometimes smooth knickers, and he liked the way their nipples sometimes hardened as they played.

Martin Stephens looked at the image and decided that she was close enough to his ideal woman. The way her eyes looked directly at you, the way her mouth was slightly parted, and the way her breasts swung. He reached out and touched the screen with his forefinger, tracing the curves of the image's breasts.

The static charge built up on the bed, snapped from his fingertip onto the screen . . .

And the screen exploded.

Red hot slivers of glass ripped into the young man, shredding his skin, peeling back the flesh of his face, his eyes, his mouth. A chunk of molten plastic caught him in the throat, burning through the skin, severing the artery, blood jetting high into the room.

And his last conscious thought was of the smiling eyes of the cartoon image . . .

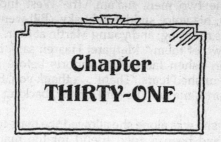

Chapter
THIRTY-ONE

TIRED and dispirited, feeling hungover even though she hadn't touched a drop last night, Margaret Haaren read through the reports, barely paying them any attention.

The accidental death of an old tramp in Kensington Gardens.

The suicide of a lonely widow.

The bizarre death of a youth when his computer exploded.

She was putting away the attending officer's report on the last incident when she stopped and looked at it again. And then checked the address of the suicide.

Both addresses were in the same private close where Frazer lived.

Coincidence?

She'd been too long in the force to believe in coincidence. She was reaching for the intercom button when there was a tap on the door and Sergeant Stuart Miller stepped into the room. She immediately knew by the expression on his face that something was wrong.

'We've just had a call from the hospital, ma'am . . .'

She came slowly to her feet, heart suddenly

pounding. The young officer, Martin Moore . . .

'It's the two men, ma'am,' the West Indian said carefully, his voice suddenly husky. 'Bill went around three this morning; and young Martin at four.'

'The two of them?' Margaret Haaren sank back into the chair, ashen faced. The reports before her eyes swam in unshed tears. 'Thank . . . thank you, Stuart.'

'I'm sorry, ma'am,' he said lamely, backing from the room.

When she was alone she allowed the tears to fall; Bill Russell had been a good friend for too many years. When a woman PC had been a curiosity, a rarity, something of a freak, he'd accepted her for what she was, and when she made inspector she'd requested him as her sergeant.

There was a knock on the door and Stuart Miller reappeared, a cup of tea balanced precariously on top of a sheaf of reports. The inspector accepted the tea gratefully.

'He was a good man,' Stuart said respectfully.

'He was a fine officer and a good friend,' Margaret said slowly. 'And now we can lay three deaths at this scarred man's door.'

'Yes, ma'am.'

When she looked up her green eyes were cold, implacable. 'I want the man who did this. And Jonathan Frazer knows him!'

Silently Stuart Miller handed over the sheaf of brown folders.

'What's this?'

'List of possible suspects, cross-referenced with Bill's old and present cases, further cross-referenced with Jonathan Frazer's friends and business associates. The latter list is by no means exhaustive, but it's the best we can do.'

'Any matches?'

'Nothing at the moment, ma'am.'

She looked up into Miller's brown eyes. 'Frazer's dirty, I can feel it. I want an exhaustive check into his background. Bank accounts, records, everything. He's a material witness and possible suspect in a multiple murder case, we should have no problems getting the clearances.' She drank her tepid tea in one quick swallow. She knew what she was doing now, she had done it before: she was using work to ease the pain of her friend's death.

The sergeant leaned forward and took the cup from her desk. 'We could also try leaning on him, ma'am,' he suggested quietly.

Margaret Haaren nodded slowly. 'I haven't ruled that out either.'

Jonathan Frazer went through his wife's clothing with a fine-tooth comb, and then proceeded meticulously to check through her chest of drawers, cabinets, on top of her wardrobe, the dressing table. He was looking for evidence of his wife's infidelity.

He was aware that if he stopped to think about what he was doing, the madness of it would strike home, and he would begin to question his own sanity.

What was he doing?

Why was he doing it?

After an exhausting day, he had imagined he'd seen something in a mirror – a fantasy – and on the basis of that he had allowed all his repressed fears that centred on his wife's fidelity to come flooding to the surface, and now here he was pawing through her things like some cheap private detective.

But it had been so real. The image had been so real.

Was it true, or just some bad-minded wish?

Where was Edmund Talbott?

She felt like shit.

The only time she'd ever felt like this was when

she'd had a hit of bad hash in Paris.

Manny Frazer dressed slowly, her every joint aching, her breasts heavy and painful, her stomach feeling bloated. On impulse she checked her calendar, but her period wasn't due for another two weeks, so it wasn't that . . . unless it was coming early, brought on by the trauma of the last few days. And that was certainly a possibility.

She pulled on her usual black tee-shirt over black jeans, and looked at herself in the mirror. She looked ghastly, her face pale and wan, her eyes sunk back into her skull, dark-rimmed and bloodshot. She ran her fingers across her head. The stubble rasped loudly. She'd only had it cut a few weeks ago, and yet it seemed to be growing very quickly this time.

. She had no real memory of her nightmare the previous night. She remembered waking as her mother had turned on the light, and even then at that particular moment, the horrors were fading, but she had insisted that the light was left on, and it took a long time before sleep finally claimed her.

She met her father in the corridor and he stopped, obviously surprised by her wretched appearance. 'I think you should go back to bed, sweetheart,' he murmured, kissing her forehead.

'I'm OK, Dad, just a bit whacked out after the last couple of days.' She attempted a smile. 'You're not looking so hot yourself.'

'I didn't sleep very well. Nightmares,' he explained.

'So did I. Didn't Mother tell you?'

'I haven't seen your mother this morning. I haven't seen much of your mother since she came back from her Swiss holiday, and when I did see her it was at your bedside in hospital.'

Manny stopped. 'Then she didn't tell you . . .?'

He looked at her in surprise. 'Tell me what?'

'Last night she told me she was going up to Scotland

to that skiing resort this morning.'

'She said nothing to me,' he murmured.

Manny linked her arm through her father's as they walked slowly downstairs. 'Do I get the impression that all isn't sweetness and light between the two of you?' She caught the blank look of dismay on his face, and continued ruefully, 'I am eighteen, you know. I'm no fool. And you don't need to be a genius to guess that you're both going your separate ways.'

'It's true,' he admitted. 'In the last couple of years, our differences and interests have become more and more pronounced. I'll be thirty-nine next birthday. It doesn't bother me, ageing never has, maybe that's because I worked with old things all my life. But your mother . . . well your mother will be thirty-five next birthday, and she dresses and acts as if she's ten years younger.'

'That's not so unusual. It's a last-ditch attempt at retaining her youth,' Manny said with all the seriousness of an eighteen-year-old.

'Thirty-five is not over the hill,' Jonathan gently reminded her.

'No spring chicken either,' she laughed. She stopped at the bottom of the stairs and turned to face her father. 'But you still love her don't you, Dad?'

'Yes,' he said seriously, 'yes I do.' He was surprised to find that he meant it. And he liked to think that she still loved him.

'Well, if you still love one another, surely you can sort out your differences,' Manny asked, looking into his troubled eyes.

He nodded. 'If we both still love one another,' he agreed.

Maybe he should think about trying to answer that question.

'Don't turn around, Mister Frazer.'

Jonathan froze, his hands locked onto the wheel of the Volvo Estate. He had just climbed into the car and the garage door behind him was humming upwards, flooding the garage with morning light. He recognized the voice immediately. The accent was vaguely Irish, he decided, perhaps a soft Irish country accent. 'I was wondering when you'd get in touch,' he said, glancing into the rear-view mirror. Edmund Talbott's coal-black eyes regarded him unblinkingly.

'Things have become very difficult, Mister Frazer,' Talbott continued.

'The young policeman you hit died,' Frazer said coldly.

'I will not be taken into custody,' Talbott said simply.

'Why not?'

'Mister Frazer, perhaps I have not explained myself fully. My family have been the guardians of the mirror for generations. It was our task to keep it inert, to keep it safe from the world, not to allow it to feed its hunger for souls and blood and human emotions. It needs these for nourishment, it needs these to survive. Eventually it would have *died* – if you can apply that term to it – of hunger. And we were so close, so close. It wouldn't have happened in my lifetime, but in the next generation perhaps. It was weak, so weak.'

'What happened?' he asked, without turning around, watching the man's eyes in the mirror.

'It was my fault. I had to go away to a site meeting in Saudi. It should have taken no more than forty-eight hours, it took the best part of a week. When I returned to Ireland, I discovered that the house had been burgled and that the mirror and a few other antiques were gone. The burglars were local lads, who knew that the house was empty. One of them did odd jobs around the garden and knew there were some antiques in the house. That's the official story.

'I am inclined to think that the mirror exerted its

influence on the youths; paradoxically it can most easily influence the strong-willed and the weak. Ordinary people, with ordinary lives and ordinary worries crowding their ordinary minds are quite safe from its extraordinary powers.

'The rest of the story, I think you know.

'They took the mirror, wrenching the heavy cloth covering from it, exposing the glass. Once uncovered it began to feed. It took the life of your male assistant first, and then the female, and since then it has been feeding on the blood and energy of those all around it, growing stronger with every soul it takes.'

'The police say the auctioneers have no record of having sold the mirror to me, nor is there any record with the haulage firm.'

'The records are probably computerized. The mirror probably deleted the records,' Talbott said simply.

'But what about the people who sold me the mirror? The assistant I was dealing with; the auctioneer, the truck driver who delivered it? Surely they must remember it?'

'You have no conception of the power of the object you're dealing with,' Talbott said quietly.

'But what you're suggesting is impossible . . .' Frazer began.

'Do you know anything about astral projection, Mister Frazer,' Talbott asked suddenly, 'or the astral plane?'

Jonathan shook his head.

'When one sleeps one's spirit – the astral body – leaves the physical body and moves onto the astral plane. This plane may be a "physical" place or it may be a state of mind, I don't know. I merely accept its existence, and use it. There are various levels on this astral plane, and with skill and practice and determination, it is possible to move from plane to plane, to move one's physical body through space – as

I did when I visited you in the hospital room. You weren't dreaming, Mister Frazer, I really was there.

'On another level, a higher level, it is possible to see the souls of the newly dead leave their bodies. Some hover uncertainly about the corpse, others fly away to freedom, others are trapped.

'The astral plane is disturbed at the moment, Mister Frazer. There is a presence, a force rippling through the usually placid domain. It is like a giant whirlpool, sucking everything around it into its circle. I have stood on the very edge of the plane and watched this *thing*. It is the non-physical manifestation of the mirror, Mister Frazer, a whirlpool of all the emotions, the energies, the blood and sweat and semen, the pain and anger that had fed the mirror down through the ages. It is enormous, ravenous, ravening.

'And it is moving.

'People died around you last night, Mister Frazer. Innocents. A woman across the street cut her throat to be with her husband who had been dead twenty years. Fooled by the image. A young boy had his face shredded by the glass from an exploding computer screen. Entranced by the image on the screen. A tramp stuck his head under water in the fountains in Kensington Gardens and drowned. Beguiled by the image.

'And do you know what else I saw last night, Mister Frazer? I saw the mirror feed. I saw it drink the blood of sacrifice. I saw it accept the emotion of passion.'

'Does the mirror only show the truth?'

'Invariably. It rarely needs to lie. It counts on the fact that truth, like most things, is addictive. And the images on its surface are the ultimate narcotic; people return to them again and again.'

'Do you want me to destroy the mirror?' Frazer asked, not sure if he could in any case.

'NO!' Talbott shouted. 'Break it, and you have a thousand mirrors, each one complete and whole in itself. Anyway,' he chuckled, 'I doubt if you'd get within a dozen yards of it with evil intent. The last person who even thought about that paid a terrible price . . .'

Frazer suddenly knew he was talking about himself.

'I cannot come and take the mirror from you now,' Talbott said, suddenly sounding distant and tired, 'but cover it, for God's sake, cover its surface with a heavy black blanket and turn it away from the moonlight. It will begin to weaken almost immediately, although it will take it a long time to return to some sort of quiescence. But when all the police activity has died down, then I'll arrange to take the mirror from you and have it shipped back to Ireland.'

'And then?'

'Then?' Talbott asked, puzzled. 'What do you mean?'

'What happens when you bring it back to Ireland?'

'Then the whole process begins again. I don't even know how or why it was created. The mirror is ancient, and the glass, its method of construction, and the materials are older still. I don't know what magic, what natural forces went into its creation. But this is one of the most potent occult forces remaining in the world today; there is no way to hurry it along. In a couple of hundred years' time, perhaps someone will have figured out some way of destroying it. But I doubt it.'

'But what happens if it continues to feed?'

'Every soul makes it stronger. It will kill and kill and kill again, and no one knows to what end. Maybe it is significant that it has always been activated during the bloodiest events in human history. It has to be stopped, Mister Frazer, and only you or I can do that . . .'

As Frazer watched, the eyes in the mirror closed as the voice faded. He swivelled around in the leather seat . . . and discovered that there was no one in the back of the car.

Chapter
THIRTY-TWO

WITH infinite care, Doctor John Dee removed the cork stopper from the glass jar. Blood flowed from the glass and ran along a series of tubes which fed it into a series of narrow branching glass tubes that were positioned directly over the seven foot tall mirror. The liquid, thick and glutinous, ran down the length of the glass.

It congealed about half way down into a sticky mess.

'It needs human blood,' Kelley remarked.

Dee nodded distractedly. Animal blood had no effect on the glass, which meant that there was some element unique to human blood which activated it. And yet his own researches into human and animal blood had shown that there were minimal differences between the two. So the difference had to be metaphysical.

In the dim and warped reflective surface, Dee saw the door behind him open and the woman approach. She was naked as usual and as she neared him, he saw the ripples of power flow down the mirror's surface, sparked by her proximity.

'Feed it with human blood,' she whispered, her breath tickling his ear, 'then it will show you wonders.'

Dee stepped back away from the mirror and put his

209

arm around the woman. Her flesh was chill and damp.

'I've been walking in the gardens,' she explained before he could ask the question.

'The villagers and staff will think you're a witch,' he said softly.

'Do they not already think you are a witch?' she murmured.

Dee bowed in acknowledgement. Some weeks ago he had finally persuaded the woman to move to his home at Mortlake on the outskirts of London. She had travelled at dead of night, the mirror carefully swathed in sacking, packed between sacks of feathers and strips of leather. It had taken six strong men to manoeuvre it up the narrow winding stairs to Dee's own study at the top of the house.

Since then he had experimented endlessly with it, attempting to recreate the fleeting images he had glimpsed on that first occasion.

And with little success.

The mirror became active in the woman's presence, he knew that. And she was the most exciting, the most erotic women he had ever encountered. Perhaps it was her natural magic firing his lusts, or perhaps it was simply that she rarely dressed, and usually wore little more than a cloak to cover her nakedness. At times he ached for her, and yet, despite Kelley's assurances that she desired him, she had shown no signs of it. She touched him often, pressed herself against him, crowded him, but never with anything other than seemingly innocent intent.

And he still didn't know her name.

He had asked for her name countless times, but all she would say was that when there was a time for names, he would know hers.

The only other way to activate the mirror was to use human blood. He had experimented with animal bloods and found them to be useless: in fact, they were worse than useless because they befouled the surface of the glass, clinging to the sticky black grit that covered the face of the mirror and were difficult to remove, but he was still reluctant to take that final step into smearing the glass with human blood. It smacked too much of witchcraft, and he was not a witch, he was a scientist.

The problem was that he had mentioned to the Queen that he was in possession of a scrying glass of extraordinary powers, and she had pointed out to him the obvious potential for observing England's enemies. He cursed himself now; he had never been discreet. Now, she was beginning to put pressure on him to produce results . . . and he knew from experience that her patience was not limitless and that often the favourite of today was the villain of tomorrow.

He needed to be able to show something to the Queen . . .

John Dee looked over his shoulder at Edward Kelley. 'Can we get some human blood?'

'My lord, in London, one can buy anything.'

'Pure blood,' the woman murmured. 'Neither diseased nor tainted, preferably the blood of a virgin or a child.'

Kelley nodded again, bowing this time to hide the smile that twisted his thin lips. He had coached the woman well, but she was also a natural actress . . . but then, if this was successful, then her reward would be great indeed.

This time the blood had an immediate effect.

John Dee stood three feet away from the mirror, the woman standing at his left shoulder, Kelley in the background, while the blood slowly flowed down the length of the glass, slicing through the grime, leaving long ovals of clean glass in its wake.

For the first time, Dee saw himself clearly in the

mirror, tall and thin, grey-haired, grey-bearded, the voluptuous raven-haired woman standing behind him.

And the the glass clouded.

The grey-haired, grey-bearded image in the mirror had been replaced by a tall dark-haired man, with sharper harder features than Dee's. His short goatee beard was jet black.

Standing beside him was a young woman, ragged, dirty, no more than a child . . . except for her eyes, which were cold and cunning.

Behind them a tall, gangling youth, with a shock of fiery red hair, his head bent, his eyes squeezed shut in what looked like fear.

Dee turned slowly, beginning to realize what he was seeing. He looked from Kelley to the woman and then back to the glass . . . these images were from the past, this was Kelley, the woman and himself as youths.

But the image had changed.

Naked and aroused, he sat in the chair while the woman made love to him with extraordinary abandon.

The glass clouded, and strange images, blood and fire, the flash of a knife blade descending, arising bloodied, writhed across the glass.

The image of the woman. She was still naked, though now her belly had swelled and her breasts were full, the nipples dark. Dee was standing behind her, his hands on her shoulders.

Doctor John Dee started forward, trying to make sense out of what he was seeing: was this the future definite or the future possible?

The woman lying on the ground, her legs spread wide, her body sheened with sweat, her head thrown back. A bloody head appearing between her legs, and then Dee reaching in and drawing out a girl child, raising her high as if in triumph or offering.

Dee looked at the woman by his side, saw that she too was staring intently at the glass. He glanced back over his shoulder, but Kelley was crumpled on the ground, his head buried in his hands, obviously terrified by the pictures flowing across the glass.

A child. Four or five, naked, with hair flowing down to the base of her spine. Her hands were raised high above her head and were visibly glowing with twisting energies. She straightened her hands by her side, pressing downwards with her palms, and then she shifted, rising upwards . . .

Dee looked at the woman and she turned her large dark eyes on him. The girl had the woman's eyes and Dee's long face. He gripped her shoulder, ignoring the mirror in his excitement. 'It is our child. The child of a new generation of man . . . a race in tune with the natural magic of the universe.'

And the woman smiled. 'It is our destiny.' She turned to point at the glass. 'Watch,' she whispered.

There were new images on the glass, images of blood and fire and a face. Wavering, indistinct, the face assumed a demonic cast, the teeth drawn back from stained teeth, the curling black hair spiked with grease, the eyes wide and staring. He was dressed entirely in black with a broad ruff stained with blood and the knife in his hand was thick with gore.

'An evil man,' the woman whispered, 'who brings evil to the Queen.'

'It's Essex,' Dee whispered, 'but it cannot be, he is one of her most loyal subjects.'

'But ambitious?' the woman suggested.

'Ambitious,' Dee agreed.

'He should be taken away from the Queen,' she said softly.

Dee nodded his head in silent agreement. He turned abruptly from the mirror and almost stumbled over Kelley who was still crouched on the ground, his head buried in his hands, his face screwed up in terror, tears on his cheeks. He had bitten through his lips and the blood had run down his chin. Dee kicked at him cursing him for a coward and staggered from the room.

As soon as the door closed, Edward Kelley rolled over onto his back, a broad smile on his lips.

'Well,' the woman asked.

'You were magnificent,' Kelley said, 'I might almost say possessed,' he added with a smile.

'He's leaving,' she said.

Kelley rolled to his feet and joined the woman by the window. They watched the carriage sway across the rutted track towards London. Doctor John Dee was a troubled man; he was about to bring his Queen bad tidings about her favourite, and he wasn't looking forward to it. It had even spoiled his excitement at the thoughts of sleeping with the woman, of conceiving a child on her, and the power that that child would hold within its hands. The first of a new generation indeed.

'What happened?' she asked. 'Where did the first images come from, those of Dee and me and you too, I think, many years ago?'

'That was before I could take control of the images,' he muttered, rubbing the palm of his hand to his head. He had a pounding headache, and the effort of projecting the images onto the mirror had been agony, and what Dee had taken for cowardice and an expression of fear had been intense concentration and effort.

He had lost control of the mirror at a couple of points, when it had shown the blood and fire, but in the main the experiment – and the gamble – had worked spectacularly. Previously he had only projected pictures onto the glass, simple images that lasted only fleetingly.

Kelley had stumbled on the process by chance. When the mirror had been in the wharfside den, he had taken an old women in off the streets on the pretext of feeding and clothing her, had dragged her unceremoniously down before the glass and cut her throat, spraying the glass with her thin blood. The results had been disappointing. The glass had cleared for a few brief moments, had shown a few strange and terrifying images – disembodied faces howling in what looked like agony – before clouding over again. He had been standing before the glass idly wishing that he had caught the woman's blood in a goblet of some kind and allowed it to flow more evenly down the surface of the mirror, when he had suddenly seen an image of the goblet in the glass. It had lasted no more than a heartbeat, but Kelley had been an alchemist for long enough to recognize the signs immediately. He had dragged the lifeless body of the old woman to her feet and sliced open her ragged bodice with his knife, exposing the dirty pallid flesh. He had cut through the empty dugs, and snapped the ribs beneath with his bare hands before finally wrenching the heart from the chest. Allowing the woman's body to fall to the ground, he smeared the mirror with the bloody organ and then stepped away, the remnants of the heart still clutched in his left hand, the knife in his right. He looked down at the knife, and then brought it up before his face, looking closely at it, concentrating on the triangular Italian blade, the plain wire-wrapped hilt.

And then he allowed the knife to fall to the floor.

But the image remained in the mirror.

He stared at it for five pounding heartbeats until the smeared blood dried on the glass and flaked away and the image faded.

But Kelley knew then that he could project images onto the glass with his mind.

He thought that the plan to remove Essex was his master stroke. With the Queen's favourite out of the way, she would obviously come to rely more and more on people like Dee for advice and guidance, and Dee was malleable.

Edward Kelley threw back his head and laughed aloud, even though the sound pounded through his skull, threatening to split it. Everything was coming together nicely.

And once they had Dee's child and had sacrificed it to the mirror then everything would be complete.

The trap was baited.

Chapter
THIRTY-THREE

THE trap had been baited.

With images that preyed on the fears of the human-kind, it had successfully survived through the Dark Times, and the times of Imprisonment.

It had come close on occasion to escape, to shucking off this crystal shell, but it had always been thwarted.

But these were better times, more complex times, and that suited it. The belief in its kind and its sisters had faded, they had been relegated to petty tales with which to frighten children.

Ignorance now was its greatest weapon.

It had grown in strength since it had been uncovered and had started to drink of the myriad complex emotions of the human-kind. And whereas before it had been a shadow in the Otherworld, a fetch, now it was an elemental force that swept all before it. The souls of the newly dead were sustenance to it, the dreams of the innocent and the insane fed its hunger, but its thirst could only be fed with blood and tears and semen.

It had started to extend its influence into the world of men, to hunt, taking those closest to its core, calling them with images from their own minds. It relished

217

their fear, their terror, its clutched them to its bosom, draining their lost souls of all their emotions, leaving the husks to be twisted on the whirlwind of its power.

But there were irritations. The last scion of the old enemy was at large, it had felt his presence on the very edges of the Otherworld, a thin, cold spark of hatred, carefully shielded from all influences. But as its powers increased, then so too did his vulnerability, and soon, soon, it would reach out and snatch his immortal soul from its cowering place, and that was a morsel it would enjoy.

But now it thirsted. It needed blood and sweat and semen to satisfy its craving.

The trap had been baited with subtle and beguiling images. Soon it would drink its fill.

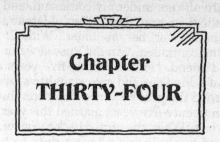

Chapter
THIRTY-FOUR

MARGARET Haaren walked away from the graveside and picked her way through the graves to where Jonathan Frazer was standing sheltering beneath a large black umbrella. She was wearing her full uniform and Frazer thought this lent her a dignity which her otherwise rather matronly figure denied her.

'I'm surprised to see you here, Mister Frazer,' she said quietly, stepping under the umbrella, deliberately bringing herself close to him.

Behind them the minister was intoning, 'Ashes to ashes . . .' and the thud of wet clay onto the wooden coffin sounded like a gunshot across the bleak rainswept cemetery.

He looked past her, his soft brown eyes unfocused. 'I suppose I felt I had to come. I felt responsible.'

The inspector said nothing. She was a great believer in allowing people to talk themselves into trouble.

'I mean it happened on my property . . . and he was investigating a crime that had happened in my . . .' he trailed off, realizing he was talking nonsense.

'I'm going straight on to another funeral, Mister Frazer. Another officer killed on your property. And tomorrow I'm attending the funeral of the officer slain in the library. I didn't really know these men, but they were police officers under my command, and I have a duty to them to find their killer.' Margaret Haaren glanced back over her shoulder. Without turning around, she continued. 'But Bill Russell was a friend, a very good friend. He was twenty-five years a policeman. That's his wife and two daughters over there. They married the year he joined the force: they would have been twenty-five years married this year . . . next month in fact.' When she turned back to Frazer, her face was a hard mask. 'I don't have a duty to find Bill's murderer. I have an obligation. I want the man who killed him, and my other two officers. I know you know this man, Mister Frazer; I know you know more than you're telling me. But unfortunately I cannot prove it – yet.' Her voice was now little more than a whisper. 'I'm going to catch the man responsible and he's going to jail . . . and I've a feeling you're going along with him. Accessory to murder is a very serious charge and doubly so when the victims are police officers. Remember, Mister Frazer, the next time you meet your friend.'

'Aunt Margaret . . . .?'

With a hiss of anger, Margaret Haaren turned around, and Frazer looked over her shoulder at a tall, blonde-haired, blue-eyed beauty. 'I'll be with you in a moment, Helen,' she snapped. 'My niece,' she explained to Frazer.

'I don't blame you for your suspicions,' he said tiredly. 'But I am the innocent here. I am truly sorry for the deaths of your officers, but I can assure you that I had absolutely nothing to do with them, nor did I know anything about them. If I knew where this stranger was I would tell you; remember, I'm the one he's been threatening.'

'Possibly you should surrender the mirror into our keeping until he is caught – at least then you can tell him the police have it.'

She was watching him closely as she made the suggestion, and she'd already guessed the answer before he said hurriedly, 'I'm not sure if I could do that. I already have some interest in it ... from collectors of glass ...' he added absently, and then he abruptly wished her a good day, turned and walked away.

The inspector nodded slowly. The mirror was the key. It linked this stranger and Frazer ... and Frazer had lied about the mirror when he had said he had purchased it in Dublin; the company there had denied all knowledge of it. It was time to take a closer look at this mirror. She wondered if she'd be able to confiscate it as evidence? She watched the man disappear through the trees, head bent, umbrella low on his head. He was in this up to his neck ... the only problem was she wasn't sure what he was up to his neck in. Extortion? Smuggling? Theft? And murder ... don't forget murder. But whatever it was, Jonathan Frazer was making her life miserable. Maybe it was about time she returned the compliment.

Jonathan Frazer sat in the Volvo parked across from the graveyard, his hands locked in a white-knuckled grip on the steering wheel. Through the ornamental iron rail surrounding the graveyard, he could see the mourners beginning to drift away from the graveside in ones and twos. He did regret the policemen's death, but there was nothing he could have done about it, was there?

Was there?

He could have given the mirror back to Talbott when he had first asked for it.

He could have done that ... and Diane and Robert and those three police officers would still be alive.

And why was he now protecting Talbott? The man was a murderer, a cold and callous murderer with some sort of occult power. The man was a killer – why didn't he tell the police what he knew?

And what was he going to tell them: the man appeared to me in a dream; I saw the man in the mirror of my car and when I turned around, he was gone? Oh, and by the way, he tells me my mirror is haunted?

Yes, he could see them believing that! He was already in enough trouble as it was. They believed he was involved with this Talbott, and that woman inspector believed that he was implicated in the death of the police officers. He wondered if she had enough evidence to hold him for questioning . . . or even worse, to confiscate the mirror.

That thought filled him with a strange, almost overpowering terror.

He savagely turned the key in the ignition, the engine screeching, and then slammed the car into gear and took off with a squeal of rubber just as the first of the mourners left the graveyard.

Margaret Haaren stood at the gate of the graveyard and watched the Volvo exceed the speed limit as it disappeared down the road. She wondered where he was going in such a hurry. She turned in time to see the pale cream-coloured Sierra pull out from the kerb and take off in pursuit, and nodded in satisfaction: she'd read the report later on.

The dry dust and leather smell of the stables was overlain with a sharper, bitter odour, a rich metallic copper tang. In the silence the maddened buzzing of a fly sounded unnaturally loud. And then another sound broke the silence, a sharp hiss of pain.

Jonathan Frazer knelt on the floor before the mirror. He was in his shirt sleeves, his waistcoat and jacket flung carelessly on the floor behind him. He had used a surgical scalpel, which he'd disinfected in alcohol beforehand, to open one of the small veins in his wrist, and blood was dribbling onto the thick bath sponge he held in his right hand. He didn't even want to think too closely about what he was doing; he preferred to think of it as a scientific experiment, and if it failed then nothing would have been lost and he'd review his alternatives. But if it succeeded . . . well, he preferred not to think about that either.

When the sponge was sodden with his blood, he reached out and rubbed it across the mirror . . . and the glass cleared almost magically, the grime wiping away cleanly, and he was able to see himself clearly in the mirror for the first time.

He grinned at his reflection. He looked ridiculous: no, worse, he looked like a junkie who'd just shot up, kneeling here on the floor, with his sleeves rolled up, blood snaking down his arm. He reached out and rubbed at the glass again, squeezing the sponge, blood trickling through his fingers and running down the glass, cutting through the grime.

So, that part of the experiment had been successful: blood did clear the glass.

But Talbott had also said that the mirror showed images . . . He stared into the glass, wondering what it would show. He had seen things in it before, dreamed dreams, seen faces . . .

He blinked as his vision blurred, or maybe it was the glass. He rubbed at it again with the blood-soaked sponge, but the ghosting around his features remained, the planes of his face, the curve of his chin, the shadows of his eyes seeming to shift, to move, to blur . . . to change.

There was shadow and shape and, finally, a face.

A woman looked out of the mirror at him!

A dominant, powerful face, strong cheekbones, slightly uptilted black eyes beneath curving eyebrows, full lips, a thick mass of hair.

The image moved.

Jonathan Frazer fell backwards onto the floor, supporting himself on his arms, as he stared horrified at the moving shapes.

The woman was moving, drawing away from him even as the background behind her became clearer, like a stage set coming to life. The image was combing her thick luxuriant hair, staring *into* the mirror while behind her a man, bald, with a huge hook of a nose, short, corpulent and naked sat on the edge of an enormous bed hung with draperies. The room was magnificent, the walls frescoed, hung with ornate tapestries and there were numerous rugs on the marbled floor. Two huge bronze doors, each one worked in fabulous detail, were just visible at the far end of the room.

The woman walked away from the mirror, and Frazer could see that she too was naked, and he watched the sway of her buttocks, the trembling of her mass of hair as she approached the fat man. His arms went out to encircle her as she spread her legs and climbed onto his lap, deftly working him inside her.

Aware of his own arousal, Frazer watched as she moved swiftly on top of him, her hands clasped on either side of his head, her mouth locked on his with a savage passion. And then the man's hands – heavily beringed, Frazer suddenly noticed – began to tighten on the woman's back, clutching at her flesh, leaving red weals in their wake. They scored long lines down her back as he gripped her buttocks, fingers digging into the soft flesh.

Frazer saw the woman moving more quickly now, pounding up and down on the man. And then she stopped. She stretched her hands out and her back arched, her head tilting upwards, face to the ceiling, the long mass of her hair falling almost to the floor behind her. Frazer saw that the fat man's eyes were squeezed shut, tears squeezing out from beneath the lids.

And then the woman's hands were at her hair. Frazer

saw the pin – at least eight inches long, tipped with what looked like a single ruby. He saw her hands come back around the man's head, brushing past his jowls, his tightly cropped grey hair, cupping his ears. She bent her head to kiss him, her mouth opening wide, fixing onto his, and Frazer saw her left hand move away from the man's head – and then back in again, plunging the pin deep into the man's ear. He thrashed in agony, but the woman still clung to him, her mouth still locked over his, preventing him from crying out, Frazer suddenly realized. The fat man's struggles abruptly weakened and the woman, who was still astride him, pushed him back, forcing him down onto the bed. His hands beat feebly at her, but she kept twisting the pin, turning it, forcing it in deeper. There was a sudden spasm and the fat man's struggles ceased.

When she was sure he was dead, the woman climbed off him, and hurried to the low marble-topped table. There was a heavy goblet and two glasses standing on the table, and Frazer immediately identified them as fifteenth-century Venetian glass. Dashing the wine from one of the goblets, she hurried back to the corpse. Dragging the bloody pin from his ear, she plunged it into the jugular, twisting and turning the pin to enlarge the opening. Blood spurted and then almost immediately died to a trickle. Holding the man's head, she tilted it to one side, catching the trickling blood in the goblet. When she had collected enough of the sluggish liquid, she walked slowly back to the mirror.

Towards Frazer.

Jonathan Frazer felt his mouth go dry, his breath catch in his throat. He had become aroused as she had made love with the man, but that arousal had passed as he watched in horrified fascination as she had killed the old man and collected his blood in the goblet. Now he felt himself becoming aroused again as she walked towards him and he saw her fully exposed for the first time: the large and heavy breasts, the small nipples erect now, the flesh puckered. Her belly was smoothly rounded, her navel deeply indented, and the hair between her thighs was as thick and as dark as the hair on her head.

The image crouched before the mirror, seemingly no more than a foot away from Frazer. She clutched the goblet in both hands and her lips were moving as if in prayer. She looked up, straight into Frazer's eyes – and threw the contents of the goblet directly into his face.

He shrieked aloud and fell backwards, his arm across his face. When he opened his eyes and looked at the mirror, he saw that the glass was clouding over *from the other side*. The greasy grime had returned and there was no sign of the image in the glass.

It was only when he sat up that he realized he had ejaculated in response to the images in the glass.

Chapter
THIRTY-FIVE

THERE was too much glass, too many mirrors around for him to be comfortable, and bitter experience had taught him that the image could work through any reflective surface.

The music throbbed, vibrating through the walls, pulsing in the air, and the pulsating multi-coloured lights made it look as if the packed cellar was moving in slow motion. Edmund Talbott reckoned that Hell had a chamber very much like this.

He had initially thought he was going to be very much out of place, but he was surprised at the numbers of older men cruising the disco, lounging at the bar, obviously watching the women; he was even more surprised at the number of young women who were dancing with them, drinking with them.

He shouldered his way through the crowd, making for the bar, already regretting coming in here. He reckoned his chances of finding Manny Frazer here were slim indeed.

He had been watching the house in Kensington through binoculars from a blue LiteAce van he'd stolen from a building site on the docks. He'd then stolen a set of number plates from a car parked in an alleyway and replaced the van's with these, and finally he'd daubed the plates and the front bumper with mud, rendering the plates virtually unreadable.

He had seen Jonathan Frazer drive up in the Volvo and hurry into the house at around one, but there had been no activity since then, and Frazer was still in the house . . . or was he in the stables?

He needed to get to Frazer, but with the police guarding the house he couldn't simply walk up to the front door, and he was too close to the mirror to even think about using astral projection. Even this far from the house, he could *feel* the coldly pulsating core of the whirlpool battering against his unconscious.

He was going to have to get into the house. He knew that the glass was already exerting its influence over Frazer. He had seen it in his eyes, had felt it and he knew he couldn't count on him to cover the glass with a black cloth. But he had two cans of aerosol black lacquer paint in his pockets and if at all possible he was going to spray the surface of the glass black. He wasn't sure how effective that would be, but it should cut the mirror's ability to show the images with which it enticed its victims.

And Jonathan Frazer was an obvious target.

Edmund Talbott was beginning to become concerned for Frazer's health. He had encountered signs – disturbing signs – on the astral that someone was feeding the mirror with blood, and yet Talbott hadn't heard of any deaths, hadn't *felt* any souls entering the Otherworld . . . which meant that the feeding was deliberate. Was the mirror more powerful than he imagined: had it taken Frazer several steps further than he imagined? If he discovered that Frazer was feeding the mirror with blood then he would kill him with no more compunction or thought than he would a dangerous insect.

The taxi had arrived a little after ten o'clock, and

Talbott saw a brief flurry of activity in the unmarked police car as it drove up the driveway to the Frazer house. The door opened almost immediately and light shafted out into the mild night air. Manny Frazer appeared, surprisingly wearing a long loose coat, and climbed into a taxi. Talbott immediately started up the van's engine and drove out onto the main road, timing it so that the taxi ended up directly behind him. The lights turned red and he used the opportunity to glance around – he had removed the rear-view and side mirrors – and saw Manny pulling off her coat. He pulled in at the next available parking space, allowing the taxi to move past him, and then pulled out behind it. He had followed it through the busy evening streets, as it cut across London and down onto the Embankment, finally turning off into one of the side streets close to the Temple. Talbott saw the brake lights flare and immediately turned in to the kerb. The taxi stopped outside what looked like a derelict building and Manny Frazer stepped out – and he immediately knew why she'd been wearing a coat when she left the house. She was wearing a tiny black dress that barely covered her buttocks, with a scooped neckline that exposed most of her breasts and when she turned to enter the building, Talbott could see that most of her back was bare. She was wearing a square pillbox-type hat on her head.

He climbed out of the van and locked it. The narrow street was quiet and almost deserted. It looked dilapidated and run down and while there were derelict buildings close to this end of the street, there was construction work taking place at the other end.

Talbott could feel the throbbing in the air as he approached the basement doorway Manny had entered, and he cringed at the thought of entering the noisy, hot interior, which was undoubtedly crammed with people. There were two large bouncers on the door, incongruous in their suits and bow-ties; they gave Talbott the once-over and, for a moment, he thought they were going to stop him, but apparently thought better of it.

The noise inside the cellar was a physical thing. He imagined he could feel the very air tremble with the sound. His head began to throb immediately and he was conscious of his heartbeat increasing in time to the pulsing of the music. How anyone could come to a place like this for pleasure was beyond him.

It took him five minutes before he finally got the barman's attention, and there was surprisingly little change from his fiver for his bottle of Perrier. He turned his back to the bar and settled his elbows on the counter, looking for Manny.

The stench in the place was almost overpowering, a combination of a hundred perfumes, both male and female, sweat, alcohol, the sweeter tang of hash and the vaguest hint of rot and damp. How could this be pleasurable, he wondered.

He sipped the water, his hard cold eyes watching the crowd. The problem was that Manny's costume was similar enough to scores of the young women present, and he knew that unless she actually passed right by him . . . there!

He noticed the hat first, the square hat he had seen on the young woman as she stepped out of the taxi. He immediately pushed his way through the crowd, following the bobbing hat, using his height to watch it move through the crowd. The pulsating lights were infuriating, making him clumsy and, if there was skill to moving through a crowded dance floor, then he obviously didn't possess it.

Manny was lounging up against a wall when he finally caught up with her. Her right leg was raised high enough to display her underwear, her head tilted back against the wall, a hand-rolled cigarette drooping between her lips. The man standing directly in front of her, his hand high on her thigh, was old enough to be her father – older probably.

Talbott shouldered his way into the couple and plucked the man's hand off the girl's thigh.

'What the fuck . . .'

Talbott brought his face close to the man's, smelling his aftershave and sweat. 'She's my daughter,' he hissed.

'She's over the age of consent!' he blustered.

Talbott's hard fingers grabbed a fistful of the flesh that bulged over the older man's waistband and squeezed. The smile on his face was terrifying. 'Do you enjoy pain?' he whispered, his voice barely audible above the throbbing of the music. 'Now fuck off!' He gave a final twist to the flabby stomach flesh for emphasis, and the man squeaked with pain before backing away from the terrifying figure.

When Edmund Talbott turned back to the girl she was gone!

It was turning out to be one bummer of a night.

It hadn't started out right and it was going to end in tears, she knew it.

She'd been feeling *off* all day, a little distracted, a little dizzy, like she'd done some grass or speed, but she hadn't done drugs since she'd come back from Paris – well not much really, a few tokes at Amanda's party a couple of weeks ago, but nothing serious.

Maybe it was just all the craziness in the air over the past couple of weeks. People she'd known had died, for Christ's sake! Surely that meant that she was entitled to feel a little crazy?

She'd planned to stay in, but late in the evening she'd taken a long leisurely bath and soaked for the best part of an hour and that had helped to waken her up. She'd climbed out of the bath and dried herself off in front of the full length mirror, curious at the peculiar changes taking place in her body. The hair on her head for example was really growing quickly and her pubic hair, which she'd only recently shaved, was now growing as well. Her breasts too, which were full, actually looked and felt heavier, and she was obviously putting on weight too, because her stomach looked slightly rounded, though when she checked it on the scales, she actually discovered she'd lost a pound. Must be something to do with her period, she decided; maybe it was coming early this month: didn't stress bring it on . . . or did it delay it? Unless of course she was pregnant. That stopped her cold. She stood, staring at her reflection in the glass, working out the last time she'd made love to a boy, and realized that that had been in Paris on the eve of her departure and she'd had a period since then and anyway, she'd been on the pill since she'd been seventeen.

Maybe a night out was what she needed. On her own . . . just go out, go wild, drink a few beers, maybe toke a few joints, find a nice guy to dance with . . .

And it was a mistake.

She'd realized that about five seconds after entering the club. In the year she'd been away in Paris, the character of the place had changed. The other clubs on either side of it had closed down, and the young crowd seemed to have drifted away, and she wasn't back in London long enough to discover the new 'in' place. The club had turned into a cattle market, with a lot of older guys cruising for girls who couldn't be older than some of their daughters. The music was a lot louder too and the coloured strobes that she used to find so exciting now only confused and disorientated her. All the old faces were gone – except Miriam, who'd been the hat-check girl when she'd last been there and who remembered her. As Manny had checked in her coat, Miriam had slid her out a joint with her ticket, 'Help

232

ease the pain,' she grinned, nodding to the dance floor.

She'd been relaxing against the wall when this creep had come up to her; short, slightly pudgy, with a shirt open down to his navel. He slid his hand up her leg, saying nothing, concentrating on looking meaningfully into her eyes – which translated as a leer – and she was contemplating kneeing him in the balls when this bouncer had come up and shoved the guy away. She'd wanted none of this, and didn't want to be leaned on by the bouncer. God alone knows what he thought she was, dressed in this get-up. She was sorry she'd worn it now, especially here, where some of the girls leaning against the walls were eyeing the men over with a more than professional interest. She wouldn't be at all surprised if some of the bouncers were in on the action, and she certainly didn't want them to think she was a freelancer. In Paris anyway – and London, too, she assumed – girls working without a pimp tended to end up hurt.

So, while the bouncer was having his few words with the creep, she slid away from the wall, ducked into the cloakroom and grabbed her coat from Miriam, promising she'd call her tomorrow, and was up the stairs and out of the place before either man even noticed she'd gone.

The fresh night air hit her with an almost physical blow and she stood swaying on the street for a moment, desperately resisting the temptation to vomit. She'd only had one drink, but whatever had been in that joint had been good shit.

Taxi or walk?

Commonsense said taxi, so she walked.

It was a little after eleven, a mild calm night in the middle of summer, and the city seemed almost relaxed, all the sounds were muted, and the pulsing of the club faded rapidly as she walked away from it.

She came out onto the Embankment and stopped.

She was close to the Embankment tube station, and it was only a few stops on the Circle Line to High Street Kensington which was only a five minute walk from home. But stoned or not, there was no way she was going down the underground on her own dressed like this; that wasn't just asking for trouble, it was advertising.

She walked to the water's edge and looked down to the right towards Westminster Bridge, breathing in the soft night air, trying to clear her head before making a decision and, anyway, there was no way she could go home like this. Her dad would still be up and she didn't want him to see her dressed like this, or in this state, so she had an hour or more to kill.

She had been staring into the flat reflective surface of the water for a few seconds before she realized what she was seeing.

There was a face beneath the water. Looking up at her. An oval face, with prominent rounded cheekbones, full lips and dark uptilted eyes.

And it was watching her. The mouth opening and closing, calling to her.

More and more of the body came into view – the shoulders, the chest, the arms, hands, fingers, raising upwards, reaching for her, clutching at her, coming closer to the surface, rising up out of the murky waters – and when the body broke the surface Manny knew it was going to pull her in.

And she couldn't move, couldn't scream. Could only watch in horrified fascination as the woman came up out of the glassy water.

She was familiar, desperately familiar with the face, and the portion of her mind that remained coolly practical was trying to work out where she'd seen the face before . . . the same portion of her mind was also advising her that this was nothing more than the shit she'd been smoking.

But she knew that this was something more than a hallucination, this was too real, the image was too powerful.

She was falling, cool, long-fingered hands reached for her . . .

And locked around her shoulders!

'You were swaying to and fro when I saw you. I knew you were going to fall into the water.'

Manny Frazer looked up into Edmund Talbott's scarred face and then fainted gracefully into his arms.

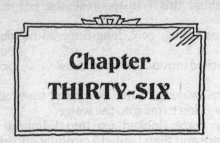

Chapter
THIRTY-SIX

HE had given blood on dozens of occasions, and it was a simple, straightforward task, with absolutely no pain, merely resulting in a mild discomfort in the crook of his arm. So extracting a pint of his own blood should have been no problem – or so he thought.

It had taken him the best part of two hours to get close to three-quarters of a pint. His left arm was one enormous bruise and the ragged puncture in his vein now almost spitefully refused to close. The bathroom sink and mirror were speckled with blood and the stink of his own sweat was heavy on the pine-scented air.

Jonathan Frazer looked at the glass beaker full of the viscous liquid, and wondered if it was enough. He looked at himself in the bathroom mirror, surprised at the deep shadows beneath his eyes, the lines on his face. He looked old, he decided, old and tired.

He ran his fingers down through the stubble on his chin, scratching. He hated being unshaven; shaving was practically the first thing he did each morning, and usually again just before tea. He had shaved this morning, just before the funeral . . . surely he didn't need to shave again. He stopped, and then stepped out of the bathroom to look at the red flowing figures on the digital clock on the bedside locker.

Two minutes past midnight.

He stared at the clock, watching the digits change from two to three. Where had the time gone? It had seemed to slip away while he'd been staring into the mirror . . . looking at Cecilia.

A smile twisted his lips. Thinking of Cecilia made him turn to look at the bottle of blood again. He must be out of his fucking mind even to consider it!

But he had seen something in the mirror, he reminded himself. And now he was going to see if he could see it again. He was conducting a scientific experiment. If nothing happened he could feel foolish, and he could curse himself for being seven sorts of a fool. But he had seen what blood did to the mirror, it wasn't going to fail.

Wincing with the ache in his left arm, working slowly and painfully, he cleaned up the bathroom, wiping away all traces of the blood, flushing the evidence down the toilet. As he came out of the bathroom he glanced at the clock again.

Twelve-thirty.

He had the house to himself. Manny had gone out, for the evening he suspected, so he had plenty of time. He'd spend an hour or so with the mirror, and then give it up. He looked at his wife's dressing table, and wondered where she was, whose arms she was in . . . well, if everything went according to plan, he'd soon know.

He began to giggle then, the sound high-pitched and hysterical in the empty house.

They'd been married about seven years when she'd had her first affair. Wasn't it men who were supposed to get the seven-year itch? She had a lot of time on her hands then: the nanny looked after Emmanuelle during the day, Jonathan had been busy building up and expanding the business. She'd been bored.

And it wasn't entirely her fault, Jonathan was as much to blame.

The first flush of passion that had brought them together had worn off and Jonathan had seemed quite content to allow it to bubble along at a simmer. But she needed him to be a little more responsive, a little more demonstrative in showing his love for her. A peck on the cheek in the morning, another at night when he came in from the shop and, by bedtime, he was usually too tired for lovemaking, except at the weekends.

But at the weekends she usually arranged a dinner party or organized a night at the theatre with friends, with the result that when they returned home, *she* was usually too tired – or too drunk – for lovemaking.

They had also become a little bored with one another.

So, given the combination of circumstances, was it any wonder that she looked outside her marriage for satisfaction? Her first lover had been a neighbour, a foreign diplomat stationed in London. His wife spent much of the time abroad and he'd been lonely. Theirs was a purely physical relationship and it had lasted on and off for nearly three months, and had taken place right under Jonathan's nose – although she was quite convinced that, unless he had actually come home and found them making love in the bed, he wouldn't have noticed. The affair ended when her lover was posted abroad, and Cecilia Frazer was just as pleased; she was becoming bored with him anyway.

It had been a year before she had taken another lover, this time on the first holiday she gone on on her own. He had been a French student, about ten years her junior, waiting tables to earn money to put himself through college for the coming term.

The following year there had been another holiday

romance . . . and then after that, well, it almost became a habit. Jonathan's idea of a holiday and hers differed tremendously and, once the precedent had been set that they should holiday apart, it became a habit. Finding a lover for the duration of her two or three or four week holidays was now part of the fun.

This year had been a little different however. She had met up with an English ski instructor in St Moritz, whose contract had terminated a few days before her holiday was due to end. She had persuaded him to stay on as her guest in the same hotel he'd once worked . . . not that he needed very much persuasion. Again, he was much younger than her – she preferred younger men – and he was a glorious and accomplished lover, always careful to ensure her own satisfaction first, before taking his own. They'd flown home together and he had invited her to follow him up to Scotland if she got the chance, where she could continue her 'ski instruction'.

It was an invitation she didn't want to refuse . . . but she couldn't justify going off on another holiday having just come back from one. Could she?

But, when she arrived home, Jonathan had been in shock at the death of the horrible Farren man. He'd been stamping around the place in a foul temper; there'd been police everywhere, and while the social circuit had suddenly rediscovered her, she knew they were only looking for tasty titbits of gossip; she had finally decided, well, why not? She had a choice: she could go off to Scotland and enjoy herself with someone she liked, or she could stay at home, miserable with someone she didn't really care one way or another about. Maybe that was what was wrong with their marriage: they didn't really care for one another, weren't really interested in one another, they had become too bound up in their own lives, their own petty interests. Where had the sharing gone?

She'd still hesitated about making the final decision, because she felt that in some ways it might be a final decision. But when Jonathan started actually sleeping in the stables, well . . .

At least with Colin she knew where she stood. Their relationship – if that's what you wanted to call it – was almost purely physical. He was eight years younger than her, and his energy and boyish enthusiasm made her feel like a teenager again.

Cecilia Frazer lay back on the bed and watched the young man undress, pleasantly sated by the two bottles of wine they had drunk over dinner. Colin Marriner was tall, broad-shouldered, slim-hipped with a shock of thick black hair and a perennial tan. And Jonathan – skinny, pale-skinned, short, greying black hair, with the beginnings of a paunch – compared very unfavourably with him. But then Colin kept himself in condition; Jonathan didn't.

She turned her head to look at herself in the dressing-table mirror, kicking off the single sheet, running her hands down her naked body. She thought she kept herself in pretty good condition. A good body, maybe a little too slim, small firm breasts, and a flat stomach and narrow waist. The muscles in her thighs were clearly delineated now from all the skiing which made her seem slightly out of proportion . . . maybe she'd go to the gym and work on her shoulder and chest muscles. She brushed the palms of her hands up across her flat stomach, aware now that Colin was watching her. Maybe she'd think about slightly bigger breasts too, the new implants were apparently absolutely amazing.

Cecilia turned back to Colin, cupping her breasts provocatively. 'What would you think if I had them made bigger?'

The young man laughed. 'I like them just the way they are,' he said, climbing onto the bed between her outstretched legs, leaning forward to delicately kiss each nipple.

The blood had already begun to turn sticky and tacky by the time he had reached the stables and settled himself before the mirror, squatting about a foot away from the glass. With infinite care he uncorked the glass jar and the dry air of the stables was immediately tainted with the copper stench of blood. Lifting the bottle, he poured the thick liquid – turned black and tar-like in the wan light coming in through the windows and skylights – onto the sponge. The pale cratered bath sponge turned black and heavy, and he immediately pushed it against the glass, squeezing it when it touched the surface, liquid snaking down the glass in twisting runnels. He rubbed the sponge in a quick circular motion, slicing through the grime, opening a window at about eye level. Wincing with the pain in his left arm, he reached into his shirt pocket and pulled out a small colour photograph of Cecilia and held it up before his face, squinting in the dim light at the vague picture. He dropped the sponge and splashed blood directly from the glass beaker across the glass, creating a shallow arc that dripped blood down its length. Jonathan Frazer vigorously rubbed the blood onto the mirror, concentrating intently on Cecilia, squeezing his eyes shut in an effort to visualize her clearly, her face, her eyes, her hair . . . but the picture wouldn't come. How could you live with someone for so long and not be able to visualize their face? When you stopped seeing them, he realized, when you stopped looking at them. He opened his eyes and looked at the photograph again. It had been taken late last year in that skiing resort she'd gone to in the French Alps. She was wide eyed, smiling, looking tanned and relaxed . . . the way she always looked after lovemaking.

A flicker ran down the length of the glass, blue and red and green.

Frazer lowered the picture and quickly threw more blood onto the glass.

The second ripple moved far more slowly down the length of the tall mirror and coalesced around the spot where he'd rubbed in the blood. The colours and twisting shapes reminded him of oil on water, and then, as he watched, the thick black blood disappeared . . . absorbed into the mirror, leaving tiny dark flakes in its wake.

There was a small amount of his blood left and he was just about to throw it onto the glass when Cecilia Frazer's face appeared.

It was the face in the photograph, wide-eyed, smiling, tanned, relaxed, but larger, life-sized, three-dimensional.

It was staring at him.

And the eyes blinked. The mouth twisted into an ugly smile, showing long yellowed teeth. The eyes blinked and blinked and the head dipped, until all he could see was the top of her dyed ash-blonde hair, the roots black and coarse. The head came back up again.

Frazer fell back away from the mirror, flinging the sponge at the image in the glass. His foot struck the glass jar, sending it crashing against the frame, the bottle shattering, blood staining the wood.

The face in the mirror leered and grimaced. It was still Cecilia's face, but subtly altered, changed. The tanned skin had assumed a leathery appearance, the eyes seemed deeper in the skull, further apart, the cheekbones more prominent, the teeth longer, the expression mocking, long moist tongue licking the cracked lips lasciviously.

He understood, on some deep unconscious level, that it was still Cecilia he was looking at, but now he was seeing another aspect of her, as if the mirror had stripped away layers of deceit and subterfuge, revealing her true character.

The face abruptly shrank in size, as if it was falling away from him, drawing him forward, until his face was inches from the glass. The spreading oil of colours obliterated everything and then twisted, and shifted, curling into shapes, resolving into a series of tiny pictures which fluttered past like wind-blown leaves. There were images, faces, pictures – a woman, a naked body, an infant, a face with long waving hair, Cecilia's face convulsed in ecstasy, Edmund Talbott's, Manny's, a tanned youth, blood and flames. Abruptly they stopped, one image resolving itself on the glass.

He was looking into a bedroom, a hotel bedroom, by the furnishing and decor. The angle was low, a few feet off the floor, and looking directly onto a bed on which two naked figures writhed together, arms and legs locked around one another. He frowned, wondering what he was supposed to be seeing, and then he heard the high-pitched gasping pants of a woman approaching orgasm.

It was Cecilia's voice.

A smile of something like triumph locked onto his face, pulling his lips back from his teeth. The experiment had worked, was working. He pressed up close against the glass, staring deep into it, wishing he could be closer to the bed, trying to make sense of the angle, wondering how he was seeing them, trying to make sense of it in relation to his own position in the room. He looked around; what was missing from the picture? And then he suddenly realized that he was looking *through* the dressing-table mirror!

The woman's gasps had now been augmented by a man's panted grunts, and Frazer was forced to sit, watching and listening to the couple reach their orgasm together and then finally collapse in a heap on the bed, where they lay breathless and gasping for a

243

few moments, until the woman rolled out of the bed and approached the mirror.

Maybe he had been hoping – desperately hoping – that his mind had been playing tricks with him, and that it wasn't Cecilia who'd been in the man's arms, making love to him with an abandon and energy she'd never shown with him. But it was Cecilia, the smile of sated satisfaction back on her lips now, her skin flushed with the after-effects of orgasm.

Bitch, bitch, bitchbitchbitch . . . fucking bitch.

In his rage, Frazer clawed at the image in the glass . . .

She used to think that all this talk about multiple orgasms was so much nonsense, but tonight she'd had two in quick succession. She supposed everything was possible with a considerate lover, and while Colin might be many things – brash and arrogant, ignorant too, not terribly well-educated – he had an instinctive understanding of how to treat a woman, where to touch, where to kiss, to lick, to suck.

Reluctantly, Cecilia Frazer swung her legs out of the bed, and padded towards the bathroom. She wanted to stay in bed with Colin, to feel his arms wrapped protectively around her, but two bottles of wine and a bout of energetic lovemaking were not compatible: her bladder was about to explode.

The flicker on the dressing-table mirror caught her attention.

She stopped and looked behind her at the bedroom wall, wondering what was reflecting off the glass, making the shimmering rainbow patterns on the surface of the mirror. She could see nothing obvious. She leaned forward, looking deeper into the glass, frowning now. There were shadows in the glass. She reached out to touch the surface of the mirror with her fingertips – and the glass exploded outwards!

Cecilia Frazer screamed as the slivers sliced into her naked skin, gouging at the flesh in her face . . .

Jonathan Frazer howled with delight as his slut of a wife reeled away from the glass, her flesh nicked and torn, four long scratches running down the right side of her face, under her chin and into the soft flesh of her shoulder.

Looking exactly as if someone had clawed at her!

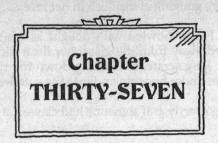

Chapter
THIRTY-SEVEN

A dot, a spot, a circle of white in the distance. Growing. Expanding. Moving. Taking on shape, shadows appearing, planes forming . . . becoming a face.

Wide-eyed, open-mouthed.

Terrified.

Screaming.

Emmanuelle Frazer awoke with the scream ringing in her ears . . . and then she realized that the scream had been hers. She sat bolt upright in the bed, both hands pressed to the side of her face, staring wildly around her.

Where was she?

Her last memories were of leaning over the river, and feeling herself falling and the hand grabbing her and the face of the ugly scarred man.

The scarred man.

The scarred man was sitting in a chair facing her, elbows resting on the arms of the chair, fingers laced together. He was wearing a black polo neck jumper over black trousers and, with his dark eyes fixed on her face, he looked positively evil.

246

She scrabbled for the thin blanket that covered her, dragging it up to her chin.

'Who are you? What am I doing here? How did I get here?'

'You're like your father,' he said quietly, 'he asks too many questions too without waiting for an answer.' He stared at her for a moment, and then he said quickly. 'I am Edmund Talbott, and I saved you from falling into the Thames. You are safe here.'

Manny wasn't quite so sure about that.

'You know my father?' she asked.

'In a manner of speaking. We have met a couple of time. Has he not spoken to you about me?'

She started to shake her head and then the fragments fell together. 'You're the big scarred man who wanted to buy the mirror,' she whispered, horrified. 'You killed Diane and those policemen.' She was too shocked to be even frightened.

'I killed the police officers, that is true,' he nodded gravely, 'but not the young woman. The image killed her.'

Manny nodded gravely. She was in the presence of a madman, and all she had to do now was to humour him until he fell asleep and she could escape. There was only one door in the dingy room and he was sitting right beside it. There was a newspaper-covered window to her left but she had no way of knowing what was on the other side. It could be a blank wall for all she knew, or they could be six storeys high.

She looked at the man – Talbott, had he said his name was? – noting the lines of the scars and wrinkles on his face, figuring that he must have been handsome once, before the accident or whatever had so badly scarred him. She wondered why he didn't have plastic surgery.

'The scars are memories,' he said suddenly, frightening her. He smiled at her horrified expression.

'When people look at me – and I mean really look, not a quick glance – they usually wonder two things, how I got the scars, and why I keep them and do not use plastic surgery.'

Manny nodded. Keep him talking. While he was talking he was calm and reasoned.

'I got the scars in a lift accident. I keep them in memory of my wife and son who died in that accident.'

'Oh,' she whispered, wondering if it were true. 'That's . . . that's terrible . . .'

'I attempted to meddle with something I could not control. And it didn't like it.' He touched his face. Talbott stared intently into her eyes and then added. 'But at least I knew what I was doing . . . or attempting to do. Unlike you.'

'Me!'

Talbott stared at her impassively.

'Look, I really don't know what you're talking about!' she snapped. Mistake, mistake, mistake, she thought, always agree with them.

'The mirror,' he said quietly.

'The mirror?' She looked at him blankly and then said very softly, 'The mirror. What about the mirror?'

'Why don't you tell me about it?' he said maddeningly.

'Look Mister . . .'

'Edmund Talbott.'

'Look Mister Talbott. I know nothing about this mirror. I've seen it, it's in my father's storeroom. And three people that I knew have died around it.'

Talbott brought his fingertips up to his lips, the palms of his hands pressed together. His finely developed senses told him that the girl was telling the truth . . . and yet he had seen the whirlwind in the Otherworld feeding off sexual energies that were undoubtedly female. Was it possible that the mirror was using her without her knowledge? It was unlikely,

248

and yet ... not impossible, and there was so much about the mirror and the images that it controlled that he did not know. The last person in his family to have a full understanding of the mirror had been his grandfather, whose knowledge of the occult was extraordinary, and who had counted many of the modern figures in the occult revival amongst his students. The stroke that had robbed him of most of his faculties including speech and the power of his hands had been a terrible tragedy ... or so Talbott had thought until he discovered that before the stroke his grandfather had been talking of putting the history and the legends surrounding the mirror down onto paper.

'Have you ever seen – or experienced – anything strange or curious around the mirror?'

'What do you mean, strange or curious?'

'Tell me what you think I mean,' he said coyly, unwilling to lead her on.

Manny considered for a moment, 'I don't like it, if that's what you mean ... it's ... it's creepy. And I saw a face in it once,' she admitted almost reluctantly.

Talbott nodded. 'What sort of face?' he asked gently.

She closed her eyes, remembering. 'A woman's face ... a ... a woman's face.' She opened her eyes again, shaking her head. 'That's all I can remember. Why? What is it about this mirror? Is it haunted?'

He shrugged, a wry smile stretching the scars on his face. 'Yes ... no ... I don't know. It is evil, it attracts evil, it disseminates evil, that is all I know. It is ancient and deadly.'

'I don't see what all this has got to do with ...' Manny began, but Talbott held up a hand, stopping her.

'The mirror works through people, controlling them, using them to feed its appetite. It shows people things, sometimes it shows them what they want to see, more

249

often than not, it shows them what they most fear. You may or may not choose to believe this if you wish, but I think you've seen enough over the past couple of weeks to know that what I'm telling you is the truth. Now you will also admit that your father has been acting strangely of late . . .?'

Manny suddenly nodded. 'I thought this might have something to do with Dad. He has been acting strangely, but then strange things have been happening around him . . .'

'. . . ever since he bought the mirror,' Talbott finished for her.

'So what are you saying to me? Are you telling me that this mirror has some sort of control over my Dad, that it's possessing him?'

'No, I'm not saying that at all,' Talbott murmured. He was watching the young woman carefully, wondering how much to tell her, wondering how much she would accept. Usually, the young were always so open to ideas . . .

'I am saying that your father is seeing things in the mirror . . .'

'What sort of things?'

'Whatever he most wants to see, whatever he fears most. I don't know. He will keep going back to the glass again and again, feeding it, becoming addicted to the images.'

'What do you mean *feeding* it?' Manny asked, the significance of the words suddenly sinking in.

'The glass is dirty, grimy, greasy. Only blood will clean the glass, only blood will fire the images. Blood and sex.' He saw the sudden colouring on her cheeks, and pressed on. 'The intense emotion of orgasm can also fire the mirror. But I think perhaps you know something of this, eh?'

'I think I want to go home,' Manny said suddenly.

'Why, what have I said that frightened you?'

'Nothing. Shit! But everything you said frightens me. Magic fucking mirrors, blood, sex, images; you're a crazy person!'

'I'll not deny that. But everything I've said to you is the truth.' He came suddenly to his feet and crossed the room to stand towering over the girl. 'Now someone has been feeding the mirror with blood – your father, I believe. Someone else has been feeding it with sexual energy – you, I believe.' Manny started to shake her head, but Talbott pressed on. 'But you see, since you know nothing about the mirror, I can only assume that you've been doing this unknowingly. Have you been having strange dreams lately, erotic dreams?' he asked suddenly. He saw the answer in her eyes and continued relentlessly. 'Usually the female is a willing part of the conspiracy, giving freely of herself, deliberately feeding the mirror. But not you. You're so close to your father, so close to the mirror that I suppose it was only natural that you should be caught up in it.'

'I have been having ... strange dreams,' Manny admitted in a whisper, 'erotic dreams. When I wake up I realize, I've ... I've ...'

Talbott patted her shoulder. 'I know. I know,' he said quietly. He straightened and crossed to the window, peering out through a tiny rent in the newspaper across the silent streets in the general direction of Kensington. Even in his waking state he could still feel the vague disturbances in the Otherworld.

'What can I do? Can you help me? Can you help my father?'

Edmund Talbott turned back, shaking his head slightly. 'I don't know,' he said truthfully. He looked down at the pale-faced girl, wondering if it wasn't too late for them all.

He glanced at his watch. It was three-thirty. 'Was

your father going out tonight?'

She shook her head. 'When Mother's away he rarely goes out.'

'Where is your mother?'

'She got a bit fed up with Dad – or at least that was her excuse – and went up to Scotland for a little break. She said she'd come back when all this was over and done with.'

Talbott nodded thoughtfully. At least that was one less problem to take care of. 'You know there are police watching your house. They're watching for me,' he added unnecessarily. 'Can you get me back to the house posing as a boyfriend?'

'Why?'

'I asked your father to cover the face of the mirror with a black cloth. But I don't think I can trust him to do that.' He dug his hands into his pockets and pulled out the cans of black paint. 'I want to get close enough to the mirror to do the next best thing.'

Manny nodded, looking at the cans in horrified fascination. She felt almost physically sick at the thought of spraying the mirror with the black lacquer paint.

Chapter
THIRTY-EIGHT

NOW . . . now . . . now . . . NOW!

It had tasted his blood, savoured it, felt his touch upon the imprisoning crystal, it had turned his dreams, his fears, into reality, allowed him a taste of power, given him a glimpse of possibilities.

And the blood had been good, so good; almost fresh, still bright with energy.

The whirlpool of energy that whipped through the Otherworld began to vibrate, to shiver with trembling energy. Vivid reds, vibrant greens, sulphurous yellows cut across the placid grey landscape of the astral plane and a deep violet stain spread across the greyness, twisting, turning like a coiling cloud, dispelling the drabness of the Otherworld. Fragments of the whirlpool began to break away, lurid clouds flashing across the plain, spinning curls of lambent colour. But deep within the core of the whirlpool of power the twisting energies latched onto the presence before the crystal cage, feeding it, as it had fed them. It had never been so close to freedom before.

It called up the Image from its memory.

Jonathan Frazer rocked back and forth on his heels,

tears streaking his grimy face. The *bitchbitchbitchbitch*. She thought she could fool him, but he'd got her in return.

And the experiment had been successful.

The mirror was some sort of psychic resonator, he decided. It obviously magnified thoughts or emotions, or possibly the blood was what originally charged it, allowing it to create the psychic link between people or places, translating the image through the nearest mirror, or possibly any reflecting surface would do. When he'd lunged at Cecilia, he'd obviously overloaded the mirror at the far end of the connection, causing it to break, the glass slicing into her skin.

Jonathan Frazer sat back nodding quickly, rubbing his sleeve across his eyes, convinced that his explanation was at least plausible. He was sitting cross-legged on the floor, staring speculatively at the mirror, mentally and physically exhausted by his recent encounter, when he noticed the flickering, deep in the core of the glass. It was a slow, flesh-coloured pulse and, as he watched, it grew from a tiny spot to an egg shape, and then larger, into a pale-coloured sphere. Colours, indentations, shadows began to appear on the pulsing ball, and just as Frazer realized that his heart was throbbing in time to the entity in the mirror, it assumed a definite form and shape and substance.

There was a woman in the mirror.

The woman he had seen before, Dee's and Kelley's companion. The woman with the long hair and the uptilted black eyes, the mysterious nameless woman.

But he had never seen her so clearly before, never in such exquisite detail. It was almost as if she were standing on the other side of the glass.

Jonathan Frazer came slowly to his feet and discovered that she was about his height. But whereas her legs and groin were clearly delineated, her breasts and head were still slightly shaded. He stooped and picked up the still damp sponge, rubbing it across the glass, squeezing hard, smearing the last of the sticky blood onto the glass, clearing the dirt. Her features immediately came clear. Her eyes were wide and pleading, her mouth working, her hands outstretched.

She was attempting to communicate with him.

She was a spirit, a ghost, trapped within the mirror, he was convinced of it. And she wanted to be free.

'How?' he asked, mouthing the word clearly. 'How can I help you?'

The image's mouth moved slowly, her full lips forming words. But did she say *feed me* or *free me*?

Frazer pressed the palm of his hand against the glass, and the image on the other side did the same, matching his fingers with hers.

Feed me?

Free me?

It didn't matter. He'd do both.

Chapter
THIRTY-NINE

SHE had first felt it in the cab, the strange tingling deep in her groin, the itching in her fingertips and toes, the pressure on her breasts. She was conscious of her heart pounding, of her shortness of breath.

And it was due to Edmund Talbott's proximity.

When Edmund Talbott had leaned over and tapped on the partition separating them from the cab driver, asking him to pull over, she'd been delighted. She needed the air.

Manny stepped out of the cab and into the shadows and watched Talbott pay the cab. She could make a run for it now if she wanted to; she knew these streets well. She was about a hundred yards from home and she was sure she'd get to the police car parked outside her house before this madman caught up with her. But she didn't run.

She had found that her attitude towards Talbott had changed as she'd approached the house. He seemed genuine, and certainly everything he told her fitted in with what she already knew. She could feel the power radiating from the man; he was dangerous and a killer, and yet she didn't feel threatened by him. He spoke of strange energies, powers and places with intimate knowledge, which she found fascinating. And while she had at first doubted his story about his wife and child, as he had continued to speak she found she had less and less reason to mistrust him, and now she found the whole idea of him keeping his scars as a memento to his dead family almost romantic.

And, of course, she didn't want him to harm the mirror.

Talbott waited until the taxi had pulled away and walked over to Manny, moving in under the trees that overhung the road, blanketing her in shadow.

'You know what to do?' he asked gently. 'Do you still want to do it?'

'I want to do it.' She slipped her arm through his. 'You are my boyfriend; I've known you for years. You're a little drunk so you're coming home with me for the night. Goodness knows what you'll think of me,' she said archly.

Edmund Talbott smiled and said nothing. What he hadn't told the young woman was that if the police saw through the ruse, and there was every possibility that they would, he would have to kill them both, and then all thoughts of subtlety went out of the window. Killing so close to the mirror would only draw its attention down on him. He would then have to get to the mirror as quickly as possible . . . and God help Manny and Jonathan Frazer if they got in his way.

Manny led him through a series of side streets and lanes, her high heels clicking loudly on the pavement, the sound unnaturally loud in the pre-dawn silence. He glanced at the glowing green dial of his watch; it was a little before four, the dead time of night. More suicides were committed at this time of the morning than at any other; this was the time when the nightmares held sway, when dreams turned ugly with returning consciousness. This was the time when the astral body began to return to its fleshy host. It was a time of memories.

They stopped at the entrance to the cul-de-sac. The unmarked police car was still parked across from the Frazer house. Edmund stared at it for a few moments, but could see no movement inside. He smiled; he hadn't chosen to come here at this particular hour without good reason: this was also the time when the human body's imperative to sleep was at its strongest.

They wove drunkenly down the street, Talbott's head dipped low on his chest, stooping to disguise his height, Manny clinging to him, her arm around his broad waist. She could feel the heat coming off the man, she was close enough to smell his strange scent, a curious bitter-sweet aroma of herbs. She was also aware of the effect he was having on her. Maybe her heart was pounding, her flesh was tingling because she was about to do something illegal and dangerous, but she didn't think so. She was becoming aroused, and it was Edmund Talbott's fault.

The two police officers were asleep in the car. Mouths open, they both had their arms folded, one leaning against the left window, the other against the right.

Maybe there was a God after all, Talbott reflected, resisting the temptation to smile.

He shivered as they passed in through the gates, a deep shuddering chill that wracked his body, causing him to stumble. Manny held him as he attempted to catch his breath.

'What's wrong, what's the matter?'

'I can feel it,' he muttered through gritted teeth. 'It's strong, so very strong.' He held his head up, almost as if he were listening and when he looked at Manny, his eyes were wide in alarm. 'It's fed recently. I can taste the blood on the air.' Blood and the faintest hint of sex. His large hand closed around Manny's arm, almost dragging her up the driveway. 'Come on.'

'What do you mean, it's fed?'

'Blood,' he murmured.

'My father . . .?' she asked in alarm.

'I can't think of anyone else.'

The power of the image was strong here. He concentrated on building the defences around himself which he hoped would prove effective. Every element of his consciousness had to be withdrawn into himself; he had to force himself to think about one thing only, something simple, if even a portion of his unconsciousness went into the Otherworld then he was lost. This was the very heart of the whirlpool. He could almost *see* it towering over the house, grey and sere, twisting, turning, with faces both human and demon within it, could almost hear the howling of the ghost wind, hear the wailing of the damned . . .

STOP IT!

It knew he was here. It was attempting to lure him, to beguile him into thinking about the deadly glass.

Was he strong enough to withstand the blandishments of the mirror? He had to be. He touched the cans of paint in his pockets.

Manny let herself in by the hall door. It was easier and quicker to make their way through the house and out through the kitchens than it was to go around through the gardens. She turned as Talbott came into the hall and then stopped, frozen by the expression of horror on his face.

'Mister Talbott . . . Mister Talbott . . . Edmund . . .?'

'The mirror,' he whispered, squeezing his eyes shut, 'for pity's sake, cover the mirror!' He fell to his knees clutching at his face, covering his eyes with his hands.

Manny whirled around. There was a large free-standing mirror in the hall at the bottom of the stairs alongside the coat-rack. She could see herself and Talbott reflected in the glass. And then she blinked.

Talbott's image had briefly flickered . . . and so had her own. As she watched the glass clouded. Emmanuelle Frazer approached the mirror slowly, touching it with her fingertips, her heart pounding convulsively. She could no longer see her face in the glass. There was a misty grey oval where her face should be.

And Edmund Talbott's reflection showed him lying on the marbled floor, his clothing ragged and shredded, his flesh torn and bleeding.

The scream caught in her throat as she spun around. Talbott was unmarked. 'Edmund . . .?' she whispered slowly.

And Edmund Talbott slowly took his hands away from his eyes. He had caught a brief glimpse in the mirror as the door had swung open, and in that instant he knew he was lost. That face, those eyes, the soft auburn hair, the gently curved lips. Even covering his eyes couldn't remove the image that had been seared on his brain. Now he could smell her in the room, that cologne she favoured, feel the heat from her body, and then – the final touch – her voice. Soft, gentle, husky, her Irish accent strong when she whispered, 'Edmund?'

It was Elizabeth, his wife.

And where was Edward, his son? He must be around here somewhere.

'Edmund?'

He'd been away too long, too many business trips, and he'd missed her. She'd missed him too. She was kneeling on the floor before him, her arms around his neck, kissing him with a passion he didn't ever remember her demonstrating. He could feel her tongue against his lips, pushing, probing, her hands working at his clothes, fumbling with buttons. And he was aroused, so aroused; he wanted her, he wanted her so badly. He tore at her black dress – he'd never seen her wear it before – exposing her breasts, and then rent the dress down to her groin, ripping it apart. He fumbled at her breasts, her nipples larger than he remembered them, but then she was nearly five months pregnant, her breasts were bound to be heavier, her nipples larger than usual, darker. She had almost pulled his shirt off, buttons were popping and skittering across the floor, and now she was working at his belt, snapping his zipper open, dragging his trousers down. And those eyes, so wide, so expressive, so full of love and warmth and need. Her mouth, now flat against the side of his head, whispering obscenities in his ear, urging him to take her . . . take her . . . take her. And his own passion reaching a stage where he simply had to have her here and now on the floor and he knew she was five months pregnant and he didn't care, and then he was inside her and she was wrapping her legs around him, pulling him in deeper, her fingers clawing at his flesh, as she thrust herself at him. She'd never done that before, she'd always been passive in bed, but obviously his absence had fired her blood, and he found himself pounding savagely into her, grunting, savouring her whimpering and her little gasps of pain, concentrating now on his own release, feeling it building deep inside him . . .

She wasn't sure when it started exactly. She'd knelt on the floor, wondering what was wrong and put her arms around him, and then he was kissing her and the pressure she'd felt building up inside her, the coiled tension, seemed to unwind, and she found herself returning his kiss with a passion that surprised even her. The tingle of electricity in her limbs continued to shudder through her body, concentrating in her groin, on her breasts, and when he had rubbed his thumbs across her sensitive nipples, the first orgasm had taken her, snatching at her breath, increasing her already racing heartbeat to an almost frightening level. She could feel the power coming off him, raw, naked energy that flowed from his body into hers. When he entered her, her second orgasm had shivered through her and she had clutched at him, wanting all of him inside her, acutely aware now of his body against hers. His chin and stubble rasped against the soft flesh of her cheeks. She was speaking to him, shocking herself as she urged him on, encouraging him to take her, guiding him with pornographic detail. He began to pound into her, his large hands tightening on her breasts, twisting the nipples ... and hurting. His pounding had become painful, her lubrication suddenly seeming to have vanished, and the rasp of flesh against flesh was agony. She attempted to push him off, but his weight was pressing her down. She flailed at him with her fists, but his face was locked into an impassive mask, his eyes blank and unseeing, spittle dribbling from the corner of his mouth. His hands began to convulse on her breasts, digging into the soft flesh, leaving long weals in their wake, scoring the skin, drawing blood in places. She attempted to scream, but his mouth was on top of hers, his tongue pressed against her lips. Her groin was on fire now, pure agony as he continued to batter at her, slamming against her pubic bone, attempting to push himself deeper and deeper inside her.

And then his orgasm took him.

Talbott's back arched, and his head went back, his eyes squeezed shut in blissful pleasure.

And Manny Frazer punched him with all her might in the throat!

Edmund Talbott convulsed off Manny, his eyes wide in shock, both hands clutched to his throat. She saw his Adam's apple working, his chest heaving, and then his eyes began to bulge, his face purpling as he fought for breath.

And the mirror exploded.

He knew, in those last few seconds of life, what had

happened. After all the preparations, all his precautions, he had been trapped by his own stupidity. He realized now that he'd been made to come here, here where the mirror was so strong, where the power of the image was absolute. How it had played with him, showing him the image of his long-dead wife – he wondered what poor Manny had seen – and then taken his lust and inflamed it. And it had been a long time since he'd slept with a woman. It had fed off the sexual emotions the two of them had generated: what a triumph that was for it. And then it had turned the emotion of lust to fear for the woman, making what he was doing no more than rape. It undoubtedly took extra pleasure in that: sex by force was probably a delicacy to it.

It had lost him in the few seconds after his orgasm had wracked his body. The feeling of horror was matched by his revulsion . . . and then he'd felt the pain. It lanced through his throat, impacting the trachea, blocking the air passages and his deflated lungs began to scream for air almost immediately. Coolly, almost calmly, he realized it was a death blow.

And the mirror exploded.

He raised his head and watched the mirror at the bottom of the stairs dissolve, long slivers of glass erupt outwards, lancing their way towards them, moving almost slowly through the air, glittering, sparkling, lethal.

Edmund Talbott's last conscious thought was to throw himself forward atop Manny, wrapping his arms around her, shielding her as the glass tore into his body, shredding the flesh on his head, shoulders, back and buttocks, cutting down to the bone in many cases, laying open a whole section of his spine, spears of glass penetrating his kidneys, ripping into his lungs.

It had taken ten years, but the image had finished

263

what it had set out to do. Edmund Talbott wondered what would happen now to Jonathan and Manny, and everyone else who came in contact with the image.

He was surprised to find that he still cared.

Chapter FORTY

'**PERSONALLY** gentlemen, I don't give a fuck what your excuses are. You let him walk right past you and rape the girl in her own fucking hallway! I'm bringing you both up on charges.' Margaret Haaren stalked right past the two plain-clothes officers standing at the gate. Neither of them attempted to offer any excuses: there were none to offer. The first they'd known of the attack of the girl was when a screaming, naked and bloodied female had hammered on the windscreen of their car, jolting them both awake. Her bloodied handprints were still smeared across the glass.

The inspector stalked up the gravelled driveway, almost shivering with rage. So you did your best, no . . . you did more than your best because you were a woman in a man's world and the best wasn't good enough. You had to give a hundred per cent plus ten. And when the Chief Inspector had asked for a report in person, you told him the situation was under control and that you had two of your best men – best men, *Jesus* – watching the house and that there was no way the scarred man was going to get within a hundred yards of the house. And this was only yesterday; this was the Chief Inspector telling you –

warning you – that they needed a result, and fast. The bodies were beginning to mount up here and far too many of them were police officers. And what happened? Fucking animal waltzes in past the two *best* men on the gate, gets in through the front door and brutally rapes the daughter in the hallway. The only good thing to come out of all of this was that she'd actually killed the guy. Punched him in the throat and then dropped a mirror on him, ripping him to shreds in the process. He was probably alive when that had happened too, his throat completely closed, unable to scream. Well, it couldn't have happened to a nicer guy.

The technicians had finished by the time she arrived and the body had been removed to the morgue, but the hallway still looked like an abattoir. There was glass and blood everywhere, splashed high on the walls, the backs of the doors, some of it even speckling the ceiling. It stank too. The sharp copper tang of blood was everywhere, but the bitter stench of urine and the sweeter, cloying odour of excrement was discernible too. She had once been in a room where an irate husband had blown apart his wife and her lover in their bed with a 12-gauge double barrelled shot-gun. It had smelt the same.

Sergeant Stuart Miller came up and stood beside her, saying nothing, allowing her to absorb the atmosphere of the place.

'How's the girl?' she asked eventually.

The West Indian made a face. 'She's upstairs, refusing to go to hospital, with the family doctor in attendance. She's hysterical,' he added slowly, 'but I've seen enough hysterical women in my time to know when it's being put on a bit for our benefit.'

'How's the father taking it?'

'Oh, he's a cool one all right. If I didn't know any better, I'd think he was smoking some weed or

266

popping a few smarties. I'm not saying he was uninterested in what had happened to his daughter, but it's as if it didn't really affect him one way or the other. He didn't impress me. I know how I'd react if it was my daughter . . .'

'I don't think our Mister Frazer is a very nice man,' Margaret Haaren agreed. 'What about the mother? Where is she?'

'On holiday in Scotland; skiing on one of those dry slopes. Neither of them wants her told.'

'Just one big happy family, eh?'

Stuart Miller nodded. 'How do you want to play this?'

'By the book; I'm picking up flack from upstairs. They were looking for a result – well, they got that, but I've a feeling it's not going to be enough. A live body would have been nice.'

'What about Mister Frazer?'

'Nothing would give me greater pleasure,' she said with feeling.

As she began the procedure of working through the exact sequence of events, she tried to establish why she disliked Jonathan Frazer with such intensity. Rarely had she become so emotionally involved – if that was the right word – with one of her suspects. It wasn't a new feeling, but it was usually reserved for rapists or child molesters. What had Frazer done to deserve her ire?

He'd lied to her. He'd looked at her and decided he was cleverer than she was; he'd decided that he could run a scam on her and she wouldn't pick it up.

And he was involved directly or indirectly in the death of more than one police officer, one of whom had been a very good friend.

There was something wrong here.

She stopped in the doorway and examined the sketch one of the attending officers had prepared of the scene, and then flipped the page to read through his initial notes on the man's injuries.

The scarred man – no identification present on the body – had been in a state of partial undress, coat and shirt lying on the floor – still there – his trousers down around his ankles, still wearing one shoe; the other was lying on its side in a pool of thickening blood.

His back had been shredded, glass everywhere, long slivers actually penetrating deep into his flesh.

According to Emmanuelle Frazer she had pushed the mirror over on top of him.

Margaret looked up.

And what had she done then? Lifted it up and wheeled it back to its position at the foot of the stairs where it was now?

Skirting the blood on the floor, she stopped in front of the mirror, looking closely at it. The glass was broken outwards, which was consistent with it having been dropped onto the ground. Crouching down she examined the castors. The mirror was obviously an antique. The heavy gilded frame ended in four legs, each leg ending in a carved animal claw clutching a ball. Licking her finger, she ran it across the floor directly in front of one of the legs: a faint ring of grime appeared on her finger, with a corresponding white mark on the floor. Surely if the mirror had been moved those heavy wheels would have left some marks on the marble tiles. She stood and looked closely at the mirror, and then, clutching it in both hands, she attempted to lift it. It shifted slightly, but didn't move. She knew adrenalin lent strength . . . possibly giving a terrified woman the strength to drag the mirror on top of her assailant. But to wheel it back again? The fact that the mirror hadn't been moved added more credence to the theory she was developing.

Margaret Haaren walked half way up the curving staircase, stopped and looked down, visualizing another scene, creating another set of circumstances to fit the facts.

When Stuart Miller, still standing in the hallway, saw her smile, he immediately started up the stairs. 'Yes, ma'am?'

'Where is Mister Frazer?'

'Having a little lie down, ma'am. He looked shagged,' he added.

'As if he'd been up all night?'

'Something like that.'

'Is he still there?'

'There is an officer on the landing – for Miss Frazer's benefit of course,' he added with a smile.

'Of course.' Her lips pulled back from her teeth in a humourless grin. 'Let's go and talk to Miss Frazer first, and we'll see what she has to say for herself.'

WPC Carole Morrow came to her feet as the door opened and Inspector Haaren and Sergeant Miller entered the room. 'How is she?' the inspector asked, looking at the girl lying on the bed, eyes closed, scores of tiny nicks from flying glass on her face. In the pale dawn light her flesh looked grey.

Manny Frazer's large brown eyes snapped open. 'She's as well as can be expected having been beaten and raped while your men slept outside. Much fucking good they did me!'

The inspector immediately sat down, putting herself on a level with the woman, unwilling to tower over her. 'I know what happened,' she said gently. 'The men will be dealt with. I'm not making any excuses for them.'

Manny Frazer subsided back onto the pillows.

'Do you want to tell me what happened?' Margaret Haaren asked gently.

'I've already told her what happened,' Manny snapped, jabbing a finger at the WPC, 'and then I told the doctor what happened, and then I told another

269

policeman what happened. How many times do I have to tell what happened?'

'Tell me,' Margaret said firmly.

Manny sighed audibly, and then she took a deep breath. 'There was a knock on the door late last night, early this morning. I thought it was Mother coming home. I shouted through the door, asking who it was, and the voice said, "Taxi; just dropping a fare." So, I was convinced then it was Mother. I thought I heard footsteps moving away on the gravel, so I opened the door. It was this guy, big ugly scarred guy. He pushed me into the wall, threw me to the ground, ripped the clothes off me and raped me. There was a struggle; I punched him in the throat and then I pushed the mirror down on top of him. I then ran out and got your men. They were both sleeping,' she added.

Margaret Haaren nodded. 'That's essentially the same story you told my officers. But now I'd like you to tell me the truth.'

Manny sat up in the bed, the covers falling down, revealing the scrapes and grazes on her breasts. 'What the fuck d'you mean "the truth". I told you the fucking truth.'

'Tell me again how you pushed the mirror over onto the man,' the inspector said quietly, her cold green eyes locked onto the younger woman's face.

Manny looked away. 'I . . . I punched him in the throat. He was holding his neck and gasping for breath and . . . and I sort of slid out from beneath him and grabbed the nearest thing, and that was the mirror, and pushed it down on top of him. The glass broke . . . and then I lifted the mirror off just to see if he was still alive.'

Margaret Haaren noticed that there was a slight sheen of sweat on her top lip and she wouldn't meet her eyes.

'The umbrella stand behind the door was nearer than the mirror,' the inspector said very softly. 'There are a couple of heavy walking sticks in it. Good solid weapons.'

'What?'

'The mirror is about eight feet from where the man attacked you. It would take two of my officers all their strength to lift the mirror . . . but then the mirror hasn't been moved, has it?'

Manny Frazer looked from Margaret Haaren to Stuart Miller, and then back at the inspector. 'What are you saying?' she demanded.

'I'm saying that you're not telling me the truth.' She smiled humourlessly. 'And suddenly, what's justifiable homicide turns into murder. Do you know what I'm saying?' she murmured.

'Look . . . look, I've told you what happened. Now I'm not saying another word unless my father is here. Or my solicitor.'

'You've been watching too much TV, my dear.' She turned and looked at her sergeant. 'Charge her with accessory to murder.'

'What . . . what . . . what are you talking about?' Manny's voice had grown shrill, strident.

'Where was your father last night, Miss Frazer?'

'I don't know.'

Margaret Haaren stood up suddenly. 'We will make arrangements for you to be taken to hospital . . .'

'I'm not going to hospital,' Manny said firmly.

Stuart Miller stepped forward. 'Miss Emmanuelle Frazer, I am formally charging you as an accessory to the murder of one Joe Bloggs. Anything you say say will be taken now and may be used in evidence against you later. Do you understand what I am saying?'

'I didn't murder him!'

The inspector half turned her head, and the sergeant looked up from his notebook. ' "I punched him in the throat. He was holding his neck and gasping for breath . . ." ' he read.

'You're under arrest, Miss Frazer. We will be taking you to a hospital for a check-up and then you will be brought to the local station for questioning.' She turned abruptly and walked from the room.

Stuart Miller caught up with her on the landing. 'What do you think?' he said softly.

'Get rid of the rookie WPC and substitute someone older, a maternal figure she can talk to. Have her run through the horrors of prison scenario. I'll talk to her later today and we'll see if she still sticks to her story.'

'And Mister Frazer?' Miller asked, stopping outside the bedroom door.

'Suspicion of murder, conspiracy to murder, and whatever else I can think of.'

'How do you read it?' he asked, genuinely interested.

'I think the scarred man was attempting to extort money from Frazer. He's tried threatening him, killing off his employees, and maybe he tried to kidnap the daughter, or maybe it was rape as an example. Frazer comes in. There's a struggle. The guy is thrown against the mirror, and suddenly he ends up dead. The only problem is,' she admitted, 'there's not a lot of glass around the base of the broken mirror.'

'Most of it ended up in the dead guy's back,' Stuart Miller reminded her.

'So we'll have Mister Frazer down at the nick for a few questions. Let him sweat too; let's see what happens. This will be a pleasure,' she grinned, turning the handle and walking into the bedroom.

The room was empty.

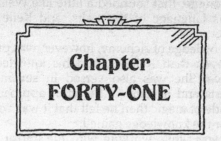

Chapter
FORTY-ONE

SHE was a demon, John Dee had decided. Some creature from the pit.

And he was fascinated by her, completely under her spell.

They had been married for the best part of a year now, although the priest Edward Kelley had produced had been of dubious antecedents, and he wouldn't have been surprised to find discover that the man had been a Papist. And he didn't care: he loved the woman.

It had been an extraordinary year in many ways, and he sometimes thought he knew just as little about the woman now as he did on the occasion of their very first meeting. He still had to learn the woman's name. She subscribed to the old pagan tradition – still current in some magical circles – that there was a magic in a name, and to give that name freely and without thought to another person delivered you into their power.

She rarely spoke, and more often than not he seemed to find her in a trance, her cold black eyes glazed, looking at something only she could see. Often she talked through Kelley when he was in a mediumistic trance. She would speak some alien foreign tongue, that sounded a little like Welsh or the barbarous language of the Celts, and Kelley would translate.

Her knowledge of alchemy, however, was profound, deeper even than Kelley's, and his knowledge was impressive. She was also versed in several of the arcane arts and if some of her craft approached the darker side of magic then he felt that it was worth it in return for the knowledge gained.

But it was while working with the mirror that her extraordinary abilities became evident.

He had watched her perform – if that was the word, and it seemed so base a word for what she did – before the mirror every month when the moon was full. Standing naked and proud before the glass, she would arouse herself with complete abandon and then, at the precise moment of her greatest passion, he would spill the blood down the length of the mirror.

The resultant images were profound, vivid, terrifying and completely exhilarating.

And they had brought him recognition at Court. Although he was already a favourite of the Queen – she had even allowed him to predict the precise time and day for her Coronation and he had prepared several natal charts for her – with the virtual banishment of Essex to Ireland, he was one of the few persons at Court she asked for advice.

And she believed in magic.

In so many ways she was so practical, so level-headed, so firm in her convictions, it was difficult to believe that she should ever vacillate in any one thing. And yet she was quite prepared to take and act upon advice from outsiders.

But Dee's greatest advantage was that his advice was *good* – so good. The mirror's images were never wrong. Indeed, the Queen had been so curious about the quality of Dee's information that he had been obliged to inform her of the mirror's existence, and had promised to show it to her when the moment was propitious.

And now the enigmatic woman was pregnant.

They had made love . . . no, that was not the correct term. They had engaged in congress together every night for two weeks, but there was no love involved in it, their coupling had been in the manner of a scientific experiment. She had been in control at all times.

Dee had thought he would have found some difficulty arousing himself as the nights progressed, but when the time came, one look at the woman's naked body had been enough. They had coupled in front of the mirror, with the woman on top, and she always ensured that the great passion took them simultaneously. Then the mirror would explode into sights and visions that Dee was sure must emanate from Hell. There was so much to see, so many images, from all the ages of man, from times he had heard about, places he had read of.

One image he particularly remembered. It showed the woman and himself standing side by side holding a child by the hands – a female child – raven-haired, grey-eyed. He saw the child drop its parents' hands and approach the mirror, stretching out its long-fingered hands towards the glass . . . and the mirror came alive with sights, vivid and animated.

'A magical child,' the woman had whispered, watching the mirror over her shoulder. And then she had crouched lower over Dee, pressing her full breasts against his thin chest. 'This night you have impregnated me.'

He didn't need to ask her how she knew; her natural magic would surely have told her. And later, when he worked out the birth date of the child, he discovered that it was due around the mid-winter solstice.

Now when she came to the mirror, heavy with her child, her breasts and belly swollen, he found he could still watch her with the same satisfaction, feel the same desire. Now she squatted on the floor before the tall glass and proceeded to arouse herself, the colours flowing down the glass, the images flickering in rapid succession ... but one image in particular kept recurring ... that of a knife rising and falling ... rising and falling ... silver when it fell, red with gore when it rose ...

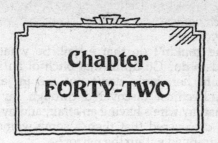

Chapter
FORTY-TWO

. . . A knife rising and falling, rising and falling, silver when it fell, red with gore when it rose . . .

Jonathan Frazer came awake with a scream. He sat up in the tiny smelly bedroom and rubbed his face with his hands, feeling his stubble scratch against his skin. He felt and looked like shit. He swung his feet out of the bed and then rested his elbows on his knees, his head buried in his hands. How had he got himself into this situation, he wondered dully.

How?

Why?

Why had he run away? He raised his head and looked into the speckled mirror on the battered dressing table beside the filthy sink. His eyes were deep sunk, the flesh tight across his cheekbones, his expression haunted.

He'd been frightened, terrified to be more exact. He was so close – so damned close – to the solution of the riddle of the glass that he couldn't afford to be put in jail or taken in for questioning. Not now, not when he was so close.

He wasn't finished with Cecilia just yet.

And then there was the image. He'd made a promise to her.

Feed me.

Free me.

And he couldn't do that in jail. So what was he supposed to do? Go up to that bitch of an inspector and say to her, look, don't put me in jail at the moment, I've just discovered through my magical mirror that my wife's having an affair, and by the way, I've also discovered that there's some woman, some creature, trapped within the mirror?

Oh sure, she'd like that. She already suspected him of conspiracy or whatever; she'd use any excuse to haul him in, and then use whatever influence she could to keep him in.

They were probably looking for him now. They might even suspect that he had something to do with Talbott's death.

And what was he going to tell them when they finally caught up with him? He'd heard a crash of glass and come down to see his daughter lying naked beneath Edmund Talbott who looked like a piece of meat off a butcher's slab?

'And how did the glass get there, Mr Frazer?'

Oh, the mirror broke of its own accord and the glass flew through the air at him. Actually, I believed the woman trapped in the mirror sensed the danger to my daughter and was protecting her the only way it knew.

And you believe that, Mister Frazer.

Absolutely. Why, less than an hour previously, I'd watched my wife in bed with another man. Go and ask her, see if she had scratches on her face.

Yes, he was sure they'd believe that.

So he'd made up the simple story of Talbott raping Manny. It was plausible enough to be true. He was raping her, she struck him a lucky blow that immobilized him and then Manny had dropped the mirror on him. He didn't think they'd investigate too closely; Talbott's death tied things up neatly.

When he discovered the police officer posted outside his bedroom door, he knew he had a problem. They were going to take him in for questioning, and neither his nor Manny's stories would stand up to serious questioning.

Getting out of the bedroom was simplicity itself. The large double windows opened out onto a small balcony which was positioned directly over the sloping conservatory roof. The only problem he'd had was making sure he didn't put his foot through the glass in the conservatory roof. Keeping to the bushes, he'd crept out through the narrow gateway that led out into the lane that ran along behind the house.

So now he was on the run. That brought a smile to his face. He looked at his reflection in the glass. He was thirty-eight years old, and all his previous encounters with the police had been for parking fines, and now here he was, a suspect in a murder hunt.

He'd got sixty pounds in his pocket, and his plastic cards . . . but if he used them wouldn't the police be able to trace him that way? Anyway, he spent eighteen pounds for a night in a grotty B&B on the edges of Soho, and so far this evening he'd had three women of various ages and condition knocking on his door asking him if he was looking for any company.

What he needed now was a plan. Running away had been spur of the moment, now he needed to do something more constructive, more long-term. Obviously, he was going to have to clear his name. He'd need to talk to the inspector, make her listen to sense.

And he needed to get back to the mirror again. He wanted to see the image again.

Feed me.

Free me.

Yes, and he was going to have to work out some way

of freeing her, releasing her spirit. Talbott would have known ... but he was beginning to wonder if everything Talbott had told him had been the truth. Maybe Talbott knew of the existence of the woman in the glass and wanted to keep her for himself. Now wasn't that a much more plausible explanation – inasmuch as anything was plausible – than his story about some vampiric mirror. Yesyesyesyes. He nodded fiercely. Talbott wanted the woman for himself; that's why he wanted the mirror.

Jonathan Frazer stood and crossed the room, swaying slightly, suddenly realizing that he hadn't eaten in more than twenty-four hours. He searched through his jacket pocket, looking for a slip of paper, and a pen, finally finding his 22 carat Gold Cross pen and two theatre ticket stubs – *Les Misérables*, the last time he and Cecilia had been out together. He smiled, remembering. It had been a good night. The smile faded as he turned the ticket stubs around in his hand. Unfortunately, there had been far too few good nights in the last few years of their marriage. He stood looking at the stubs for a moment before returning to the bed – there was no chair on the room – and sitting down.

On the back of one of the tickets he began to list his imperatives.

Clear my name.

Clearing his name meant going to the inspector and talking to her, but she wasn't likely to believe him without evidence. And what evidence had he got? He couldn't exactly bring the mirror to her, could he?

And why not?

Why not bring *her* to the mirror, let her see for herself? His hand was trembling so much now that he could hardly write. It was so obvious. So simple.

Return to the mirror.

He needed to feed it some blood again. It would be

280

hungry soon; he could almost feel its craving. He needed to get back to the mirror to have another 'look' at his dear wife. And he wanted to see the image.

Getting back into the house might prove to be difficult; the police would undoubtedly be watching it. But he didn't need to go back to the house. He could go directly to the stables. Surely they wouldn't be watching the stables? With Talbott dead would they even be watching the house?

Blood.

He was going to need some blood. He rolled up his sleeve and looked at his left arm. The flesh was still darkly bruised and tender and he didn't fancy trying the same trick with the other arm. Maybe that was another reason he was feeling dizzy.

What about animal blood?

That didn't *feel* right. Surely it would be wrong to feed the glass with the blood of one of the lower creatures? Was it possible to buy blood, he suddenly wondered, staring blankly at the mildewed curtains. Hadn't he read that you could buy anything on the streets of London? So what did you do? Go up to someone on the street and ask them could you buy a pint of blood? Were there haemoglobin pushers and plasma junkies?

He began to giggle at the idea.

And what was the going rate for a pint of blood? Was there a set rate depending on its purity and age, and did the price go up according to its age, like old wine?

If one of the street girls cost you twenty pounds for an hour and there were eight pints of blood in the human body, did that not work out at two pounds and fifty pence per pint?

He started giggling again. He loved the very thought of going up to a girl and saying, 'Excuse me, could I buy a pint of your blood?' The smile faded from his lips. What was the first thing she was going to do? . . . run to the nearest policeman and say she'd been approached by some freak. The newspapers would have a field day with that, 'Vampire on the Streets of London.'

Nonononono . . . this was going to be done subtly. He wondered if it was possible to work out some way to get blood from a body without the person knowing. Now, think about this; there had to be some way. How did hospitals take blood . . . well, he knew how they took blood, but the donors were awake, but they could just as easily be asleep. So, he was going to have to put his donors to sleep. Drink? Drugs?

Cecilia had sleeping pills back in the house: shit – she had a whole pharmacy in the house!

OK. So he got these sleeping pills, administered them to his donor, in a drink presumably, and then when she fell asleep he'd take a pint of blood. He'd be gone by the time she woke up, and if he did it properly she'd never even know what he'd done.

He glared at his expression in the mirror opposite. Of course she'd know what he'd done. She'd have a fucking big hole in her arm! The face in the mirror was fierce, twisted, the warped glass giving him a depraved expression. And maybe the sleeping tablets wouldn't have any effect, maybe the pain would bring them awake. And what then?

Why was he giving himself all this grief; why the fuck didn't he just kill one of the tarts? Who was going to miss them? Wasn't exactly as if they were important. Dirty, diseased whores. Spreading their filth, sapping the vitality of honest men like himself. Why not make them serve a higher cause? Bitches should be honoured to feed the image.

Jonathan Frazer began to shudder. He pressed both hands to his head, feeling the pressure, the pounding deep in his skull, sure it was going to burst. Not enough sleep, not enough food. He was going crazy, thinking like a crazy man.

. . . A knife rising and falling, rising and falling, silver when it fell, red with gore when it rose . . .

He barely made it to the sink before he retched up a thin bile. He stayed, crouched over the sink, feeling his stomach churn as the sickening images, the vile thoughts that crowded at his mind, pushed their way in, insinuating themselves into his consciousness.

He was tired and hungry, emotionally exhausted. He'd sleep. He'd feel better when he awoke.

It was late into the night when he awoke again. There was no longer traffic on the street outside, no longer traffic outside his door. He turned over on the soft, sagging bed, and found himself staring into the pale oval of the dressing-table mirror. As he watched a pale flickering oval appeared, not quite a face, twisted, misshapen, ugly. It cleared once – for a single heartbeat – and the mouth worked.

Feed me.

Free me.

Who was going to miss them? They were unimportant. Dirty, diseased whores. Spreading their filth, sapping the vitality of honest men like himself. They should be honoured to serve a higher cause, to advance the cause of science, the exploration of the paranormal.

He moved through the filthy streets, watching the people part before him, acknowledging him on some deep subconscious level as their superior. He could feel the power flowing out of him now, could almost see it. He lifted his left hand and peeled off the leather glove. Yes, his pale flesh was surrounded by a pale bronze aura, shot through with particles of red. He saw one of the women standing lewdly in an alleyway, her ankles exposed, staring openly at him. He glared at her, his thick eyebrows drawing into a straight line across his forehead, drawing his lips back from his teeth in a sneer and she quickly looked away.

How easily these animals were controlled.

They were cattle, to be led, to be used.

What visions he had seen in the mirror, what sights! Mysteries beyond comprehension, carriages without horses, birds of metal, velocipedes without pedals, buildings standing impossibly tall.

But he was astute; he recognized that what he was seeing was some future tomorrow and he saw the precursors of those fabulous articles all around him. If he were astute, he would be able to invest in the correct properties, the proper stocks and shares. And that income would allow him to continue his experiments. He had all the time in the world. By feeding the glass he was becoming immortal, he knew it. Already he felt stronger, sharper. He had seen his aura turned from the colour of mud to bronze, when it turned gold he would be undying.

And then of course there was the image.

Once he had freed her he would have everything he wanted, everything he needed.

One more should do it . . . well, one or two.

The newspapers had given him the names of the last four, Nichols, Chapman, Stride and Eddowes, not that he was really interested in the names anyway. You didn't give cattle names, you gave them numbers. He'd had to do the last two together because he'd been disturbed. But that night, aaah, that night he'd felt *alive*. He'd felt his aura flaming like a raging fire. He felt that all he had to do was to reach out and touch someone to make them burst into flames.

He smiled savagely, remembering.

And now he needed blood again.

His mistress hungered.

It was late now, after midnight certainly, but the streets of Whitechapel were still busy, but there were no *decent* people on the streets at this time. He wasn't sure how long he'd been walking; latterly time had ceased to have any real meaning for him, and he suspected that this was because of his immortality. Did the ever-living appreciate the passage of time? Mankind was intimately aware of the passage of time because each passing day brought him closer to his death . . . but if one did not die, then there was no passage of time to appreciate. He stopped suddenly, pleased with the proposition.

His mistress hungered.

He was aware of her hunger as an almost physical ache, and he knew that if he didn't appease it soon that hunger would grow into an all-consuming, ravening need.

It was raining heavily now, and many of the whores had gone for the night, earning their pennies on their backs, and those few who remained were likely raddled with disease, their blood thin and poisoned.

He turned into Commercial Street just as the woman came out of the squalid public house. She was younger than most, mid-twenties he would guess and pretty in a vulgar sort of way. And drunk.

'How much?' he asked directly, taking her arm, manoeuvring her down the street into the shadows. He'd do her the first opportunity he got, some dark alleyway.

'Not so rough, guv. Impatient, ain't ye?' He detected an Irish accent.

'How much?' he repeated.

'Two bob.'

He laughed. 'A shilling.'

'Make it one and six, guv and you can stay the night. My lodging's just around the corner in Miller's Court, just back of Dorset Street.'

It would be good to work indoors, out of this teeming rain which might wash some of the precious blood away. 'One and six,' he agreed, and then asked, 'is there a mirror in your room?'

She looked up at him blearily, her eyes red-rimmed, bloodshot with the alcohol. 'Aye, there is.'

'Excellent.' He wondered why he hadn't thought of it before. Fresh blood spilt directly onto the glass, what images would he see then, what visions?

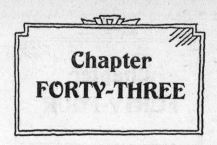

Chapter
FORTY-THREE

IT remembered that time.

It had been a time of strength and power. It had been strong then, so strong, feeding on the emotions of the man and the blood of the women. Curious that it should have remembered that now when it had so many memories to call upon.

They were crowding closer now, all those bloody memories, of times of strength and power, of blood and killing.

The memories were flowing out, into the servant.

Teaching him.

Showing him what he needed to do.

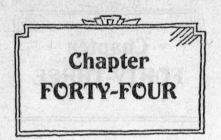

Chapter
FORTY-FOUR

SHE stood naked before the mirror, combing her hair, the smile fixed on her face, her gaze vacant. She looked into the glass, idly wondering how long it had been since she'd last had hair to comb. By rights her tight haircut should have lasted most of the summer, but it had sprouted with extraordinary rapidity, until she now had a straightforward short haircut that no one could object to. Another couple of weeks at this rate and it would be flowing down her back.

Manny Frazer ran both hands through the hair, pulling it back off her face, noticing the way her cheekbones seemed more prominent, her eyes slightly sunken, her lips thicker.

The first thing she had done when she'd gotten out of the clutches of the inspector was to have a shower, a long hot shower, washing away the grime, the smell of the hospital and the police station. They'd treated her like shit, she decided, like a criminal, and she'd get her father's solicitor to bring a case against them, wrongful arrest, something like that.

If she knew where her father was.

That woman detective had been very curious about

his whereabouts; she'd practically accused him of killing Talbott and being involved in the deaths of the other policemen. Well, she supposed he was, in a roundabout way.

Where was he? Where was he likely to go? Had he a special club he liked to go to? A friend? A mistress? Where was her mother? What was his relationship with her mother? What was her relationship like with her father? Tell us again what happened? Tell us again . . . and again . . . and again . . .

After a while she just refused to answer any more questions until her lawyer was present. But she hadn't been charged with anything, the woman told her, she was simply helping them with their enquiries.

Finally, they just let her go.

Now the police presence outside her house was much more visible. There was an officer stationed on the gate and the unmarked car out front had been replaced by an official police car.

Margaret Haaren's last words as Manny had climbed into the police car, had been, 'If your father contacts you, let us know immediately. We are very worried about the state of his mental health.'

What shit! What utter shit. They didn't give a toss about the state of her father's health. They were going to try and pin something on him. The woman had more or less said so.

She pulled on a heavy robe and wrapped a towel around her still damp hair. She walked around the house, looking into each room, checking the windows, locking the doors when she had finished. She felt tired, a little freaked too, like she'd just come down off a trip, but then again, it was the middle of the afternoon and she had been up all night . . . and been attacked too. She'd every right to feel freaked out. Everything was a little jittery, colours seemed sharper, brighter, edges were more defined, and she had the impression that objects were moving at the corner of her vision. She needed a good night's rest . . . and some food, she decided, coming into the kitchen.

She made herself a tomato sandwich and a cup of tea and then opened the back door and sat on the veranda, the bread clutched in both hands, chewing it slowly and carefully, her eyes wandering over the garden. It was a gorgeous evening, mild and quiet; the sounds of the city were a very distant hum, and the sunlight coming in over the tops of the trees was a rich warm gold, deepening to purple.

She finished her sandwich and drank the almost cold tea and then wandered around the garden, breathing in the moist warmth. She stopped beside the stable door: it was ajar.

Her heart was beginning to pound as she walked up to the door and pushed it open. There was no sign of the heavy lock – perhaps the police had it – and the bolt had been neatly folded back . . . just the way her father did it. She stopped. And then a broad smile spread across her face. Where else would he go? She stepped into the room and called, 'Dad?'

The heat and musty closeness took her breath away. The skylights were washed with light, diffusing gently into the room, and the air was alive with swarming motes and spots of dust.

'Dad?' The room swallowed her voice.

Maybe she'd been wrong . . . or maybe he had been here and had slipped out . . . and of course he wouldn't necessarily know that she'd be back so soon. Manny made her way into the room, breathing in the dry air. She shared some of her father's interest and enthusiasm in antiques and, like him, she had often found peace of mind in this place. Some of the objects had been here for as long as she could remember. They were always going to be fixed *tomorrow*.

And in the centre of the room, in the middle of a

veritable maze of antiques and artefacts, was the mirror. It had taken the late evening sunlight and darkened it, turning it a deep, iridescent purple, the same shade as a bruise. She stopped before the glass, squinting against the glare from the sunlight, barely able to make out her reflection.

Talbott had believed that this was responsible for everything, and she couldn't help but think that maybe he was right. He'd talked a lot of nonsense, asking her all sorts of strange questions about her own feelings towards the mirror, about what she'd seen there . . .

The face.

She remembered the face. A woman's face.

He'd said the mirror controlled people, using them to feed its appetite. She'd half believed him then, but now . . . standing before the glass, she wasn't quite so sure. She reached out, rubbing her finger along the dirty surface.

The glass is dirty, grimy, greasy. Only blood will clean the glass, only blood will fire the images. Blood and sex. The intense emotion of orgasm can also fire the mirror.

And she remembered her own dreams, the erotic dreams that left her exhausted.

But it was only a mirror, wasn't it? She desperately wanted to believe that it was just a mirror, just an ugly antique mirror and she was crazy even to think about that madman's words. He'd been insane, he'd killed people, he'd raped her . . . and he'd died with his back cut to shreds protecting her.

She closed her eyes, remembering him crouching before her, both hands clutched to his throat, his face purpling, eyes bulging. She'd been facing him, both hands pressed to her mouth, desperately resisting the urge to throw up. He'd been looking at her, and then *past* her. She'd heard it, too, a snapping, popping, cracking sound. She remembered the look on his face, that look of horror, and then he'd thrown himself forward on top of her, covering her entire body with his, his arms cradled around her head.

She'd struggled violently, as she felt him shuddering, gasping, twitching, grunting.

She'd thought he was in the throes of orgasm, until she felt the liquid running down her body, down her face, her arms, her legs. And Talbott was unmoving. With one violent heave, she managed to roll him off her . . . and that was when she saw the blood, the glass . . .

Manny Frazer opened her eyes.

And the image looked back.

Unblinking, wide-eyed, dark-eyed, solemn, the woman regarded her impassively.

Manny looked at the face and recognized it. No, that wasn't true . . . she didn't recognize it: she *knew* it. Only the face was visible, the body was in shadow. She knew the face, the lines, the wrinkles around the eyes and lips, the curve of the nose, the point of the chin, the way the teeth indented the bottom lip, the weight of the hair on her head. She knew that face as well as she knew her own.

Manny was surprised that she felt no fear. But looking into those wide unblinking eyes, she knew that there was no evil in them. She reached out, touching the glass, tracing the lines of the woman's face. She wasn't beautiful, but that was part of her allure. She would have found it easier to believe that a beautiful creature was evil: surely something powerful would create for itself a beautiful image. Wasn't the devil supposed to be handsome?

But this woman, this image, was so ordinary, only the eyes, the extraordinary eyes, uptilted, wide, quizzical, lent it a mystery. And the hair. Yes, the hair was very beautiful: thick, dark, moving slightly in some unfelt breeze. Manny Frazer reached up and ran both hands through her own short hair, pulling her

292

fingers through its thickness.

Why had Talbott hated this woman so? Why had he wanted to cover the surface of the mirror with black paint?

Why did he fear her?

Because he could not possess me.

Manny looked into the glass, looking at the face, white against grey, the hair black and solid against the greyness. She felt no fear ... merely a sense of wonder, of curiosity. She looked deep into the mirror and spoke aloud, 'Why did Talbott fear you?'

Because he could not possess me.

'Who are you?'

The image closed her eyes, shaking her head slightly, almost sorrowfully.

'Can I help you?.'

Feed me . . . free me.

'How?'

But the image was fading, moving away from Manny, the hair swirling around its face as if blown from behind. She touched the glass, feeling a sting as something snapped from the mirror to her fingers, like static, but the image had vanished.

Manny crouched before the glass for the best part of an hour, staring at it, but no further images came. When she began to nod off, she came slowly to her feet and made her way back up to the house, careful to leave the stable door ajar, the way she had found it.

She would see the image again. She was sure of it.

Feed me . . . free me.

Hadn't Talbott said that the mirror fed on blood and emotion . . .?'

Feed me . . . free me.

She fell into bed, still wrapped in her dressing-gown, the words running around her head in a monotonous refrain.

Feed me . . . free me.

Chapter
FORTY-FIVE

. . . Fresh blood spilt directly onto the glass, what images would he see then, what visions?

When Jonathan Frazer woke, he knew exactly what to do.

Cold, detached, he stood in front of the full-length mirror watching her undress behind him. The moonlight streaming in through the skylights and the barred windows turned her hair silver and black, and washed the colour from her skin, leaving it alabaster, flawless. Her nipples were dark coins against her flesh, her groin in shadow.

Jonathan Frazer reached out and touched the glass, tracing his fingers over the reflection of her breasts. The surface of the mirror felt slick, greasy. He spread his hands on the glass, splaying his fingers, and for a single moment he imagined he felt the surface of the glass shift, soften, meld beneath his clammy palms. When he took his hand off the glass, he found no sweaty print on the surface.

The woman – he suddenly realized he had forgotten her name, but no matter, she was cattle – was standing naked with her hands on her hips, watching him, her whole stance suggestive, aggressive.

'What's wrong? Shy?'

'No . . . yes . . . I mean this is the first time . . .'

'Take your time. You're paying for it.' She wandered around the huge room, peering at the numerous antiques and artefacts that were clustered along the shelves, touching the faces of the broken clocks, the figurines with arms or legs or heads snapped off, an enormous glass jar filled with pennies, her fingers trailing along the surfaces, humming tunelessly to herself.

'You could do with a light in here,' she said suddenly, reaching for the light switch beside the door.

'DON'T. Don't,' he repeated more gently. 'I prefer the dark. It's much more romantic, don't you think?'

The woman looked at him, nodding slightly, a smile on her painted lips. She was twenty-two years old and had been on the streets since she was sixteen: she didn't know the meaning of the word romantic. She had also done it in some strange places, but never in what looked like a converted barn at the back of some posh house. It was filled with some of the most amazing rubbish she'd ever seen in her life; it looked almost like an antiques shop, except that everything was broken. She wasn't sure if he worked at the house she'd briefly glimpsed as they'd made their way in through the back gate, or if he owned it. But he acted like a married guy – you could always tell – and he was used to money, she was sure of that. He'd agreed to the fifty notes she'd asked without even blinking, even though it had been a slow night and she'd have agreed on thirty. He'd also agreed to an extra tenner for the inconvenience of taking her off her patch.

All in all, it was going to be a good night.

Frazer watched her in the mirror as he slowly undressed. The moonlight slid off her body, touching it with mystery, lending it a grace which she didn't possess, hiding the bruises along her upper arms, the puncture marks behind her knees. She was heavy breasted, no longer slender and even the make-up didn't disguise the haggard lines in her face. But Frazer wasn't interested in how she looked. He had deliberately chosen one of the more common-looking women in the bar, figuring that it might take a little longer for someone to come looking for her.

He knew what to do, he had done this before: picked the plain girls, the common women, the raddled, the drunken, the debauched, those who would not be missed, and even if they were, who would care for a shilling whore? He saw her stop before a sixteenth-century Venetian goblet, reach out and touch it with a tentative fingertip.

In the mirror the goblet moved.

Frazer spun around – the goblet was part of a pair and priceless – but the woman hadn't lifted the glass, merely touched it.

His heart began to trip.

She was here.

He swung back around to the mirror, staring hard at the vague reflection of the goblet in the glass. It *was* moving. As he watched, fingers – pale, golden, perfect fingers – appeared around the stem of the glass. The wrist and arm that flowed into the air were also flawless, so detailed he could see the tiny fuzz of hair on the arm. Shoulders, breasts . . . the image of the body flowing downwards, like frost on a windowpane. The long slender column of a neck . . . and then, finally, the head.

Vaguely transparent, black-eyed and raven-haired, the image raised her head and looked at him. Her long-nailed hand lifted the goblet in a parody of a toast, while her left hand moved lasciviously down the length of her body, caressing her heavy breasts, the palm of her hand moving across one nipple, and then continuing downwards, across her slightly rounded belly, into the coarse dark hair between her thighs.

Her mouth opened, strong yellow teeth against a glistening tongue. She was speaking to him, but he heard nothing, the only sound now the thundering of his heart, the harsh rasp of his breath.

The image lifted the goblet, mouthing the words slowly, 'Feed me.'

Ice cold hands wrapped around his body, folding on his stomach and he yelped with surprise.

'I should have guessed you'd be a watcher.' The woman – Susan . . . Suzee, that was it – rested her chin on his shoulder and stared into the mirror.

'What . . . what do you mean?' he whispered hoarsely.

'You've spent all your time looking into that old mirror. I bet you like to look at yourself. Watch yourself while you do it.' She indicated the shadowy room with a jerk of her head. 'You've got all these fancy antiques, I bet you've got some fancy antique clothes too. I'll bet you like to dress up in them and look at yourself in this old mirror.' She looked disdainfully at the plain ugly frame, the slightly warped, speckled glass.

Frazer said nothing. Standing directly before them, he could see the shimmering image, the goblet raised in its hands.

'Look, if this is going to be an all-nighter, we can negotiate a new price . . .'

'No.' Frazer spun the woman around so that she was facing the mirror, her arms limp by her sides. Standing behind her now, he moved his hands across her stomach up beneath her breasts.

'I knew you'd be a looker,' Suzee said, smiling tightly. He was a weird one all right, but harmless.

He pressed his cold lips to the back of her neck, slowly working around to the side of her throat. She tilted her head to one side, closing her eyes, leaning back into him. She could feel the dull pounding of his heart against her back. At least he was gentle . . . maybe she'd convince him to fork out for an all-nighter. She'd exhaust him in the first hour and then have a comfortable night's kip.

'Keep your eyes closed,' he murmured. His hands moved up onto her breasts, palms flat against her nipples.

Suzee began to relax. This guy was taking his time: she'd get an all-nighter out of him, maybe even breakfast too. Might even enjoy it.

His right hand moved away and she could feel him stretching out. Probably got one of those fancy sex-toys. Or an antique sex-toy; he was into antiques. And that meant he had money. Maybe if she was extra nice to him, he'd become a regular . . . maybe put her up in a little flat somewhere . . .

'Say mister,' she began, opening her eyes, 'how about . . .?'

The knife was eight inches of razor sharp steel, double-edged, needle-pointed. As Frazer's left arm locked around her body, holding her upright, the blade tore into the left side of her throat, and then ripped across. Hot dark blood gouted across the mirror, hissing on the greasy glass.

Suzee's scream died in a liquid gurgle. She scrabbled weakly for the blade, slicing through her fingers.

Frazer flung her up against the glass, pressing the side of her face against the mirror, pumping blood smearing down the length of the glass, dark and ugly, hissing loudly like water dropped onto a boiling hot surface.

And then it disappeared . . . absorbed into the oily surface of the mirror, vanishing without trace.

The woman abruptly stopped struggling, and the flow of blood pumping from the wound in her throat slackened. Frazer stepped away from the torn corpse, allowing it to slump to the ground. He pressed the palm of his hand into the single bloody stain that remained on the glass, and then lifted it away. There was a dried flaking brownish crust on his skin.

He was moving away from the mirror, the realization of what he had just done beginning to sink in when the image appeared.

The figure was close to the surface of the glass, arms and legs spread wide, displaying herself to him. He could just about make out his own reflection through the woman's glorious body. She pressed herself against the glass, her breasts flattening themselves against some unseen barrier.

Frazer reached for her, forefinger tracing the outline of her breasts through the glass, moving upwards along the line of her throat, touching her lips.

Her tongue darted out – and he felt it!

Like a cat's tongue, harsh and rasping, it sent an electric spark through his fingertips into his entire body. He spread his hand on the glass about her face, pressing hard into its surface. It felt soft, almost resilient, palpable . . . like flesh.

And then the woman began to lick his hand, tiny pointed tongue darting, flicking at his skin, arousing him almost unbearably. He lifted his hand, looking at it in wonder – the dried blood had vanished, the image had licked it off.

Jonathan Frazer stepped forward, over the body of the prostitute and pressed himself to the glass, willing himself through. The image mimicked him, moulding her body to his, her eyes wide with longing, mouth open, breasts heaving. His own orgasm took him suddenly, shuddering through him, exhausting in its intensity, his fluid splashing onto the glass . . . and was absorbed into the mirror.

*

Frazer awoke as the cold light of day unmercifully illuminated the room. He was stiff and shaking, his body wracked with shivering, and there was an iron bar deep in the pit of his stomach, bile in his mouth.

The woman's corpse was a grey and twisted thing curled around the base of the glass. There was surprisingly little blood, and it looked like nothing more than an empty sack. Disposing of it would not be a problem.

He came slowly to his feet and approached the ancient mirror, reaching out to run his fingers down the length of the glass. It looked brighter, cleaner this morning, his own reflection in it seemed crisper, sharper. Its surface still felt slick, slightly greasy, but most of the speckling had vanished.

Pressing both hands to the glass, he peered into it, attempting to see something – anything – out of the ordinary, but all he saw was the reflection of the cluttered stables.

No matter.

He had established contact – physical contact – with the woman in the mirror, the image. Blood had given her substance: he would give her enough blood to make her whole.

Chapter
FORTY-SIX

EMMANUELLE Frazer opened her eyes.

And knew immediately that something was wrong.

The room was dark, cold, the sheets covering her heavy body were coarse, rough, foul-smelling. She sat up with a strangled shout, the covering falling away from her body, revealing breasts that were heavy and painful, the nipples large and dark. There was movement beside her and in the wan dawn light she saw the old grey-haired, grey-bearded man roll over and look at her.

This was a dream.

This was a nightmare.

'Mistress?' he asked, his accent strange, guttural, rural.

She had seen this man before, in her dream, this man and the red-haired, red-bearded man.

'Mistress?' he asked again. 'Is it time?'

'Aye,' she murmured. 'Find Kelley.'

She could hear herself speak, the words pounding in her head. This was a dream. This was a nightmare. And she had no control over it.

The old man – his name was Dee, she realized – threw back the covers and hurried from the cold room,

301

a vaguely comical figure in his long soiled night-shirt. She swung her legs out of the bed more slowly, gripping the edge of the coarse, rustling mattress with one hand, her other hand resting on her swollen belly, wincing as the child kicked and kicked again.

Aaah, the agony of the past nine months, to feel her body change so, alter, her flesh becoming misshapen as the thing grew inside her like some foul parasite, robbing her of everything she possessed, her rather dubious beauty, her dignity and her ability to control men. Who would look at a pregnant women, an ugly deformed creature?

But it would be worth it – it had better be.

Kelley had sworn . . . and thus far he had delivered all of his promises.

And now the door was opening and the red-haired, red-bearded Irishman was in the room, his eyes aflame, a rare smile on his lips. 'It is time,' he hissed, 'I told you it would be tonight.'

He had; he had prepared a natal chart and had been able to predict the moment of the child's birth almost to the hour, but then he had even chosen the night for her to become impregnated by the old fool, Dee.

'Where's Dee?' she whispered.

He jerked his head upwards. 'Gone ahead to prepare the room. Can you walk, or will I carry you?'

'I can walk,' she hissed. She was not completely helpless. She wrapped a cloak around her nakedness and strode from the room with as much dignity as she could muster. However, halfway up the stairs to the tower room where the mirror was kept she had to stop as the birth pangs twisted her almost double and then Kelley had swept her up in his strong arms and carried her effortlessly up the rest of the way, murmuring softly to her, telling her that it would be soon now, so soon, and then they would have accomplished everything they had worked so hard for – absolute power for him, immortality for her.

And there was a price to be paid, but that was only right and proper: everything in this life had to be paid for. That was what had convinced her that Kelley's offer had been genuine in the first instance. If he had told her that he could make her immortal with no cost to herself, then she would have known that she was being used. She was earning that immortality now. She had earned it over the past nine months.

'The child is mine,' Kelley reminded her, his breath warm against her ear.

'You think I want it!' she asked indignantly. 'What about Dee?'

'Once the child has been given to the mirror, Dee will be ours, a puppet to be used and controlled to our will. There is nothing we will not be able to accomplish. Absolute power . . .'

'And immortality,' she added.

'Forever and ever . . .' he said and kicked open the door to the tower room. 'Is everything prepared?'

'All is in readiness,' Dee said eagerly.

A couch had been positioned directly facing the mirror, water bubbling in the great copper pots over the blazing fire, clean linen towels piled on the wooden table beside the couch.

Dee had wanted to bring in a midwife from the local village to assist with the birth, but Kelley had been against it: too many questions, too much gossip, he had argued. What would the villagers say if they heard that a child had been born in the topmost room of Dee's house, in front of a huge mirror, with Kelley in the background, chanting the proper incantations? Not even the Queen would be able to save him from the resultant scandal.

Kelley had midwived women before; he would do it.

The contractions were regular now, deep and

powerful, and she barely made it to the couch before the waters broke.

Manny Frazer opened her mouth and screamed.

She was the woman, seeing what she saw, feeling what she felt, aware of her thoughts.

And yet she was apart.

She felt she was hovering somewhere in the background, behind and to the woman's right, calmly looking on.

The dream and the nightmare inextricably entwined.

The room resembled a scene from hell. The only illumination came from the blazing fire, roaring up the chimney when Dee worked the bellows, casting wildly dancing shadows across the walls and the mirror. They hunched before the fire, Dee like some warped demon; Kelley, with his hair and beard metallic in the firelight, like an ancient idol.

The ripple that flowed down the glass was like oil on water, twisting, curling rainbowed, vaguely metallic colours.

And then the flickering began deep in the core of the glass, a twisting, shifting pulsing ball of light that throbbed in time to the woman's contractions.

On the couch facing the mirror, the woman screamed her agony. She was bathed in sweat, her skin a warm copper in the light, her sweat blood red, and when the blood came just before the birth of the babe it was black.

She saw a distorted reflection of herself in the glass. The warped glass had turned her flesh yellow, twisted her legs, turning them into something like an animal's, her full breasts looking flat and wasted, while her face was a parody of a skull. Only her hair was alive, coiling, twisting, turning, winding around her face with some bizarre life of its own.

The woman looked down through her spread legs at Kelley. Hunched before her, he watched her with an expression that was almost feral, eyes wide, lips parted. He was chanting solidly, lips barely moving, grunting a monotonous chant, calling, promising, promising, promising. He eagerly reached for the child's head when it appeared, his touch surprisingly gentle, pulling the head towards him, turning the body, drawing it out, and then finally – triumphantly – holding it up by its feet. It was a girl; but that was no surprise, they had known all along that it would be a girl. The child opened its mouth and wailed, the sound pitiful, like a seagull's mewling, the tiny noise almost lost in the room, swallowed up in the roar of the fire and Kelley's guttural chanting.

The images in the mirror went wild.

A face appeared, and then another and another and another. Countless faces, some no bigger than a fingernail, others the size of a palm, male and female, young and old, eyes wide, mouths open, silently crying, calling, shouting, screaming, pleading. When the child was finally birthed, sliding out into Kelley's bloodied hands, the mouths closed, the countless eyes fixed on the bloody bundle between the woman's legs.

Kelley lifted the child in his hands, still attached to the mother by the umbilical cord, and turned to face the mirror. The mouths and eyes opened again, and then began to dissolve, fading away, like melting ice or wind-blown dust until only one face remained, tiny and sexless, close to the centre of the mirror. It was a woman's face, and it was so perfect it looked almost like a mask, with its bronze-gold skin, jet black hair and huge green eyes. As it grew larger, seeming to approach the surface of the mirror, the rest of its perfect naked golden body appeared from a gritty milk-white background. When it was life-size, it reached for the squalling child with both hands, fingers long and slender, fingernails long and curved.

Kelley smiled at the golden image, lifting the child even higher.

Manny screamed when she saw him produce the knife.

Deftly, surprisingly neatly, he snipped the umbilical cord, spattering the mirror with blood. The image touched the score of tiny droplets on the glass, and they vanished, drying to a dry crust and flaking away as she brought her fingertip to her mouth.

The image reached for the child again, but Kelley shook his head . . .

'Later,' Manny saw him mouth.

. . . and her face twisted, turning ugly, beast-like for an instant, her hair raising up around her head. And abruptly she was gone.

Kelley turned away from the mirror and wrapped the child in a pure linen cloth, cleaning its face and eyes with the corner. He leaned over the woman. 'Your daughter, Mistress.'

The flesh was soft against her breast, the babe's mouth opening automatically, and she could actually feel the movement in her breasts before the milk came. She felt the child latch onto it, feeling the pulling and then the release that was almost orgasmic in its intensity.

'I don't want it,' the woman hissed.

'For appearance's sake,' Kelley murmured, eyes drifting up to where Dee had left the fire and was hurrying towards them. He straightened and smiled. 'You have a daughter, sir.'

Dee looked at his wife with the baby now sucking at her breast. He ran his fingers through his wife's thick sweat-damp hair and kissed her forehead. 'Our child,' he whispered. 'A child of the New Age.' When he looked up, his eyes were bright with unshed tears. 'A child of magic.'

Kelley nodded, face twisting into a parody of a smile, 'A magical child indeed.' He touched Dee's arm. 'Let us leave your wife to rest.'

As soon as the two men left the room, the image returned. The golden skinned, black haired woman pressed against the glass, staring hard at the sleeping woman and the child. The hunger in her eyes was almost tangible.

And then she looked *up* . . . behind and to the right of the sleeping woman. She looked at Emmanuelle Frazer. Her lips twisted in a wide smile. Her thick black hair suddenly battered itself against the glass, coils and strands striking and striking against the surface of the mirror. Her large green eyes caught and held Manny's, and she reeled back with the almost physical blow. The woman's mouth was working, mouthing words, and she was pointing to the child . . . and to the knife.

Manny shook her head violently. No.

The creature smiled and the planes of her face subtly altered. She was still golden and beautiful, but her burnished flesh was now dulled and tarnished, her eyes seemed to have sunk deeper into her face and her cheekbones looked sharper. She had been golden and innocent; now she was ancient and exuded a palpable aura of evil. Her mouth twisted and she spat at Manny, green slime dribbling down the surface glass.

But the woman was awake now, staring in horror at the figure in the glass. Instinctively, she clutched the babe to her bosom and screamed, the sound tearing from her throat. The image instinctively spat at her too, a gobbet of the green fluid passing through the surface of the glass, splattering onto her face, searing into the flesh to the right of her eye.

Manny screamed with the pain, the fire in her face.

Manny screamed with the pain, the fire in her face.

Manny rested her forehead against the cool glass of the bathroom mirror. She was bathed in sweat, her pyjamas sticking to her skin, and yet she felt cold, chilled through to the bone. She looked at her face again . . .

The skin from the corner of her right eye, almost

down to her jaw bone, was red and raw, leaking a pale watery pus.

Chapter
FORTY-SEVEN

THIS was only Toni's third night on the street and she was still terrified. Her two friends who also worked the streets told her that the first night was the hardest and then after that it got easier. But the second night hadn't been any easier and she was absolutely terrified with the prospect of another customer tonight.

Frankie, who lived in the flat further down the hall, told her that she should be able to get three or four punters a night, and at forty quid a go that would mean she was earning between a hundred and twenty and one hundred and sixty notes *per night*.

The first night she'd managed one guy. She'd been shaking, but he'd been so drunk he hadn't noticed. She'd been so sick, so ashamed afterwards that she gone right back to the flat and washed herself again and again, imagining she could still smell him – stale sweat and beer and sex – on her skin.

The next guy on the second night had been so nervous that she felt almost sorry for him, but again, she'd washed and washed herself, scrubbing away the smell, knowing she could never erase the memory.

She hated it, she'd never be able to get used to it, not

the way Frankie or Joy did. But she had to do it, she needed the money desperately.

It had started when she'd lost her job – and she'd been bloody lucky that they hadn't pressed charges, but she supposed it would have cost the shop more to bring her to court to sue her for stealing three tee-shirts. And it couldn't have happened at a worse time: she was four months pregnant and just beginning to show. Maybe that had been another reason the shop manager hadn't pressed charges but simply dismissed her on the spot without a reference. Without a reference she stood absolutely no chance of finding another job.

She'd borrowed some money just before the baby was born. None of the regular lending agencies would give it to her, and she ended up dealing with a 'private finance company'. Later, when it was too late, she realized they were quite simply loan sharks. When they'd asked her if she was working, she'd lied and said yes.

When they discovered that she couldn't pay back the loan, they'd become very upset. Now they had this guy coming around every day demanding the money, threatening her, and the last time she'd seen him deliberately looking at the baby as he told her that people who didn't pay him always had bad luck.

She'd spoken to Frankie, telling her the story, hoping – but not asking – that she might give her some money. She knew Frankie had plenty of cash; she had her hair done two or three times a week, and she always wore the latest fashions. Frankie hadn't been any help though, except to make the suggestion that she go on the streets.

Toni had immediately dismissed the idea out of hand, until Frankie had started to tell her how much money was to be made from it, and as long as you were careful and picked the johns and didn't go with any crazy looking guys, never got into a car with more than one person and avoided some of the sleazier pubs, you'd be all right. Oh, and you always made sure to take your pill and you didn't do it with guys who wouldn't wear a condom.

She owed three hundred pounds; it had started out at one hundred and fifty, but the interest mounted up rapidly. Frankie had pointed out to her that three nights on the street at three clients a night would take care of her problem and leave some money left over to buy herself or baby Stephanie a present. And you never know, maybe she'd end up liking it, and be able to earn herself a few bob every week; Frankie knew women who only did it at weekends or mid-week, just for a night or two, earned themselves enough money to carry them through to the next week. And yes, some of the husbands knew about it: but if you were on the dole with a couple of kids to bring up and a mortgage to pay and the bills just mounting up, what other way was there to earn money . . . except maybe go out and rob a bank.

Toni knew she'd never like this. She enjoyed sex, but only with someone she loved, or at least thought she loved. But there was nothing pleasurable in this. This was a necessity.

She hadn't even dressed 'whorishly' and yet she felt as if everyone knew what she did, and everyone was looking at her. She'd come into the bar tonight with Frankie and though she'd been here nearly two hours – and Frankie had been in and out with two different guys, and she charged fifty quid – so far no one had shown the slightest bit of interest in her. Maybe she looked just too respectable.

Frazer looked at her closely. He'd noticed her the moment he'd stepped into the bar, a slim, dark-haired, pale-skinned young woman, nineteen, maybe twenty.

He'd watched a tall coffee-coloured woman appear and chat to her for a few moments on two occasions before disappearing with two different men. He knew what *she* was, but the younger woman . . . He closed his eyes, squeezing them tightly shut, attempting without success, to call up the figure of the image. He looked at the woman through slitted eyes.

Did it matter what she was? She was cattle. Flesh and muscle and bone . . . and blood. Especially the blood. She was an animal to be butchered and sacrificed to the image.

He leaned back against the wall, his left arm extended, feeling the pressure of the knife against his forearm. It was a risk wearing it, of course, in case he was picked up by the police, but it gave him such a feeling of power, of control, of authority.

Jonathan Frazer sat forward, and stared into his glass of Coke. Reflected in the dark surface, he saw his own haunted expression, his deep sunk eyes, the lengthening stubble on his chin, the new lines around his eyes.

The image looked at him.

Startled he looked up.

And saw the beasts.

The people were still there, but surrounded now by thin glowing ovals of light. As they moved, the ovals shifted, moving with them, sometimes hardening to a reflective surface, then dissipating to reveal, not the person beneath, but the flickering image of an animal, a fleshy beast with the attributes of a human, a man with the face of a swine, a woman with the huge eyes of a cow, a small man with the feral features of a rat. The shimmering ovals were wan pinks and delicate greens, pale blues, insipid yellows . . . except one. The woman at the bar was bathed in a warm blood-red light that was so intense he could barely make out her features beneath it.

Jonathan Frazer was on his feet before he was even conscious that he was moving. The beasts parted before him.

Toni watched the guy move through the crowd and knew instinctively that he was making his way towards her. Tall, thin, with a three-day growth of beard on his face, there was directness about his gaze that she found disconcerting. His clothes were good quality, but looking a little crumpled now, as if he had slept in them.

Watch out for the crazies, Frankie had warned her.

He stopped in front of her, saying nothing, simply staring at her. She attempted a smile but found she couldn't meet his eyes.

'You shouldn't be here,' he said hoarsely. 'A girl like you is too pretty, too good to be doing this.'

Surprised, she looked up, staring into his eyes. She thought she saw genuine pity there. But Frankie had also warned her about this type, too, the type who wanted to save her from herself.

'You're new,' the man moved in beside her, and she caught a faintly musty, damp smell from his clothing. 'Let me guess: a husband unemployed, the rent due, bills to be met or maybe you've lost your job?'

Toni nodded. Was he a pimp . . . a social worker . . . police maybe?

He shook his head, drawing his fingers through thin black hair that needed a wash, pulling it back off his face. 'It doesn't matter, does it? What matters is that you've been forced into doing this.'

'Are you going to tell me there's another way?' she asked boldly.

'No,' he shook his head, surprising her. She expected him to give her an answer; everyone had an answer to her problem. 'If you see this as the solution to your problem, then so it is.'

'I owe money you see,' she said suddenly, surprising herself. 'Three hundred pounds to a money lender. He's grown threatening. I think he's going to hurt my baby if I don't give him the money.'

'How much do you charge?' the man asked gently. Now the shadows beneath his eyes lent them compassion.

'Forty.'

'How long have you been doing this?'

'This is my third night.'

'And how much have you earned so far?'

'Eighty,' she whispered.

'Come with me then, and I'll pay you two hundred and twenty pounds on one condition . . .'

'What's that?' she asked fearfully, expecting to discover that he wanted her to do something kinky.

'That you ask me no questions . . . and you never go back on the street again.'

She had no trouble agreeing to those conditions.

Now, she wasn't quite so sure.

She had been reluctant to bring him back to the flat; there was only one room and the baby slept in the cot in the corner, and when he suggested his place she had immediately agreed. When she asked where his place was, he said Kensington. She'd immediately thought he owned a place in Kensington, but as he moved down the back lanes behind the tall, elegant houses she realized he only worked there. Maybe he was a butler or a gardener or something. Gardener, she realized, when he led her through a fancy gate into a high-walled garden. There was a long low building running along the length of one wall and he made his way along a paved path and pulled out a key. She heard him muttering when he discovered that the door was already open.

'Do you work here . . . is it OK for you to be here?'

The last thing she needed to happen was to be done for trespassing or breaking and entering.

He looked back over his shoulder at her. 'The house is empty; everyone is away. I'm . . . I'm looking after things. I work here,' he added as an afterthought.

Toni followed the man into the dark interior of the long shed, wrinkling her nose at the dry, musty smell . . . similar to the smell that clung to his clothes. A hand – dry and cold – reached out of the darkness and found hers, pulling her into the building. 'The fuse box has gone, and I'm not sure how to fix it,' he murmured, his voice little more than a whisper. There were objects piled high all around, but with an almost uncanny knack, he led her deep into the pitch-dark room without bumping into anything. As her eyes adjusted to the dimness, she could make out the vague squares of the windows and similarly lighted rectangles high in the ceiling. The man – she realized he hadn't given her a name and hadn't asked for hers in return – dropped her hand and moments later she heard the rasp of a match being drawn across sandpaper and a tiny yellow light flared. He put the flame to a tall white candle, creating a warm circle of yellowish light.

There was an enormous mirror in front of the candle that helped reflect the light. She looked into it. The glass was old and warped: she imagined she could see shapes twisting in the darkness behind her. And then she jumped, her hand flying to her throat as a pale face materialized out of the shadows behind her right shoulder. The dancing candle-light lent him a ghastly expression, the shadows under his eyes and the stubble on his cheeks endowing his face with a skull-like appearance. He moved around in front of her and handed her a thick wad of ten pound notes.

'You can count it; there's thirty there. The extra's a bonus . . . buy something for your child with it.'

Toni put the money into her bag without counting it. 'I think I can trust you,' she said, smiling.

'I think you can,' he agreed, his lips drawing back from his teeth in an imitation of a smile.

Without another word, Toni began to undress.

Skinny, Frazer thought, flat-chested, narrow-hipped, her stomach still carrying the weight of the child. He watched her undress without the slightest flicker of emotion and when she was naked he came around behind her and stood with his hands on her shoulders staring into the glass.

'What do you see?' he asked curiously, wondering if she saw the woman standing *behind* him.

'You . . . me . . .' the young woman smiled.

He urged her forward with his hand in the small of her back. Her flesh felt cold, clammy. When she was close to the glass, he reached out and touched it, his fingers pointing to the darkness beyond her shoulders.

'What do you see?' he asked again.

'Shadows,' she whispered. Her skin began to ripple with goose flesh. Frankie had warned her about these guys, the crazies. Humour them, her friend had said, humour them and when you get your opportunity, run like hell.

'What do you see?' she asked hoarsely.

'Shadows,' he said with a smile. He moved around behind her until he was almost completely obscured by her body. With both hands he drew her hair back off her shoulders. 'I thought candle-light would be more romantic, don't you?'

'Yes,' she whispered.

'Do you know there is an old wives' tale that if you stand a lighted candle before a mirror, you will see the face of your lover behind your left shoulder?' His face suddenly appeared over her left shoulder.

316

'Does this mean you're going to be my lover?' she asked coquettishly.

'Absolutely,' Frazer whispered, his hands at her hair again, then moving down to her throat, across her breasts, onto her slightly rounded stomach. The woman closed her eyes and rested her head back on his left shoulder.

Frazer drew the knife out of his left sleeve. It was a twelve-inch mid-nineteenth-century Japanese Tanto. Designed for piercing lacquered armour, it slid effortlessly into the woman's flesh just about her groin. He felt the tremor run up her body and the fingers of his left hand locked around her throat as he savagely ripped upwards, eviscerating her, flooding the mirror with gore. He pressed the widely spasming body against the glass with the weight of his own body, eyes and mouth wide with savage glee. This shouldn't be some nameless whore, it should be his slut of a wife. She was no better than them. They did it because they had to; she did it because she enjoyed the rutting. She was a beast, cattle. She should be in his arms now, with the knife buried between her breasts, her body cut open, slaughtered like the beast that she was. He threw back his head and screamed her name aloud, 'Ceciliaaaaaaaaaaaaa . . .'

She awoke in absolute agony.

She opened her mouth to scream, but it was as if an iron band were locked around her throat. The pain in her stomach was incredible. The pain intense, just above her groin.

It was an appendix . . . no, it couldn't be, she'd had it out.

An ulcer, a burst ulcer, a bleeding ulcer.

She'd made love with Colin earlier that evening. They'd ended up on the floor with him pounding away as they both screamed and grunted their way to orgasm. Maybe he'd damaged her, ruptured something . . .

Cecilia Frazer threw back the bedclothes and desperately attempted to raise her head to look at her stomach, every movement an agonizing effort. She was bathed with sweat, her hair sticking to her head. She managed to raise her head a couple of inches so that she could look at her reflection in the mirror of the dressing table directly opposite the bed.

She could see nothing . . .

She could see a thin red line on her flesh!

The pain was a live thing now, boiling inside her, ripping up through her body, pure and absolute agony. Her head dropped back to the pillow, eyes squeezed tightly shut, tears squeezing from beneath the tightly closed lashes and then with a monumental effort she managed to lift her head the few inches to look into the glass again.

Her flesh was parting, the skin folding back, almost neatly, to reveal the raw muscle beneath, and then that too was parting to show glistening organs.

With a sudden wrench, her entire stomach was sliced apart, lengths of intestines coiling onto her skin, curling onto the bedclothes. Blood and thick gobbets of flesh spattered everywhere, the walls, the ceiling, the mirror.

The pain took her, wave after wave washing over her body, in surges of ever-increasing intensity, finally concentrating on the spot between her breasts. The pain took her and finally claimed her as she heard something bestial howl her name in the distance.

Jonathan Frazer knelt on the floor of the stables in the blood and tattered flesh of the woman and pressed himself against the glass, staring intently into it. He could see the image of Cecilia Frazer lying naked on a bed, arms and legs splayed.

318

She had been torn apart from groin to breast.

Colin Marriner awoke with the dawn as usual. His dreams had been particularly vivid and he was aroused. He rolled over, his arm going across Cecilia Frazer's breasts.

And then he sat bolt upright recoiling from the chill of her flesh.

Her eyes were wide open and her skin was clammy. He pressed his hand beneath her breast. There was no pulse.

He closed her eyes sadly. He was going to miss her; she'd been fun and he had genuinely liked her. But at least she'd died peacefully in her sleep. That was the way he wanted to go.

Chapter
FORTY-EIGHT

AN ecstatic shiver rippled through the enormous whirlpool, vibrating deep in its core. The pulse throbbed throughout the Otherworld, bringing dreamers all across the city abruptly awake, shivering from their nightmares; children awoke crying at shadows, and one by one, the dogs of London began to howl . . .

Joe Gerritty came awake with a start from a startlingly vivid, erotic dream. He rolled over in the bed and turned the digital alarm clock on the bedside table: the glowing green letters read 2:21.

Jesus Christ! But if he'd told those people once, he'd told them a hundred times that their fucking mutt kept him awake howling outside his window. And he'd just done thirty-six hours straight because two of the other orderlies were sick and they were already short staffed with the health service cut-backs.

When he worked days the dog kept him awake at night.

When he worked nights their kids kept him awake during the day.

Well right now he'd just about had enough.

The big man staggered out of bed and pulled on a pair of ratty jeans over his pyjamas. He hauled on a polo neck jumper and slid his feet into ancient carpet slippers before stamping downstairs and into the kitchen. Pulling back the curtains he peered out into the high-walled backyard. The fucking dog was running around in a cirle in *his* yard – wouldn't do it in its own yard, oh no – howling its head off.

Gerritty wrenched the back door open and pitched an empty tin can at the animal. It missed and clattered off into the darkness, but the sudden sound made the animal stop and it turned to face the big man, a growl beginning deep in its body. The dog was a nondescript mongrel, but big and wiry with a mangy black coat that left hairs everywhere. Gerritty reached for another can and tossed it at the dog. This one struck it squarely on the nose.

Without a sound, the animal leapt for the hospital orderly. He saw it coming and slammed the door in its face, seeing his own reflection in the glass . . . but the animal kept coming, exploding inwards through the glass, its teeth finding and locking on his throat even as the shards of flying glass ripped into the big man's face, destroying his eyes, disembowelling the dog.

Kenneth Pearson awoke with a pounding in his head that was positively frightening. He sat up in bed, holding his head in both hands, imagining he could actually feel it throb.

OK. So he couldn't drink . . . what was it, how much . . . eight pints . . . why, that was a gallon of cider. So maybe eight pints had been one too many . . . or seven too many.

Thanks be to God his parents were asleep when he got in; they would have been less impressed. Drinking cider was something yobs did, not nice middle-class kids, from middle-class suburbia. Mind you, at the time he could see the attraction of it, and he especially remembered the attractions of that girl . . . what was her name?

He shook his head savagely . . . and then wished he hadn't. The pain in his head was excruciating and he needed to puke. Christ, his parents were sure to hear him throwing up. He'd have to use the downstairs loo.

The young man staggered out of bed, and discovered that he was still dressed, but his brand new Levi jeans were stained and the heavy black leather motor-cycle jacket hanging on the end of the bed had a long strip hanging off it.

With his stomach roiling, he hurried down the stairs and ducked into the toilet in the narrow corridor between the kitchen and the stairs. Leaning straight-armed against the sink, he stared into the mirror, squinting against the pain in his head. He felt he was going to die. He squeezed his eyes shut, feeling beads of sweat begin to pop out on his head. He rested his head against the cool glass. Why had he ever agreed to go out with the rest of them? It wasn't as if he even liked cider . . . it wasn't as if he even liked alcohol; Coke was his drink.

The pain had assumed a regular throbbing, which abruptly intensified to absolute agony. Kenneth Pearson's head automatically snapped back and then shot forward, smashing into the glass. The throbbing flowed away with the sharp, liquid pain. He continued to pound his face into the shattered glass, until there was no more sensation . . .

Sara Tynan was not exactly drunk; she'd only had two, or was it three, glasses of wine. She was mellow, she was relaxed, and humming gently along to one of the golden oldies on the late night show. She half remembered the original appearance of the song but that was no indication of her age. Songs that were only a year old were turning up as golden oldies or classics nowadays. They had a short shelf life.

The lights turned red and she slowed the Fiesta, allowing it to roll to a stop. The doors were all locked, but she kept the car in gear and her foot on the accelerator. She'd heard of lone women being attacked in their cars while they sat at traffic lights, and while this was not one of the seedier parts of the city she was still taking no chances.

Anyway, the traffic lights really should be turned off like they were on the Continent.

The lights changed. She was already moving as she glanced in her rear-view mirror . . .

Something in the back of her car was looking at her, large black eyes regarding her expressionlessly. The scream caught in her throat, became a whimper. She tried to look away but found she couldn't. She tried to stop the car but couldn't. Her foot was stuck to the accelerator, pressing it deep to the floor, the engine howling in first gear.

The eyes crinkled as if someone was smiling.

And the spell was broken.

Sara Tynan managed to scream once, as her headlights illuminated the massive plate glass windows of the electrical goods showrooms, hidden behind a metal grille. The car hit the grille, ripping most of it out of its frame, bringing it down around the car, entangling it as it continued on into the shop front, televisions, videos, cameras, and computers, most of which were still plugged in, exploding into showering sparks and acrid smoke.

Several hours later, when the car was cut free by the fire service, it was discovered that the falling metal grille had sheered through the windscreen of the car, completely severing the woman's head.

It took no more than a heartbeat to regain control. But

that had been enough. The overload had shivered out across the Otherworld, upsetting the delicate balance between the two planes of existence.

Little damage had been done, and it had drawn some sustenance from the deaths.

But it would have to be very careful now. Very careful. This was the critical time. Freedom had never been so close. Never had it been so vulnerable.

Chapter
FORTY-NINE

IT had been a shitty day. Every so often you got them when one thing just piled on top of the other. By noon, she knew from experience that she might as well go home for all the work she was going to get done.

Margaret Haaren sat on the edge of the bath, pouring bath salts into the swirling water. She only stopped when the water began foaming up spectacularly. She realized then that she'd emptied half a jar of crystals into the bath when usually a capful would do. She was tired, dead tired, physically as well as mentally, with an ache that went deep to her bones.

There was a gentle rap on the bathroom door and Helen, her niece, popped her head around the door. There was a large mug of tea in her hand. 'Thought you might need this. You look shagged.'

'I am. Thanks love. I know this hasn't really been much of a holiday for you . . .' she began.

'Look, don't worry about it. When you're not here, I simply *have* to go shopping and go out and enjoy myself,' she smiled widely.

'I was going to take you to the museums, the galleries, but it's just been crazy the past couple of weeks . . .'

The teenager ran her fingers through strands of her blonde hair, pulling it back off her face. 'Well, you know, it is such a chore having to wander around London,' she smiled wickedly, 'but I suppose I could find it in my heart to forgive you. Look,' she added seriously, 'I know what it's like; so, don't worry about it. There's a copper or two in my family too. Now, go on, have your bath, relax. I'll see what I can do about making dinner.'

'That would be lovely.'

'Be a miracle, too,' Helen muttered.

The water was as hot as she could bear and she almost had to force herself beneath the bubbles covering the surface. Tiny beads of sweat gathered on her forehead and ran down the sides of her nose. Once she was beneath the surface of the water, with only her head showing, the water lapping at her chin, the trick was not to move, because that agitated the water and the hot water stung. Closing her eyes, resting her head against the bath, she deliberately reviewed the day's events before pushing them aside, dismissing them until she returned to the office in the morning.

Jonathan Frazer's wife Cecilia had turned up dead for starters.

Died in her sleep in the arms of her boyfriend . . . what a way to go! That had been fine, people died in their sleep every day . . . until the emergency autopsy she'd requested – and the Scots were very efficient about such things – had revealed that just about every internal organ in the woman's body had ruptured and that her intestines were in pieces – literally!

She'd spoken to the doctor who'd performed the autopsy and in a light West Highland burr he'd told her that in thirty years of practice he'd never seen anything like it: 'it's as if the woman was cut open . . . except that the dermis is still intact!'

That in itself had been weird enough, until the body

of a young woman had been pulled up out of the river. The one whose belly had been sliced open! The one whose wounds matched Cecilia Frazer's!

That's when it got downright scary.

The body had been identified as that of a Toni Kane, a young unmarried mother who'd found herself in financial straits and had gone on the game to make cash. Her friend, who was also on the streets, told them that this had been her third night out.

Third time unlucky.

Added to that, a second body had been fished out of the Thames by the River Police. Although lots of the extremities had gone – fingers, toes – the face was still reasonably intact and one of the lads who worked vice had identified the body as that of Susan – Suzee – Burton, who'd been on the game since she'd been a kid. She'd had her throat sliced open.

Other than the fact that both had been killed with a knife and both worked on the streets there was no obvious connection. But when both bodies came from the river, there was a very good possibility that you had yourself a killer with a pattern: knife, prostitutes, river.

And then there was the bizarre connection with Cecilia Frazer . . .

Which reminded her that she had better go and tell the Frazer girl in the morning.

Where was Jonathan Frazer? He was still at large. She wondered how did he fit into all of this . . . because he was connected. She was convinced of that.

Why hadn't she come?

He'd fed the mirror with blood, why hadn't the image come?

The answer came slowly . . . because he'd used up the energy, the power in the blood, to strike at Cecilia.

Yesyesyesyesyes.

The power – the energy – was in the blood.

The blood had called the image the first time, given her substance as well as sustenance. The second time the blood had – what? – given his thoughts substance.

What was it Talbott had said, '*Once it is fed its powers are limitless.*'

Jonathan Frazer prowled around the mirror, approaching it, then standing back, almost teasing himself with its proximity and his knowledge that he could bring it to life, that he could call forth the image. That he could make it do his will.

All he needed was blood. And this world was full of cattle.

But not ordinary blood. Not tainted blood. He needed fresh blood, pure blood . . . virginal blood.

The thought stopped him cold. He stood in front of the mirror, nervously running both hands through his lank hair, pulling it back off his face and then twining his fingers together around the back of his head.

Yes, fresh blood, pure blood, virginal blood. Surely the power of the mirror was proportional to the purity of the blood?

Jonathan Frazer looked up, tongue licking dry lips, eyes narrowing as a smile twisted his lips.

He'd been a fool!

Hadn't Talbott told him everything he needed to know!

The mirror needed a male and a female. The male to feed the mirror, the female to provide the blood. And hadn't the mirror already put its mark on Manny, hadn't it saved her from Talbott; hadn't Talbott told him that she would be different?

She was the chosen one.

Moving unhurriedly, Jonathan Frazer lifted the Tanto and wiped the blade in his sleeve. Flakes of dried blood and a darker, harder substance fell away. He didn't think he'd need the knife, but there was no harm in being prepared anyway.

He slipped out of the stable door and moved silently along the path that led up to the house. There was a light on in the kitchen and he could see Manny moving around the room, wearing a heavy towelling dressing-gown. He parted some leaves, peering closely at his daughter. How long ago had it been since he'd last seen her – a day, two days, three days? – but in that time her hair had grown dramatically.

A broad smile creased his lips. The image's hair was long. Now, it was creating her in its own image.

The pain in her face had abated around noon and the red swelling and burn-like mark had gradually faded as the afternoon had worn on. The dream was still vivid though, especially the image of the golden woman or creature, or whatever it had been.

And the baby.

She rubbed her breasts. They felt tender, heavy and the flesh around the nipples particularly was darker, oozing a thin colourless liquid.

What was that term . . . psychosomatic? Like when you imagined yourself to be pregnant and your body began to change as if you were – a phantom pregnancy. But could a dream, even such a particularly vivid one such as she'd had, bring on this change in her breasts and leave the red burn mark on her face?

What if it wasn't a dream?

Manny Frazer carried the kettle to the sink and stared out of the window into the garden as it filled. The evening light was grainy and already you could see where the year had turned and the days were drawing in.

What if it wasn't a dream?

The first time she had seen a face in the mirror it had been that of the woman who was to become Dee's wife. Yet, if she was to accept the evidence of her dream, there had been a woman who had appeared to *her*. Had Dee's wife somehow replaced the previous image? She shook her head. Maybe Talbott would have been able to explain it to her. The little he had told her just wasn't enough. He'd said that the mirror was evil and that it possessed people . . . like her father, like herself. Was she possessed? She didn't feel possessed, but then if you were possessed, would you necessarily know it, or would everything just seem normal?

Certainly what she'd done with Talbott that night hadn't been normal . . . something had definitely been controlling her that time. She shivered, and then yelped as cold water poured over her hands.

Maybe she needed a little holiday. She'd try and contact her mother in the morning. Go and spend a few days with her.

And then she screamed.

A face had appeared at the window.

The kettle crashed onto the tiled floor, spilling water everywhere as Manny just stood there, frozen with horror.

When she looked again, the face was gone, leaving her an impression of wild hair, round eyes, and a fixed, maniacal grin.

The kitchen door swung silently inwards and the figure stepped into the room, a sour, damp odour preceding it. She squeezed her eyes shut and opened her mouth to scream. 'Hello Manny,' Jonathan Frazer whispered.

'Dad . . .' Manny's eyes blinked open. 'Dad?' she said again, looking at the man who bore only the vaguest resemblance to her father. 'Oh Dad.' She ran over and wrapped her arms around him, wrinkling her nose at the smell. 'Dad, what happened? Where did you go? I've been worried sick.'

Jonathan Frazer pressed grimy fingers to his daughter's lips, quietening her. 'No time for questions. Come on, we've something to do.'

'What? What have we got to do, Dad?' Manny asked in alarm. Her father's hands were busy with her hair which had started to grow at an alarming rate. Some sort of hormonal change, she realized suddenly, and that would certainly account for the changes in her body, the marks on her face! She twitched her head back away from her father's hands. 'Dad, are you OK?'

He nodded vigorously. 'I'm fine, I've never been better.'

'Do you want something to eat? You look tired.' There was something desperately wrong with her father.

'I'm not hungry. I'm not tired.' He reached for her hand. 'Come on, we've got to . . .' he stopped and smiled secretively. 'Well, I think you know what we've got to do, don't you?'

'No, Dad,' Manny whispered, 'why don't you tell me?'

'Come on, come on.' His hand found hers and he pulled her out through the open kitchen door and down the path towards the stables. 'I suppose I haven't really been thinking you see. Talbott told me that there would be changes, little things out of the ordinary . . .' His hand went to her hair again, 'But I suppose I've just been too busy to notice. And of course I should have realized that there would be two . . . male and female. He created them in his own image, the yin and the yang, the two making a whole . . .' He was babbling now, making no sense.

'Dad, Dad,' Manny whispered, feeling the tears start to her eyes, the burning in her throat. 'Come on, you need a rest, a break, you've been working far too hard. I was thinking of heading up to Scotland to where mother's staying . . .'

His harsh laugh broke the evening stillness. 'Don't bother. Your mother's dead.'

Her voice was a hoarse angry rasp. 'Dad? What are you saying?'

He glanced sidelong at her and Manny suddenly realized that she was looking at a stranger. 'She's dead.' Jonathan Frazer's smile became a leer. The knife suddenly appeared in his right hand. 'I cut her from crotch to sternum. The bitch was rutting with some punk. Serve her right. Fuck her!'

Manny pulled her hand free and took three steps backwards. 'You're not my father,' she accused. 'My father would never say such things. What's happened to you?'

'Oh I am your father.' He moved the knife through the air. 'Now, be a good little girl and come on . . .'

'I'm not going anywhere until you tell me what's going on.' She took another step backwards.

He shook his head in exasperation. 'We need to feed the image.' He lifted his head, sniffing the air. 'She hungers. I can feel her hunger.' He turned to look at her, his eyes like coins. 'We need to feed her your blood. Only your blood can make her whole.'

Manny Frazer turned and ran.

She lost her slippers almost immediately, and then ran on the gravel, the stones cutting her feet. She cut across to the grass, feeling it wet with dew, slippery beneath her bare feet. She cast a quick glance over her shoulder . . . and her heart almost stopped with fright.

Her father was loping after her, bent almost double, gleaming knife clutched in one hand. There was a wide grin fixed to his lips, showing most of his teeth, and she could see saliva dribbling down his chin.

Manny raced into the bushes. They caught and snagged her dressing-gown, slowing her down, eventually completely entangling her. Her struggles only enwrapped her further in the branches. Finally, she wriggled free, the branches tearing at her skin and raced for the house, her naked flesh goose-pimpling.

She heard her father crash into the bushes, and then there was the definite rip of cloth.

Up the steps, across the patio, footsteps pounding on the grass behind her, now pattering on the stone flags, through the kitchen door, slamming it behind her, turning the key, realizing that the madman was not going to stop, racing out through the kitchen door as he came through the glass door in a cascade of glass and wood, out onto the slippery hall, falling, scrambling to her feet, fumbling with the locks on the front door, hearing the kitchen door snap open, someone stumbling on the hall floor, and now down the gravelled drive, screaming, screaming, screaming, footsteps crunching on the gravel behind her, a harsh voice panting, cursing, and now out onto the cul-de-sac and the white lights close, too close, a scream of rubber echoing her own scream.

And the pain.

And silence. Blessed silence.

Chapter FIFTY

AND silence. Blessed silence.

The screaming had finally stopped and the silence brought her from her sleep. She'd dreamt of a grey landscape and a whirlpool of faces, of mouths opening and closing, their howling like that of the wind through stone, relentless, incessant.

And then silence.

When she awoke Kelley was bending over her, a large hand pressed to her mouth, a forefinger pressed to his lips. His bright green eyes were dancing in the light from the fire which had been built up to keep the winter chill away.

'It's time,' he murmured, his Irish accent pronounced now, betraying his nervousness.

'Dee?' she murmured.

Kelley grinned. 'Asleep, a little tincture in his ale to ensure he remains that way for a while.'

The woman came up out of the bed, only the heaviness in her breasts betraying the fact that she'd given birth in the past three months.

Kelley caught her up in his arms, pressed her naked body against his. 'Tonight, I will make you immortal,' he whispered. He released her and she went to the cot and lifted out the sleeping form of her daughter, Madimi. She looked at it without interest: the child had been necessary for the completion of tonight's exercise. Nothing more. She felt nothing for it; she had deliberately prevented herself from developing feelings for it.

Even though the fire had been kept lit in the tower room, it was still cold, the chill radiating from the stones, emanating from the mirror. She hung back, loath to approach the slab of glass, touching her face where the *thing* had spat at her the night the child was born . . . or had that been a dream? Certainly her face had borne the red burn mark the following morning.

She had described the creature, the golden woman, she had briefly glimpsed in the glass, but Kelley had dismissed her fears; he knew the history and lore surrounding the glass – after all, his family had been its guardians down through the ages – and he had never heard of anything like that in the mirror. He reminded her that she had just given birth to a child and that the body's humours needed time to settle and, added to that, she had just consumed a glass of brandy which had been laced with a soporific . . . so that it was only natural that she should see something. His words held a ring of truth in them and he dismissed the mark on her face as nothing more than the blood, which had been excited and agitated by the birth settling close to the skin. It had faded before the day was out as he promised, and she had eventually forgotten about it.

Until now.

She looked at the mirror again, and abruptly found she could remember the creature in the glass in perfect detail. She looked at Kelley again, but he was moving around the mirror, preparing for the ceremony that would give him ultimate power and give her life eternal. He felt her scrutiny and glanced back over his shoulder, brows creased in concentration.

'Second thoughts?'

'None.'

'You know what has to be done?'

'Yes.'

'You will have to be strong.' He turned away and picked up the deep copper bowl, in which was lying a long razor-edged sliver of flint, one end of which had been wrapped in thread which had been coated with tar to form a handle.

'Will there be pain?'

'An instant. Nothing more. Followed by an eternity of bliss.' He turned back to the mirror. A deep purplish pulse had already begun deep in the core of the glass. 'You see, it knows, it senses our presence. Come, come, bring the child. It is nearly time.'

There was an astrological chart spread out on the floor, its edges held down by small copper pots. It had been carefully calculated, and the interconnecting circles with their lines of relevance and reference bisecting them into neat arcs had led him to the inescapable conclusion that tonight was propitious. Kelley had been working towards this moment for so long now . . . for most of his adult life, in fact.

And now only seconds separated him from power, incredible occult and magical power.

Edward Kelley stepped back from the mirror and began to strip off his clothing: this ceremony must be performed unclothed, to allow the body's aura to be washed in the mirror's energies.

When he was naked, he took the flint knife and scored the palms of both hands in two long crosses, hissing slightly with the pain. Placing the knife back in the copper bowl, he pressed his bloody palms against the glass.

The rippling in the mirror warped and abruptly coalesced into a series of twisting colours, vibrant, vital. There were hints of faces, features, eyes, mouths.

Kelley stepped back from the glass, the two bloody crosses on the surface fading, drying to a brownish flake. The woman had come up behind him, placing both hands on his shoulders, her breasts brushing his bare back, her nipples hard against his skin.

'It's coming,' he whispered. 'Get the sacrifice.'

The woman turned away and lifted the child from its swaddling clothes, dropping them to the floor. She walked around in front of Kelley, holding the still sleeping child in both hands, offering it to the glass.

The multitude of features on the glass had begun to coalesce, to form hideous masks, with multiple eyes, numerous mouths, teeth, ears.

She continued to hold the child as Kelley came around and crouched before her, sitting cross-legged on the ground. He placed the copper bowl directly before him and placed the flint knife carefully on the ground to the right of the bowl.

The woman handed the babe down to him. When he placed it in the bowl, the coldness of the metal brought the girl wide awake. Bright blue eyes regarded Kelley expressionlessly. Kelley lifted the stone knife. This was the ultimate sacrifice, an unbaptized virginal female, and while it would have been preferable to find a pubescent virgin on the verge of menses, where the energies of woman and girl were still in flux and all the more powerful because of that, the sacrifice of the baby was the next best thing.

With his eyes fixed on the centre of the mirror, Kelley called the image forth. He lifted the knife and placed it against the child's throat.

And pressed.

The mirror came to a blazing, vivid life.

They were the daughters of Phorkys, the third son of Pontos.

Theirs was a terrible power, theirs was an elemental

337

strength. With no conception of time, they had ruled this world before the creature known as man had crawled down from the trees. They had watched it shed its hair, watched it walk upright. They had been old when the first villages had been built, ancient when the first of what the man-kind would call civilization had taken its first faltering steps.

The soft-skinned ones knew of them and the rest of their kind that the humans called gods, and they offered sacrifice to the Triad as was their due. It amused the daughters of Phorkys to allow the human-kind to hunt for them, to feed and honour them.

Until the human-kind grew envious of their powers. They turned away from the old gods and began to worship gods created in their own image. And the Ancient Ones, who had come to depend on the human-kind for sacrifice and worship, and who fed off the petty fire of human emotions and the blood of their sacrifices, had felt their powers wane.

This was a Time of Fear.

The man-kind had grown strong by then. They had perfected weapon-craft and metal-working, they had mastered the secrets of fire and they knew some of the secret lore.

So the Triad and the others like them, the Ancient Ones, had moved on, leaving the world of men, going into the secret places, the hidden valleys, the floating isles, the barren lands. There they would conserve their waning powers and wait for the world to change, as it surely would.

But still some of the human-kind pursued them, drawn by lust or envy or anger or hate. So the Triad created a legend of terror to keep the man-creatures away, but even this failed. The legend drew the foolhardy and the brave and, occasionally, the cunning.

Once there had been three, Stheno, Euryale and Medusa.

And then the man-kind, Perseus, had come and slain Medusa with cunning and a weapon of metal.

The two remaining sisters grew frightened then. They were three, and the three were one, and even though a part of them was gone, they could still survive. But if another part of the Triad were to be slain then they would be lost forever, for all time. So the two creatures that the man-kind called Gorgons created a vessel that would carry them through time, rightly guessing that with sophistication would come ignorance. And with ignorance, they could become whole again, for within them both they held the seeds of their sister, Medusa.

But what would entice the man-kind, and yet remain unsuspected in their world?

The Gorgons noted that the humans were vain, and liked to admire their reflections, and so they conceived of a huge mirror, a gateway to the Otherworld, where their kind, the Ancient Ones the humans called the gods, still reigned. And Stheno sacrificed her sister, Euryale, and set her spirit into the glass to prepare the way, and then she flayed the flesh from her sister's bones and spread it out behind the great mirror to keep the magic alive, to allow it to become active when blood was spread onto the glass. The blood . . . or any human secretion – would seep through the glass and soak into the skin, bringing forth the ancient magic. Stheno then took her own life, spreadeagled across the mirror, allowing her own thin ichor to seep into the mirror, allowing herself to become absorbed.

Then was the Time of Waiting.

In the beginning they had come close to escape on many occasions. The men-beasts were controllable. They needed two: the male to supply the blood to soak the skin, to bring the magic to life. The female was the sacrifice and the host for Stheno. And once they had the host, once Stheno could come forth, she would raise Euryale and together they would be able to bring forth the Medusa.

But they hadn't counted on the wiles of the human-kind. The beasts had always had their magicians, their mages, sorcerers and witches. But these were primitives with only the merest trace of power, and of no account. But their powers had grown, had magnified, until they had breached the Otherworld of their own accord. And some of them had grown fearful of the huge mirror and the threat it had represented and had eventually sent it away to the land at the edge of the world, and set guardians over it, turning it into a crystal prison.

But they were patient and human-kind was weak.

The passage of years actually suited it. The human-kind became soft, weak, gullible. In this decadent age, what power would be theirs for the asking?

All they needed was a host . . .

'It's time,' Kelley turned to look up at the woman. He came smoothly to his feet. 'You understand. All your blood must leave your body, for blood carries the corruptions which bring age.'

She nodded. She stepped over the copper basin with its pitiful bundle and pressed herself against the mirror. The glass was cold against her naked flesh.

She turned her face slightly, pressing her cheeks against its coolness, feeling its sensuous touch against her breasts, belly and thighs. She shuddered, spreading her arms to clutch the edge of the plain wooden frame, opening her legs to the touch of the mirror's moist surface.

She felt her nipples hardening, her breathing quickening.

'Forever and ever?' she whispered.

The shadowy figure behind her – barely glimpsed in the mirror's dull surface – moved closer. 'Forever and ever, unchanging, unchanged.'

'Yessss,' she hissed. She closed her eyes, visualizing herself spreadeagled up against the mirror, face to face, breast to breast, belly to belly with her own image. Her heart began pounding with ever-increasing force, almost as if it were pressing against the glass, and the heat moved down into her groin . . . At the very moment her orgasm took her, wracking through her body, the thin silver of sharpened stone rippled through her throat.

Ultimate pleasure became absolute pain.

Blood hissed and steamed on the glass. Her mouth opened in a soundless scream and, as the shadowy figure moved closer, bending his head to her face, her lips moved, words forming, bloody froth bubbling on them. 'Thank you.'

Kelley held her against the glass as her blood poured onto the surface of the mirror, quickly disappearing into the greasy interior of the mirror.

He could barely contain his elation. He knew the secret of the glass. Perhaps he should try to remove the back of the mirror to allow him access to the hide of the Gorgon . . . but perhaps that might not be such a good idea.

Kelley looked at the glass again, a frown creasing his brow. According to his studies, once the blood had drained from the woman's body, the corpse should become animated by the image.

He took his hand away from the corpse and stepped back. The body crashed to the ground . . . but its reflection remained in the glass. Where was the golden woman?

But this was no reflection, this was the image, naked and complete, its hair waving around its head in a parody of the legend of the Gorgon. He looked at the corpse on the ground and frowned in puzzlement. What had happened? What had gone wrong?

The creature, the image of the woman he had just slain was mouthing words in the glass, repeating them over and over again, until he finally understood their meaning.

'The body was impure, diseased. The body must be virginal in every way. We have taken its soul, its reflection. We cannot take its physical form.'

It reached for him, arms outstretched, palms flat against the glass. Kelley pressed himself against the mirror, almost feeling the woman's warm flesh against his. He pressed his lips to hers, feeling her breath, warm and moist against his cheek, her tongue against his lips, probing, opening them.

And then she whispered. 'You have failed us!'

The tongue that broke through the surface of the glass and shot into his mouth was rasping, hooked, forked. It filled his mouth, insinuated itself down his throat. He attempted to scream, but couldn't. He attempted to pull away, but couldn't. The foul tongue was deep in his body now, he could feel it squirming, coiling, moving.

And he couldn't breathe, couldn't even vomit.

Couldn't breathe.

And now the hair was changing, twisting, turning coiling, melding together, tiny heads forming, black polished eyes, tiny darting tongues.

The image was changing, twisting, altering, her features running, melding together, elongating, a beast-like snout forming, long tusks digging into its own flesh.

It opened its mouth, wider, wider, wider, its tongue still lodged deep in his throat, its fangs growing, now great slab-like teeth coming up from the lower jaw, snapping at his face, scraping against the glass, threatening to break through.

With a final convulsive effort, Edward Kelley wrenched himself away from the mirror, stumbling backwards across the bodies of the woman and the baby. Blood streamed from his mouth.

In the mirror, the beast devoured his tongue with great relish.

Chapter
FIFTY-ONE

SO, the body had to be pure and virginal in every respect. He'd known that, his instincts had been right all along.

Jonathan Frazer crouched before the mirror in the stables, watching the images slowly fading from the glass. He'd been feeding the mirror with his own blood for most of the evening, and he was dizzy and faint, but now he knew the secret of the mirror. However, he could still hear the plaintive cry of hunger, like a distant keening in the back of his mind. His mistress hungered. And he was going to feed her, but now he knew just what she wanted, what she needed. She needed a virgin's blood and she needed a virginal body as a host.

He tried to think but his thoughts had been so confused over the past few days. Which of his friends had teenage daughters, and virginal daughters at that? Weren't teenagers supposed to be much more promiscuous these days in any case? How was he going to find a young virgin?

Well now let's see, who says it had to be young? Maybe the image would prefer an older, stronger body when it came back to this world . . . but it still had to be a virgin.

He curled his legs up under him until he was sitting cross-legged. He dropped his head onto his clenched fist, his elbow resting on his knee, and closed his eyes, considering. Maybe someone unmarried, a spinster . . .

Moments later, his head snapped up, his deep brown eyes bright, glittering. He began to chuckle and then laugh, the sound coming from deep within his body. But when it reached his throat it was high-pitched and maniacal. Maybe he might get to kill two birds with one stone. This time the laughter left him convulsed, rolling around on the floor, clutching his sides.

In the silence of the hospital room, the regular blipping of the machine, the gentle sussuration of the ventilator sounded very loud indeed.

WPC Carole Morrow looked up as the door opened and then straightened as Margaret Haaren stepped into the room. The inspector raised her eyebrows questioningly and the young policewoman shook her head. Standing at the end of the bed, the woman sighed, looking down at the bandaged form of Emmanuelle Frazer.

The girl was alive . . . but just.

She was lucky to be alive too. Two broken legs, broken hip, shattered kneecaps – even if she survived, and that was somewhat in doubt for the moment – she'd never walk properly again. She also had a cracked skull, concussion, broken ribs, and because she'd been naked when the police car which had been alerted by her screams had hit her, she was badly skinned, a mass of cuts and bruises.

What Margaret Haaren wanted to know was why she'd run screaming from the house. Why was she naked?

A search of the house had revealed the shattered

kitchen door but nothing else. The stables had been securely bolted and padlocked and a room-to-room search from attic to basement had disclosed no one, nor were there any indications that anyone had been in the house. The officers watching the house had seen no one enter or leave.

And there was still no sign of Jonathan Frazer.

Where does a man who is basically a loner go? He'd no real friends to run to; he didn't drink so he couldn't take solace in a bottle, and to the best of their knowledge he was still in the country. There was an APB out on him now, the divisional police forces had been alerted, as well as the Irish police and the European police forces. Margaret Haaren picked up the girl's chart and quickly scanned it. Too many years of doing what she was doing now – standing at the end of a bed looking at a victim or a witness or a villain – had made her an expert at reading charts.

'Did she say anything?' she asked, without looking up.

The WPC shook her head. 'She was mumbling and moaning earlier, but nonsense words, something about a baby, that's all I got.'

The inspector nodded. 'Stay with her; if you've got to leave the room for any reason, make sure the officer outside steps in.'

'Yes, ma'am.'

The inspector replaced the chart and folded her arms across her broad chest, looking at the young woman.

'Do you think *he* was responsible?' the WPC asked, looking at Manny Frazer again. They both knew she was talking about Jonathan Frazer.

'Didn't they teach you never to speculate without facts?' the inspector asked, smiling to take the sting from her words.

'They told me to use my imagination,' the young

officer said simply. 'I think she was running from her father.'

Margaret Haaren nodded but said nothing. Privately, she agreed. The two officers in the police car had said they were responding to terrified screams. They were parked at the entrance to the cul-de-sac, so that anything coming into the close would have to pass them. They had driven up fast, lights on but sirens off, the screams becoming louder, more piercing as they neared the Frazer household. And then the naked young woman had run straight out in front of the car, and there was absolutely nothing they could do about it. She hadn't even been looking where she was going, she had seemed to be looking over her shoulder.

She was being chased.

Who . . . and why?

'I'm going to the Frazer house,' she said to the WPC. 'I'll be there if you need me.'

'Yes, ma'am.'

Tommy Hinge didn't like the term 'peeping tom'. It certainly didn't apply to him. He simply walked around the grounds of the flat complex where he lived and if he happened to see someone undressing in a window, well, he could hardly be blamed for looking, now could he? After all, he was only human.

He'd lived in these apartments for three years now, a retired postman, or at least that's what he told people. His discharge from the Post Office had been anything but honourable. Misappropriation of post was the charge.

Bullshit.

Over the years – because he'd often used their services himself – he'd become expert at recognizing the plain brown wrappers that came from the companies supplying adult toys and playthings. He knew all the innocuous sounding names by heart.

He'd taken the first one out of sheer curiosity and discovered it held a treasure trove of Swedish porn. And after that ... well, he was hooked. He never thought someone would complain ... and after all who were they going to complain to – consumer affairs? Excuse me, but I didn't get my blow-up doll ... my vibrator's gone missing in the post ... my spanish fly seems to have flown. But that's exactly what had happened. Someone had complained, obviously someone without any shame or embarrassment at all. Since all the thefts had occurred within his postal district, it wasn't difficult to find the culprit. The department's fraud section had sent a few trial packages through the post and of course he'd fallen for it and lifted them.

And that was that. Only the fact that he'd nearly forty years service saved him from a court appearance.

The meagre pension he got from the state ensured that he couldn't treat himself to any of the glossy new mags, and porno mags rarely appeared on the second-hand shelves, so he'd had to find new ways to amuse himself.

He'd discovered the pleasures of peeping by accident. He'd been out for a stroll one evening, when he'd chanced to see a young woman in one of the corner apartments undressing. She'd forgotten to close her blinds fully, and he'd spent ten of the most pleasant and exciting minutes in his life simply watching her.

After that it became a ritual, and now his ambition was to see every single woman in the apartment block naked or as near naked as possible. High on his list was the woman in the corner apartment on the second floor, Mrs Haaren, a filing clerk in the local cop shop. A big woman, mature, masculine – just the type he preferred. And she'd got a young one with her at the moment, a niece apparently. Blonde, skinny, but pretty: he'd like to add her to his collection.

He'd been standing in the hedge beneath the trees for

nearly an hour before he saw the light go on in the apartment. From this position, at the edge of the grassy knoll that led down to the ornamental pool, the apartment, although it was on the second floor, was almost directly opposite him. Raising the tiny field glasses to his eyes he looked into the room. He'd already pre-set the focus. There was nothing visible yet, but there was some compensation in the fact that she hadn't pulled the curtains yet. He knew from experience that if the curtains weren't pulled the moment a person walked into the room, then the odds were greatly improved that they wouldn't pull them at all. It was surprising how so many people didn't. Why, just tonight he'd watched the widow two apartments down from the Haaren woman dressing to go out. He'd seen nothing he hadn't seen before but it was the thrill of watching unobserved that aroused him now.

Footsteps sounded on the path and Tommy shrank back into the deeper shadows. He knew he was virtually invisible – he'd bought himself a black tracksuit and then peeled off all the decorations and reflective strips – but he certainly didn't want to run any risks.

He watched the figure move swiftly by and was suddenly glad he couldn't be seen. There was something about the man, the way he moved, the expression on his face, the smell . . . yes, certainly the smell, like old decayed meat, like blood. It frightened him.

The figure stopped almost directly across from him and consulted something in his hand, finally standing back and looking across at the windows. And then he stepped backwards into the bushes, not two feet away from Tommy. Maybe he was in the same business. The man abruptly grunted in satisfaction and walked briskly away from the bushes.

The peeping tom gave a sigh of relief. He turned his

attention back to the Haaren woman's apartment.

So how many *M. Haaren*s could there be in the Central London telephone directory, eh? And the very fact that it was an initial convinced him that it was the same woman.

He was surprised to find she lived in an apartment; he'd have thought she'd have had a little place of her own. But then he supposed that an apartment was ideal for a single woman, living alone, not often home.

He stopped when he came into the landscaped grounds of the apartment complex and checked the address again, counting the apartments from left to right . . . yes, there was a light on in the apartment he had assumed was hers.

He swore when he stepped into the foyer. The large double doors ahead of him were locked, while on either side of the doors was a series of letterboxes and tiny grilles alongside the names. He found *M. Haaren* half way down on the left-hand side and pressed the bell.

Her heard a click and then crackling static. 'Yes?'

'Bouquet for Inspector Margaret Haaren from Flora International.'

'Come up. Second floor, apartment number 9.' The door opposite buzzed loudly.

Smiling Jonathan Frazer pushed his way through the door. The lift was already waiting and he immediately stepped inside. As he pressed the button he touched the comforting pressure of the knife strapped to his arm.

Aaah, showtime.

Tommy Hinge smiled broadly as the woman, wearing a towel around her head and another wrapped around her body moved towards the door. She stopped, her head turned sideways as if she were asking a question and listening to the answer.

And then she was stepping back, opening the door . . .

Jesus Christ.

It was him. The man with the smell. He was moving into the apartment, a knife in his hand, pressing it against the woman's throat, his face so distorted with hate it was barely recognizable as human.

The knife had been in his hand, and at the woman's throat before he realized it wasn't Margaret Haaren. It was some blonde teenager, vaguely familiar, though he'd no conscious thought of ever having seen her before.

'The Haaren bitch, where is she?' he snarled.

The young woman looked at him wide-eyed, mouth open in shock.

He pressed the knife against the slender column of her throat, the razor sharp edge parting the skin, blood from the cut snaking down to stain the towel wrapped around her breasts. 'Answer me!'

Her throat moved. 'Working,' she whispered.

Frazer swore. He slashed at the beaded curtain that separated the kitchen from the rest of the apartment, wooden beads and shells scattering across the floor.

'When is she back?'

'I don't know. Later, maybe. Tomorrow.'

All the energy seemed to drain out of Frazer, the knife dropped away from the young woman's throat and his head dipped.

'Say mister,' Helen began, 'you could be making a mistake. Margaret Haaren's a cop.'

'I know that,' he snarled. And then he suddenly looked up, his eyes bright, glittering. 'I know you.'

She started to shake her head.

'I know you,' he repeated. 'I saw you at the funeral.' He squeezed his eyes shut, remembering. He'd been talking to Margaret Haaren and this young woman had come up behind her, and called her 'aunt' and Margaret Haaren had called her . . .

'Helen,' he said, his eyes snapping open.

'Yes,' she said, surprised he knew her name.

Jonathan Frazer smiled, lips drawing back from his teeth in an animal snarl. He moved the knife up before her face, allowing the light to reflect into her eyes. 'Tell me, Helen,' he whispered, very softly, 'are you a virgin?'

Tommy Hinge winced as he watched the man speaking intently to the young woman. The hatred in his face was almost palpable and terrifying. He watched him snatch the towel from the girl's head, exposing damp blonde hair and then wrench the towel away from her body. The girl's head and shoulders were shaking as if she were crying. The man was nodding now, as if satisfied, and then he pointed away with the knife and then walked behind her, his left hand on her shoulder, the knife resting against her right shoulder close to her neck.

The light in the bedroom snapped on.

Tommy's hands were trembling so much now he could barely hold the binoculars. He was surprised when he saw the young woman dress, pulling on a tee-shirt, climbing into jeans, lifting a denim jacket off the back of a chair. The light went off in the bedroom. The couple moved through the apartment, and now they were at the door, the man's hand still on her shoulder, but the knife was no longer visible. The light went out.

Tommy Hinge lowered the binoculars, desperately wondering what he was going to do. He was still wondering when the pair walked right past him, the man's grip so tight on the young woman's shoulder that he could see the whiteness of his knuckles.

He waited until they had rounded the corner and then he stepped out after them, abruptly glad of his black tracksuit and his rubber-soled trainers.

Chapter
FIFTY-TWO

SHE was trapped in a crystal, in a huge block of ice. Everywhere she looked there were reflections . . . but it was not her own reflection she was looking at. She raised her arm and a dozen figures – no, a hundred, a hundred hundred – male and female, and obscene combinations of both, raised their arms in silent mimicry. She hammered on the surface of the glass and a thousand arms hammered in perfect syncopation.

Now she was in a glass coffin, and it was growing smaller, constricting, shrinking, contracting. She began to scream, but there was a vacuum within the crystal cage, and there was no sound. She began to hammer on the surface of the block of ice, ignoring the mimicking hands, ignoring the slack and gaping faces, beating, beating, beating against the glass . . .

Until it cracked.

It tumbled down around her in huge razor-sharp shards, the glass cutting into her body, slicing into her flesh, hammering into her legs. Dear God, the pain in her legs.

Emmanuelle Frazer opened her mouth and screamed.

*

'What happened?' Margaret Haaren demanded.

'She came awake about ten minutes after you left,' WPC Morrow said, trying to remain as calm as possible. She could still hear the woman's terrified screams in her ears. She took a deep breath and continued. 'She screamed for at least five minutes without a break. Her heart machine was going crazy,' she added.

'Then what?'

'By then the doctors had injected her with a massive sedative. It should have knocked her out completely; it didn't. She grew calm. She looked around and spotted me. I said, "Hello Miss Frazer, how do you feel?" '

'And?' Haaren said through gritted teeth. Did she have to drag out every particular word by word?

'She closed her eyes first and when she opened them again, she started to cry. She said, "He's got a knife. He's going to kill me. That's not my father." She started crying then. She's still crying.'

'Right.' The inspector had put her hand on the handle of the door when it suddenly opened and a tall blond-haired, blue-eyed doctor stepped out. He looked about eighteen.

'I'm sorry, no visitors,' he said imperiously.

'Don't be ridiculous,' the inspector said, ignoring him.

Manny Frazer had calmed down by the time the inspector stepped into the room. She was still dreadfully confused, and she hadn't got a clue how she had ended up back in hospital. She looked up into the inspector's broad face and smiled in recognition.

'How do you feel?' Margaret Haaren asked gently. She took the girl's bandaged hand in hers, stroking it lightly with the fingers of her left hand. The girl was eighteen, the same age as her niece, she suddenly remembered.

Manny's mouth worked but no sound came out.

'Can you tell me what happened? It's important.'

'I'm hurt bad, aren't I?' Manny's voice was cracked and raw.

'The doctors say you'll be fine. You were hit by a car when you ran out of your drive. What made you run like that?'

Manny's large brown eyes, almost lost now behind the bruises, opened wide and her breathing began to quicken. The now silent heart monitor showed increased activity on its tiny square screen.

'Gently, gently now,' the inspector murmured. 'You were being chased. Who was chasing you?'

The bloodshot eyes opened wide. Her voice was a ragged whisper. 'He's got a knife. He's going to kill me. That's not my father.'

'Who's chasing you, Manny, who is after you?'

'He's got a knife. He's going to kill me.'

'You're safe now, Manny. There's no one after you now. Tell me who it was. You know who it was, don't you?' she demanded. 'Tell me.'

Manny's eyes opened wide. 'It was my father.'

'So, it was your father.'

'But it wasn't.'

'The man looked like your father,' she said patiently.

Manny attempted to shake her head and then stopped, realizing she was restrained. 'It was my father. But he was different.'

'He had a knife, Manny. What did he want to do with the knife?'

'He wanted ... wanted to kill me ... no ...' Her breath died away to a ghostly whisper, and Margaret lowered her head to catch the words. 'No, he said he wanted to sacrifice me. To feed it my blood to make it whole.'

'Feed what, Manny. What did he want to feed?'

'Mother!' Her voice rose to a hoarse shout. 'Mother. He said she was dead!'

Margaret Haaren stopped, her own heartbeat beginning to trip along in rhythm to the girl's. There was no way Manny could know about the death of her mother.

'He said he'd killed her. Said he'd cut her from crotch to sternum, that's what he'd said. Said she was with someone.' Her fingers tightened convulsively around the inspector's, blood beginning to seep through the bandages. 'Is it true?'

'Your mother is dead, Manny,' the inspector said slowly.

'Did . . . did Dad do it?'

'I believe he did,' Margaret said.

Manny lay back on his pillows, eyes closed.

'It's not his fault, Manny. He's not well. He needs our help, yours and mine. Now, tell me, what did your father want to feed?'

'It's that mirror. It's possessed him. Talbott said it was evil, and then it killed him. And it would have killed me,' she added wonderingly. 'He was going to kill me and feed my blood to the mirror.'

'Where is he, Manny?' Margaret Haaren said loudly. 'Where is Jonathan Frazer?'

'He can hear it, feel its hunger. It's making him kill to feed it.'

'Where is he, dammit?'

'In the stables. He's in the stables, and he's going to feed the mirror. He's going to kill tonight!'

Margaret Haaren was already moving towards the door when it snapped open and WPC Morrow's pale face looked in. She handed the inspector a walkie-talkie. 'Emergency feed, passed through from the station.'

'Haaren,' she said crisply, turning in the doorway to look back into the room, but Manny Frazer was sleeping again, only the rapid movement behind her closed eyelids evidence that her sleep wasn't peaceful.

'Miller, ma'am.' The West Indian's accent was abrupt and pronounced.

'What's wrong?' she murmured, stepping outside the room, closing the door behind her. Carole Morrow stared anxiously at her, until Margaret jerked her thumb and the young WPC stepped back into the room.

'We got a report from a member of the public about half an hour ago that a man roughly answering to Frazer's description was seen to kidnap a young woman at knifepoint. The citizen followed them to Frazer's house in Kensington, where he was picked up by our men for loitering. Our lads didn't believe his story so we sent a car around to the address where he said the young woman had been taken from.'

'And.'

'I've verified this myself, ma'am. Everything checks out. Ma'am,' he added, and she instinctively knew that it was bad, 'he's got your niece, Helen.'

She was back in the crystal prison, a flat oblong of glass spinning slowly across a grey and drear landscape. She was spreadeagled in this glass, trapped, her mouth open, screaming, screaming, screaming.

And there, in the distance was a towering funnel, lightening wrapped, vari-hued. As her crystal prison spun nearer, she recognized it as a whirlpool, but no ordinary whirlpool this. In the grey silence it exuded a barely perceptible hum, a high-pitched keening. Instinctively she knew that herein were the trapped souls of aeons. If the whirlpool had a name then it was Agony. There were faces in the whirlpool, hundreds of tiny faces, mouths and eyes wide, pleading, begging, crying for release, from all races, from all times. Close to the top of the whirlpool there were whole bodies of the recently dead circling around, caught in the great tidal pull of the circle, and further down, nearer the bottom, there were only parts of features, partially glimpsed eyes, mouths, tongues, lips. She felt its pull, the wrenching deep within her as the crystal prison bucked and warped. It dragged her forward and suddenly she was within the whirlpool, sucked into the funnel, and she was spinning, spinning, spinning, down and down and down, deep into the core of the turgid greyness.

Now she could hear the song of its captured souls, and this song was Desolation.

The rectangle of crystal fell further, deeper into the core, and now the partially glimpsed features were no longer human or even animal, but something of both. Here were the creatures of myth, of legend, of faith and fancy.

Abruptly the greyness was broken by a rain of tiny white lights which streaked past her. Vivid, pulsing with their own inner life, the droplets spattered all around her, calling to her, drawing her down even further, even deeper . . . until she saw the opening ahead of her. It was a small rectangle, but growing, growing, growing as she rushed headlong towards it.

There were figures in the rectangle. A man naked, standing before the opening. A woman, naked, bound and blindfolded lying on the ground behind him. Behind her strange and curious artefacts.

Recognizable artefacts. Antiques.

The man standing before the opening was familiar. Dear God, but he was familiar. He was close now, so close that she could see what he was doing . . .

He was masturbating and his seed was streaming past her in long thin streamers and elongated globules, drifting back up into the core of the whirlpool. Feeding it.

She came to an abrupt jarring halt. She was on one side of the mirror.

And Jonathan Frazer was on the other.

A figure stepped past her out of the greyness and looked at Frazer.

359

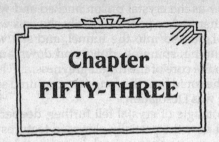

Chapter
FIFTY-THREE

HE'D masturbated furiously, spilling his seed onto the glass while calling up the image. She had appeared at the precise moment of orgasm. She pressed up against the glass, staring at him, her eyes wide with desire, her long hair battering against the glass.

'I've got her,' he whispered. He glanced over his shoulder at the bound, gagged and blindfolded young woman. 'A virgin. Unsullied, unblemished.'

The image smiled at him.

'Tell me what to do,' he whispered.

Feed me. Free me.

He remembered fragments of the pictures he had seen of Kelley the night he had sacrificed the woman and the child. The copper bowl, the stone knife. But were they necessary? Surely all the image desired was the blood of the sacrifice.

Frazer stood, leaning forward against the glass, the palms of his hands resting against the glass. In the glass the image mimicked him. He could feel the flesh of her hands against his, see the way her breasts flattened against the glass. He brought his face close to the mirror, close to the dark-haired, dark-eyed woman's face. 'Tell me what to do.'

The image's stone-hard eyes flickered to the bound woman. *Feed me. Spread her on the glass. Bring her to the moment of her greatest passion. Then sacrifice her. I will take her life substance, and when she is nothing more than a husk, I shall possess the shell. I shall be made flesh again.* Her tongue flickered out and he imagined he felt it brush against his lips.

'Soon,' he promised, 'soon, soon, soon.' He turned to look to the girl.

'Now, now, now!'

Margaret Haaren lifted the .38 from her bag and swung open the cylinder. There were five copper-coloured rounds in the gun; regulations demanded that the chamber beneath the hammer should be kept empty. She surreptitiously slid another bullet into the gun. She had a very good idea that Mister Jonathan Frazer was going to be shot while resisting arrest.

The entrance to the cul-de-sac had been sealed off and the residents of the surrounding houses had been evacuated. There were marksmen situated in the houses opposite. Jonathan Frazer was armed and considered dangerous.

The Chief Superintendent himself was in charge of this operation. His softly-softly approach was famous – or infamous – and she knew he'd more than likely spend the rest of the night in the van talking to the snipers and the observers before making any decision, and by that time Helen could be dead. Manny had told her that Frazer would kill tonight.

Now the press were starting to arrive.

Of course, she'd forgotten about the press. Whatever chances they had of taking Frazer by surprise were going down the toilet, right now, while the Chief gave an interview.

Stuart Miller materialized by her side. There was a flak jacket over his uniform and the holstered pistol looked incongruous on his hip. 'What would you say if I told you there was a back way in to the house?'

Margaret Haaren looked at him and then glanced over at the Chief. 'I'd say lead the way.'

They slipped through the crowd and walked back almost to the entrance of the close. The sergeant stopped, his eyes moving to the left, the inspector following the direction of his gaze. It was just another garden . . . no, it wasn't just another garden. The opening was incredibly narrow, barely wide enough for a person to walk in single file down its length. Without a word, she slipped into the leafy darkness, Stuart Miller following her without a sound.

This was how Frazer had managed to get into the house without them knowing! This was how he'd slipped in and out when he'd chased his daughter. The lane was almost in total darkness, the only light coming from the houses. She counted four gates and stopped at the fifth. This one? She glanced back over her shoulder at Stuart. The West Indian was almost invisible in the darkness and she almost missed his nod. She heard the snap as he removed his gun from its holster and held it up by his head. Clutching the gun in her right hand she carefully ran her hand over the flaking wooden gate, eventually finding and pressing the catch. The gate swung inwards without a sound.

The girl was spreadeagled on the mirror, arms and legs tied to the four corners. She had struggled and kicked until he had laid the flat of the cold knife against her breasts, promising to cut her deeply unless she shut up. When he'd pressed her up against the glass, she had winced, pulling away from the chill, but again he'd used the knife to urge her forward.

She wasn't to know that he wasn't going to cut her – the image wanted the body whole and undamaged. No, he wasn't going to cut her . . . well, not just yet.

He stood back grinning widely. From where he was standing it was as if the young woman were embracing the image, breast to breast, thigh to thigh, belly to belly. He looked into the image's dark eyes, shivering at the dark hunger he saw there, the longing.

He came up behind the bound girl and ran both hands down her sides; her flesh, though silky soft, still felt harsh to his fingers, her hair coarse and brittle.

She was a beast. Cattle to be used.

He sank to his knees behind the bound girl and ran both hands up the insides of her thighs, finally stopping deep in her groin, his fingers probing, stroking, pressing, rubbing.

In the mirror he could see the image mimicking his movement, arousing herself, her eyes locked on his face, her tongue moving lasciviously across her lips. The invitation in her eyes almost physical.

Where there had been only dry flesh beneath his fingers, now there was moisture. Deep in the corners of the mirror, he could see the first tentative curls of shifting power begin to twist and weave.

He looked at the knife resting by his left hand. At the moment of her greatest passion he would kill her. Soon. He could feel her muscles begin to twitch of their own accord.

The stables were locked – but from the inside this time. The lock was missing and the bolt was thrown back.

Which meant that there was someone inside.

The windows were all blocked up and some of them seemed to have been recently painted over or covered.

Margaret Haaren pressed the side of her face against the door and listened. For a moment she heard nothing and then, faint, muffled, she heard the quiet sounds of a woman panting, the unmistakable sounds of a woman approaching orgasm.

She stepped away from the door and looked around.

She couldn't go through the door, and the windows were barred. There was a tree overhanging the stables – and she remembered that there were skylights in the roof. If she got up onto the tree . . .

Stuart Miller saw her look from the tree to the roof and shook his head. 'Don't even think about it, ma'am.'

'Give me an alternative,' she snapped.

'Let me go out and get the tactical boys. They can blow the door, we can pile in, hit Frazer and grab the girl.'

'Go and get them,' she said and pushed him away into the darkness. Easing down the hammer on the pistol, she stuck it into the pocket of her coat. She waited until she heard the gate close softly behind him and then headed for the tree. She hadn't climbed a tree since she was a child, but she supposed that, like riding a bike, it was something you didn't forget.

The girl might be a virgin but she was reacting violently to his stroking. Although she was tied to the edge of the frame, she was now actually clutching at it for support while her body bucked and shifted, pressing herself hard against the glass, using its chill as a stimulus.

Frazer guessed that the image had something to do with the girl's extraordinary level of arousal.

And now her orgasm was beginning. Deep shudders were wracking through her body, her buttocks were clenching and unclenching and her stomach muscles were almost rippling. Her breath was coming in great heaving gasps. She started to cry out, short grunting sobs that quickly lengthened, deepened. Her head was thrown back and he guessed that beneath the blindfold, her eyes would be squeezed tightly shut.

Jonathan Frazer stepped back and allowed the woman's own passion to do the rest.

He lifted the knife in his right hand and approached the young woman. It was only a matter of seconds. But the moment had to be right, it had to be perfect.

Margaret Haaren swung from the branch onto the roof of the stable with surprising delicacy for such a heavy woman. She crawled to the nearest skylight. She could see nothing. Gritting her teeth, she crawled, inch by inch to the next. She pulled the gun from her pocket as she crawled. Just give her one good shot at Frazer. Below her the grunting, moaning sounds had reached a crescendo.

And then silence.

Gripping her hair tightly, Jonathan Frazer plunged the knife deep into her jugular, and then dragged the blade back across her throat. The woman's shudders continued, but now they were of a different character. She slumped against the glass, and hung there, suspended by the ropes binding her to the frame. The blood from her torn throat gushed onto the glass, warm and salty, steaming slightly, hissing, bubbling.

The mirror exploded into a maelstrom of light. Jagged streaks of colour ran from one edge of the glass to the other. The image reached out to match the position of the young woman tied to the glass. Only now when it pressed itself against the glass Frazer clearly saw the glass bow outwards. He saw its fingers stretch the surface of the glass like jelly, and then break through one by one, and wrap themselves around the girl's face, pulling her close to the glass to where its lips pressed against the glass around the gaping wound in the woman's throat. Its tongue – long and dark and moist – lapped at the spurting blood.

Frazer came to his feet and stood behind the woman, pressing her slumped head close to the mirror so that the image could suck at the blood. The image looked at him once, and he shuddered with the promise in its eyes, before it returned to licking, sucking, drawing the last remnants of life from the young woman. Frazer watched it for a moment, and then he too bent his head to the wound and tentatively tasted it with the tip of his tongue.

Margaret Haaren's hand trembled as she lined up the sights. Almost directly below her, Frazer was bent over Helen who was tied up to a huge mirror. There was a dripping knife in his hand and he was licking at her neck where she could see a bloody wound.

She took a deep breath, held it, and pulled the trigger.

Jonathan Frazer glanced up into the image's eyes – and found himself looking at a nightmare.

She is mine! the beast roared.

Whiplike tendrils of hair shot out from the mirror, as if they were breaking the surface of a pond and wrapped themselves around his head, holding it tight, pulling it to the glass.

The image's mouth was opening and closing, her teeth lengthening, the upper incisors growing, gouging into the flesh of her chin, scoring through the flesh. Threads of thick dark saliva dripped onto her breasts. Her eyes were changing, the whites disappearing, turning black, the pupils lengthening, becoming yellow and slit-like. The face became the mask of a beast, like a boar with curling tusks and leathery verminous skin. The mouth opened and opened and opened, drew back ... and erupted through the mirror.

The forked tongue lashed at his eyes, destroying the retina, the lower jaws clamped into the flesh beneath his chin, the fangs in its upper jaw tore into the soft flesh behind his eyes and then it bit down, sheering off the whole front of his face.

The bullet shattered the skylight, continued down, entered the crown of Frazer's head and blew off most of the lower portion of his face, spattering gore across the glass. He was dead before he hit the floor.

Although another shot was unnecessary, Margaret Haaren calmly shot him in the back of the head as he lay on the floor. At close range, the .38 bullet tore off what was left of his face.

EPILOGUE

STUART Miller came up and stood beside the inspector, grinning broadly.

'What's got you so happy?' Margaret Haaren asked.

'The Chief's just about to throw a serious fit. You stole his limelight. He was in the middle of his speech about "a considered response to this delicate situation" when you blew Frazer's head off.'

'He'd cut her throat,' she said tiredly, watching the ambulance crew carry out Helen on a stretcher. Light bulbs flashed. 'He'd made a puncture in it and was drinking her blood like some vampire.'

'I've heard about that. The need for blood is some obscure medical condition, some deficiency,' Stuart Miller said mildly. 'But the other stuff, the vampire stuff, the black magic rubbish is some sort of sex trip.' He jerked his thumb back over his shoulder. 'We found some women's clothing over there. Remember those street girls who ended up in the river? I'll bet you my pension we've got ourselves a connection.'

'Good.' She handed across her pistol. 'Check this in for me will you? I'm going with the ambulance.'

'Give my regards to Helen, eh? Tell her she's a really lucky girl.'

'You can say that again.'

When Margaret had looked down into the room, she

had immediately assumed that Frazer had cut her niece's throat. But when they'd finally broken down the door, and she'd rushed to her side, they'd discovered that there was only a small nick in the side of her throat and that the girl was already beginning to open her eyes.

For one instant they'd stared at Margaret Haaren completely devoid of expression, and then a smile fixed itself to her lips.

'Hello Aunty.'

In her glass prison, Manny Frazer screamed and screamed and screamed . . .

NOTES

John Dee and Edward Kelley were real historical characters. Dee, who was Elizabeth's spy, was one of the Queen's closest advisors, prepared regular horoscopes for her, and did choose the date of her Coronation.

It is a matter of record that John Dee married twice: the name of his first wife is unknown, and she died mysteriously after only one year of marriage.

Following the woman's death, Queen Elizabeth visited Mortlake, home of John Dee, to view the marvellous mirror she had heard so much about, but she inexplicably refused to enter the house and insisted on viewing the mirror in the gardens.

The real name of Edward Kelley, or Kelly, was Talbott.

The mirror, albeit in slightly smaller form than described here, exists. Its face is kept perpetually covered with a black cloth.

DREAMER

Peter James

The last time Sam had the dream, she was seven years old
and that was the night her parents were to die. Twenty-five
years later her childhood is but a bad memory. Now
married to a wealthy Eurobond dealer, she has a child,
two homes and a highly successful career. An enviable
lifestyle. But for Sam it is becoming a nightmare. Because
the childhood dreams are returning – and this time they
are coming true . . .

Gradually and subtly, the dreams of the night foretell the
disasters of the day – and no-one believes her, nothing
can help her. As psychiatrists, clairvoyants and dream
therapy fail her, she is left to confront the evil alone,
without knowing its name: hallucination, premonition,
reincarnation or psychic projection? Whatever it is, it
won't relinquish its hold. And then Sam starts dreaming
her own death . . .

0 7474 0577 6
GENERAL FICTION/HORROR

SWEET HEART

Peter James

The Estate Agents described Elmwood Mill in Sussex as
'a delightful 15th-century mill house in outstanding
secluded position'. That they said nothing about its
disturbing atmospheres was hardly surprising – especially
as Charley was the only one who felt it. Her husband
Tom said she was imagining things. Charley, after they
moved in, knew otherwise. She was *remembering* things.
Yet she had never been to Elmwood before in her life.

But had she known it in a previous life? As the haunting
begins to invade her everyday life, Charley resorts to
hypnosis – but each session ends with a feeling of doom
and terror. There is something hidden that the hypnotist
cannot reach. Something that was safely buried in her
past – until now . . .

0 7474 0895 5
GENERAL FICTION/HORROR

RENEGADES

Shaun Hutson

Immortality – the ultimate secret. David and Laura
Callahan, like others before them throughout the ages,
will stop at nothing in their perverted quest for it. But for
Callahan, a multi-millionaire gun runner, eternal life has
never looked less likely: he is being hunted both by a
renegade group of hired killers and by two British
counter-terrorists. And nobody knows who hired the
killers – or why . . .

In a race against time, a trail of violence and terror leads
from a desecrated church in France, to London, and on to
strife-torn Ireland where modern terrorism battles against
ancient powers and a terrible secret is revealed. A long-
forgotten secret that will threaten the lives and souls of
those involved. And when the final confrontation comes,
the living will envy the dead . . .

0 7474 0791 6
HORROR/THRILLER

THE BLACK FEDORA

Guy N. Smith

It is Festival Week in Lichfield and the cathedral city is teeming with people; some resident, some invited, and some not . . .

Benjamin – leader of a hippie peace convoy, a man with a mysterious past and a destructive purpose

Kosminski – the Polish Premier, ambassador for communism, and for the horrors of a gone but not forgotten era

The police – a force to be reckoned with, not above corruption

The Bishop – guardian of the Lichfield Gospels, lifelong believer in God – and the Devil

Haggard – the man in the black fedora. He knows no one, but inspires a chilling, creeping fear in everyone

There will never be another festival like this one . . .

0 7474 0730 4
GENERAL FICTION/HORROR

THE WALKERS

Graham Masterton

It didn't take long for Jack Reed to decide to convert the huge gothic building in the woods into an idyllic, up-market country club.

But behind the ornately carved walls of The Oaks lurks a past that was anything but idyllic. Sixty years ago the house was an asylum, home to crazed psychopaths – all of whom disappeared one night, never to be seen again.

Now the empty rooms echo to the soundless screaming of the madmen traped *inside* the brick and plaster, walking endlessly through the maze-like mansion. And now Jack's son, dragged into the hellish prison of the walls, is held a screaming hostage by Quintus Miller, leader of the insane.

Quintus took the killers into the walls. Now, he insists, Jack Reed will set them free – or his son will die . . .

0 7474 0493 3
GENERAL FICTION/HORROR

DEATH DREAM

Graham Masterton

It was a thing out of a nightmare. While mankind slept it stalked the dream-world, driving men to madness and death. The demon's bloodlust was terrible; its rage was unstoppable.

Decimating the realms of dreams was not enough – the creature hungered for the waking world. Hidden in a child's nightmares, it emerged in a riot of slaughter. None could stand against it.

And then the Night Warriors arose, summoned by the demon's evil. Powerless in our world, in dreams they are virtual gods. In dreams they will confront the demon – unless it finds and destroys their sleeping selves . . .

0 7474 0330 9
GENERAL FICTION/HORROR

Sphere now offers an exciting range of quality titles by both established and new authors. All of the books in this series are available from:

Sphere Books,
Cash Sales Department,
P.O. Box 11,
Falmouth,
Cornwall TR10 9EN.

Alternatively you may fax your order to the above address. Fax No. 0326 376423.

Payments can be made as follows: Cheque, postal order (payable to Macdonald & Co (Publishers) Ltd) or by credit cards, Visa/Access. Do not send cash or currency. UK customers and B.F.P.O.: please send a cheque or postal order (no currency) and allow £1.00 for postage and packing for the first book, plus 50p for the second book, plus 30p for each additional book up to a maximum charge of £3.00 (7 books plus).

Overseas customers including Ireland, please allow £2.00 for postage and packing for the first book, plus £1.00 for the second book, plus 50p for each additional book.

NAME (Block Letters) ....

ADDRESS ....

....

☐ I enclose my remittance for _____

☐ I wish to pay by Access/Visa Card

Number ⬜⬜⬜⬜⬜⬜⬜⬜⬜⬜⬜⬜⬜⬜⬜⬜

Card Expiry Date ⬜⬜⬜⬜